The Mark

Samantha Hurrle

ISBN: 979-8-9862801-0-3

Library of Congress Control Number: 2022909280

Any references to historical events, real people, or real places are used fictitiously. Names, characters, and places are products of the author's imagination.

Front and back cover images by Alyssa Meyer.

Book design by Samantha Hurrle.

Printed by DiggyPOD Inc.; Amazon Inc.; IngramSpark Inc. in the United States of America

First printing edition 2022.

Samantha Hurrle
7454 Ahles Road
St. Cloud, MN

To all who seek the heart of God
To all who strive to do his work
To all who suffer evil

May the lavish love God pours out to you in life be multiplied.
May He transform your tears into astounding joy and everlasting peace.
Go with God, and may you forever know the love He has for you.

*"For we wrestle not against flesh and
blood, but against principalities, against
powers, against the rulers of the
darkness of this world, against spiritual
wickedness in high places."*

(Ephesians 6:12 KJV)

CONTENTS

THE MARK

PART ONE

CHAPTER ONE

SILENCE BEFORE THE STORM

The city of Xanadai lay quiet. The vast caverns and shadowy passages of the underground city held the stillness like a prisoner. No soldiers painted with disciplinary scars guarded their posts. No one walked the passages idly or hurried about to do their masters' biddings. Not even the brats entertained themselves in the unstable caves and jagged crags that spiked the vaulted cavern. The central cavern, Sheol, the grandest of the spaces making up the city, was barren. It was a tomb lit by the glow of the molten lava that boiled nervously around the Great Temple. The expansive hole stretched for miles beyond the Great Temple into a darkness that swallowed the somber glow of the lake.

Karueq stood on the shore of that great lava pit. To his right, a narrow walkway extended from the city to the temple in the middle of the lake. At a stretch to his left rose a series of towers hewn out of the earth that served as dwellings for the people of the city. The lowliest among them dwelt at the top where the toxic fumes from the volcanic waste lingered.

The heat and the smog were nothing to Karueq, who made his home from a tower with a single room suspended at the edge of the

9

others. A balcony swept out from the room so that he may keep a watchful eye on Sheol. His charges liked to indulge themselves in rather idle frivolity, and Karueq saw to it that his leadership would undo his undisciplined predecessors' laughable work.

To Karueq, the stillness that captivated Sheol was not unsettling. He knew exactly what was happening in the Temple Sector. He did not quiver at the report of another revolt. Old habits have a nasty way of lingering, especially when the tenants of such habits are bored and frustrated. Most of his men could be reliable when properly handled, but Karueq still had a few diseased lunatics on his hands that could undo his will on them. The revolt was but a symptom that would be remedied in the same way as the one last week.

One thing did unease Karueq, something outside the rebellion in the Temple Sector, and he was the only one in all of Xanadai who knew about it and what it meant – and it would stay that way. The unpleasant distraction was a good thing this time.

In his hand, Karueq held a pendant. It was a little larger and more ornate than the pendants worn by most common soldiers, carved from glassy obsidian and gilded in gold. The six-headed reptilian beast was the symbol of Xanadai's elite team of assassins, the Brehila. Boasting the most predatory killers Xanadai had to offer, the Brehila were known for their cruelty and the many lives they had taken. Each of them had been singularly responsible for the deaths of at least ten of the enemy's soldiers and some for almost thirty. The owner of the pendant in Karueq's hand was responsible for eighty-nine.

Quiron had a particularly determined nature. Upon his acceptance to the Brehila, he had made a vow in blood to earn his hundredth kill from the death of a man called the Quiri, the protector and guardian of the enemy commander, the Elequiri. With ten more kills and the head of the Quiri, Quiron would have laid claim to all the honors and riches that could possibly be bestowed.

But Quiron would not receive such honors. In place of riches and glory there would be shame and exile. He would be hunted for the rest of his life. The Eleverians' new strategy against Karueq's armies, the Shatanala, proved to be more effective than any of them had realized. They had taken Quiron, one of their most dangerous enemies, and made him one of them.

This is the secret Karueq would have to keep. Such information would increase rebellion and spread further panic through the Shatanala. The caverns of Xanadai had the capacity to house the Prince's armies, but total rebellion would spill into the world above, Seaga, ruining the carefully calculated world Karueq was toying with above ground.

Unlike Quiron, Karueq cared nothing for taking an unprecedented number of lives. He cared nothing for the glory of which most of his men dreamed. Karueq's focus was on the ultimate prize, the one few others had the foresight to even consider, let alone focus on – the total annihilation of Eleveria. Quiron's bloodlust for the Quiri had been one component of this dream. Taking him would make the Elequiri vulnerable. With the subsequent destruction of the Elequiri, Seaga would be without the protection of the Eleverians, Israel and Judah would be trampled, and Karueq would take pleasure seeing the Prince overpower their God, Eleh, once and for all.

Karueq absentmindedly watched the tide, like that of the ocean, lap the shore and steam the rocks in its wake. He allowed the heat to envelop him like a shawl, let it sink in, felt it gently burning him from the outside in. He often stood here like this to remember that he still lived, still breathed – to know that he could still feel the heat suffocating him. This hole in the earth made the mind a stranger to itself. It was the hazy darkness, the feeling of being alone even when surrounded by an army, and the ghostly stillness in the passages snaking deeper into the earth. These elements stole perception, twisted it.

"Karueq," the voice came to him like a whispered fog yet to materialize. Karueq instinctively turned to his left.

"My lord," he saluted.

The Prince stood there with a dark, alluring air. His features were defined, handsome in the burning light flickering from the lake. A thick, heavy cloak draped the well-built form he assumed. Stately, black wings reached out from his spine and poised on either side of him. "I was informed," he began, his voice deep and graced by an easy charm, "you sent a team to track one of our own."

"I did," Karueq replied.

"You told no one why," the Prince gazed steadily at his first in command.

"Yes, Shatan," Karueq replied. "I thought you should know first as to the nature of our problem."

Karueq tossed the pendant into the Prince's hand. The Prince's eyes examined the pendant, his expression unmoved.

"The Brehila. Which one?"

"Quiron," Karueq stated.

The Prince turned his stare on him. "He is not dead, or you would have his body in your possession, not just this."

"Indeed, my lord. They turned him."

The being before Karueq retained its dark surety despite the news. There was only a brief blink changing the landscape of his face.

"I sent the team to track him down and bring back a body, only," Karueq continued.

"Call them back," said the Prince, blankly.

"He has secrets the Eleverians must never know."

"They already have them," the demon countered. "Whatever secrets he has that may be valuable to them are already forfeit and nothing will come out of diverting men we can use elsewhere."

"What example does that make for my men?"

"They need not know he is alive," Shatan replied, decidedly. "They need not know he has been lost. Recall your men, and forget this traitor ever existed."

"I don't think that's wise," Karueq said, not budging. "I cannot ignore the fact that the enemy now has one of our best in their ranks. His knowledge aside, he could damage our numbers with his skill."

"All the same, recall them."

Shatan's dismissal irritated him. "My lord, you seem to miss the point. Quiron was a Brehila. One of the best. They will notice his absence."

"The Brehila keep themselves isolated, even from each other, but to ease your concern, I leave it to you to keep them occupied so they do not miss him."

"There are only so many statesmen and priests they can eliminate before we start losing our holdings."

"You're a creative man. You can make targets for them by pointing them toward insignificant folk."

Karueq held his tongue on this point. Karueq had learned to be picky about his battles with Shatan. Both of them were cunning leaders and interested in the bigger prize, however often they disagreed on details. This dispute was a detail, a detail that concerned Karueq but held no value for Shatan. Since Shatan had ultimate power over the situation, Karueq would let this one go.

"I appreciate your concern over this matter," said the demon, reading his mind. "Your attention to the details is one of the many reasons I chose you to lead my forces."

"Save your praise," Karueq spat. "I have a rebellion to attend to."

"Very well." The ancient creature furled his wings around himself and disappeared.

Karueq dispelled a frustrated sigh and turned to the main tunnel in the back wall of the cavern. The tunnel was little more than a natural gash in the steep rock wall at the back of the cavern, but it could move people ten abreast into the greater tunnel network. Karueq disappeared into this winding network of the passages. What he would do with Quiron could wait. Plans to thwart the wretched enemy he swore to destroy would also be left for later. Karueq was in a wicked mood to squash something, and so help the next man, woman, child, or creature he found in his path.

The passages were all like this. Some were dank, some blistered with the heat from the belly of the earth, but all were poorly hewn. Xanadai boasted no straight halls or smooth passageways. The tunnels gnawed through the ground, providing poorly navigable paths between the sectors to the city. Some were carved out better than others, like this one Karueq traveled through to reach the temples. Some, like the paths to the prison, were sharp and ugly, hardly leaving any good footing to traverse. They were made at a time when the Shatanala were undisciplined and mindless. The previous commanders had made no attempts to improve them, and Karueq had followed in that great tradition. Though the tunnels were both confusing and dangerous, the Shatanala knew their city well and needed no markings to avoid getting lost.

A temple guard, dressed in his unholy finery, appeared around the bend of a particularly long tunnel – running frantically, hurrying to find help.

"My lord!" he cried upon seeing his commander. "My lord! The fifth battalion! They have overrun us!"

Karueq whipped out his sword and thrust it into the guard's belly. The guard shrieked and grunted on impact. Karueq yanked his blade out and kept walking, barely hearing the thud and clank of the guard falling to the ground and his cries of agony. The pitiful guard would survive. Karueq found no use in killing his assets. He stepped behind a pile of rubble left on the path and disappeared into a crack in the tunnel wall, unnoticed in the barren passage.

The crack opened slightly into a vein that slunk through the walls. The air grew more intimate, like stale breath. The closeness lingered as Karueq continued on to the temples. He hated the temples more than any other sector of the city. The formalities and flippant customs that were expected only disgusted him. The feeling that saturated the air is what unnerved him. The air in the temples never felt quite right, like a subtle shift in reality.

The low rumble snapped him out of his uneasiness – voices shouting. Karueq was amused as he thought about what this rebellion truly meant. Finally, after simple scuffles in the stockrooms and the prisons, someone had taken the initiative to pillage the temples, and Karueq had a good guess about who the fool was.

The tunnel came to an end. He was three stories above the floor behind a statue in a crack near the ceiling. Before him was the lofty cave that held the entrances to the temples of the greater demons. Karueq had chosen to take the long way in and follow this tunnel to avoid the rebels. He let his ears guide his gaze around the wide space. The rumble came from the temple to his left. They had a great deal of nerve to have chosen Madaka's temple as the point of attack. The looming doors to the temple space were adorned with carvings of serpents, bats, pigs, and obscene horrors that delighted such creatures as demons. Statues of the same stood guard on either side. The doors to the other temples, though not as grand, were decorated with similar images, and statues paying respect to the monsters within stood watch at the doors.

Karueq's ears alighted on distinct voices coming from the floor. Through the ghostly, purple torchlight, he could see a few of the usurpers drunkening themselves on the floor with what Karueq assumed was the temple wine.   One of the men was making unwanted passes at one of the women. These rats below had evidently grown bored of their cause and had wandered here for some personal amusement.

Karueq slipped along a ledge that crept along the wall to his left and vanished into another crack in the rock. This vein led to a concealed overlook at the back of Madaka's temple. All of Karueq's senses were poised on the cues coming from the temple. He slid himself into the shadows at the lip of the opening across from the man, Bleren, who was already watching there and gazed down on the scene. Unlike the rest of the city, the temple boasted chaos and clamor. The fifth battalion had seized control of the Temple Sector and converted the temple of their darkest demon into a central base.

Small riots were breaking out briefly in the crowded places around the central altar. The men struck each other bluntly. The women danced invitingly on the smaller altars around the temple. The temple servants were bound and detained near the ceremonial fires. Small groups of pillagers looted the demon's gold. The battalion clearly found themselves victorious.

They had sacrificed the temple's priest. He was stretched out on the center altar, his body laid open. No doubt someone had removed his heart while it was still beating. The lavish robe he normally donned was missing, and his hair had been cut off.

The man with the knife that slew the priest jumped onto the altar. He was wearing the priest's robe and threw a fistful of hair into the crowd in front of him. Karueq recognized him instantly. This was Zokul. Zokul had instigated more distractions than Karueq cared for. He had even taken his campaigns into Seaga to establish kingdoms for himself. His tactics were primitive and obvious, but they were often effective. Karueq had regrettably found Zokul's obnoxious influence of value on occasion, sometimes turning his men toward more productive but unpleasant goals. However, Zokul's attempts had never brought him this far. Taking their most feared demon's primary place of ceremony was perhaps his way of showing all who could see how invincible he could be. No one dared challenge any of the greater demons, especially not The Shadow itself. Perhaps this time, Shatan would heed Karueq's suggestion to terminate this buffoon.

"We are no longer slaves to the whim of our oppressors! Ha-ha!!" Zokul cried, rallying the entire body of his followers to his sacrilegious podium. "Ours be the comforts with which our lords have taunted us. Yes! Ours be the gold of our masters. The power!"

"The temple women!" someone shouted. The detained servants glared at the men for thinking such things. The offender received encouraging slaps from his comrades.

"The women?" Zokul spat. "Ours be the women of Seaga when we take it!"

The temple resounded with the cries of approval from the men. The women, too, joined in the uproar for the sheer glee of victory.

"Yes!" Zokul screeched. "We will take Seaga. But first, we must take all of Xanadai. Make safe our home! I count each of you as my kin, and I do it proudly!" Spittle flew from his lips. "We have taken the highest temple in this sector, and where is the Shade now? Where is he?! This whole city and its weary guard will fall to us! We will destroy the commander! Yesss. We will kill him, and I will mount his head on a pike! Ha-ha!!"

Karueq smirked at this.

"We will name for ourselves a new king in the stead of the Lord of Darkness. And a new order of priests!" Zokul stomped on the head of the priest beneath him. The uproar repeated. Zokul laughed hysterically and gasped for breath. Foam dripped from his wiry beard. Karueq almost couldn't understand why a disease like this man could garner such a following, if the tensions of the war above ground weren't so palpable.

"We are free!" the lunatic cried at last. "We are free!"

The battalion joined his dramatic hysteria. They began chanting his name, almost as if naming him the new king of their version of Xanadai. Zokul danced on the altar and the body, stirring up more petty riots and feverish growling.

Bleren stepped across the opening of the overlook to Karueq's side. He'd been monitoring the temple from here since the start of the rebellion.

"We won't let them touch you, my lord," Bleren said. "I'll have guards taken from my own forces to protect you."

"Don't waste your soldiers," Karueq dismissed. "These people will lose interest in their cause in a few hours. Some of them have already wandered outside."

"We haven't seen a rebellion like this yet."

"And what makes it so different?"

"An entire battalion chose to take up arms," said Bleren, flatly. "They had the nerve to attack Madaka's temple and sacrifice his priest. Shall I go on?"

"Madaka will take care of his property. And this priest was no good anyway."

"He was a mystic, my lord," Bleren protested. "The people listened to him."

"We can make another mystic, someone who is better at wording prophecies."

"All the same, sir," said Bleren.

Karueq sighed. "Their bloodlust is useful. Zokul will be detained again, and everything will go back to normal. They haven't done anything that alarms me." Karueq switched the subject. "Any word on our prisoner?"

"None thus far," Bleren replied. "He isn't talking, and they have given us no indication they know we have him."

"They know," Karueq assured him. "They're waiting for our move. Send a team out. Somewhere crowded – perhaps a port city. Make them believe we are holding him there and set a trap."

"Yes, my lord."

Karueq gazed down into the temple. The mutiny continued. Bleren studied Karueq's face carefully.

"Something is troubling you," he stated, finally.

"It is nothing that concerns you or your duties."

Bleren pushed further. "I am your second in command. Anything that pains you has a direct impact on my responsibilities. Especially if it involves an operation gone wrong."

Karueq met Bleren's stare. Bleren had become good at reading his superior. As understandable as Bleren's concerns were, and as perceptive as he was, he would never know what had happened to Quiron. Bleren's steady loyalty was rare in the general masses, and Bleren's first loyalty was to Karueq. Bleren believed in everything Karueq and the Prince were doing to stop the enemy. He wasn't a fool, though. He had often brutally questioned Karueq's more risky ideas and counseled him in difficult circumstances. Karueq looked on him as more than a servant, more like a son. He was fiercely trusted in Karueq's eyes, but he had to maintain some boundaries.

"As you wish, Karueq," Bleren relented on his own. "I will not press you further."

"I take my leave," said Karueq. "Stay here until Madaka returns to clean up his mess. Then, you may go back to your station."

"Yes, my lord."

Karueq stole one more glance at the angering crowd below. What little discipline they had been employing earlier was beginning to break down as political debates, bruised honor, and stolen lovers took attention away from their cause. It was how all the rebellions developed. They bent to the whim of the next crazed monkey with half a plan, and then reverted back to usual divisions.

Karueq left and slipped back through the tunnel with his broodings.

His wanderings took him further into the belly of the city. The tunnels became more disjointed the farther down he traveled. These tunnels weaved and sloped down, always down. A wave of heat rolled around Karueq as he arrived in the prison sector. He took a moment to clear his lungs and mind of the uneasiness of the temples. The prisons, though sometimes echoing with the moans and whimpers of its inmates, were easier for Karueq to swallow. At least the scariest aspects of this sector were tangible. It was the lowest place in the city. Because of how close it was to the planet's core, it was necessary to change out the guards regularly. The heat and the poisonous air were extremely potent here.

The cell aisles resembled the tunnels – disordered and meandering away through the ground. The cramped cells were stacked on top of each other. They were just big enough to wrestle the often-objecting detainee through. They had no doors. The prisoner was encased in stone that fused over the openings. Total seclusion was the idea. Being trapped with your own mind was torture, especially when at every moment you felt like you were suffocating.

Some of the cells held rebels and deserters. Most were empty, except in the few days succeeding a rebellion like today. Karueq's success in bringing relative order to the Shatanala hoard was to account for this. The only thing that still frustrated that order was the people's growing upset with the stalemate against the Eleverians. A stalemate that Karueq, remembering the pendant, now feared they were losing.

Karueq found his way to a row of cells that were similar to those above ground in Seaga – iron bars and doors that one could peer through. These were for interrogation. Isolation was not necessary, as conversation from the prisoner was strongly encouraged. And the only way out of these cells was to talk. Death was not an option.

A hulking man emerged from one of the cells where soft weeping could be heard, wearing a leather apron and carrying a large, stained, rusty hook. Upon seeing Karueq, he gave a brief bow.

"My lord," the brute saluted. "How might I be of service? Got another toy for me to play with?"

"You'll be pleased to hear I've got an entire lot of new rebel bones for you to pick through. They'll be arriving soon, though that's not why I'm here. I'm wondering if any progress has been made with one of the toys I've already given you."

"Ha! The ugly one?" chortled the massive man. He pointed down the line. "He's on the end. Still nothing, but we were expecting that."

"Yes, well I hope you're at least enjoying yourself."

"Of course! It's fascinating seeing how different he is from my usual lot."

Karueq was always struck by the boyish fascination this man had toward his cruel work. It made him unsettling despite his permanent smile.

"Find anything useful?"

"No, nothing yet. How long have I got him?"

"As long as you like."

The butcher gave a low whistle. "Then, I'll have plenty of time to find something to report to you."

"May I take him away from you for a few minutes?" said Karueq. It wasn't really a request – he could do what he pleased – but he didn't need to be brash with all his subordinates anymore.

"Certainly," he permitted, "I was just on my way out." Then he pointed his meat hook at Karueq. "But don't go taking too much of my fun away."

Karueq smirked. "I'll try to leave you a few bits of him."

The man snorted. "That's all I ask," and with that, he walked toward the passages, whistling and scraping the hook happily against the stone walls.

Karueq walked down to the end of the row and peered inside the cell. Inside was a man, carved up and broken. He was unconscious, and his straight, black hair was drenched in sweat. He looked small in this state, despite the broad sinew that filled out his body. The butcher had worked his artistry on this man, and it was a sight to behold. However, the wounds were already drying up any bleeding, and his breathing was normal.

Karueq pressed his hand to the metal plate on the door. He summoned some of the dark energy inside his belly and willed the lock to turn. The device inside the plate gave a muffled clank, and he swung the door open. He closed the door behind him and willed the lock to return to its resting place. His presence stirred the man bound to the rack in front of him. One eye opened disinterestedly and found its way to his face. The prisoner inhaled, stretching his chest as if waking up from a restful sleep, flinching only a little as his wounds opened again.

"My captor has finally found the time to visit me."

"I wouldn't be so arrogant if I were in your situation, Hunga." Karueq spat.

"That wasn't arrogance, Karueq," he corrected, blinking his eyes open and settling his focus on Karueq. "That was humor. You should try it sometime."

"I find humor in seeing you in this state," said Karueq, glancing over the torn body.

"I find humor watching you trying to feign control," Hunga chuckled. "You may have captured me, but you can't get anything you want from me." He gave an exhausted sigh. "It must be so maddening – having answers and advantages right in front of you without the ability to unlock them."

"You mistake my plans for you," replied Karueq, unblinking. "I know you won't talk. However, I know your people are loyal to each other and will do everything they can to rescue you."

"They're not short-sighted enough to come here," Hunga sighed. "If only they were, right? If only everything you are working for fell into your lap. What is it you want again?"

"We're setting a trap for them. I think they'll charge a small team with your rescue. They'll be delivered into our hands within the week, I would imagine."

Hunga blinked at Karueq. "And you are going to offer me the chance to save them? To talk and give you everything you want in exchange for not deploying this trap?"

"If I was in a good mood, perhaps," Karueq teased.

"Sorry, I'm all out of foolishness for today," said Hunga, closing his eyes and settling his head into the rack again. "Now if you'll excuse me, I was in the middle of a wonderful dream."

Karueq tore his knife out of his boot and threw it squarely into Hunga's thigh. Hunga let out a cry as the blade bit into his flesh. He braced his head against the rack. Karueq closed the distance between them.

"You will deliver the Elequiri to me!" Karueq hissed.

Hunga pulled his head toward Karueq and looked him squarely in the face. "And the Quiri, too? How about the Captain? Better yet, wouldn't you like the keys to Eleveria's gates?"

Karueq landed a blow on the hilt of the knife. Another cry escaped from the imprisoned Eleverian.

"Yes," said Karueq, calmly. "All of them. I will win them one day, Hunga. You have my word."

Hunga stared at him and didn't retaliate. His silence was what angered Karueq the most. Seeing an Eleverian's joy in the face of pain was nothing compared to his silence. Their nerve was unshakable – every last one of them. Karueq had not encountered one that would submit to questioning by him or any of the Shatanala. Their ability to withstand any methods the Shatanala used against them made them a worthy adversary.

The stand they made against Shatan was born out of their unbreakable devotion to their King. They had succeeded in turning some of Karueq's men, but no Eleverian had ever defected. None of them would abandon their vile religion and accept the offers Shatan had extended them – offers that some of the Shatanala could never dream of sharing. This is what had driven them into a stalemate. The Eleverians would not be moved, and Shatan would never give up his holdings in Seaga. Two immovable forces, both of them intelligent and fiercely determined.

Karueq yanked his blade out of Hunga's leg. Hunga's stifled yelp did not escape his lips this time. Instead, his gaze continued to bore into Karueq.

Was that pity?

Karueq wiped the blood from his knife onto Hunga's frayed shoulder. It was a rather petty attempt at taunting him, but it satiated Karueq's need for dominance in that moment. He retreated from the cell without a word – and without looking back at those eyes piercing him.

CHAPTER TWO

STALEMATE IN SEAGA

The trap for the Eleverians appeared to be taking longer than Karueq wanted. Bleren assured him the plan would work and that the Eleverians would be caught, but Karueq was impatient. It had taken Bleren a week to meticulously spread a rumor that they had Hunga above ground in Thessaly. Karueq didn't really care where he staged the ruse. He trusted his second-in-command to conduct his trick as if he were Karueq himself, but he found himself pleased with the location Bleren had chosen.

What Karueq didn't understand was why the Eleverians were taking so long to act. Hunga wasn't just a soldier. He was the Keeper of the Guard. For the Eleverians, he maintained the integrity of the army, sort of an advisor to the Elequiri and a steward of war. To the Shatanala, he was much needed leverage. Karueq had hoped that it was enough of an advantage, but the silence on the part of the Eleverians was making him wonder how valuable their prize really was. He may not be enough to tip the stalemate in their favor, even a little.

Without any progress being made down that road, Karueq turned his attention elsewhere. He still had a war to attend to. The distraction of the rebellion within the city had occupied him long enough. He looked to Seaga now. Shatan's holdings in Seaga were extensive, but incohesive. Small nations scattered around the world paid their allegiance to the Prince, and whenever one nation defected, another could be swayed back to the fold. It was a game of balance, one that Karueq had become quite good at.

Early in Karueq's leadership, more nations had been corralled into the control of the Shatanala. But in recent days, his momentum had been obstructed by the increased efforts of Eleveria. And so, the stalemate had begun. Each of them matched the opposing intensity, driven by different causes. For Eleveria, it was totalitarian takeover of all Seaga. For the Shatanala, it was liberation from that tyranny. From the moment Shatan rebelled, he had striven to give the world the same freedom he'd gained. He had in turn given that freedom to Karueq all those years ago. Now Karueq sat among the most powerful creatures in existence.

Karueq looked down into the valley and the city below, sleeping peacefully under the night sky. It was nations like this that he needed to save. They devoted themselves to vain sacrifice, offering the best they had to a protector who never showed. They wallowed in a dying hope that they would one day receive a reward for their pain.

The plan Karueq had in mind was a simple yet effective ruse he had used before. It was near harvest season, and the river had blessed the city with abundance this year. This was the time when their petty hope was at its highest. Rather than rationing tightly through the winter, the people would arrive in the spring strong and ready to work for an even better harvest next year.

The trick, then, was two-fold. First Karueq's men would destroy the crop in the dead of night and throw the people into famine. Second, the temple rising from the middle of the settlement would be burned. Thus, suffering would set in, and their protector would flee from them. After an adequate period of grieving, Karueq usually sent in some of his men to rebuild and offer the Prince's good graces. Occasionally, the people might resist for some time, but they would ultimately defect when their children's hunger pains could no longer be ignored.

Karueq signaled for the men beside him to head for the fields. He himself would go for the temple. He watched his soldiers slink down the hill toward the burgeoning fields. He imagined the scene as the sun arose, casting light on their work – the tall wheat bowed low and the livestock peppered with wasting disease. They didn't always work like this. They usually got lucky and nature would take care of this part for them, but sometimes a stubborn people needed to be brought in by force.

He took a moment to enjoy being up here on the surface. The cool breeze floating up from the river was a pleasant relief from the heat of Xanadai. He stretched his lungs with the sweet air and gazed at the pale moon glowing above. He couldn't deny the beauty the light cast around him. The stars gazed back at him without question or account. The river, too, glittered on its way toward the sea. Karueq etched the scene in his mind and tucked it away. It would give him sanity amongst the stink and blackness of the underground.

He returned his focus to his task. He kept his eyes and ears open for midnight wanderers as he made his way toward the riverbank. The lamps had been extinguished hours ago. He stopped at the edge of one house and listened. All he heard were the crickets in the grass and frogs at the river's edge. No footsteps. No dogs guarding here.

He left the corner of that house and ran silently to the city's heart. The temple loomed ahead, rimmed by the moonlight and brightened by the only torch left burning during the night. He tucked himself into the shadows of the last house. He paid extra attention to the sounds around him here. The torch cast enough light that any passersby would see him approaching. This had to look like an unnatural event, not a sabotage by flesh and blood.

Karueq heard nothing, so he slipped away from the house and into the torchlight. Movement to his right. He froze and turned his gaze to the intruder. A boy, no more than seven, stood there, a look of shock on his face. He may have been stirred from sleep by thirst – gone to draw water from the well. Karueq peered at him from beneath his hood. He couldn't let this boy go and risk the secrecy of the mission. But what to do?

He would take the child and bring him into the ranks of the Shatanala. Perhaps, if the boy yielded quickly enough, Karueq would return him to his family when the Shatanala brought aid back to the city. Then there would be a loyal servant of Shatan living among them, keeping them in line.

Karueq lowered his hood and held out his hand. He allowed a warm smile to spread across his face. He appeared every bit like a benevolent guardian, not the captor he would be to this child. The boy hesitated, but Karueq waited patiently. There was still plenty of night ahead to tear down the temple once this interruption was remedied. The brat took a tentative step forward.

Hoofbeats shattered the stillness of the scene. They pounded the ground behind Karueq. He whipped around, sword drawn. A large horse bared down on him. He sidestepped the steed and swiped at it. The horse nimbly swayed out of range. A figure on its back snapped a bow taut and released it. An arrow buried itself in Karueq's side. He let the cry of pain escape his lips but turned back and lunged at the pair.

The rider swatted Karueq's sword away with his bow. The horse threw a kick his way. Karueq dodged the hoof and sliced the horse's leg. The horse squealed and kicked again, narrowly missing Karueq's head. The rider swiped at him again and fixed the horse between him and the boy.

A sound suddenly stole his attention. It was a scream from the fields. His men were being attacked.

More hoofbeats thundered in his ears. He glanced around and saw horses coming in from both angles, leaving him a single exit – away from the boy and the temple. Karueq angrily snapped off the end of the arrow's shaft and ran to the cover of the houses.

He kept running, ignoring the pain searing through his belly. They'd found out. How had they found out? Karueq turned at the last wall and hid himself behind the storehouse. He slammed his back against the wall. His ears locked open for the sound of the horses racing after him, but nothing came. He breathed shallowly, partly to let his hearing stay clear and partly to keep his expanding diaphragm from wriggling the remaining piece of the arrow in his side.

His breathing slowed on its own. He cursed the attackers with everything in him. This had been a spontaneous attack. The Eleverians should not have been aware of their presence in the area. Karueq shook his head. He had to admit he hadn't been entirely invested in this operation. It was more of a way to pass the time than a calculated scheme, something to distract his mind. He looked around at the city and listened again. He heard the people stirring from their slumbers. Karueq left the cover of the storehouse and ran silently up the hill.

Karueq's mind ran through the damage. He wondered if he could salvage any part of this mission. Not with the Eleverians staying. The

Eleverians had this people's trust, and the bodies they would find in the fields would confirm their biases.

He continued on once he reached the top. He and his men had tucked their rendezvous point behind a smaller hill carved out by a tributary away from the lip of the bluff. It wasn't his most clever hideout, but they hadn't planned to be there long. He rounded the corner to find their rides and a lone soldier. They had come on winged beasts, the Rales. They looked sickly with their ugly, rat-like heads and their unfeathered, bat wings. Their feet were fearsomely clawed and as large as bear paws and ribs stretched their ravaged skin outward. Their tempers were short, but they could carry a rider for hundreds of miles without stopping – one of Shatan's personal creations.

The soldier rose from where she was sitting upon seeing her commander.

"Sir, our men have fallen," she stated, flatly. "I fear I am the only survivor."

"You didn't think to give your last like your brothers?" Karueq snapped. He continued to ignore his side. Especially in front of a subordinate.

"This war will not be won here," the soldier dared. "I think you also saw no use in staying."

Karueq considered her clarity for a moment. "What is your name?"

"Ingana," she replied, standing straighter.

"Hmm, Ingana." He sized her up, noticing she swept a braid across her forehead. "You could be one of my lieutenants one day if you continue thinking like that." He brushed passed her and mounted one of the more agreeable Rales. "What would you do now?"

Her eyebrows furrowed in thought, trying to come up with an answer becoming of a future officer. "I would wait and see if they stay until the evening…"

"…and then report back to me," he hurriedly finished her thought. "I expect you back with a report within a week."

The girl seemed startled by the request. "Yes, sir," she saluted.

Karueq kicked the beast into flight without acknowledging her further. The other Rales, save one, followed him into the air.

The beast pulled them into the air, each pump of its wings aggravated Karueq's wound. He circled them once over the valley to survey his losses. He could dimly see a crumpled body lying in the field below him. He guessed there were similar corpses in the other fields, save the one Ingana was assigned to. The torchlight still cast a glow in front of the temple, but it was accompanied by lamplight coming from the roused homes.

The Eleverians were still there – a small team of five. They had dismounted their horses and were embracing the people, calming their worries with lies. Karueq was disgusted by them. He couldn't wait to rip the rest of Seaga from their dirty hands. If only he could deliver the Elequiri.

Karueq turned the Rale back around. He had no desire to stay here, nor could he with an arrow in his belly. He pushed the beast to follow the pack that was leaving them behind. They glided silently on the wind, like ghosts, but the wind cracked in Karueq's ears. The pack cleared the valley and soared up into the waning night.

Karueq slowed his Rale and let the pack pull ahead. His body had let a clammy sweat erupt over his skin. He fought the urge to rip the broken arrow shaft out and relieve his nerves. However, he realized that doing so might allow enough blood loss for him to pass out. He considered returning to Xanadai, but it was a long journey, and he was too frustrated by the mission to return with a cool head. Instead, he gathered his resolve and kicked the Rale into a sprint following the river to the south. The rest of the Rales would return to Xanadai riderless and hungry. These creatures had a bloodlust that matched his armies, but their animal natures required that thirst to be satiated. They often attacked each other if not given a kill for too long. Karueq mused about the trouble they would give their handlers upon their return.

The Rale huffed along, straining against the air drag for several hours. To the east, the foothills of a mountain began to rise. Karueq peeled his eyes from the horizon and found the mountain's dark shadow spiking the sky. The mountain fed small channels many miles toward the river below. It was a nurturing place for a settlement – a settlement the Shatanala had claimed many years before Karueq came to power.

Karueq kicked the beast left and urged it to sail faster toward the black mountain. The creature squawked and squealed in protest, its membranous wings tired from the journey the evening before and the hasty journey it made now. Nevertheless, it obeyed Karueq's demands and raced east. The wind roared even louder as it whipped around them, and it dragged the chill deeper into Karueq's bones.

The butte standing above the foothills came into view. Karueq pushed the Rale into a steep descent. It gave no protest, as it knew its hard work was about to come to an end. Karueq braced his body against the impact as the oversized rodent's claws crashed to the ground in front of the palace. The force jarred the shaft in his side, making Karueq grunt in pain. The animal collapsed on its belly and snarled at him through its wheezing for the unfair, hard ride. He ignored the growls and dismounted. The animal limped away. The Shatanala had trained the Rales to hide and wait for a whistle if not instructed to stay put. This allowed the Shatanala to conduct covert schemes without the ugly, unnatural creatures raising alarm.

Karueq spotted the two palace guards on either side of the door. They were Shatanala plants, as was the nation's king inside. Karueq stood tall and looked around at the quiet city to maintain his commanding air in front of his subordinates. The stars were just beginning to fade before the sky turned gray. The city wouldn't be up for an hour or so.

He walked up the short flight of steps to the palace entrance. The guards bowed to him. They probably didn't recognize him as their commander, but he was definitely a superior.

"Good morning, sir," one guard greeted him as he opened the door.

Karueq swept past him sternly and stoically as a wave of nausea crashed over him. He kept his balance as he marched into the hall. He veered for the king's chambers and burst through the door.

The snoring king in the luxurious bed choked awake at the sound of an intruder entering his room. "Oy, who goes there?" the oaf yelped. His eyes widened at seeing the pale commander.

The sick, commanding man swayed. "Send for your physician."

Karueq's world went dark, and he collapsed.

--^--

Karueq awoke to the sun blazing on his face. He blinked at the brightness, adjusting to his sudden awareness. When his eyes stopped burning, he took a deep breath to clear the sleep away from his mind. He threw off the blankets and winced as a dull throb radiated through his belly. The arrow.

Karueq sat up stiffly and looked down. A bandage wrapped around his muscled abdomen. His curiosity got the better of him and he peeled the wrap away where it bulged concealing more bandages. A fresh scar bored into the muscle. It wasn't oozing or bleeding; rather the skin had knitted together well, protecting the fragile organs beneath that would take more time to mend. The physician had done well.

The physician, Karueq noticed, was still in the room with him. He was sitting on a cushion on the floor, busy grinding away at a mortar and pestle, not minding his patient's rising.

Karueq cleared his throat, but the small man didn't look up. His arm flurried round and round, working whatever he was grinding into a fine powder.

Karueq cleared his throat a little louder. The physician yelped in surprise and the ceramic stick flew out of his hand. The little man squelched again as it crashed against the wall.

"Report," said the commander rising to his feet and reaching for his shirt.

"Uh…" the flighty thing stammered.

Karueq sighed and pulled on his shirt. "How am I healing?"

The physician relaxed as he climbed to his feet and came over to examine the scar. He pulled up the shirt and peered at the skin eagerly, poking around at the intact flesh.

"You are healing very well, my lord," the physician appraised. "You should be fully healed in a few days. Your liver received some damage, but the arrow missed your major vessels."

"How long have I been here?" Karueq asked.

"You arrived this morning, sir."

Karueq looked out the window. The sun was in the west. It was late afternoon. He inwardly marveled at the quick job Shatanala healers could do with a little dark magic.

The little man scampered back to his cushion and rummaged through his bag. Karueq stretched his tired shoulders while he waited. The physician snatched up two vials and bounded back.

"Drink this one for your liver," he said, holding up a green tincture. "And this one for the pain." He raised the brown liquid in his hand.

Karueq took the liver cure and pocketed it but left the brown vial in the man's hand. He was pleased when the physician's mouth dropped in bewilderment and a stifled protest. He needed to feel powerful in this moment after a failed scuffle with the Eleverians. Especially a scuffle that had rendered him helpless for most of a day.

"You may go," Karueq commanded.

Karueq turned to his belongings while the physician swept up his crafts from the corner. Karueq belted his sword at his side. It restored his remaining pride. He stoked his confidence by mulling over the forty-eight Eleverian lives he had personally taken with this sword. Though he had been responsible for the plots that had killed hundreds more, he relished those forty-eight kills more than anything. Some had been singularly feared by the Shatanala and were leaders among the enemy. Others, well, Karueq would never know their names.

When he finished gathering up his weapons and donned his cloak, he pulled on his boots and strode out the door. Out in the hall, he could smell roasting meat. His stomach clenched in hunger. The sound of merry footsteps came from his right.

"Aha! My lord," the king bellowed, striding toward him amidst an entourage of stately individuals. "You're just in time. I've got quite the feast prepared. Come!"

The king ushered him with an arm around his shoulders toward the music that was coming from the end of the hall. The lord of this nation was a king named Grogun, the most loyal of the Prince's royalty. But these rulers were only royalty out here in their kingdoms. They still answered to the commander and many of the higher officers in Xanadai. To the general crowds in Xanadai, they were pawns who lived in luxury and fattened themselves on the Prince's rewards. They drew jealousy for the often rich lives they led for seemingly no work.

Their less jealous commander was more privy to their uses, however. These pawns maintained the people's loyalty for the Prince and safeguarded their holdings in Seaga. The Shatanala armies may fight the battle to win the prize, but the kings made sure their prizes remained won.

"I was expecting you to spend a few days with us," Grogun said, leading him into the banquet hall. The hall was bursting with frivolity. Musicians set the merry tone from the far wall. The noblemen of the city had been invited to partake in the gaiety. Karueq's nose scoured out the roasted flesh and fresh breads that spilled over the table. "You should stay all the same."

"As much as I appreciate your hospitality, I will only accept it for this evening."

"Very well," the king chortled. "I'm pleased you're at least staying for the feast we've prepared in your honor."

Karueq smiled curtly at the old man. He wouldn't refuse the food that was offered to him. He hadn't eaten anything since the night before, and although he was very powerful among the Shatanala sorcerers, he was still bound by the needs of his body.

Grogun set him at the head of the table and then fell into the seat to his right. A servant appeared at Karueq's shoulder and overfilled his tankard and plate.

"What brings you out here, my friend?" the king asked jovially. "I can assure you we are holding strong here."

"I don't doubt that," Karueq replied, dipping into the food. "We ran an operation in a nation north on the river."

"The little squatters' camp a hundred leagues from here?"

"That's the one."

"Some of my scouts say the Eleverians have been prowling this region lately." Grogun gestured to Karueq's side. "Is that from one of them?"

Karueq drained the tankard and wiped the remaining drops from his lips. "We were caught by surprise. I hadn't received any reports of them in the area."

"Bad luck, then," Grogun grumbled as he sank his round face into a pork leg.

Karueq mulled his words over. That was certainly one point of view. He had been reckless and hadn't considered the Eleverians would be plotting their own schemes in the area. And one of their operations just happened to be in the same place Karueq was working. Perhaps he should examine his possible conquests more carefully.

The other alternative was that he was becoming predictable. Though he thought the mission was spontaneous, he had to recognize nothing he did was ever truly off the cuff. He had gauged the season and known it was harvest time. He had taken exactly the number of men as was needed for the number of fields the city possessed. The timing might have been quick, but the variables had been calculated.

Grogun must have noticed Karueq's disappearance into himself because he cuffed him on the arm. "Ay, your luck will turn up next time. And you'll find those filthy worms nestled under your boot."

"Do you ever wonder if they think they're right?" Karueq asked, not really paying much attention. A dancer from the court draped scantily in red had caught his attention.

"Of course they do," Grogun chuckled. "Everyone thinks they're right. But let me tell you something, my lord. What do you think is more right? Wallowing through life in misery? Or enjoying the benefits life gives us?" At this the king slyly caught Karueq's eye and flicked his head knowingly at the dancer.

Karueq shook his head in dismissal. "What about their promises? You know their religion, Grogun, you spent your whole life turning these people from it."

"Promises," the king spat. "Let me tell you about promises, laddy. I've watched you since you were a boy, growing up into the mighty man you are now. Now the Prince, he's promised you rewards, has he not? And how many of those payments has he made good on?"

Karueq quickly glanced over his rise to his position. "Every one."

"Now tell me this," Grogun chomped into another pork flank. "This Eleh, he's promised a vague 'ultimate bliss' as you might say after you spend all your days trying to follow a list of rules no one can ever be expected to keep and suffering without any help from Him. And they don't even know if they are going to get it. Then, they get tossed into the pit for disobeying and spend the rest of their days paying for the treason they made against Shatan. Now tell me, does that sound at all like being right?"

Karueq smirked. If ever he had any doubts about his choice those many years ago, there was always someone who reminded him of why he made it.

"And how have these people responded to your version of promises?" Karueq asked. "For a man so sure of himself, you should have more evidence that your thoughts are correct."

"My lord, they've done completely away with Eleh. In fact, they've done away with worship all together. They serve no one, except for me of course. They throw themselves into the pursuit of wealth, power, and decadence."

Karueq grinned at this. "Wealth and power themselves can be gods."

Grogun choked on the pork stuffing his mouth. He wiped his puffy chin with a grin. "Aye," he chortled. "That they can."

CHAPTER THREE

PLOTTING AND SCHEMING

----- ----- ----- ----- ----- ----- -----

He heard the knock at the door, but Karueq continued to stare absentmindedly at the small stone in his hand. It was no larger than the tip of his finger and washed smooth by the river from which he had taken it. The stone boasted no special properties except that its pale color had caught Karueq's eye as it lay in a bed of darker stones.

The door opened, and it took but a moment for her perfume to slither toward him.

"What do you want?" Karueq asked, coldly. He turned his eyes from the stone to the temptress before him. She leaned seductively against the wall. Her long, black hair cascaded about her head. Her deeply bronzed skin shone with oil, and her red mouth curled softly into a coy smile. Her arms were covered in gold bracelets. The train of her slender black and gold dress melted across the floor.

"It's not what I want, Karueq," she answered. "It's what you want."

"Don't be a snake, Jezebel," Karueq warned her.

She leaned away from the wall and stepped around the low table in front of Karueq. Her eyes flitted over the map spilling across it. Several other stones like the one in Karueq's hand were carefully positioned inside the borders of the long-disputed land claims scrawled across the paper. Karueq marked each victory by collecting a stone from a nation's land once it fell to him.

"What do you want?" he repeated, impatiently. This priestess could wield her seductive power all she wanted. Karueq had only been fooled once. She hadn't promised him anything, per se, but she had played him for more power – power he had not been able to revoke once he finally came to his senses.

"I came because I sensed you were in pain." She reached out and caressed his aching side. He hadn't fully healed from the arrow.

Karueq scoffed and pushed her hand away. "And you wish to use it as leverage for something? To pretend you're consoling me and then wrap your slithering hands around my throat? No, Jezebel. Your tricks no longer work on me."

"Tricks?" she cooed, drawing closer to him. "Karueq, darling, how long have you known me, and you still think I'm trying to play you?" She was close enough for him to smell her sweet breath.

Karueq forced her away. "You keep your distance, witch," he ordered, maintaining his resolve. "I've known you far too long. Your charms will never work on me again."

Jezebel's expression fell and an icy sheen spread over her inviting eyes. Karueq savored the moment. Many of his more astute soldiers would give anything for this, to control even for a second Shatan's most powerful priestess. She devoured souls in return for granting wishes of wealth, love, and power, and few could escape her allure.

The snake retreated from him and threw open the drapes hiding the balcony. She gazed out into Sheol with her arms stiffly crossed.

"It's your preoccupation with your schemes, isn't it?" she jabbed, not looking back at him. "Your base desires are distracting you."

Karueq chuckled. "Even if it were true that I am distracted, it's no less than what you do to my men."

"Don't be a jackal," she spat.

"Oh, come now, priestess," Karueq grated. "You are indeed powerful. You put your charms to good use, and I'm thankful for the distraction you offer my men."

"Do not talk to me like I'm some harlot to be used," she warned, turning to face him.

"I didn't say that; far from it. You are indeed desirable, Jezebel, and had you not crossed me, I might still find you agreeable."

Jezebel's face lifted again, with an arid power. "I don't need you to love me, Karueq," she cooed. "The people believe in me, and my power comes from them. You may have them in your command, but they worship me."

"You put your stock in a fickle people," Karueq said, growing tired of her presence. "They won't love you forever. As soon as you lose their interest, I'll see to it that you become lower than a harlot."

Jezebel smiled coyly. "You want a contest then? To judge who has the most influence over this hoard? Your wish is my command. I've been given an assignment in Israel and won't be around to personally influence their loyalties. You can see if they still adore me in my absence."

Karueq wasn't surprised that he wasn't informed of this plan. Shatan knew how they quarreled, and he made it his business to keep them from interfering with each other. It did startle him, however, that Shatan was asking her to go into Seaga. Even more startling was Shatan's decision to give her charge of the enemy's stronghold.

"Surprised, my dear?" she hissed. "Are you trying to understand why he would give me such an important task while you wrestle with the Eleverian dogs?"

If Karueq were honest, he could see Shatan's reasoning behind this scheme. Her gift was careful seduction. She appeared to offer support and be a fierce ally while she plotted in plain sight. But expressing the value of her gifts was something Karueq did not need to do.

"I assume it has something to do with your womanly assets and not your knack for strategy."

Her lips thinned and her eyebrows narrowed. Jezebel glared at him, coldly.

"He's assigned you to marry the king," Karueq guessed, almost gleefully. "I'm sure you'll make him an agreeable wife, Jezebel. How many children have you decided to put forth for this animal?"

"Stop it!" the witch barked.

Karueq kept his sneer to himself. He actually reveled at the thought of this enchantress being reduced to a prop in the public eye. The lies she would whisper to the Israeli king and the plots she would weave behind the shutters of the palace would be masked by a display of submission to her despised husband. How different from the honor she experienced here.

"Alright, I don't need to mock you, now," he conceded. "But I can't have you toying with my assignments either. What are you planning to do when the Eleverians come nosing around?"

The priestess turned up her nose and spoke evenly. "I couldn't care less about those rats."

It was Karueq's turn to show offense. "They are our enemy, Jezebel - a dangerous enemy. You may have spent your life down here among our own, but you have to realize they will find out what you're doing, and they'll interfere."

"Ha! You think I tremble before a man who never shows his face and his pathetic little army?"

"That man is smarter than you think. He could bring *us* to our knees if *you* are not careful."

"Please, spare me your pittance. What do they do up there, Karueq? Tell me. Can you really say they're a mighty people when they hardly even fight us? They sneak around thinking their charitable works are doing anything."

"I wouldn't underestimate them, Jezebel."

"And if I were you, I wouldn't underestimate Shatan."

"What do you mean by that?"

"I mean you underestimate the power of the angel you profess to believe will one day overpower God."

Her words took him off guard. She noticed and closed the distance between them. Her perfume hung thickly around him.

"My dear," she whispered, forbiddingly. "If you really do believe in the Prince's cause, if you really believe that he should be the one to rule all, you should be a little more reverent of his ability to destroy Eleveria."

She left her sting clinging in his ear as she walked to the door. Karueq heard her gold bangles jingling as she left and closed the door. Karueq stood frozen, staring out into the cavern as he tried to shake her words from his mind. He was Shatan's most trusted soldier, was he not? Of course he believed in Shatan's power and his ability to overpower. He wouldn't have ascended to this position if he hadn't.

Karueq shook his head of these toxic thoughts. It was Jezebel who had spun them, and he had learned long ago to brush her words aside. She was always vying with him for Shatan's favoritism, but while she had been occupied with gaining love and affection from the people, Karueq had worked tirelessly toward realizing his master's goal.

Karueq's ill-placed musings had brought his feet from his chambers, passed the tunnels, and into the prisons. Bleren was already there to meet him, staring into Hunga's cell with his arms crossed. He was absentmindedly contemplating something. If Karueq had to guess, his loyal officer was considering new ways to break that unshakeable prisoner.

Karueq pulled himself up next to Bleren and gazed into the cell. Hunga's body showed evidence of the butcher's recent games. Karueq had ordered that he be shown the butcher's hospitality every day without fail, though he was sure the frequency of the torture would do little to break him when nothing else had.

"You've been busy, Karueq," Bleren said, breaking the silence. "Tangling with the Eleverians? Growing bored, are you?"

"I can't just sit idly while my soldiers run off to all the fun," Karueq replied.

The two turned down the aisle toward a cell a few doors down.

"You were reckless," Bleren scolded him. "What if they'd killed you?"

Karueq chuckled. It wasn't the first time an Eleverian had come close to making him answer for the lives of their comrades. "They didn't. I'm still here."

Bleren shook his head in exasperation as he put his hand on the metal plate on the cell door and it gave a soft clank. "You're really reckless, you know that?"

Karueq opened the door, and a rabid chortle reached their ears. "You know what would be really reckless?" the diseased voice cackled. Zokul rolled his head up from his spittled chest. "But you don't have the guts." He choked feverishly, his body rocking against the straps tying him to the rack. "Don't have the guts to take it. You'll never have the guts to do it! Don't have the stones!"

Bleren whopped his elbow across Zokul's face. "Quiet, you mutt," he commanded, keeping his voice level. Bleren seized the dog's jaw and forced him to focus on Karueq.

"You will submit to your master, or you will have spent the last of your days down here. You will swear it in blood, or I'll drain you by force."

"You must know by now that you can't trust me," the rebel sneered. "Whether or not I bow to you in a pool of my own blood and that of my followers, you know that by now." He stared pointedly at Karueq, and Karueq was starkly reminded of the steady soldier Zokul used to be. Now, Karueq wanted with all his might to be rid of him, but even after the revolt in Madaka's temple, Shatan wouldn't hear of it.

"I know I can't," Karueq agreed. "I can't trust you, therefore I can't release you. I could just kill you, but you've caused me so much trouble, it wouldn't be nearly satisfying enough."

Bleren reached in his pocket and took out a small, innocuous looking bit of paper, catching Zokul's attention.

Karueq continued. "Since you don't enjoy your lodging in Sheol and your duty as a soldier of Shatan, we will give you accommodations with the Rales."

Zokul was trembling, his eyes locked on the paper. "What is that?"

Bleren turned the paper to Zokul so he could see the writing. "We agreed that because of the lack of decency the Rales have when it comes to anything with flesh, we thought it would be fair to safeguard your life. So, we took the liberty of drafting this contract to bind your soul to your body."

Karueq saw the carnage flash in Zokul's eyes, the prospect of being ripped apart without ever dying shooting through Zokul's mind.

"No! No! You can't!" Zokul screamed, his eyes wild and frightened. "I have to agree to a contract if it's going to work!"

Karueq seized Zokul's left arm and pulled his shoulder forward. The Mark every man, woman, and child in Shatan's service bore was branded into the flesh of Zokul's arm. "This is your consent," Karueq hissed. "Any oath made for you in blood is valid. One drop of your blood on this paper and the contract holds."

"No!" Zokul cried. He wrenched his shoulder away. "I rescind my allegiance! I renounce Shatan! I renounce Shatan! I renounce Shatan!"

"You know you can't do that," Karueq sneered through the hound's screams. "You're in for life, and even in death you will serve him."

"I don't serve him!" he sobbed. "I haven't served him in years!"

"You're right, you haven't."

"Ok, ok!" the blubbering man pleaded. "Ok, I'll make you a deal. I'll make you a deal!"

Karueq took a step back, satisfied that he'd rattled the man, and plucked the paper from Bleren's hand. "I'm not interested in making your deal." He gathered the dark energy inside his gut and pushed it up through his shoulder, down his arm and into his fingertips. The paper caught fire, and it curled and blackened into nothing beneath the bright flames. Zokul's lips trembled, and his eyes shifted away from his master's stare.

"To tell you the truth, you rather amuse me, Zokul," Karueq lied. "I don't mind you turning my men into bloodthirsty savages, as long as they don't turn on our cause. I want to commend you on your ambition and your ability to sway my soldiers to your will. You've proven yourself as a brilliant strategist. Therefore, I am offering you the opportunity to put your skills to work for your master."

After a moment, Zokul spoke up quietly. "I have no master."

"As long as you are branded, you serve Shatan. The only thing that you control is your willingness to serve."

Zokul turned his eyes away again. He looked helpless and childlike, and Karueq was relieved at his reduced state. He knew it may only be temporary, but finally seeing Zokul break was a welcome change.

"Now," Karueq continued. "I have a special assignment for you. I am placing you in charge of finding the Quiri. Bring his body back, and you will be richly rewarded."

"Richly rewarded, indeed," Zokul sneered. "Thrown back on the rack after. There's my rich reward."

"Refuse to do this, and I will keep you on this rack until the end of your days. And I will make your days long."

"You suppose the Quiri will help you win Eleveria. You're playing too safely. You'll never win like that."

Karueq crossed his arms, and his eyes narrowed at the prisoner, "I assume by that comment you think you know a better plan."

"You don't have the guts," Zokul sneered, quietly.

Bleren sighed, begrudgingly. "What could we possibly be afraid of?"

Zokul turned his attention to Karueq only and whispered his secret. "From the inside. You must feign allegiance to them, and then break them from within."

Karueq caught Bleren's annoyed sideways glance out of the corner of his eye.

"Very well, Zokul," Karueq said, dismissively. "We'll take your idea into consideration. I'll have you released, and after you bring me the Quiri, you can enlighten us more with your ideas."

With that, Karueq turned his back on the man and returned to the prison aisle. Bleren locked the door behind them. They heard Zokul's unintelligible laughter reinvigorate and echo through the shadowy prison as they made their way toward the prison entrance. Bleren was the first to speak. "You know this already, but I wouldn't mind driving a spike through his skull. If Shatan hadn't forced you to give him this assignment, I would seriously consider it."

"You're not the only one." Karueq halted as he felt the air change. The change was subtle, but Karueq's trained senses caught it instantly. He raised his eyes to the cell door on his left. It was Hunga's. The defiant but weak prisoner's head was bowed, eyes closed, and his expression was exhausted but serene. Karueq barely heard Bleren dismiss himself from the prison.

"Using your magic won't help you escape," Karueq said through the door.

Hunga raised his head. "What makes you think I'm trying to escape?"

"I can sense your energy from here. It's not much, but it's there."

The corners of Hunga's mouth turned up. "I'm not using magic, Karueq, at least not the kind you've come to know. I'm praying."

"Praying for what? Your God cannot hear you down here, and he certainly cannot rescue you."

Hunga tilted his tired head. "You think I'm praying for myself."

"What else would you ask for right now?"

There was that look again, the one that seared into Karueq and made him feel small. Did this creature pity him from his detainment on the rack?

"Karueq, a little advice from your enemy," Hunga offered. "Unless you know what we fight for and what continues to strengthen us, you will never have a hope of destroying us."

"Enlighten me," Karueq told him.

"You would understand with open eyes, but not as you are now."

"What does that mean?"

Hunga sighed. "You see us how your master sees us, and I'm sorry that you do."

"I don't need your pity."

"It's not pity."

"Whatever it is, I don't need it."

"Yes, you do," Hunga said, quietly. "More than you know, Karueq. I can help you."

Karueq ran his hand along the bars of the door, his mouth curling anew. "Whether or not I would ever need your help, you're helpless in this cage."

"And that is why I pray," Hunga said. "So that my prayers may fill the void I'm leaving behind."

"The only void you're filling with your prayer is the space outside this hall."

The Eleverian didn't say anything in response, but his eyes told a different story. He was telling Karueq just how wrong he was with that look but knew the commander wouldn't yield his opinion.

Karueq moved to walk away but stopped at Hunga's final word. "If you want to know us," he said, "see what we do when we're not crossing blades with you."

Without looking at him, Karueq walked away.

It was a few more days until Karueq's injury was fully healed and the pain ebbed away, but he wouldn't be distracted from his schemes. Another nation had been converted to the worship of Shatan, but two more had been stolen by Eleveria within the week. His plants from these fallen nations came back with reports of toppled idols and sackcloth, and it made Karueq's skin crawl with rage. It was just another sign to Karueq that they were losing their footing. The fact that he couldn't figure out why they were slipping itched his frustration and had him carefully considering Hunga's words.

Karueq even considered the possibility that the impervious Eleverian had given him a hint, his brain possibly addled by the delirium of blood loss and constant torture. He considered what he meant by mentioning their activity when they weren't engaged in combat. Karueq had no way of knowing, of course, because Eleveria was sealed off from the world, and the location of the gate was unknown. So, he couldn't possibly know what they did in their homeland. His mind wandered to fantastical plots to expose any information about the Eleverians he could.

Finally, he called Bleren to him. His second nodded in agreement, knowing the plan, if nothing else, could undercut Jezebel's authority in Sheol - a personal advantage Karueq wouldn't turn down.

The barren temple Karueq now stood in held a ghostly illumination, very different from the violent, orange torchlight during the siege of the fifth battalion in Madaka's lair. No signs of the rebellion lingered among the altars and ceremonial fires. Madaka had purged every remnant of the siege.

Karueq was careful not to make eye contact with Madaka unless he was addressed. The Shade's mere presence prickled his spine. While Shatan presented himself attractively to mortals with his stately image, Madaka was every bit a demon in appearance. That wasn't, however, what unnerved Karueq. The Shade's presence was pure malice, fear, and despair. Karueq deliberately spent little time with him, but Madaka's station forced him to on occasion. Karueq was the commander of flesh, and Madaka was the commander of spirit.

Karueq focused instead on the Prince while persuading him of the plot he had in mind.

"Tell me, Karueq," Shatan invited him. "What have your musings been of late?"

"I've come to realize we know next to nothing about the Eleverians," Karueq began. "We don't know how they operate or why they fight us so hard. Therefore, I propose a scandal of sorts." He caught Madaka's pleased grin in his peripheral vision. "You have Jezebel stationed in Israel, and although her work there is needed, we can use her position to another advantage. The Eleverians frequent Israel for various purposes. Now, not many can resist the priestess's temptation, and I venture this could include a number of Eleverians. My lord, the Elequiri is the prize you've been seeking. The play is this, fabricate an affair between Jezebel and the Elequiri."

Madaka's smile fell into a frown, but Shatan's face remained still.

"This seems rather desperate, commander," Shatan said, simply.

"These are desperate times, my Prince."

"What are we to gain from this scheme?"

"We gain information. Whatever their reaction is or whether or not we get one, we can judge their loyalty to their leader and possibly more. It would be a distraction to them if nothing else."

"They would never believe this," Shatan stated, more than a hint of disbelief edging his voice.

"If they don't, we'll be exactly where we are now."

"Why let Jezebel do this?" the Shade's slippery voice hissed. "Claim the affair yourself. Make the Elequiri fall for you, man to man." Karueq's blood turned cold from his gaze, but he kept himself in control.

"My value to this fight comes from my ability to lead, not my powers of seduction."

Madaka snorted angrily at him, and Karueq looked away quickly. His spine shivered. He fought to keep his focus on Shatan as his master contemplated the proposal.

"Very well," the Prince said at last. "Send word to Jezebel."

"As you wish," Karueq bowed and turned sharply to leave. He heard Madaka snarl behind him as he made his way out.

CHAPTER FOUR

THE TEMPTATION OF THE TEMPTRESS

Karueq used this mission as yet another distraction, a way to clear his head and let his mind calculate the next move and the next. His meetings with Shatan usually left him jaded and disappointed. He tried not to let the words spoken become personal attacks, but when Madaka was in tow, he couldn't shake the sour feeling in his stomach.

He had decided to meet with Jezebel to discuss her orders instead of sending a messenger. As missions go, this was by far the easiest. He hadn't even left instructions for Bleren should his absence be permanent. He couldn't begin to care this time what happened to Xanadai in the few days he would be gone.

With that thought, Karueq's internal rebel kicked in. He pulled the Rale around hard and sent it soaring off course toward an Eleverian holding. A report had come in about a disaster that had crushed the city's irrigation system. The report had described blockages and breaks in the canals brought on by a flood from the river. It made Karueq wonder why this people agreed to bow to a God who let them suffer needlessly.

45

The city drew near, and Karueq landed the Rale away from prying eyes. The beast gave him a low growl, but Karueq ignored it. He listened patiently to his surroundings, on guard for an Eleverian watching the city perimeter. None came. Satisfied, Karueq made his way up to the bluff overlooking the fields. He crawled on his belly to peer over the edge unseen. Bleren had told him it was foolish to fly during the day, but of course in his displeased mood, he had ignored him. Again, Karueq rolled his eyes at his lack of spontaneity in favor of cool calculation. He had meant to come here, hadn't he? He wanted to test Hunga's words and see the enemy in action.

Below, the canals were indeed in disorder, though not as much as the report had described. The trenches needling their way from the river through the fields had already been under repair. How quickly the Eleverians worked. There he saw them, side by side with the citizens of the land, digging out the blockages and mounding the dirt at the breaks. By his count, there were seven Eleverian soldiers, one for each trench. They were easy to pick out not from their attire but from the way they carried themselves. They stood taller than the common Seagan laborers who were forced to stoop to the earth for their livelihoods. The Eleverians were as much accustomed to the posture of combat as they were to lifting the burdens of the ordinary folk.

Karueq focused on the one nearest him. He had seen this roach before. His name was Alamar, and he had a calm collect about him, save for the annoying brightness and laughter the Eleverians all seemed to have. This man frequently led non-combat missions like this one, but he could also be brutal with the sword. Karueq hated him. However, watching the proud Eleverian putting his back into the dirt also made him throw disgust toward his own camp. The stalemate stood firm with neither side forcing an imbalance. Yet, Eleveria's soldiers put effort into tasks like this, outside of war. Digging trenches wouldn't advance their holdings much, but they did it. The Shatanala, on the other hand, were always trying to heave the balance their way, never having the time or resources to throw into distractions like the Eleverians did. It disgusted Karueq.

One of the workers along Alamar's canal slipped under his strenuous effort and thudded to the ground. A cry escaped him as his leg caught on rock that sliced it open. Alamar's attention stole to him at once, and he raced to the source of the distress. Karueq watched him dive in to inspect the leg while his comrade, a woman in the nearest trench, ran to a

satchel perched on a levy and hastened to his side. The woman dropped
the satchel within Alamar's reach and knelt at the fallen peasant's head,
calming his cries. Alamar set to work on the leg. Soon the leg was covered
in a poultice and wrapped. The other five Eleverians remained in their
labors, not concerning themselves with the scene in the western trench.

Karueq's fascination gripped him as the man was invited to
stand. Gently, the Eleverians lifted the man to his feet. A look of shock
spread across his face, and he took a ginger step away from his helpers'
supportive arms, then another. He tested the leg out by bearing his full
weight on it. A small stab of pain jerked his body once, but he turned
around to the Eleverians and embraced them. The woman smiled and
returned to her trench to continue with the other workers. Alamar retrieved
a canteen from the satchel and gave it to the man, who sat down obediently
and rested momentarily from the labor. He exchanged a few words with
Alamar before the soldier returned to the trench, throwing himself doubly
into his work as if to make up for the temporary loss of the grunt.

Karueq shook his head. There certainly were differences between
the Eleverians and the Shatanala. Karueq chastised himself for not
thinking to come observe these missions of the Eleverians simply for the
sake of observing. Without an action plan clouding his mind, Karueq
could simply watch these fools and learn.

For instance, he had seen the speed with which the Eleverians'
bodies recovered. Hunga's captivity provided a convenient means of
experimenting with this. The injured man in the trench, however, was not
an Eleverian. He was a simple man with no unearthly abilities, and
Alamar had healed his leg with the speed meant for a battlefield.

As another lesson, Karueq had witnessed the innate efficiency of
his enemy. He would have expected either none or all of the Eleverians to
respond without direct orders. Yet this woman had responded on her own,
without orders and with supplies in hand. Karueq didn't know her, and so
she couldn't have had high rank. She wasn't designated for the job either,
as the satchel was within reach of any of the Eleverians, and she was down
in the trenches working with the people. Shatanala healers did not engage
in the mission until injury was apparent.

Karueq shook his head. He should study them like this
more. Perhaps bring Bleren along sometimes and then discuss what they
had seen. For now, Karueq had another thorn in his side to attend to.

The flight to Israel seemed far shorter. Karueq couldn't help mulling over what he had just seen and didn't pay much attention to the rest of the flight. When he arrived at the palace seeking an audience with the princess, he was informed by the Israeli guard that Jezebel was not present. She had, in fact, gone to Samaria to tend to her family's temple. Karueq was surprised at this. She seemed to be taking her role more seriously than he was willing to give her credit for.

The Rale was significantly less agreeable on the third leg of its flight. Dusk was settling in when Karueq reached Samaria and let his mount chirp gleefully at the prospect of rest as he landed it in front of the temple doors. Jezebel had indeed wasted none of her time away from Xanadai, and Karueq actually found himself to be relieved. She had set up a mighty refuge for two demons just outside the Israeli stronghold under the guise that she should be allowed to maintain her Phoenician family's religion. It was not an unreasonable request given Israel's propensity to allow idol worship on occasion, an allowance that further separated it from the kingdom of Judah.

She had commissioned a grand building, a permanent structure that made the holy tents used by those enslaved to Eleh appear tiny and insignificant. She had given the mortar fusing the blocks a gold finish. Thus, its sand-colored bricks could not disappear into the surroundings. She had done well to make this temple to the demons Baal and Asherah an important fixture of the landscape.

One of the guards at the door rushed to his side and took the reins of the Rale from him.

"The priestess," he demanded.

The guard bowed. "She is inside, my lord."

"Tend the beast," he ordered, and swept past the other guard unceremoniously into the temple.

Upon entering, he looked around. The temple was but one hall, and it wasn't very different from the priestess's abode underground. The walls boasted no windows and so even in the daytime, the fires around the altar were the only light. The fires themselves blazed and crackled, and they swathed the room with a sweltering heat. The slender figure in front of the altar caught his gaze. She didn't turn around, focusing her attention on the energy she was conjuring near the ceiling, a protection spell.

"I've come to seek an audience with her majesty, the princess," Karueq swept low to the ground in a sarcastic bow.

Jezebel's hand shot upward, holding the dark energy in its place and turned her smoldering gaze on him.

"Please don't interrupt me, pet. I'm concentrating."

Karueq summoned the darkness from his gut and burst it from his hands into the mass above Jezebel. The energy above exploded around the room causing Jezebel to scream. The energy wavered but a moment and then set to humming gently in its place, creating a curtain-like barrier. Karueq moved his hand forward slowly, pushing the barrier out of the hall to surround the temple. He concealed a deep inhale, his body attempting to recover from the enormous amount of energy he had just expended.

Jezebel turned on him with venom in her voice. "You fool!" she cried. "You could have killed me!"

"But I didn't, Jezebel," he retorted, releasing the barrier from his control. "Besides, you were taking too long, so I... helped," he added slyly.

"I don't need your help here," she spat.

"Yes, I know," he admitted. "I'm actually rather impressed by what you have accomplished here. I'll admit I was uneasy when Shatan granted you this task, but I'm pleased that you're taking it so seriously."

"You're not the only one who's keen on seeing Eleveria fall."

"Yes, I realize that now. Thank you for boosting my confidence in you."

Jezebel rolled her eyes at the retrospective insult. "My, your compliment is too much," she jabbed sarcastically. "Really, you speak too highly of me. I only ensnared the king of Israel, brought demons to the land to be worshiped, and slayed all of Eleh's prophets."

Karueq set his jaw. "All the prophets?"

"Oh, there's one left, but he's wandering the desert."

"One got away?" Karueq asked, vindictively.

Jezebel's eyes narrowed. "It's more than you've managed to do in decades. Besides, he'll be dead soon."

He brushed the insult aside. "Jezebel, I am here to discuss your orders from the Prince regarding the Elequiri."

"If you think I'm going to indulge you, you're blind. I have work to do here, and I'll be damned if you're going to take it away from me."

"I'm not taking anything away from you, Jezebel, I'm here to tell you that you are to ensnare the Elequiri, learn what your plan is so that I may stay out of your way, and then leave before I grow ill with your presence."

Jezebel perked up at this and raised a brow. "I'm to bring the Elequiri to Shatan myself, and you're not going to stop me?"

"That is not what this is. You are to make the Eleverians believe their leader is making his bed with you. I doubt you'll actually be able to bed him."

"I wouldn't be so quick to discount my allure, my dear."

"We'll see. Do what you want with this task. I was given no details, so as far as I'm concerned, you are to execute as you see fit."

"I agree, but darling, you're not jealous in the slightest that I'm going to unveil him instead of you?"

"I'll check my jealousy if you ever actually pull this off."

Jezebel winked and smiled. "You've come a long way to discuss one matter, dear. Are you sure there's nothing you want from me?"

"I'm never falling under your spell again."

"Don't worry, that's not what I was alluding to. As if I would ever want to be in your arms again. I believe you need a rest from the politics underground. You sought an escape from your duties, however temporary. I can offer you that."

"I am here to discuss your plan. That is all."

"Fine. I have to finish preparations here. I'll be with you shortly."

Karueq turned to leave, but Jezebel's voice stopped him. "I insist that you stay the night."

Karueq threw a glare back at her. She rolled her eyes again. "Not like that. After we've discussed this new endeavor, you may rest while I finish preparing this temple for Baal."

Karueq thought about it for only a moment. "I'll accept that."

"Good. My guard will escort you to my tent."

Karueq nodded and exited the temple.

The guards outside bowed. "The witch's tent," he commanded. The guard on his right led him away to the tent. It was a short distance from the temple and away from the city of Jezreel. Again, she had chosen her methods wisely. The guard offered him food and drink, and Karueq accepted them, ordering him to bring enough food and water to the tent to last a day, but no wine. He would not let his guard down around this woman.

Karueq stared out the temple entrance at the city and its surroundings. False gods were not allowed within Israel at this time, and Jezebel, under the guise of a political wedding, had been allowed to set up this temple in the neutral zone of Samaria. It was a day's ride by caravan road to the Israeli city. Jezebel had taken one of the Rales with her upon departing, so her time was well spent in preparation for her nuptials. Once she became queen, Karueq doubted she'd make use of the beast and would instead lead her wavering subjects on pilgrimages to the temple before planting a few shrines in Israel itself. Although he harbored a deep distrust of her, he had to admit that she was a clever snake and a worthy delegate for the task at hand.

The sky was dark. From the entrance of the tent, Karueq looked at the moon, like he had so many times before. The moonlight shone brightly in the cloudless desert sky, illuminating the landscape and putting the stars to shame. He briefly wondered why he only ever stopped to look at the sky when the moon was out, before realizing that it was the only bright thing that ever drew his eye. Underground, there were shadows and meager light cast around from fires and the lava of the lake in Sheol. Above ground, he only came out at night, as his presence was usually secret. If ever he came out by day, like this afternoon, he was on his guard and never looked up at the brilliant sun blazing down on him. He made a pact with himself to go out to the sea after their next victory and do nothing but bathe in the sunlight and wonder at the blue expanse of the sky.

The guard came back laden with food and a large jug of water. He dismissed the inferior man before rummaging through the supplies - roasted meat, loaves of bread with fruit baked in, fresh greens, and cakes larger than his fist. Karueq nearly scoffed at the food. Of course, she would insist on the best of everything she could get her hands on, but he found it silly because she was out here alone doing work, and staples should have sufficed.

As if on cue, the priestess entered the tent and helped herself to a lamb leg. Karueq wiped his hand off on his cloak and dipped it into the jug. His fingers grabbed a fistful of what lay at the bottom and came back up.

"Something wrong, Karueq?" Jezebel asked.

"You must be very comfortable indeed to put berries in your water," he replied and dumped the berries back into the jug.

"Just because I'm out on mission doesn't mean I can't enjoy the luxuries I've already won."

"You have work to do here. Are you certain you're not neglecting your duties?"

"Where is that confidence you showed me in the temple? I've got my affairs under control, Karueq, but I am still the high priestess of Xanadai, and I can obtain comforts you deny yourself."

Karueq briefly thought about this. He did deny himself many of the rewards Shatan had offered him for victories he had won. However, his work was not done, not until Eleh's defeat was realized.

He plucked a scrap of meat from the sack. "Now then, what is your plan?"

"Humor me, Karueq. You've been traveling with nothing but your head to occupy you. You must have a plan for how you would execute this task. What would you do?"

Karueq ripped a mouthful from the bone. "I would send letters to him as if the affair is already going on. Now that you are stationed above ground, you could use that to your advantage."

"Mmm, and what would you say?" she encouraged, slyly.

"That's your area of expertise, not mine."

"That's a pity. I would have loved to hear if you could come up with anything better than what I already sent," Jezebel chuckled, sipping a cup of wine.

Karueq's eyes narrowed. "You've already started?"

"Why yes, Karueq!" she cooed. "I've been toying with the hearts of men for many years. I know how to fake a love affair, and I'm surprised you thought to come up with the same thing."

"What did you do?"

"I sent a letter to him, giving in to the passions of having fallen in love with him and desperately wanting him to be mine. And then I begged him to run away with me. We've both grown so tired of the battle for the heart of Seaga, and we want to give in to the passions of love," Jezebel continued her plot, enjoying revealing what she had come up with. "We're running away to the wilderness. Eleh's followers are always drawn to the wilderness for some reason. We'll run to the desert and leave this whole war behind us."

Karueq chuckled. "Have you been plotting your own desertion?" Karueq jabbed.

Jezebel turned her cold stare on him. "I've been toying with men's hearts for a long time, Karueq. I know what they want, and I find a way to give it to them. That is how seduction works. In your case, well, you were so broken when you were corralled into the army that you begged me for respite."

"Enough," Karueq ordered.

"Too painful a memory to bring up, Karueq?"

"No, we just have no time to spend on reliving your lost conquest."

"Lost conquest? I let you go free. Though I do wonder, my dear." Her cold stare was replaced by an inquisitive eye. "What was it that broke you so?"

"Nothing broke me," Karueq replied simply. "So that's your plan? Implore the wretch to run off with you?"

"Yes. And Karueq, it'll work. Not only will it shake the faith those filthy cockroaches have in their leader, but he may in fact come running to me."

Karueq thought for a moment, and although he wouldn't tell her, he was satisfied with the plan. Her quick wit would ensure the letter was at least believable on her end. Whether or not the Eleverians took the bait would be his concern. He wouldn't make any assumptions about their play now. He would wait, unbiased, for any reply to Jezebel's letters and draw conclusions then.

"I take your silence as agreement. I have a few more preparations for the temple so Asherah and Baal can rule in peace here. Those Eleverian dogs would be foolish to come after them in the temple. Did I mention I've already started a drought to break the people's will?"

Karueq finished his mutton and dropped onto some of the extra pillows in the corner away from the bed.

"Oh, Karueq dear," Jezebel cooed at him from the entrance. "You may take the bed. I won't be joining you tonight." With that, she flicked the curtain closed behind her.

Karueq rose from the pillows and rolled onto the bed. He immediately drifted to sleep, a tactic ingrained in him for missions. His dreamless sleep passed without incident until he awoke to a hand on his shoulder. Feeling the weight of someone else's hand, he whipped out the knife from his boot and pressed it to the throat of his intruder – the guard from the temple.

"Please sir," the frightened man squeaked. "The priestess sent me to bring you provisions for your journey."

Hearing the intruder was no threat, he sheathed his knife and waved the guard away to fasten the supplies to his Rale. He rubbed his face and rose from the bed. Lamps had been lit – nightfall. Jezebel had indeed let him rest until he could fly in the cloak of night.

Karueq's journey back to Xanadai was long and failed to amuse him, but he wanted to mull over the information he had gained from his little errand and what his next move might be. He would break the stalemate somehow, but he was unsure if this was the path that led to that end. So, he took his time getting back, taking a few days to return to the city.

He mused over creating natural disasters to further occupy the Eleverian forces with their silly little side missions. He could distract them that way, but it was only a matter of time before such charitable interactions in Seaga gave them a stronger foothold among the people. He couldn't allow them to build upon the reputation they had with those they helped. No, Karueq wouldn't be able to gain ground there. He would have to settle for the identity of the Elequiri and dismantling their power structure, which as of yet was still shrouded in mystery.

Maybe Jezebel's letter would shake the integrity of Eleveria's confidence. Perhaps a simpleton among them might defect, or at least let slip some secret they were holding. Karueq could use that. He could use anything given to him, but the Eleverians were careful never to give him anything. They kept their secrets. All he knew about them, all they would allow him to exploit, were they're tactics in battle and they're missions in Seaga.

Thus, the stalemate couldn't be broken by the Shatanala. Karueq would take a city, and another fell to the enemy. The stalemate wasn't broken by the Eleverians either. Shatan had made certain many centuries ago that Xanadai was both as secret and impenetrable as Eleveria. Karueq saw to it that it stayed that way. A venerable punishment awaited those who would jeopardize the underground city.

As Karueq was musing about the protection given to the city, he came to his first of several checkpoints. He dug his heels into the Rale's sides and forced it to climb higher and double back. Anyone tailing him under the waves of the sea would lose him here. The cloud cover at this checkpoint made it impossible for someone to track him from below, especially at night. He soared away from that turn, maneuvering beyond the islands that made up other checkpoints to a small, lonely reef. There, he landed and waited. He kept his ears tuned to his surroundings. Any whisper of a sound and Karueq would be forced to return to the first checkpoint and choose a different path.

The Shatanala were very careful about entering Xanadai. Most of the common Shatanala soldiers sent out on missions never returned to the city, as they were not trusted to shake tailers and maintain secrecy. If they did, they were shuttled in when a distraction was being waged elsewhere, keeping the Eleverians occupied in some battle or another. The agents who did make frequent trips into Seaga were trained to exhaustion about reentry. The checkpoints remained the same, but the agent could never take the same path to the checkpoint twice. Although Karueq made the trip more than any other Shatanala, he wouldn't let himself have an exception. He created more intricate patterns and traveled varying distances to avoid using his previous paths.

His ears picked up no sound. Only the breeze from the waves licked over him. He looked up at the moon one last time before making his descent underground. A tiny veil of clouds wrapped the moon's brilliant shine and muffled it, but Karueq still wondered at its radiance. It calmed the tension he was clenching between his teeth, and then he noticed the salty air and the coolness of the night. He needed this on occasion. It kept the heat and vapors underground from addling his mind.

With his lungs clear and his mind sharpened by the scene, Karueq kicked the Rale into flight once more. He flew low over the water, not needing to draw attention from whatever prying eye might still be out there in the dark. Soon, he came to an ashy stump blackening the water - the volcanic entrance, long inactive. The peak of the volcano barely breached the water's surface. It was visible just enough for those who were looking for it.

Karueq cast a purple fireball into the opening, a signal that let the guards know a Shatanala was arriving, and dropped the Rale into the center, letting it parachute to the bottom of the column more than a hundred feet down. They landed with a thud. Karueq leapt from its back. The guards surrounding the landing, seized the Rale and led it away, while Karueq was left to gather his bearings on the ground and stride away into the tunnels toward the city.

He rotated his neck as he approached the tunnel system. He was looking forward to a very much needed spar with Bleren to loosen his body from the long flight. Their spars also usually doubled as meetings, so he would tell his second about his happenings above ground.

No sooner did he reach Sheol before he was halted by the sound of someone calling him. "My lord!" the voice yelped. Karueq turned around with a cold stare.

"What?" he sneered, irritably.

"My apologies, my lord," the young soldier began. "We were ordered to direct you to the prisons when you arrived."

"On whose authority?"

"General Bleren."

"Did he say why?"

"He only gave one word. Thessaly."

CHAPTER FIVE

THE CAPTAIN

The jagged tunnel opened into the prisons, and Karueq looked around. No, the prisoners were not being held in the forward cells. They would be sealed into the tombs furthest from the entrance. This prey was too valuable to risk an escape. The cells were special commissions of Karueq's own design. Not only was the prisoner encased completely within the wall, but the cells were enchanted to freeze so that there was little energy to be used by the inmate.

He weaved his way through the aisles until he came to a group of ten soldiers standing at attention in front of Bleren. Bleren turned at the sound of his footsteps.

"My lord," he saluted. "You received my message."

Karueq nodded, a raw smile spread over his face. "I did, and I must say, after my errand, this is very good news."

"They're awake," Bleren informed him. "I think they're praying."

Karueq scoffed, "Eleh's ear is not strong enough to reach them down here." His brow perked up. "You managed to catch more than one?"

"Yes," Bleren said, "five of the Eleka Guard." Karueq's pulse fluttered as Bleren spoke. "We caught them three days ago while you were away."

Karueq turned his attention to the smooth wall on his right containing the cells. "Well done, general," he said, absentmindedly.

Encased in the stone were five of their most feared enemies. Karueq could hardly believe it. The Eleka Guard never participated in missions to bring aid to Seaga. They only ever engaged in combat with the Shatanala, brutally and directly.

Not only were they feared, but Hunga had been the only prisoner they had ever been able to capture and bring to the city. Every other Eleverian was either rescued, escaped, or died of their injuries before he could imprison them here.

Hunga was turning out to be a very valuable catch indeed. The Eleverians had been blinded by his importance to their cause, so much so that they sent their elite team to Thessaly to bring him back. Bleren's plan wasn't the only thing to credit with the success. He wondered if the Eleverian forces were breaking down in the absence of their Keeper.

"Five Eleverians isn't the only gift I've brought back from Thessaly with me," Bleren went on. "One of the prisoners is their Captain."

Karueq turned a pleased smile on his protege. "A gift indeed. Has the Prince been informed?"

"I have," a voice behind him spoke. Karueq turned about and executed his customary salute of the demon.

Shatan's gaze was fixed on the wall, ignoring his men. Karueq could see his mind working. He had waited a long time to possess the Captain of the Eleka Guard, especially in the confines of Xanadai. Next to the three greats of Eleveria – Elequiri, the Quiri, and the Keeper – this was a great prize indeed.

Karueq cleared his throat. "May I be so humble as to suggest we not simply stand here? I don't believe you'll get an unprompted response from the wall."

Shatan shot him a glare. Karueq didn't normally invade the Prince's authority in front of subordinates, but he was anxious to begin. He, too, had waited far too long to capture the Captain, and he would relish taking part in breaking such a strong spirit.

Shatan didn't delay in order to put Karueq in his place. He nodded, and Karueq stepped forward to place his hand on the wall. He gathered the energy in his belly and raised it to his palm. It pulsed through his hand as he willed the enchantment to disable. His other hand found the knife in his boot as the rock melted inward. The cold air hit him like a thousand needles.

As soon as the shivering body inside was visible, he seized it and slammed it against the wall outside the cell. He slid the knife against her throat and waited.

The breath falling from her lips fogged the blade on her neck. Her hair stuck together, frozen in dark clumps from cold and sweat. Her skin, which used to be bronzed by sunlight, was blue and icy. Her wrists were tied behind her and the binds were enforced with witchcraft as an added measure. Shivers from the bitter cold in the cell rippled through her body and shuttered her breath. Her lightweight armor had been taken away. Only her light clothing had provided protection from the freeze.

Her eyes were shut, and Karueq watched them carefully. She was awake, but the shock of the heat outside the cell kept them tight.

"Look at me," Karueq ordered.

The woman opened her eyes. Her focus wandered around for a moment, and Karueq noticed warily that she was regaining control of her shivering muscles.

"Look at me!" he barked.

She locked gazes with him. He studied her carefully, making sure she was lucid enough to speak. She was indeed in control of her senses. He could tell because she was studying him, too.

"Your new king has a proposition for you, Captain," he said, holding his composure. "I suggest you be awake for it."

She glanced at Shatan. A confident smile crept onto her thawing face.

"I h-have no k-king but Eleh," she replied.

Shatan responded. "It is time you start calling me 'master'."

"N-not for an et-ternity," she stuttered. "I will d-die first, and you know that."

"Not master in the sense that your God demands. He has abandoned you here."

"You really don't know Him, do you, Shatan?" Her shivering ceased, although her muscles remained rigid under Karueq's hand while they continued to warm.

"But I do," Shatan answered. "I knew Him long before He created you."

The color rose back into her face, and the shivering stammer stopped. "Yes, Shatan. You did know Him, but you shouldn't make Him your enemy when you no longer know Him."

"I am not concerned with Him; I am concerned for you, Chelia. He has abandoned you here among His enemy."

Chelia turned her eyes back on Karueq. "Are you hearing this?" she asked with an arched, grinning brow. "He has concern for me. Is that what he told you to suck you in?" Karueq's anxious disgust thickened his blood.

"Young one, I am offering you pardon and refuge," Shatan said, a mist of gentleness trickling through his words. "I ask nothing from you. You will find peace here."

"Young one?" she grinned. "Asking nothing in return? My, my, how generous. I feel so cared for." She turned her attention over her shoulder, inspecting the straps binding her hands together and probably feeling out the energy tying them.

"I make my offer to you perpetual," Shatan continued. "You may have all the time you need, but when you are weary of your struggle, I will save you and give you everything your heart desires. It's such a pity for a strong woman like you to be bound to such a fool God."

She locked her eyes on the demon, abandoning her exploration of the binds. "Do not insult my King."

Karueq's blood chilled from the ice in her tone and the fact that she didn't flinch. She wasn't even blinking. This was why the Captain of the Eleka Guard was so feared. She stared down the most powerful demon in Sheol with a daring, challenging eye even as a knife pressed against her throat and she was helpless to do anything. She answered to no one except the Elequiri, making her predictable only in her conviction and steadiness. This woman was dangerous and her campaigns with her team always ended in blood.

"You dare challenge me?" Shatan growled.

"You insult my King and threaten my people. You frustrate our efforts to bring peace to Seaga. You imprison my men in the belly of the earth. Yes, I challenge you, Shatan, and that is my perpetual answer to your perpetual offer."

Karueq felt his eye twitch and he pressed the knife further on her throat. Chelia broke eye contact with Shatan and turned her unnerving stare on him. His attention was caught for but a moment from her eyes by a thin red line snaking its way down the blade. He had misjudged his advance.

"Your threats mean nothing," she hissed, bringing Karueq's eyes back to hers.

Shatan snorted. "I know you will not yield now, but in the meantime, I have something you want." He nodded to Bleren who ordered two of the soldiers at the wall out of the aisle. They hastened away. All the while, Chelia's breath remained steady, and her gaze on Karueq never wavered. His skin crawled under that stare.

A moment later the soldiers returned, dragging a limp body between them. This momentarily distracted Karueq. Chelia checked him in the shoulder and plowed a kick into his stomach. He fell hard on his back.

"Hunga!" Chelia called and dropped to her knees in front of the body. Her bound wrists forbade her to reach out to him, so she dropped her face lower to take a closer look at him. Karueq lunged at her from the ground and pinned her from behind.

"You witch!" he bellowed into her hair.

"Hunga, answer me," she begged the body beside her. Karueq punched her mouth.

A low sigh escaped Hunga.

"Hunga! You're alive!" she cheered, despite her assaulted jaw.

"Barely," he answered. "What took you so long, Captain?"

"These gentlemen invited us to Thessaly by mistake. My apologies."

Karueq braced himself on his right knee and yanked her from the ground. He threw her back in her place against the wall. She grunted at the impact but shook the pain off quickly.

"Oh, is that all?" Hunga teased.

"Enough," Shatan spat, breaking into the reunion. "Captain, you aren't yet enticed by my previous offer, because you have no self worth. You think you are disposable."

"I *am* disposable, demon breath."

"However, I know you do not put yourself above your comrades, so I am making another offer."

"I advise you to revisit our previous conversation. My answer remains."

"That is not what I want from you at this time."

"My allegiance for the safety, life, or freedom of my friend here?"

"No. I will eventually win your heart. I am patient, but I want something from you in the meantime."

"What might that be?"

"I will trade his freedom for information."

"You must be desperate. Surely your well-trained spies can share their secrets with you. What more can I tell you?"

"I want the identity of the Elequiri," Shatan said plainly.

Laughter. It peeled from Chelia's steady breath like a cascade and made Karueq's spine shudder. Hunga contributed a small laugh and shook his head. Chelia's laughter finally broke enough to address Shatan.

"The Elequiri?" she giggled. "That's what you want? All of our secrets, all our strategies? The reason we fight you?" Karueq's instincts jolted at this, "And you want to know *that*? The Elequiri? You're chasing a ghost!" She turned to Karueq. "Commander, tell me he's joking."

Karueq's elbow hit her sharply in the jaw again. "Answer him, Captain."

She took a moment to wiggle the soreness from her jaw, her laughter lost but not her grin. "I have an obligation to protect the identity of the Elequiri," she explained, "as do my men and any citizen of Eleveria you meet. You will never see the face of your enemy unveiled."

Shatan nodded to Bleren who began disabling the remaining cells. "You will surrender him, Chelia."

"You will never win, Shatan." She steadied her gaze on the devil again only for it to be broken by the commotion of Bleren's men. Teaming up in pairs, they were removing the other four shivering bodies from the wall and restraining them.

Karueq knew each of these soldiers. The first out were Hanai and Honai, twin brothers that were always seen together on missions. Karueq's soldiers knew that if ever they saw one of them alone, they were to be on the lookout for the other. Next was a woman, Henara. She was considered the most diplomatic member of the Eleka Guard, but she still was as brutally skilled in combat as the rest. The last was a relatively new face. Aryngo was a young man who had only recently been seen among the Eleka Guard, a new member learning the brutality the Guard was known for. Karueq never underestimated any of this team, even the newcomer, because like the Shatanala's Brehila, these were the best of Eleveria's men.

Aryngo was the first to open his eyes, and Karueq inwardly cursed their bodies for adapting so fast to the heat. He sized up the two men holding him, still shivering. "Uh, u-usually I'd like to be asked before I'm grabbed, fellas."

"You th-think they prefer to grab you over me, Aryngo?" Hanai piped up.

"Why else would they be getting so close?" Aryngo replied, sizing up the brute clinging to his right arm and shoulder.

"Silence," Shatan hissed.

Aryngo turned his attention to the devil before him and glanced at Hunga bound on the floor. Karueq saw the terrible, rash idea behind his naive eyes and pitied his next move. The young man twisted his arms out and threw off the men holding him. He lunged at the soldiers restraining his comrades and clubbed them. A tussle erupted. In the fray, Aryngo's eye caught the Prince and clambered his way out of the fight.

"Aryngo! No!" Chelia ordered. Her words were lost on the young man. Shatan raised his hand forward and squeezed the air, his fist twisting and curling. Aryngo grunted midrun and doubled over, clutching his stomach.

"Shatan, enough! You deal with me!" Chelia demanded.

"Your dog attacked *me*, Captain." Shatan wrenched his fist even further. Aryngo's groans turned to screaming.

"Enough!" she cried. "Enough, Shatan! You've made your point!"

Shatan let his hand relax a little but kept his invisible grip on the writhing body before him. "I have not yet made my point."

"Captain," Aryngo's small voice made it through the clench in his teeth, "take his deal."

"What deal, Aryngo?" she asked in warning.

"He wants a trade for our freedom, doesn't he?" he whimpered dryly, no doubt knowing how out of line he was being. "If Hunga is included, take it! Then our mission is done."

Chelia stared at him bewildered. The strong, certain facade was broken and she looked lost. "Aryngo…"

"Don't betray us like he did." Tears began weeping out of Aryngo's eyes, and Karueq didn't believe it was just from the pain.

"Quiet, Aryngo."

"You don't have to defend him down here."

"Quiet!" she hissed, her commanding demeanor returning suddenly.

Aryngo's face twisted in pain again and he looked back at his comrades, again effectively restrained by the soldiers they were trained to kill. Their reactions were mixed - disbelief with a bit of sympathy. Karueq couldn't believe what he was seeing and hearing.

Chelia hastily readdressed the Prince. "We understand, Shatan. You want us to think you're really scary. If we say you are, will you let him go? He's new at this."

Shatan's hand twisted anew, and Aryngo choked and groaned in response. Karueq kept his eyes glued to the woman in his hand but couldn't help hearing the brutal pain behind him. He would not be distracted again, but her quickness didn't make that matter.

In an instant, Chelia kicked his knee backward and swept his legs from beneath him. She pushed him aside, her hands somehow free, and hurtled at Shatan.

A thunderous blast shook the prison, and Karueq was hurled into the tunnel wall. His vision danced and his head pounded. He staggered to his feet, willing his head to clear. His legs gave out, but he caught himself on the wall and found his bearings.

His swimming vision cleared and what he saw stunned him. Shatan had been flung to the ground a few yards away. The creature within him laid there - a sick, hopeless creature. The skin, a mere membrane with a dull pallor, stretched over the thin diseased skeleton. He was bald and hairless, his stately wings replaced by those of a starved bat. His eyes were empty but somehow flashed with rage.

Chelia stood between them, staring the demon down. Her stance was shaky but ready to spring upon him again. Her fists were clenched tightly at her sides. Her wrists were split from where the cords had restrained her. The cords themselves rested on the ground by the wall.

Chelia interrupted the silence, her voice thick with adrenaline. "Save your breath for the day you beg Eleh to take you back. Touch my men again, and you may not get that chance."

Karueq's instinct snapped. Despite her challenging posture, he saw that she was weak from whatever power she had just unleashed. He sprang forward, jumped over Aryngo, and shoved her back against the wall where she belonged with a thud. She crumpled against his shoulder and gasped for breath. His forearm locked under her jaw, forbidding her to move. After a few breaths, she picked her head up, and that piercing gaze again found him. He settled himself beneath it. Their sideline war wasn't over, and she would exploit another opportunity to dominate him should he give her one when her strength returned.

Shatan found his voice again. "You have made a grave mistake, Captain." His stately appearance had returned, which Karueq could see in the corner of his vision. "My perpetual offer to you still stands, but you will pay the price for your actions today."

"I suspect you would exact that price no matter what I did," she growled.

"Indeed," Shatan agreed. He turned to the soldiers, the ones holding the other four and those standing over Hunga and Aryngo. "Kill them all, but leave the Captain."

Chelia's eyes went wild at the command. Karueq braced himself against her, preparing for another escape. Instead, she tilted her head upward and screamed into the prison.

"ELEH!!"

Karueq's blood froze. He broke his stare and found Shatan. Shatan was equally as confused. He couldn't fathom why she would call for help that would never arrive.

Then Karueq heard it. A low hum coming from the prison entrance. Karueq peered down the aisle. Then a cool wind hit him, breaking the feverish heat that seared them. There was power there, raw and terrible. It flooded his blood and his bones. It gusted to a strong wind, and Karueq had to shut his eyes against it, bracing himself. He felt Chelia slipping from his hands no matter how hard he gripped her. Then the wind stopped.

Karueq opened his eyes and blinked around. The soldiers were shaken, their hands empty. Shatan was staring down the aisle, stunned beyond words. Karueq's eyes fell to the cords on the ground.

Gone. They were gone. Somehow, the terrible wind had the power to usher away those that it wished.

Eleh.

"My lord," Karueq said quietly, finding his voice. "Tell me I'm wrong about what just happened."

"Kill them," Shatan answered shortly.

"I don't understand how you expect me to do that without them here."

Shatan's voice broke into his mind though his lips didn't move. *"Your soldiers."*

This wasn't the answer Karueq was looking for. He sent his thought through the space between them. *"Shatan, you can't think that…"*

"Do it!" Shatan barked aloud, whipping around. Then he hushed his voice. "Do you want another riot?"

With that, Shatan furled his wings around himself and disappeared in a whirlwind.

Eleh, the monster. He stole them! Never had the Shatanala had to fear His presence in their territory, certainly not in their nest! He had swept through the caves and taken his people away, the cheat!

Karueq let this atrocity boil the energy coursing through him. It surged like fire. He whipped around and let it fly from his hands like lightning. The stunned soldiers surrounding him screamed and then crumpled to the ground.

Bleren stood aghast. "Karueq…"

Karueq hated doing that, killing his men for something they had no control over. He had no need for sentiment, but they were part of a larger army that could dwindle quickly if he did this frequently. He would have rather sealed their mouths or threatened them somehow if they leaked what they had witnessed.

"Karueq!" Bleren pleaded again.

"You are no longer needed here," he commanded.

"What just happened?" His protege couldn't hide the concern in his tone.

Karueq turned to him sternly. "You know exactly what happened. Leave me."

After a brief, unadulterated pause, Bleren left the aisle. Karueq's next thought was reckless, very reckless indeed. His thoughts grew darker and the chaos in his mind erupted as he stalked out of the prisons and through the tunnels. His jaw was set, forbidding his rage from breaking through just yet.

He emerged from the tunnels into Sheol. The boiling lake answered his anger and his frustration. It was as if it, too, had enough of the impossible restraints Shatan exacted. It, too, was furious that the balance had slipped through their fingers without them knowing. He marched across the bridge into the Great Temple. The vast, open atrium was lit by the lake and a fire burning behind the wide altar at the far wall. The pristine, regal temple paying homage to his impotent lord further enraged him. He whipped out his sword and shredded the ornate banner that had the audacity to stand next to him.

"Shatan!" he roared into the high ceiling. "Shatan!"

"Stand down!" the demon ordered, appearing in front of the altar.

Karueq wasn't in any capacity to obey. "You are going to tell me exactly what happened back there!"

"I don't need to answer to you for anything."

This dismissal throttled his anger. He compressed the energy in his gut and released it in an explosion of lightning. The vessels and basins shattered and the banners tore apart. Karueq stared unblinking at Shatan. Shatan returned his stare evenly before speaking.

"I don't need to answer you for what happened," he reaffirmed. "You are to continue as you were."

"Continue as if nothing has changed?!" Karueq cried in disbelief. "I can't continue to fight your war on the surface if you can't protect your territory down here where your assets are! You led me to believe that this was a stalemate! That we were equally matched to them, and it was only a matter of time before we tipped the scales! You charged me with that! You directed me with that in mind! Answer me, Shatan! How badly are we losing?!"

"We are not losing!" Shatan growled.

"What do you call that?!" Karueq pointed toward the tunnels.

"Nothing of consequence."

"Nothing of consequence? Let me tell you what that incident told me. They know where we are. This city's location is not a secret. It also tells me that our enemy can come in here at any time and destroy us! And these secrets were doubtlessly leaked by Quiron, the traitor you told me not to hunt down! That doesn't concern you?"

"No, and let me tell you why. Yes, Eleh was able to infiltrate our base. He was able to extract his soldiers, but we need not concern ourselves with this. He has never made a presence here, and I doubt He will make an appearance again. As for the display of power, He only took the Eleverians. He didn't touch our men, or you, or me. I'm disappointed you were distracted by the performance like those wretches I had you destroy."

"And Quiron? He is spilling our secrets to them."

"Nothing he could know would bring us to our knees. I thought you were better than this, Karueq. Do you doubt me?"

Karueq's eyes narrowed, and he was reminded of Jezebel's comment regarding his belief in Shatan's power. He sighed once to steady himself. "Regardless of the damage that was or wasn't done in the prisons, this means we have lost ground. I fear thinking how long they've had the advantage."

"What advantage?"

"Our city isn't a secret. They know how we operate, and they have been slowly thwarting us above ground while we wait down here for just the right weakness in their defenses."

"Is that what you've been doing? Waiting, indulging yourself in sloth?" Shatan challenged him.

Karueq rage boiled again, but he kept himself steady. "I have done more than you give me credit for. You only approve one in ten of my plays."

Shatan smiled wryly. "It has made you patient and kept the fire of hatred and desire burning within you." Shatan walked down the steps of the altar toward his commander. "Your plans would not be nearly so effective if you weren't so thirsty to do something, to thwart the Eleverians, to attack any weakness they may have."

"It has made me bitter," Karueq responded. "It has made me suspicious."

"Is that such a terrible thing?"

"You're not at all concerned that He can destroy the city?"

"He is not powerful enough," Shatan said, assuredly. "There's a reason He won't be God forever."

"Sir!" a new voice interrupted.

"Not now," Karueq snapped, not turning around.

"I have a message for the Commander," the man insisted. Shatan's eyes flickered, and Karueq realized the voice was familiar. He turned around.

It was Zokul. The lunatic stood before them with an eerily pleasant look on his face.

"What is it?" Karueq spat.

"The Elequiri wishes to meet with you."

"The Elequiri? You were supposed to be tracking down the Quiri."

"Indeed. You sent me out with that in mind." He smiled. "But I was unsuccessful. My message, Commander. The Elequiri wishes to meet you at this location." Zokul handed Karueq a small sheet of etched wax.

"Where did you get this message?" Karueq asked warily.

"From the Elequiri."

Karueq's eyes widened. "Did you see him? Tell me everything!"

"Oh, of course I did, more than you trained any of us to look for. I saw the very face of your enemy."

His phrasing gave Karueq pause. "Your enemy?"

Zokul just gave Karueq that unsettling, serene smile again in reply.

"Who is he?"

"I'll never tell you," he replied, then turned to Shatan. "I am no longer bound to you, Shatan." Zokul removed the shoulder piece from his armor. Where his brand should have been, a thick, ugly scar marred his skin. "I belong to Eleh."

"You do not," Karueq hissed. "Who is the Elequiri?"

"You will never know," Zokul said, still calmly beaming. "You will never see the face of the Elequiri unveiled."

"No!!" Karueq cried. He pulled his sword from his side and plunged it into Zokul's body. The lifeless body fell backward with a thud. His face remained tranquil, even in death.

Shatan turned and backhanded Karueq. "You lout! We could have gotten answers!"

"No we wouldn't have!" Karueq spat at him, ignoring the sting of the blow. "Their hold on him was likely too strong, and you know it. I am done playing games that lead us nowhere. I want answers, Shatan, real answers. That nation is a mystery to us, and we won't be able to regain any ground we've lost until we know something. Anything! Do you understand me?" He wiped the corner of his mouth. "I am going to meet the Elequiri. No tricks or traps. They are a generally forward people, and it would do us well to play by their rules one time. Once we know something, you can have your way."

Shatan stared at him long and hard.

"I'm not asking permission," Karueq added.

"Fair enough," Shatan replied. "If you are unhappy with the way I've been leading you, go your own way and see what becomes of it. Remember, you are young to this world. You have much to learn."

"And old men do well to learn from the young," Karueq dared.

Shatan's face hardened. His somber but authoritative expression reminded Karueq of one very important fact. He might not agree with Shatan at every turn, but this demon had been fighting this war for thousands of years, and he had been able to grip the hearts of millions of men, women, and children in Seaga. He had amassed an army from the creation of his enemy.

"Go," the demon said.

Karueq gave a small bow and turned to leave. His attention was stolen by Zokul's body lying across the floor, and he remembered the reckless thing the man had said before his fateful mission. "One more thing," he added, his eyes still on the body. "This traitor did give us something we could use. He suggested we infiltrate the Eleverian ranks by feigning allegiance to them." He threw a glance over his shoulder at Shatan. "Think about it while I'm gone."

CHAPTER SIX

THE FACELESS MAN

Karueq sat at the entrance of the cave, staring at the Mark on his shoulder. Dusk had set in, and he didn't have very long to wait. He knew this area well. It was a neutral site beyond civilization where the Shatanala and the Eleverians claimed no territory – yet. He had arrived early to the summons the Elequiri had sent and set up camp in this den at the edge of a lake. A tree grew above it, and its roots encircled the entrance, keeping the soil stable so that Karueq always found it open when he came here.

Every other time he'd come here, it had been with a team to retrieve one of his officers, prisoners the Eleverians were relinquishing. Now he was coming to answer the Elequiri's call and try to get answers. He'd considered whether this was a trap. No doubt he had a very large bounty on his head, at least among the Eleka Guard, but if they were trying to trap him and collect, so be it.

He didn't care now because the escape the Eleverians made from Xanadai still weighed heavily on him. It astounded him, and even with Shatan's reassurance that all was well, Karueq couldn't help doubting the Shatanala's ability to hold them back. There was too much uncertainty. It seemed to have shattered his careful orchestration up here above

71

ground. He bitterly thought of all the years he had toiled to gain a firm grip on Seaga. He felt now that it had all been an illusion. All he had accomplished, in the name of the one whose Mark he bore, was for naught.

He closed his eyes and forced these toxic thoughts down, clamping their howling mouths shut. He opened his eyes again and looked up at the sky. The moon shone down on him, tossing its bright rays around the lake and making the soft ripples dance. Focusing on what he could see brought him back to the task at hand.

He strapped into his armor, lingering but a moment to behold the Mark again. With his frustration at his lord itching beneath the surface, he needed to remain grounded in what he was doing and who he served. The Mark gave him a visual reminder of that devotion. With forced but strong conviction, he belted his sword at his side and left the cave.

As he followed the stream from the lake toward the tree line, a wisp of black smoke materialized and swirled on the ground ahead of him. The hair on the back of Karueq's neck rose and prickled. His spine tensed. The smoke rose to form a thick column and then dissipated revealing the form of Madaka.

The shade sneered at him. "You are a fool, Karueq," he hissed.

Karueq remained silent. The shade's unnerving presence enveloped him, suffocating him.

"Are you planning on defecting to the Elequiri tonight?" he asked, his voice slippery and mocking.

"That would please you, wouldn't it?" Karueq hated this demon with everything in him, and the demon had always despised him in return.

"It might have been the scheme you told Shatan of before you left, and the fact that you came alone. It also might be your consistently arrogant attitude toward your master."

"You question my loyalty?"

"I question your resolve to serve the one who gave you everything," the shade replied with glittering eyes, echoing Jezebel's words from weeks before.

"That is not why I serve him."

"Do tell me why."

"He will bring Eleh down one day, and this enslavement will be at an end." Karueq's conviction steadied as he spoke. This exchange made his skin crawl and made him sick, but it did do him good to be reminded of his choices before going in to face the enemy.

Madaka glared at him. "Be sure you don't forget it."

"If you have complaints against me, take them to Shatan," Karueq growled back. He sidestepped the creature and continued his march to the trees. A soft, indignant rustle behind him and the malice being swept from the air told him Madaka had disappeared. He paused for a moment to rotate his neck and release his tense muscles. He rubbed his face, and the chill in his nerves dissipated. He felt like a powerful commander once more.

The forest was hushed. The ancient wood of the trees groaned and murmured as Karueq passed them following the stream. They looked on their guest without interest, resting peacefully in their old age. The undergrowth was thick, but not impassable, and it rustled with his steps. The younger trees beneath their old ancestors seemed to reach their branches out to him. The air was dense and humid. A light breeze gusted in from the perimeter, and the leaves trembled in response. The moonlight failed to penetrate the heavy canopy above.

A lone owl appeared, floating over the undergrowth, causing Karueq to stop and place his hand firmly on his sword. It didn't make a sound as it landed on the branch ahead of him. He quieted his breath. The owl surveyed its surroundings with interest and then noticed the man staring at it. It tilted its head at him, studying him curiously. Karueq's hand cautiously left his sword. This bird wasn't involved in the summons he had been issued. Satisfied there was nothing of interest, the owl spread its wings and left the branch, gliding deeper into the forest.

Karueq watched it disappear. Then he listened for any sign the Elequiri was around. Only the groaning of the trees and the tickling sound of the stream answered him. He picked his way carefully through the undergrowth, minding his surroundings with the greatest care. His ears were fully peeled as he wandered deeper into the shadows.

The forest grew darker, and he relied on the sound of the water trickling along to guide him. He'd decided not to light his way so that his presence would be as unnoticed as possible. He considered the possibility of the Elequiri being off his guard and perhaps he could be subdued and captured if he didn't see Karueq coming, but the real reason he wanted concealment was for his own safety. The Elequiri was the most powerful and dangerous of the Eleverians. If they wanted to end Karueq's reign of war and blood, not one of them matched him as well as their leader.

A silvery light glowed quietly in the distance ahead of him, illuminating from the bottom of a ravine. Karueq left the stream as he approached, deciding to descend on the source from an alternative route. The ground rose gently to an outcrop overlooking the trench, and from here he could see the source of the light. Near a shallow pool of water in the floor of the ravine, with its outstretched hand supporting a silver ball of light, was a hooded figure – the Elequiri.

Karueq surveyed the ledges surrounding the ditch and saw no signs that there were others keeping watch. He let himself assume they were alone, he and this ghost. The figure didn't move. Karueq was reminded not for the first time of the Elequiri's notorious nature for being unreadable. He couldn't tell if he had been made, if the man under the hood knew he was near. It didn't matter anymore. He couldn't delay the meeting by being too cautious. He'd made his decision to come alone, and he had decided that the Elequiri truly would talk with him rather than skewer him.

Karueq swung himself down into the pit with his opponent. He pulled his sword, poising it securely at his side, and walked slowly and carefully forward. He saw beneath the lightweight cape the Elequiri's own sword was belted at his waist. His entire body was concealed beneath gloves, long sleeves and pants, and sturdy boots. From this angle, the hood concealed the black mask that always covered his entire face. Nothing about the Elequiri had ever been identified.

Suddenly, the Elequiri turned on Karueq and thrust his hand out, a wall of energy bursting forth from it that sped through Karueq and enveloped him. The sounds of the forest were muffled as if Karueq's ears had been filled with cotton, and he felt a subtle but distinct pressure wrap around his mind.

"Put away your sword," an indistinct voice, magnified and low, spoke to him. This was how the Elequiri communicated. His voice had never been identified because he always masked it behind this cloud of power. He was too good at making himself anonymous. Though Karueq tried his hardest to break the enchantment, he couldn't hedge the wall around his mind.

"You are armed," Karueq replied, his voice muffled slightly in the magic barrier. "Why should I put away mine?"

"You may keep it at your side," came the Elequiri's voice again. "I give you my word, I will not draw mine before you draw yours."

The Elequiri voluntarily swept his cloak from his side, exposing his sword. The Elequiri's blade was well known. Chema was its name, a symbol well associated with its owner. The sword's jewel-colored hilt without cross-guards glinted in the silvery light. The Elequiri waited.

Karueq sheathed his blade but kept his hand resting on it. "Why did you decide to meet me now?"

"You did not come at my call for my benefit. You have questions you want answered. I will allow you to ask them." Even with the Elequiri's voice masked, his tone haunted Karueq. His manner of speaking was confident, gentle. Among the few closest to Shatan, it was agreed that a possible reason for the Elequiri's secrecy was that he made appearances out in the open under another name, that they had seen his face before, but nothing inspired his memory.

"Reveal yourself, coward," Karueq demanded.

The Elequiri said nothing.

"You think you can hide behind a mask while your people die by our hand? Your arrogance is killing your men."

Again, nothing. He waited for Karueq's questions. Karueq chose to lead with a damning question. "When did you corrupt our high priestess and beckon her to your bed?"

Nothing.

"I know about your little love affair."

"A trick fabricated by you to tarnish the faith my people have in me."

"Come now, man to man, what was it that interested you?"

"There is nothing about your priestess that interests me, except the saving of her soul, and none of my men believe you."

"I would question the Eleka Guard. They seemed to feel otherwise."

Again, the Elequiri was silent, and Karueq didn't know where else to pursue this line of questioning. He took a deep breath, not breaking his gaze from the mask under the hood. "Alright," he relented. "How did Eleh get into my city?"

"You feel you have lost ground. You assume He was ever unable to penetrate Xanadai's defenses. You assume the Creator is not master of what He created. The highest power given to Shatan was bestowed on him by Eleh."

"If your God is as all-powerful as you say, why hasn't he crushed us and ended this war?"

"He protects us, but He does not interfere with human will. The escape you witnessed was a display of His promise to not abandon any of His people if they call on Him."

Karueq scoffed. "He abandons you to a life of suffering. He wages war with your bodies and souls in return for a thankless reward."

"You do not know who you are fighting against. You do not know why we fight so fervently for Him. Have you seen the joy - the happiness - in the eyes of my people ever be dimmed?"

Karueq replayed the countless Eleverian faces he'd seen in his head, the last of which was the unbreakable face of Hunga. They had incarcerated him for nearly a year, but the smile on his lips and the light in his eyes wouldn't give, even in extreme exhaustion. "A false hope can seem strong," he challenged. "Fools laugh at pain from the shroud of an addled mind."

The Elequiri didn't respond. Karueq understood that the answer he'd received for his question was all he would get. He asked his next question. "Our soldiers you've turned – especially a certain assassin taken more than a year ago – how have you done so?"

"They come to the light of their own will. We do not offer them anything except for Eleh's grace and love. They accept it and are freed."

Karueq itched to rebuke the Elequiri's definition of freedom again but brushed it aside. "What information have they exposed about us and our strategies?"

"They have not shared anything with us, and they do not join us in direct war with you. The Eleverian army is made of Eleverians alone."

Karueq blinked, confused that they would so foolishly dismiss leverage. "What do you do with them?"

"We set them free," the voice explained. "We break their shackles and let them go. This is what we did for Quiron and all your soldiers whose eyes have been opened."

Again, his answer was finished. Karueq hesitated. He had one more question to ask, but he wondered if this was the right time and place to ask it. After a moment of quarreling with himself, he decided he had nothing to lose. "I've been told by two of your subordinates that we would do well to understand you. They specifically mentioned your reason for engaging with us. I'll ask you now. Why do you fight us?"

"Why do you think we fight you?"

"Do not play games with me," Karueq warned.

"I am not toying with you."

Karueq sighed in frustration. These riddles were going to continue, and he would have to sort through them later. "You fight for control of Seaga."

"You are very wrong," said the voice. "Shatan fights for control of Seaga and to make himself a god, plunging all into the darkness with him. You may never understand in this lifetime, but we fight to stop Shatan from taking innocent people away from Eleh's peace, innocent people like you."

Karueq's jaw tensed, and his eyes cast their daggers at the mask - innocent indeed. If the Elequiri would ever see him, Karueq, as innocent, he would have to forget decades of his people's slaughter, decades of outliving those who were bound to keep his identity secret. He would have to forget the horrors Karueq had committed on Seaga's people in order to secure them and bring them back from Eleh's cruelty.

It was time to turn the focus of the discussion away from Karueq's questions. "I don't expect you to accept, but we are making you the same offer we gave to your Captain."

"I assure you that neither myself nor the Captain will ever accept an offering from Shatan."

"You seem very sure of yourself, and very sure of your officers including your Captain. If I may," ventured the calculating commander, "her faith in you seems very blind indeed."

"I'm sure you must think that."

Karueq decided not to push the point any farther. Chelia had indeed been viciously defensive of this man while her party revealed their disappointment in him, but he didn't want to press the matter in case his insistence caused Jezebel's ruse to fall apart. "She will be ours, Elequiri. Once you disappoint her and she loses faith, your Captain will fight for us."

"I see you have no more questions." The Elequiri's confident tone did not cease. "The reason I brought you here is to discuss a new law my people have put in place."

"I care nothing for how you rule your people," Karueq jabbed.

"This is a matter that affects you, Commander. We have amended our law. No longer will we take the lives of your people. We will continue to fight you, but we will only subdue your soldiers. Never again will we be responsible for ending your lives."

Karueq couldn't believe his ears. "This is cowardice, Elequiri."

The Elequiri paused then said, "I acknowledge the decision for this law is purely for ourselves. You might call it selfish or foolish, but we pay dearly for every life we take. Where your forces receive glory for these atrocities, too many of my people suffer pain and regret. A soul cannot make a different choice in death, and your soldiers' current choices rest with Shatan. We are ridding ourselves of the consequences of such action."

"How do you intend to defend yourselves?" Karueq asked. "You are giving us a greater advantage over your small numbers."

"A small, strong army can match a large, weak army. You will not be any stronger than you were before we adopted the law."

Karueq couldn't figure out the ploy. They gained nothing from this law. By adopting mercy for the Shatanala, the Elequiri was dooming all of Eleveria. The pain and regret the Elequiri spoke of could only come from one source. Their guilt-dealing God made them regret the power and effectiveness they had that the Shatanala had come to fear.

"Do not underestimate us," the Elequiri cautioned.

Karueq pried. "Why tell me this? You should keep this information to yourself so that we would never know. Now we have an advantage to pursue."

"You have no more an advantage than you did before. Your victories will be no more than they were before. I reveal this to you to strike fear in Shatan's heart."

Karueq hesitated. This was very unlike the Elequiri to be so open and forthcoming. By telling him the endgame, he had given up what he hoped to win, and Shatan would not cower before mercy.

"I have also come offering you peace," uttered the voice behind the mask. "Eleh offers you the same freedom He has given to so many of your soldiers."

Karueq's eye twitched. "I will never bow to Him."

"I hope you reconsider. He loves you and wants you to be free from the chains Shatan has placed on your soul."

With the hand Karueq still had on his sword, he drew it and steadied it at his side. He would not ignore this threat. "My answer stands."

The Elequiri's hand found Chema's hilt and pulled it from its scabbard. "You pulled your blade."

"You threatened my freedom."

"We will never force you to turn. As I said, your forces defect voluntarily."

"Be that as it may," said Karueq, gathering the energy in his gut. A violent shockwave blasted from his free hand toward the Elequiri, crashing into him. Immediately the sounds of the forest returned and the pressure in Karueq's temples ceased.

The Elequiri recovered his footing and assumed a defensive posture. Karueq was already on him. He swung his sword, connecting hard with Chema. The shrill clang of metal echoed loudly with each blow as the two engaged in single combat. Karueq maintained his offense, but the Elequiri's defense held strong.

Karueq sent another shockwave thundering into his opponent. This time, the Elequiri crossed his arms in front of him and then threw a powerful defensive current back at him. The combined energy blasted into Karueq sending him tumbling backward, but he rolled himself out of the fall, ignoring the crushing soreness that erupted over his body.

Karueq saw movement to his right as he dashed back into the fight. Another hooded figure with a red mask was upon him – the Quiri. Before he had time to react, a massive blow landed on the side of his head and his world went black.

--^--

Karueq's eyes flew open, and he immediately sprang to his feet, fists curled, ready to fight. His eyes danced around the dark ravine – searching, waiting. His ears perked up and scrutinized every crackle and creak of the forest surrounding him. He was alone.

He charged his energy and conjured an orange light between his palms, illuminating the shadows. Still nothing showed. He spotted his sword on the ground just beyond his reach. He cursed himself for losing so quickly.

How convenient for him the Eleverians had decided against killing before he faced down not only the Elequiri, but his personal bodyguard as well. Had that not been so, Karueq most certainly would have faced his death here. The Eleverians were foolish indeed to enact such a law. They could have thrown the Shatanala into a panic by cutting him down.

The walk back to his camp was quicker than the journey in. He found the stream again and followed it out of the aged forest. He met no one along the way, as expected. When he left the tree line, the sky was beginning to brighten. He'd been knocked out for several hours, and there was no hope of tracking his assailants down. Instead, he broke camp and returned to Xanadai, sifting through the riddles the Elequiri had so kindly given him.

He considered his chances of capturing the Elequiri or at least beheading him during their discussion. With the Quiri watching from the shadows, it would have been unwise to attempt, even if Karueq had brought a small army with them. What the Eleverians lacked in numbers, they made up for in stealth and skill. This allowed them to fight in small groups, dispatching only as much as one Guard division at a time.

Karueq knew he could crush them by launching massive assaults on them with a large portion of his army, but this war was being fought for hearts and souls, not land and resources. Displays of power such as that did not keep their prizes for long, so Karueq and Shatan opted for smaller bouts of combat in return for leaching into the lives of the ordinary Seagan people.

Now, even that method seemed to be damned. Eleh had displayed his power. His army was dealing in mercy because it was certain it could. Quiron and Zokul had defected, along with others whose names Karueq couldn't care to recall. Karueq couldn't deny they were losing the war.

The only way to gain anything back and to continue the victories Shatan needed was to cut the head off the monster. They needed to undo the Elequiri.

The Rale descended into the pit, and Karueq dismounted. His return to Xanadai would begin with a much-needed discussion with his second.

Bleren came at once. "My lord, you summoned me," he said as soon as he walked into Karueq's chambers.

Karueq turned his attention from the map before him. "I did. Sit."

Bleren reclined himself in the chair opposite his master. He rubbed his face tiredly. "I have news for you also."

"I suppose I could do with a little good news. Go on."

Bleren sighed, "Unfortunately, it is not all good news I bring you."

Karueq's hand found his face and he rubbed his temples. "Of course it isn't," he groaned. "Very well. What blunder do I have to fix this time?"

"If it were up to me, you wouldn't fix anything. Israel is in jeopardy. You should just let Jezebel fall."

"Jezebel? You know I can't do that. Israel can't fall away again."

"I don't think we can hold it this time. My spy stationed in Persia brings back a report of Jezebel's dealings. He came back late from his assignment, and when I asked him why, he said he heard a disturbing rumor of prophets hidden in the countryside of Israel. He knew Jezebel had vanquished these prophets to quell Eleh's influence. It might have worked, but one from the king's court, my spy tells me, hid no less than a hundred of them in caves carved out of the hills. The courtier has been providing supplies for them unnoticed by the queen. No doubt there are Eleverians stationed in the area to protect them."

"Is that all?" Karueq inquired, begging there to be no more.

"Again, no. The prophet Elijah has come forth."

The conversation Karueq had with Jezebel concerning her accomplishments in Israel returned to him. She had claimed to kill all but one prophet but assured him she would wipe him out, too. So much for the brief moment of faith he had in her.

Bleren continued. "He has issued a challenge to Jezebel's demon, Baal. An altar sacrifice in which the true God lights the fire."

Karueq's mind made a quick comparison between this test and Eleh's ability to enter Xanadai. "Baal and Asherah combined couldn't win such a contest."

"As I said, Karueq, I would let Jezebel fall were the response up to me. We should put our resources back where they belong, back into infiltrating Israel's heart from the ground up, not from the court."

"I doubt we'll be able to do that under the circumstances," Karueq said dryly.

"What circumstances are those?"

"Our complete and utter failure to know just how powerful our enemy is has been our greatest weakness, and it is a great weakness indeed."

"You've been listening too much to our prisoners."

"Yes, the prisoners we've lost."

Bleren closed his mouth. He had a habit of silencing himself when Karueq was getting impatient. Doing so prevented him from encouraging Karueq in what he deemed were toxic thoughts.

This time, Karueq wouldn't be brought down so easily. "There is one way we could undo all the damage that has been done. We can use Zokul's plan and infiltrate their ranks."

"My lord, I beg you to abandon any thoughts of this scheme," deterred the less seasoned man. "Zokul was a disease, and he was so against us that he defected. Would it not stand to reason that he would want us to lose more of our soldiers to them? How many men would you send in only for them to be turned. Even Quiron could not withstand them."

Karueq contemplated Bleren's sudden mention of Quiron. He had indeed told his second what had happened to that cruel assassin, but Bleren had seen little interest in such information. The fact that a member of the Brehila defected did not seem to pique his interest at all. Now, he used that example of treason to try to sway Karueq's decisions.

Bleren continued, seeing he had caught his master's attention. "Abandon this plan, and don't think of it again."

"What would you have me do?"

"Refocus our efforts like you did in the beginning. Before I came to your service, tales of your victories inspired us as boys. You collapsed kingdoms and attacked the Eleverians with a strong arm. Do away with schemes spun from the shadows. Send out teams from our ranks to the nations and take their hearts. Find the Eleverians where they interfere and crush them."

"Things are not as simple as they used to be, young one. The Eleverians are stronger than they were, and they have made Eleh's grip harder to break. We must take this war to them, and that zealous idiot has given us the only scheme that has even a possibility of working."

Bleren shook his head. "And how many of our men will you sacrifice to this plot? Ten? A hundred? All of Xanadai?"

"Only one."

Bleren scoffed, but then his eyes darted pointedly at Karueq. The commander sat behind his careful map unblinking.

"Absolutely not," Bleren growled.

"Who better fit to attempt such a thing?"

"No, my lord. If you are so bent on testing Zokul's theory, then send anyone, *anyone* else."

"I trust no one with this, not even you."

"If you ever attempt this, I'll detain you."

"Careful, Bleren. That is treason."

"It is treason to speak of what you are so fixed on."

"I am not going in blind. I have the best chance of withstanding them."

"You have no idea how they are turning our forces. You may be the least susceptible and stand strong against them, but you may also be the most susceptible we have, and if it is the latter, you will be lost."

The conclusion Bleren came to was a plausible one. Depending on their method, whatever weakness in his forces they were exploiting, he could fall quicker than even Zokul himself who despised Shatan and the doctrine the Shatanala clung to.

"Fair enough, my friend," he agreed. "For now, I will arrest this scheme."

"Nothing would please me more," Bleren said, still wary. "Perhaps my other information would suit your fixation better. We may have a lead on the identity of the Elequiri."

Karueq smiled, willing himself to believe Bleren's assertion. "Go on."

"A team of mine made contact with the Eleka Guard while you were away. The entire Guard were present in the assault on our holdings in the East, save one. Aryngo was absent."

Karueq considered the timing of this information. The information was to be sure, but Karueq had occupied the Elequiri's time while the Guard was engaging Bleren's men. He remembered how brutally Shatan had tortured Aryngo in the prisons, but he also knew the Eleverians healed quickly, and the rest of the team was already actively assaulting Bleren's tasks.

"How can you be sure?"

"I'm requesting reports from all our forces and spies to report on any sightings of the Guard surrounding your recent meeting with the

Elequiri. It seems they have been campaigning in teams for weeks, finally converging on our base in the days before the meeting. Aryngo disappeared just after.”

Karueq considered the information with intrigue. So, Aryngo had indeed been out in the field despite his treatment down here.

“Very good, continue to monitor Aryngo’s movements. Report back to me anything, whether he is absent or active, and spare no details.”

“Yes, my lord. Is that all you require of me?”

“For now, yes. We will make arrangements to send reinforcements and aid to Jezebel later, but for now, I must rest.”

Bleren stood up to leave with a sly smile. “I really wish you would just let the witch fall.”

Karueq smirked at his insistence. “In due time.”

CHAPTER SEVEN

BATTLE ON THE MOUNT

The Great Temple glowed quietly following the clerics' daily worship ceremony. The lay people had dispersed in silence, as was customary. Karueq shook his head in amusement at the theatrical dignity the horde showed in the presence of their prince. Shatan demanded their honor, and they surrendered it on occasions like this, though they still ransacked other sacred places. The rebellions never came close to the Great Temple, but Karueq wondered if one day they might be so bold.

With the masses gone, he was left sitting on the steps of the altar, turning his boot knife over in his hand, letting his mind wander to a great many things. He puzzled over the meeting with the Elequiri. He tried to understand what the roach's play was. The Eleverians already had a far smaller army than he himself commanded. Yes, they were effective in small numbers, and as of yet, the Shatanala had no plans to deploy large numbers against them. However, the summons in Israel could change that.

It didn't make sense for the Elequiri to be so forward about unnerving Shatan. The Prince would not be moved and he certainly did not fear flesh and bone. To Karueq's knowledge there was nothing that frightened the great demon. There had to be another reason.

The play could be to make the Shatanala careless. Being given an advantage could blossom his men's egos and make them feel untouchable, but the Elequiri had to know he would never tell his subordinates this information. He would only report the law to the Prince, which looped Karueq's thinking back to the Elequiri's words.

Shatan's words broke through his thoughts. "We have a great many things to discuss, Commander," his buttery voice echoing softly in the barren temple.

"Indeed, we do," Karueq replied, staying seated.

"First your report from the Elequiri."

Karueq caught a hint of intrigue in the demon's voice. "Surprised I came back remaining in your service?"

"I am pleased with your fortitude and your desire to continue serving me well," Shatan replied. "I am well aware that this war has frustrated you, especially with the developments of late. It pleases me greatly that your conviction and good judgment have not waned because of these unfortunate events."

"You may see my resentment with some of your orders – especially when you do nothing to pervade our failures – but my faith in your campaign against Eleh won't be shaken."

"Good," the demon murmured. "Now, the Elequiri. What did he have to say?"

"Several things." Karueq turned his eyes back to the twirling knife as he recalled the details of the meeting. "The most important point is that he has imposed a new law on his people. They are going to cease killing our forces and instead wish to extend mercy to us."

Shatan's eyes shifted away as he considered this news, although his expression didn't change. Karueq continued. "He said they wish to strike fear in you, your majesty. I consider it pointless and only a means to increase our power against them."

"He gave you another reason for this law. That isn't their only play."

"He did say the law is mostly a selfish move on their part because they experience regret when they kill – and that souls can't change their choices in death."

"That is a much better reason."

Karueq's earlier reflection surfaced. "Another reason why I continue to follow you. You have never demanded that we go against reason like their guilt-dealing God."

"What say you about this information?"

The commander gave the knife a deft flip in the air and caught it by the blade. "I don't understand. I can't fathom why they would create such a law, much less tell us about it."

The Prince tilted his head ever so slightly. "You know why they made it, that may tell us why they really told you."

"Why? So they can boast about their self-righteous behavior while they fall to us in greater numbers?"

"They are indeed self-righteous, but it is not about boasting. It is about atoning."

Karueq puzzled this suggestion over. "You mean to say they are giving us an advantage to pay for the lives they took."

Shatan turned his gaze out beyond the temple. "It's an idea. What else did you discuss?"

"I had questions about Eleh's intrusion in the prisons. He said Eleh has always been able to penetrate our defenses." Here, Karueq pointed his attention directly at the demon. "Is this true?"

Shatan paused as if considering his answer. "What do you think?"

"I do not want to guess. I don't want riddles. I want a real answer."

"I know you do," the Prince relented with a smile. "That is one of the many reasons I lifted you to your position. Yes, Eleh is able to penetrate these walls and always has."

Karueq swallowed against the shiver rising in his spine. "That doesn't concern you?"

"You are letting fear and doubt corrupt your insight. Why should this concern me? For that matter, why should you be concerned? He is indeed all powerful, I've never denied that, but He does not come down here unless those He deemed as chosen are in our custody. He considers all those that I have gathered to be lost and damaged. He abhors this place and all that I've rescued. You have seen for yourself that He does not truly care for any of His creation. He tosses them aside when they are at their weakest, and I come to their aid to raise them from their despair. I do for them what no one did for me when I fell from grace.

"This is the ultimate stalemate, Karueq. We do not invade each other's territory, we allow His creation – you, your soldiers, the Eleverians, and all in Seaga - to choose their side. You are my means of persuasion from His treachery just the same as the Elequiri is His means of swaying them to Him. That, Karueq, is the true nature of the war. The persuasion of the masses to His side or the side of freedom." Shatan raised his hand out toward Karueq. The knife flew from his hand through the air between them and landed in Shatan's hand. The fallen angel studied it for a moment. It had an ivory handle and no apparent value, except that which both Karueq and Shatan knew.

"You wanted to be sure of my conviction before telling me this," Karueq guessed, feeling his pride swell at his performance in this test.

"Yes, Commander. It is easy to give your all to a cause when it is easy and there are victories at every turn, but it is far more difficult to have faith in something that appears to be a worthy but failing crusade. Now, I have seen you at your weakest, when you would no longer have faith in me, and you were tested by the enemy into turning away from me, but you remained loyal to me." He handed the knife back to his commander.

Karueq took it gingerly. "He did offer me immunity if I deserted."

"I'm pleased to hear that."

"He also rejected our reciprocal offer."

"He will bow to me one day."

"We can only hope. We have more to discuss - Israel." He sheathed the blade back into the strap on his boot. "One of our spies came back with news of prophets hidden in the hills, alive and being supplied by a man in King Ahab's court."

At this, Shatan turned away and looked out through the pillars holding up the temple dome, across the lake and into the darkness beyond. "How many?"

"The spy reports that as many as a hundred have been omitted from Jezebel's campaign."

The demon's face soured, reflecting Karueq's own thoughts on the matter. One hundred of Eleh's prophets, persuasive men and women who lived and worked alongside the Israeli people, had the potential to sway the people back to Eleh's side if they emerged. Even without the impending threat of Elijah's contest, Jezebel's operation was exposed to failure. Karueq cleared his throat. "As troubling as this news is, my lord, it does not disturb me as much as the other bit of intelligence the spy reported."

Shatan turned back to him, his face dark and bitter.

He continued. "The prophet Elijah has come forth, issuing a challenge against Baal. It will be a display of power in which the more powerful deity lights a sacrificial fire to consume an offering. My lord, we can't lose Israel again."

"She will not lose it, and Eleh will not win," was Shatan's firm answer.

Karueq kept his further wariness of their victory to himself in light of Shatan's renewed faith in him and his own belief in Shatan's power. "What resources does she have?"

"She has been stationed in Israel long enough to know them and their hearts." There was a hint of callousness in Shatan's violent expression.

"My lord, I do not wish to undermine her authority on the matter, but I am not entirely confident in her devotion to the task. I acknowledge my personal misgivings with her, but it stands to reason that her failure to eliminate all the prophets shows evidence of carelessness, or at least weakness. I suggest we not leave this matter to her alone."

"What do you suggest, Commander?"

"The contest can't be ignored. Unfortunately, I don't believe we can win it, but we can't let Israel's people dismiss us completely."

"By creating a spectacle?" Shatan asked.

Karueq's calculating mind dug into the challenge and began plotting. "The Eleverians will suspect an attack on the site. They will reinforce the boundary around the sacrificial grounds to keep any interference away. If we want to salvage any part of Jezebel's mission, we must draw them out by creating a diversion. If we send our forces to attack the people, we can engage them and decrease the numbers they can muster around the altar, and if we cause chaos, we can assert our holdings in the aftermath, just as we do elsewhere."

"Would the Elequiri be there?" the demon asked.

"I think we would do well to not assume anything he would do."

"If he does interfere, what would you do?"

Karueq was struck with a bold idea. To capture the Elequiri in the midst of the chaos they were about to both unleash and fight with, they would need more than luck and audacity. "We could never press an advantage on him with such conflicts already burdening us. Marching on the Israelites will take all the strength we can spare from resisting Eleh.”

"If the Elequiri interferes,” Shatan interrupted, firmly staring his commander down. “He will go after Jezebel and overthrow her.”

"An apt assumption, my Prince,” he said begrudgingly.

"In the event that this happens, you will be there to protect her. We cannot let the queen come to harm.”

A tepid snort escaped Karueq. “I beg your pardon, prince, but you mean to take me away from my station as commander to sit with the priestess like a woman minding her brats?”

"You scoff at your responsibility?” the demon asked, his tone of warning slicing from his tongue. “Your charge is two-fold. You will make a move on the Elequiri if he shows, and if the people turn to uprising, you are to protect Jezebel so that she may continue to control the people.”

Karueq's eyes fell to his hands. He stared hard at them, keeping his rage in check. He was the commander of the most powerful military in the world, capable of single-handedly bringing nations to their knees, and he was being ordered to sit out this crucial battle with a woman he despised.

Shatan interrupted his thoughts. “Do not place your pride above the prize. I am indeed giving you perhaps the most important part of this mission - the Elequiri, commander. Your ambition is one of the reasons I chose you to lead my forces. Now put your ambition into this task, and win.” With that, Shatan furled his wings around himself and disappeared in smoke.

--^--

The preparations had been hasty, but there was little time to spare. The challenge would commence in the morning. Karueq had managed to bring a sizable hoard to Israel, drawing not only on the stock in Xanadai, but calling in agents and squadrons from their missions near the unsettled nation.

He had divided them into three groups. A sizeable group would accompany the demons to the sacrifices. There, they would engage with the Eleverians who would try to interfere with the challenge. The largest group would spread through the main settlement and reaching out to the satellite encampments to spread the Eleverian soldiers thin. They were to fight the Eleverians and not attack the Israelites unless the Eleverians refused to engage with them. The last group, comprised of a few Brehila assassins, would hunt the prophets down and put an end to their nuisance. Wherever they had started to roam, no matter who was hiding them, the Brehila would find and kill them.

Karueq himself would miss these skirmishes entirely, and he cursed Shatan the whole journey until he reached the doorstep of the palace. He swept past the guards and the servants to the tower containing the counterfeit queen. He knocked on the door and heard a cooing voice inside beckoning him in. He pushed the door in and stepped into the hazy room. Her voice slithered through the perfume from the bed.

"Karueq," she cooed. "Have you come already? Would you be a dear and bring me some wine?"

Karueq's temper blazed up. He picked up the wine flask and hurled it at the wall just above her head. It smashed and the liquor splattered on her head as she shrieked.

"Who do you think you are!" she screamed. She jumped from the bed. "Do you know who I am here? I am queen! I am royalty!"

"You treacherous wench," Karueq accused in an even tone. "You have failed to win this people, and you have failed to fulfill Shatan's orders. You are no more royalty here than you are in Xanadai. Instead of attending to your tasks, you have become drunk on your title and gluttoned yourself on luxuries." He threw a flask of perfumed oil at her, and she shrieked. "Tell me, your worship, was it Elijah that you failed to kill when I last visited you?" He picked up the bowl of fruit on the table and hurled it at her.

"Stop it!" she shrieked, barely dodging the heavy bowl. The ripe fruit smashed into her and left stains on her nightdress. "Did you come in the late evening to taunt me? We have work to do tomorrow!"

"*I* have work to do tomorrow," Karueq corrected, "my men have work tomorrow. You will be detained so you will do no more harm to the charge Shatan has left you. You failed to destroy the one prophet that now threatens everything we have built here."

"I made one mistake, you jackal. One!" she spat.

"Don't be a child. Your ability to overlook your duty and cocoon yourself in – " he gestured around the room, "– all of this astounds me. You have accused me of not believing in the cause and for neglecting my conviction. You don't seem to have any ambition but for comfort and decadence. Not only should you have won Israel by now, but the kingdom of Judah waits at your doorstep to be claimed as well."

"I am their queen. I have their hearts. They will never sway from me because they love and adore me. Just as your soldiers love me, even in my absence."

"They have already forgotten you."

"No, they haven't. And neither will these people, especially when their old God fails to light His fire."

"You've brought drought, famine, and subjugation upon them. They won't love you forever. You are to be under my command tomorrow. I will come back in the morning. Try to be presentable for your wavering people."

He left her still stinging from the jab. A loud crash resounded against the closed door as he walked away. Tomorrow would not be easy already, and he had just stirred the beast. He hoped that he had put enough of a fire in her to perform well tomorrow – to entertain the Israelites' image of her.

He slept fitfully in a room above the queen's chamber, waking a few hours before dawn while the world still slumbered. He would not let the witch misunderstand his presence at her side, so he had found the room with a window above hers. He could still hear any troubling sounds while they slept. He dressed quickly, strapping more weapons to his body than he usually carried. With his sword belted to his side, he left the palace quietly. He arrived at the edge of the city, past the dwellings and the storehouses. Bleren waited for him there.

"Good morning," his second greeted him.

"Good morning. Are your soldiers in place?"

"Ready for their orders once I give them."

"Good." Karueq noticed the stars were beginning to dim. "I appreciate your steady loyalty, general. It makes missions like this easier."

"Are you sure you can't leave the priestess to dance with the Eleverians?"

Karueq chuckled. "You know I would rather be out here where I can be of use, but the prince doesn't want her to come to any harm if she is to remain here and rule."

"I wager you will simply sit in the tower and watch the spectacle uninterrupted."

"Then perhaps I'll have to draw a few rogues in. It would be good practice. Do you have any questions for the day?"

"No. You were clear when we arrived. I won't disappoint you, my lord."

"I know you won't. I expect a full report at the end of the day." Karueq turned away and left. He wandered back through the city but didn't return to the palace yet. There was one more person he needed to talk to.

He turned toward the shrine standing proud among a few tents. This shrine belonged to Baal, the demon whose name would be invoked during the challenge. Pillars of free-standing rock stood at the entrance. They served as idols and props of worship for those loyal to the demon. He pushed the door aside and entered the small building.

Inside were statues and ornaments all made of precious metals and gilded in gems and stones, and the space was filled with expensive tapestries. The interior glittered, an unholy dwelling for an unholy spirit. He had to credit Jezebel's influence when he saw this. Even the people's wealth was subject to her design.

A cloud of smoke filled the room, blocking his vision and assaulting his nose. Before he remedied the smoke himself, his vision cleared, and the smoke gathered together before the altar. It materialized a magnificent horned beast with leathery wings and a stern expression - the demon, Baal.

"To what do I owe your presence?" The demon's voice was deep, but it lacked the authority Shatan conveyed.

"I am not here for you," Karueq dismissed him. "You should be with the rest of the demons preparing."

Baal hissed, "I do not take orders from you."

Karueq's proud authority flared up. "My orders come from Shatan, your master. Disobey me, and you disobey him. Go."

The horned spirit gave a low hiss once more, wishing to defy this order from a mortal, but it obliged and disappeared in smoke. Karueq immediately turned his attention around the shrine. It appeared to hold no other being, mortal or immortal.

"Come out of the shadows," he commanded.

A figure in black dropped conspicuously from behind a statue to his left. The figure's face was partially concealed by a hood that extended seamlessly from his close-fitting tunic. A dark red sash bound his waist. This man was one of the Brehila. He lowered his hood to reveal the sinister war paint marking his stern face.

The assassin bowed. "Commander."

"Have the others come, Farroh?"

"Indeed."

"How long will it take you to extinguish the prophets?"

"Not long." Farroh's short answers were normal for the Brehila. They didn't spend their time with company, rather they worked alone and preferred it that way.

"I have an additional assignment for you. The Elequiri may show himself, and I am placing you and your brethren in charge of bringing in his protector. I want the Quiri alive if possible, but if he must be killed, bring back his body."

"Understood."

Karueq pulled a set of small wood rods from his pocket and handed them to Farroh. "Keep a count of your kills. I will reward you proportionally." The rods were meant to be notched to keep an accurate count. Karueq wasn't nearly as interested in rewarding these ghosts as he was in making sure all the prophets were accounted for.

"Understood."

"Good luck," Karueq said as he turned to go. He wouldn't see Farroh or his comrades until they returned to Xanadai. He would reward them with those comforts the Brehila deemed wouldn't addle their minds and cause them to slip their abilities. They were never rewarded with women or wealth. Their prizes usually took the form of raw materials they used to build weapons and improve their craft. Occasionally he enslaved a demon to their command in order to build their power.

Karueq returned to the palace just as the sky was beginning to gray. The servants were up and beginning the day's work. There was a little more work for them today, as Jezebel had hurriedly planned a feast to honor her impending victory.

By the time Jezebel stirred in her bed, Karueq had been sharpening his knives for an hour while sitting by the window. He despised his assignment and longed to be out with his men. Instead, he sat in the corner of the queen's chamber watching her blink awake. She stretched, stripping the sleep away from her neck and limbs before her eyes fell on her brooding guardian. A scowl drew itself across her face and was only broken by a yawn.

Karueq turned his eyes back to his whetting stone as she rose from the bed. The soft scraping sound against the metal marked out the passing morning as the priestess languishly adorned herself, detailing her appearance. Karueq admitted she had never looked more regal. Her long, ebony hair cascaded about her, her skin shone with oil, and she sparkled with precious jewelry in a long, royal gown. She returned to the bed and reclined, picking at the food on a table near her.

It wasn't until she reached for the wine that he spoke. "Don't," he commanded simply.

"I'll decide to listen to you later, swine."

"If you're attacked by an Israelite or Eleverian, you will wish for your sobriety."

She defiantly poured out a cup. "That's what you're here for." She drained the red drink, and he found his protest to be absent. He set to work inspecting his labor. He heard a frustrated sigh from her direction. "When does this abomination start?"

"Everything is in place," he explained. "Your priests and prophets should have slaughtered the bull and the demon hoard should be gathering strength."

"One demon is more than enough to light a fire, Karueq."

"Eleh and His soldiers are involved, and we're not taking chances. Shatan agrees with me that using a host of demons will break through whatever barrier the Eleverians place on them, and they will be able to hold back Eleh's fire."

"Baal and Asherah together have held this nation with me better than Eleh ever did. They could do it on their own."

"We are not taking chances."

"And where has that carefulness gotten you?"

Karueq slammed the knife he was holding into its sheath. "I have never taken any chances, and as such, I have successfully engaged with Eleh on all fronts. You have taken too many chances here, Jezebel. You should have treated it like your temple in Xanadai. No mercy, no excuses."

Jezebel drew to the window and looked out at her adopted country. Her face was set. He saw the fire in her eyes again, the burning blaze that swallowed the strong and the foolish, the fire that made her loved and feared.

"Then that is how I shall be today," she said, a tone of warning in her voice. Her eyes flitted to him, glittering with a passion. "No man, woman, or child will question my authority. Not even you, my dear." She walked to the door, opened it, and gave orders to the guard there. "Take every guard, soldier, and priest you can find and spread the word. Go to the Mount and wage battle with the false God's men. You will personally bring me a report of the outcome and all that happened. Go."

The guard hurried away.

Karueq interrupted Jezebel's thoughts. "You're leaving the palace open to attack."

She turned on him. "You and I are enough to keep the world at bay."

"If the Elequiri shows?"

"Then you and I will have our own little private contest to behead him."

Karueq caught something moving in his vision and he looked out the window. Down below the tower, a man walked carrying a sheaf of grain. He was dressed like a commoner, but something about where he was walking didn't seem right. He eyed the man until he disappeared among the buildings surrounding the palace. Karueq scanned the rest of the scene outside. The people were set to their daily labor while keeping an eye on the Mount. A few of the townspeople here and there were disguised Shatanala soldiers, and Karueq could pick them out quickly.

He noticed another man walking about, this one with tools in his hand. He did not concern himself with the Mount, and Karueq recalled the man with the grain hadn't either. The man suddenly halted in front of a group of the disguised Shatanala. He appeared to converse with them. His hand moved a fold in his clothing away, discreetly revealing a sword. Karueq smiled wryly. The odd men were Eleverian soldiers blending in. The challenge was set. The Brehila were silently attacking the remaining prophets. His soldiers were stationed around the city and had already drawn part of the Eleverian army away from the Mount.

The Mount itself, holding the hoard of demons and some of his best soldiers, was still. He glanced at the sky, the sun blazing above, and then looked to the ground. The tower's shadow crouched near the base, retreating from the sun. It was past noon.

"They should have lit the fire by now," he told his snake companion.

"Give it time," she said, confidently. "They will not disappoint me."

"Are you prepared to change your tactic if they do?"

"If they don't light the fire, I can assure the people Baal is not to be tested and he does not need to prove his existence to a flighty crowd such as them, and then I will deepen the famine to chastise them."

"What if they reject you because of the famine?"

"A starving people is easy to quell. You exploit this fact yourself, do you not?"

Karueq didn't respond.

Suddenly, a body launched through the window and landed on its feet in the center of the room. Karueq's reflexes kicked in. He flung one of his newly sharpened knives at the intruder and whipped out his sword. Without flinching, the woman caught the knife and tossed it back to him – Chelia.

She crossed her arms and leaned her shoulder against the wall, calm and confident. Karueq stood on his guard, hand on his sword. "Not much of a show your 'gods' are making, your highness," she taunted Jezebel. "Though I must say, your prophets are making quite a spectacle. They've been chanting to the sky and the earth and the… I forget what else. It's all quite confusing."

Jezebel squared herself on the young Captain. "The power they are building with ritual and chanting will only add to the spectacle when fire consumes everything on that mountain."

"I look forward to seeing whatever your demons are waiting to unleash," the girl egged. "You really think Eleh will lose to the hoard of Hell, don't you? Even if your forces were a thousand-fold greater, He would have no trouble keeping their fire away."

Jezebel turned on Karueq. "Kill her, Karueq!"

Karueq shook his head in amusement. "This is your battle."

Chelia leaned off the wall and closed half the distance to Jezebel. "You have defiled this nation long enough, Jezebel. The King is taking His people back."

"His people?" The priestess let a peal of demoniac laughter escape her. "How many times, Captain? How many times do we have to seduce them without any effort? How many times must they break their backs building temples in honor of our demons for you to realize they have no love for your pitiful God?"

"How many times do they come running back to Him? They do love Him, witch. They know Him and love Him. Sin tempts and seduces, but it can never hold them forever. They always return to Him."

"Not all," Jezebel defended. "Not all of them return."

"Yes, Shatan has ensnared a few." A glimmer of sorrow appeared in Chelia's eyes but was quickly replaced by her usual amusement. "Your forces on the other hand are very given to turning to Eleh, your queenship. How many of your personal servants have we brought to the light in the last year alone?"

Karueq glanced at Jezebel. Her expression ran cold. He hadn't heard of her servants defecting.

"We will keep what we have," Jezebel said, defiantly.

"Yes," Chelia smirked. "I'm sure you will. Know that I applaud your efforts and think very highly of your determination and fortitude."

Karueq stepped in before the snake scared the Captain off without the opportunity to recapture her. "How many men have you brought with you?"

The Captain turned to him. "Oh good, strategy! I love this kind of talk with you. How many do you think I have with me?"

"I don't know. You have disguised yourselves."

"Ah," she said knowingly, "you saw the exchange in the square between my men and yours. What would you say if the Elequiri brought the entire nation here to confront you?"

"That is far too bold for your kind."

"What if I told you the Elequiri bid only five of us to come?"

"How will you hold the Mount?"

"The Mount?" The Captain's head cocked to the side. "Have you been up in this tower all day?"

Karueq didn't answer.

Chelia peered at him. "Elijah is alone, Karueq. We have no men up there."

Karueq's head reeled. The bold prophet was unprotected, and he had half an army surrounding him.

Chelia must have seen this calculation. "Eleh is protecting him, Commander. Don't do anything foolish."

"Karueq, kill her," Jezebel warned.

Chelia ignored her. "The Elequiri is not making an appearance either. Whatever you were hoping this contest would be, it isn't going to happen. This isn't a glorious battle. This is Eleh bringing His people back to Him."

"You will not win," Karueq insisted.

A soft bell sounded through the window. The three enemies paused their many personal wars and looked out toward the Mount.

"You know what that sound is, highness," Chelia said to Jezebel.

"The evening sacrifice. Yes, I know."

"Your time is up – no fire. Your 'god' has failed. Now it is Elijah's turn."

Jezebel's wrath blazed anew. "We will hold Him back! My demons are powerful!"

"Powerful enough to be controlled by a mortal like you?"

"I am more powerful than you could ever hope to be."

"You misunderstand my ambition." Then she addressed Karueq again. "Have you come to know why we fight, yet?"

Karueq's mind itched. Here it was again. The invitation from the Eleverians to figure them out, to know them and then destroy them.

"I'd say not," Chelia dismissed him.

Jezebel barked. "I've heard enough! Kill her!"

The Captain's smile faded and was replaced by an earnest look, like a pleading child. "Listen. I am here to offer the both of you asylum. Jezebel, you especially are in danger. When Elijah has prepared the bull and Eleh lights His fire, Israel will come back to Him. I expect Shatan will deal with you severely. Come with us."

The witch spat on the Captain. Chelia didn't flinch at the insult as it landed on her shoulder, her pleading expression unchanged.

"Never!" cried Jezebel.

The Captain turned to him. "Karueq, you have the same offer. Come away with us. Be free of your shackles."

"You would do well to join us, Captain," he replied, turning the offer back on her. "Shatan would be pleased to have a skilled leader like you."

"You will grow tired of extending that offer, Commander."

An explosion of darkness burst from Jezebel. It blasted into the Captain, but she raised her hands just in time. The energy hurled her against the wall, the impact breaking some of the stone and no doubt her ribs. Jezebel had meant to kill her, but she had saved herself just in time.

Karueq turned on Jezebel. "Shatan wants her alive!"

"He gave me no such orders!" The witch threw a second burst of darkness at the Captain now crumpled against the wall. This time, Chelia saw it coming and blocked it with everything she could muster, despite her injury. The energy dissipated around her, and she sprang up, darting for the window.

Karueq stepped in her way and sliced at her. She ducked his blow and jammed her elbow into his leg. Jezebel's attacks had taken much out of her, and he quickly recovered from her blow, grabbing her by her braid and flinging her to the floor.

She gasped to breathe but rolled away as he brought his knee down to pin her. She whipped her sword out and swung it at him, narrowly missing his shoulder. His sword missed her stomach by inches.

Their private battle was interrupted by a sudden scream. Jezebel was clutching the window frame. A column of fire and smoke, blazing bright orange instead of violet, extended from the Mount to the sky - Eleh's fire.

Chelia slammed Karueq's sword out of his hand and kicked it across the room. He instinctively reached for the twin knives strapped on his lower back but was halted by Chelia replacing her sword in its scabbard.

"Come with me." She breathed heavily from the exertion, but she locked eyes with him. "Both of you, while you can."

In a flurry, Jezebel turned back to the room and expelled a thunderous blast of power. Karueq's head spun from the impact, but he braced himself, absorbing as much of the energy as he could. It burned through his veins and screamed in his bones. With a heavy push, he finally swallowed it into his gut.

His eyes flew open. Jezebel stood before him, breathing hard with rage and indignation. Chelia was gone.

"Where is she?" Jezebel spat, accusation in her tone.

Karueq's latent disgust for this woman kindled anew. "You must have saved her with that spell," he jabbed. "Tell me Jezebel, are you aiding the Eleverians?"

"Don't do that to me!" she cried. "Where is she?"

Karueq ignored her question and stepped over to the window. The fire was still ablaze, consuming the bull of the sacrifice on the Mount prepared by Elijah and sending the smoke to the sky. He calculated the loss and how he might get it back. He considered ordering his men hidden among the Israelites to begin a massacre. At this, he noticed the Israelites about the city were falling prostrate toward the Mount, worshiping Eleh once more.

"Priestess, your influence in Israel is over," he said plainly. "I'm taking you back to Xanadai, and Shatan can deal with you."

"My influence is not over," the witch seethed. "I have the bed of the king. I still have power over them."

Karueq shook his head, completely unamused. "You neglected your duties when you had the world worshiping you."

"I work better from the shadows," she spat.

Karueq considered the tiny flicker of worry in her eyes. She was afraid. Shatan had never been forgiving. Karueq would love to see the witch burn and be stripped of her power. He relished the idea.

Jezebel grabbed his arm in earnest, trying to wish away the damnation in his thoughts. "You said yourself we cannot lose Israel."

"You have already lost it."

"These lice can't keep focus on anything. Today, they bow to Eleh. Tomorrow, they forget him. I will regain my hold on them, trust me."

Her expression was serious, her eyes wild. Karueq couldn't deny that she could keep the king astray, and perhaps by proxy the people. They could not, indeed, lose Israel completely in light of every other loss they'd suffered.

He sighed. "As you wish, priestess."

CHAPTER EIGHT

THE WHIMPERING SOLDIER

"You let Jezebel stay?" Shatan growled. Karueq had given him the report of all that had happened in Israel. It was an utter failure and unlike anything they had anticipated.   Their three-pronged attack had been for naught.

Bleren reported there had indeed been no Eleverians on the Mount, and the division of men around the sacrificial site was useless. They had watched the contest from their hiding places and left the scene without tasting the blood they so craved. Bleren also reported he'd imprisoned many of them, because they'd been shaken by the swift result of the contest, and he didn't want to risk them spreading hysteria.

His second had personally commanded the division in the city. Bleren's own eyes had counted the number of Eleverians among them. There were only a handful of them lurking about, making themselves known to the Shatanala sparingly, which had confused Bleren and stopped the attack on the Israelites. With the result of the contest, Bleren had ordered minor sabotages of the city's infrastructure. As the purpose of the army in the city was to draw the Eleverians out en masse, this second plot failed.

The final defeat came from Farroh's report to Karueq of the assassinations on the prophets. Farroh had fallen to his knees at Karueq's feet, telling him the Brehila had found no prophets, and produced the wooden rods still intact. When Karueq asked him how they had failed so completely, Farroh stated the prophets had not been in the city nor the surrounding countryside. They searched until dusk but found no sign of their prey. With this, Farroh removed the red sash from his waist and voluntarily left for the prisons to be placed on the rack until his commander saw fit. Such was the Brehila leader's pride in his craft.

"Yes, my lord," Karueq answered Shatan's indignation. "She insisted she could keep hold of Israel through the influence of the king."

"She is saving her own skin. She knows the escape of the prophets is on her head."

Karueq argued with him, "I still contend that we can't just let Israel go. We need to hold it."

Shatan turned away and looked out from the shore across the lake into the darkness. Karueq simply waited for him. The fire searing in Shatan's eyes would frighten most of the Shatanala, but Karueq knew the rage was directed elsewhere so it didn't unease him.

"Very well," the prince decided. "She can stay, but her next infraction will be her undoing."

"I couldn't agree more with that, my lord. Might I detain you to discuss new strategy?"

"What new scheme have you concocted?" the demon asked with little interest.

"My general has deduced the identity of the Elequiri."

The demon's expression was cautious. "Who is it?"

"Aryngo, a member of the Eleka Guard."

"The worm that tried to attack me in the prisons?"

"One and the same. Bleren reported to me that in the time surrounding my meeting with the Elequiri, Aryngo was seen in the field. During the meeting, however, he was absent."

"Was anyone else tracked during this time?"

"Yes. We monitored the Eleka Guard with the most intention, but he is the only one not to have been seen during the meeting."

Cold calculation filtered through Shatan's stone expression. He was considering everything that Karueq himself had already contemplated. The more Karueq thought about it, the more he believed in the speculation. Aryngo was new to the Eleka Guard, but he wasn't inexperienced or naive. It was particularly uncharacteristic of the Eleverians to display such hasty, ill-conceived behavior as Aryngo had shown during his capture. This might, convincingly, be an attempt to mask his stoic, measured personality. How convenient, too, that the leader of the Eleverian army be among the most daring of them, the ones that fought hand to hand with their enemy, constantly monitoring the changing landscape of the war.

Karueq's intrigue had brought his mind back to the exchange made during the capture. Aryngo and Chelia had spouted a healthy exchange about the plot Jezebel had set on them. It was Aryngo who expressed disappointment with the Elequiri. It was the Elequiri's trusted combat officer, Chelia, who participated in his charade. Karueq had been cautiously, very cautiously convinced Jezebel's letter had been convincing, but now he saw that the Elequiri may have used it to aid his mask while in enemy custody.

The calculation twitching at the corners of Shatan's eyes stilled. "Does he know that we know?"

"I very much doubt it, but even if he does, we must act."

"And by act, you mean…?"

Karueq spoke frankly. "We take him out."

Shatan's face fell, and his stern expression melted Karueq's interest in the conversation. "I forbid you from killing him."

Karueq's mouth closed, although his grim brows pulled back in objection.

"You disagree," Shatan observed.

"I do."

"Why?"

"If I can get near enough to him for an opportunity to strike, why are you hesitant to take it? He is the only thing keeping you from your dominion."

"There is much concerning this war you do not know. More to victory than destroying mortal men."

"Because you think I'm incapable or because you're afraid to tell me?"

"You think I operate on fear?"

"Only when it comes to you admitting you are vulnerable."

The image of the demon blurred faintly, and the creature beneath threatened to emerge. Before it could, the image remerged, the stately prince caging the beast. After a moment, the demon reached out and removed Karueq's pendant from his neck. Karueq watched in confusion as the demon cupped his hands around the pendant. The seams between his palms and fingers glowed for a moment. He then held up the pendant in front of his commander. It appeared the same as before, no alterations whatsoever. "If you insist on destroying him now in your eagerness to act," Shatan began, and Karueq's lip stiffened further at the criticism, "you will take this."

He dropped it into his commander's outstretched hand.

"There are things I haven't told you, and I will not divulge them now. When you find him and are in position to carry out your wish, place your pendant on him. If it glows white, you are still forbidden to kill him. If it remains unchanged, you may do with him whatever pleases you."

"What does it mean?"

"You are not in a position to exact such inquiries from me. Go, and do what you must."

The demon furled his wings around himself and disappeared in smoke. Karueq inspected the pendant in the absence of his master. He considered all the possibilities for what it could indicate. He couldn't imagine what Shatan could want from his enemy beyond a courteous death. Nothing Karueq could think gave him reason to use it.

It took Karueq a few months to meticulously devise his plan. When he wasn't attending to his other charges, he was absorbed by reports from the field about all movements above ground, especially those of the Eleka Guard. Karueq didn't just want his prey followed. He wanted to know every detail he could about where his company might be at any given moment and what they were doing. He wanted to be certain of their actions and find a way to ensnare them again.

This time, Karueq had no bait, but with the recent victory at Mount Carmel, there were hints of their confidence being inflated. He was noticing an almost imperceptible pattern to their movements. He called on Bleren often, and they discussed strategy for hours. When his second left, Karueq's mind would continue to be consumed by his schemes.

Finally, the right scheme with the right timing arrived. The Eleka Guard moved in pairs against small offenses by the Shatanala. They were likely to be found in the ones baited by demons, and even more likely if the demon was slow to infiltrate the town. Hasty takeovers usually resulted in a larger Guard party. So, Karueq sent two demons to a settlement just outside of Israel's reach, ordering them to make trouble little by little. He traveled to the town a few days later and set up camp a few miles away. At his instruction, seven Brehila, disguised as travelers, entered the town several days after him and took up lodgings in some of the homes. Two of them took over a tent on the edge of the town and dispatched the inhabitants.

The trap was set, and Karueq judged he would only have to wait a week for the Guard to arrive. In the meantime, he waited and watched, always from afar. He was cautious to not be seen and kept his movements around the countryside minimal. He wouldn't let himself rush any aspect of this plot.

They appeared five days after the Brehila arrived, in the late afternoon. During one of Karueq's long surveillance sessions, he noticed a pair of travelers enter the town. True to his predictions, they entered the home of an off-dwelling family as if seeking lodging for their tired feet - the lair of his planted assassins. From this distance, Karueq could only guess from their attire that these travelers were a man and a woman. His heart thudded in his chest. The man could be Aryngo.

Karueq's senses sharpened, and he took a moment to memorize every detail of the town that he could see. His eyes flitted over the tents, the people, and the livestock ambling about. He saw what he was looking for. A smith was busy beating an iron shaft into fashion. Karueq followed the rhythmic thumping carefully. His timing must be perfect.

From the slit in his arm guard, he retrieved a flat, metal piece that was pointed at both ends. Fixed to the metal face was a shard of gray stone - the signal he had chosen. He couldn't be sure that the Eleverians weren't keeping watch or that they hadn't brought a third member to lookout. He had to rely on the predictions he made and hope they kept the pattern they'd exhibited for several months.

He slipped away from his post just enough to accomplish his move. From here, a scout would see him. It was a delicate game he was playing. Pushing the thought of discovery out of his mind, he refocused on the beat of the smith's hammer. He counted to himself before rising slightly from his meager cover and hurling the flat piece into a beam supporting a tent. It connected with the wood in time with the smith's hammer.

Karueq exhaled, releasing the tension. The only people to notice the signal would be the five assassins he planted elsewhere in the town. In two hours, those men would join him outside the city.

He waited patiently at the rendezvous, his camp outside the town. The first of his team slid beside him into the tiny rock crevasse less than an hour after he planted the signal. The others arrived within an hour.

Karueq drew the knife from his boot and carved out the attack plan in the dirt. The five assassins knew the plan already, but Karueq wouldn't leave anything to chance on this mission. Too many opportunities had slipped through his hands. If Aryngo was indeed in their trap, Karueq was going to catch him.

The sky began to gray. Karueq and his men filtered out to the surveillance point, keeping enough distance and time between them to minimize notice. They were staged perfectly to descend on the tent as soon as the town began to turn in for the night. Karueq's eagerness twitched. He had been mentally preparing himself all evening in case Aryngo was absent, but he couldn't help hoping.

Then someone came out of the tent. Karueq inhaled sharply and his eyes widened. It was the woman. Karueq's mind raced through what could be happening inside. They were supposed to stay in the tent until nightfall. Then they would slip away and attack the demons, expelling them from the town. Maybe they had figured out the trap and subdued his men. Perhaps she was going to hunt the demons herself while her companion took care of the assassins.

Karueq wasn't going to wait for an answer. He signaled for a rapid move, and the six of them dashed to the tent, unconcerned if they were seen by the townspeople in the coming dusk. They descended on the entrance.

Karueq was the first inside. Without taking the time to do a proper survey of the room, he lunged at the man. He pinned him but then found himself on his side, his target loosed from his grasp. He sprang up and delivered a sharp kick as the Eleverian engaged the five assassins now inside. The Eleverian thudded to the floor and three of the men pounced on him, pinning him to the ground while he struggled. The others latched onto the remaining free limbs.

"Get him up," Karueq ordered. His men erected the man to his knees, coordinating their movements so none of them lost their hold. Karueq caught sight of the two planted assassins passed out on the floor from the corner of his eye. The remaining five Brehila stretched their catch between them, and the one behind him yanked his head back by the hair. It was Aryngo.

"Commander," Aryngo snorted, his voice slightly raspy from his throat being stretched back. "What a surprise to see you here."

Karueq drew his sword and whipped it across Aryngo's smug face, lacerating his cheek from his ear to his chin. Aryngo grunted forcefully. The ugly gash bled.

Karueq looked to his men. "Beat him."

Two of the men released their hold on Aryngo to do their commander's bidding while a third clamped a hand over his mouth while his body remained stretched out by two others. Aryngo groaned through the gag with each break in his bones. The cries grew louder as the torture continued, and no amount of fighting back could break the holds on him.

Satisfied that his body was sufficiently broken, Karueq said "Enough". The disciplined men immediately arrested their frenzy and stepped back. The third man released Aryngo's mouth, allowing him to take desperate, shuddering breaths. Karueq stepped in front of Aryngo and looked into his eyes. He saw a great deal of pain there, matched by the residual groans in his breathing. However, he was disappointed to see defiance still radiating from those same eyes, clear and fierce.

Karueq wasn't about to use Shatan's slippery interrogation methods now. "We have caught you, Elequiri."

Aryngo's expression darkened.

Karueq went on. "You were very clever to play the young fool, but you have been arrogant since Mount Caramel. You've become predictable in recent months."

The defiance radiating from his enemy's eyes cut through him. Finally, Karueq could see for himself the fury of his masked foe. He grinned. "You thought you could hide forever."

Karueq removed his pendant and slipped it over Aryngo's head while the latter struggled unsuccessfully to avoid it. Karueq waited a moment, and the pendant remained unchanged. He smiled, savoring the satisfaction of what he was about to do.

"And now I will exact my revenge on you for all the trouble you've caused me." Karueq pulled back his sword, relishing this moment of power.

A sharp pain shot through his arm, and he grunted. An arrow shaft protruded from his flesh. The two free assassins rushed the entrance of the tent.

The intruder engaged them swiftly with the shaft of her bow and subdued them before Karueq could turn on her. It was the woman, and the woman was Chelia.

"Let him go, Karueq!" she hissed. Karueq couldn't believe his eyes - the Elequiri and the Captain on the same routine mission.

She whipped another arrow from her quiver and pulled it into her bow in a single fluid motion, aiming straight at him. "Let him go."

"No, Captain. I'm not letting this opportunity go again."

She shot him through the stomach. His vision went white for a moment and he grunted loudly. She nocked another arrow and aimed it between his eyes, her face set with a vicious rage he had never seen her possess. "The next one goes through your skull, Karueq. Let him go."

"Captain!" Aryngo barked through gritted teeth, and Chelia's attention shifted to him. "You will not break my Mercy Law, even for me."

Horror spidered across her face at his command. Karueq was shocked that she had probably meant to kill him with the arrow poised at her shoulder.

She turned on him again, now more pleading than commanding. "Let him go."

Karueq shook his head at her. "Not again, Chelia. Say goodbye to your beloved leader."

He swung his sword back up. Again, her arrow shot through his arm, but he wouldn't be stopped now. With as much force as he could muster, he lunged forward and plunged his sword through Aryngo's chest.

Aryngo inhaled sharply at the impact, but no cry escaped his lips. His eyes found Karueq for a moment, with that look of pity he'd received far too many times. Then, they closed forever. His body sagged, and the men dropped him to the floor.

Chelia lunged forward and swiped at the men with her bow. They all turned on her. She tried to break past them to get to the body, but they held their ground. Karueq ripped the arrow from his arm and rammed it into Chelia's back, straight through her lung. She stumbled backward, gasping. One assassin lunged at her. She sprung out of the way just in time. Without looking back, she rolled out of the entrance.

Two of the assassins went after her, disappearing from the tent. Karueq stopped the third as he moved to follow.

"When you catch her, bring her back to Xanadai - alive."

The man nodded, then slipped out to join his brethren.

Now alone, Karueq's attention turned to Aryngo. He lay partially on his side, with his face forward. Karueq was honestly dumbfounded they won this one, and he contemplated all that this could mean. The war against Eleveria was over, and the Shatanala could focus their attention on winning the rest of the world. He was eager to hear what the Prince's next move would be.

He relived all the encounters he'd had when this man was under the mask; the skirmishes, the careful meetings, the fleeting sightings when he hoped to uncover him. If not for the arrows still lodged in his body, he might not have awoken from this trance. He lowered himself to the ground and took a few deep breaths to focus on his condition. These injuries were not as severe as the arrow he took a few years ago when he fled to Grogun's city. He would survive them without immediate attention.

He reached down and snapped the shafts off as close to his skin as he could. The one in his abdomen tugged horribly on his skin, and he shook his head to clear it from his attention. He pressed gently on the tender flesh around the wounds, deciding he should learn a few healing spells so he wouldn't have to rely on physicians each time.

The body still lay beside him, a bloody and broken mess, yet Karueq was caught by his expression. The face was a mess from the bruises and the blood oozing from the gash, but beyond that, there was something beckoning the commander from those closed eyes. Even in death, a bitter death at that, there was peace whispering from him.

Karueq shook his head. If the Eleverians remained stubbornly relevant after tonight, he may have to learn to quell his intrigue.

A figure slipped into the tent quietly - one of the assassins.

Karueq felt his face fall to a scowl before he addressed him. "Speak."

The Brehila simply said, "She escaped."

Karueq's hand found his forehead, and he rubbed it. Of course, he could never hope for a total victory in any of these missions. "Very well. We will return without her." With a last glance at Aryngo, he said, "Bring the body."

CHAPTER NINE

LOSING GROUND

----- ----- ----- ----- ----- ----- -----

Karueq approached the altar alone. On his shoulders, he carried the broken body of the Elequiri – Shatan's prize. He bent down at the top of the steps and slid it face up onto the altar's gilded surface. The eyes were closed, and that peaceful bliss persisted.

He heard a soft wind swirl beside him. "You've done well," came the Prince's voice. The two of them stood in silence at the sight before them. Karueq had wondered if he would ever see this day. He figured he would die gloriously in battle or quietly on some mission, and his successor would be standing here victorious with his master. Nevertheless, the body of the Elequiri lay before him, lifeless, unable to respond to his schemes and destroy his plots.

"What is our move now?" Karueq inquired.

"We rip Seaga from Eleh's grasp," Shatan said clearly, his velvety voice hardly containing his pleasure. "Expel the Eleverians from any holdings they have and sweep the world into our hands. I trust you to lead the campaign."

"I will not disappoint you, my lord."

"I know you won't." The demon disappeared with a fiery grin.

Karueq remained where he stood. Plotting could wait a few more moments while he relished his victory.

He turned around when he heard slow, reverent footsteps advancing to interrupt him. Bleren approached him and eyed his right side. The first thing Bleren always noticed was Karueq's imperfect posture from the wounds he'd left unattended. However, Bleren didn't comment on it, rather turning his focus to the body on the altar. "You succeeded." His congratulations were plain, unastounded.

"We have won against Eleveria."

"I hope you're right about that," Bleren said, hinting at something Karueq had yet to be told.

Karueq sighed. "What have they done?"

"I don't relish spoiling this moment of victory for you, and I hope it's nothing. Several of our teams have gone missing."

"I only just killed their leader yesterday. I'm not concerned with an operation he ordered while he was alive."

"I know the timing is quaint, but we haven't had this kind of loss before."

"This man grew bolder after we lost in Israel. I have no doubt that we'll have to push hard against them for a few weeks, but they will crumble without him."

Bleren's arguments were quieted. Karueq relied on his counsel, but there were several occasions when the younger man let his opinions occupy too much of his foresight. He would have to learn to keep his vision on the ultimate prize and let his subordinates worry over details if he was to carry Karueq's mantel after his death.

Another set of footsteps echoed beneath the grand dome of the temple. The two turned from the altar to find a young soldier approaching them.

"I apologize for my intrusion, my lord," she said, bowing deeply. "I have just arrived from Israel."

"Make it quick, soldier." Bleren did nothing to hide his scolding tone.

Karueq recognized the braid sweeping across her forehead, but he couldn't place her name.

"Several of our teams went missing. They defected to Eleveria."

Karueq muttered to Bleren. "You didn't tell me it was the teams from Israel disappearing,"

"I haven't heard this information yet," was Bleren's excuse.

The girl continued. "Additionally, Israel is in upheaval. Ahab's reign was condemned after the death of a vineyard keeper. The Israelites anointed a new king who then killed Ahab himself in battle and other leaders in the area."

Karueq was shocked and surprisingly delighted at this news. He allowed himself to let go of his immediate hopes for Israel. Yes, he would like for that cursed nation to remain under Shatanala control, but Shatan had dismissed it to Jezebel's charge. He would very much like to see that witch fall from her throne. However, his pleasure at this was inappropriate at the moment.

He turned to Bleren. "Send teams to hunt down every last traitor out there. Find out if we have anyone holding a grudge against them. Vengeance is a useful motivator."

The girl with the braid spoke up. "If I may be bold, Commander, I wish to lead one of these teams."

Bleren wasted no time scolding her. "You are a subordinate with no rank. You will lead - if and when - you have proven yourself able to hold the position."

"With all due respect, General, I wish to be tested with haste."

"Why is that?" Karueq asked. Usually, inferiors speaking out of turn irritated him to the point of dealing out swift consequences, but this one spoke plainly without disrespect.

"I've heard rumors that you were plotting to kill the Elequiri," she began, "and it is no small prize that you have presented on the altar of the Lord of Darkness." She gestured to the body behind them. "You have won a great victory, Commander, but I know the work is just beginning. I can do far more to realize your vision than I do in my current post."

"What sort of trial do you propose?"

"Send me as head of one of these teams. If I fail to bring down no less than twenty defectors, I will forfeit my position and my life. If I bring in at least twenty of them, I request a modest rank among your officers."

Karueq considered her for a moment. "Your attitude would be better suited to the duty of a Brehila, which you must usually be born to, or procuring royal status in one of our holdings above ground."

"I appreciate your assessment of me, Commander, but I still propose that I would serve you best carrying out your orders directly."

Karueq saw Bleren's attention turn to him from the corner of his eye. Karueq addressed him. "She's in your charge, therefore the decision is yours."

Karueq left the temple to let the two of them sort out the request and made his way to his chambers.

From the balcony of his chamber, he looked upon a quiet city. His eyes wandered over the crooked towers around him where his soldiers made their homes. He heard the occasional eruption of voices - some laughing, some angry. Such was the atmosphere that freedom brought, and Karueq felt his determination at maintaining this freedom surge, even if it was temporarily at the expense of his own pleasure.

Although, he decided, he would take part in some of the revelry that would follow in the next few days. News of the Elequiri's death would race through the ranks and incite celebrations with the energy shown in the sacking of Madaka's temple. He felt he should punctuate his dark scheming with some good wine and a festal sparring game. His sword arm flexed eagerly at the thought.

A physician worked on his wounds thoroughly while he reflected. Chelia's arrows had indeed found their mark. Although the man peering at them assured him they would have never threatened his life, the placement of the wounds would slow him down for a while.

There was a knock at his door. He blinked away his imaginings before permitting the intruder. "Come in."

The door opened, and Bleren entered. "I'm sorry to bother you, my lord."

"Must you ask for approval on your decision with that girl?" he growled, a little irritated at the interruption.

"No. You already granted me approval."

Karueq studied him for a moment before waving the physician away. He suspected his trusted general wasn't here to give good news or useful intelligence. "What do you need?"

Bleren watched the physician close the door behind him before answering. "Perhaps to know what you plan to do with a summons issued by the Captain." He held up a message clutched in his hand.

"A summons?"

"Yes. She requested you to meet her."

A smirk cracked Karueq's face. "She wants to exact her revenge on me for killing her precious leader."

"Possibly, if she is that emotional about it." Bleren handed him the message.

Karueq read it carefully, his curiosity mounting.

Commander,

Please meet me in the forest where the Elequiri gave you our Mercy Law. I will be there tomorrow morning before sunrise. Please come alone – I promise you no ill will. As proof of my word, I will remind you that I stayed my hand, and I will not dishonor his memory by betraying the Law now.

Chelia

Karueq looked up from the paper. "You want to know my decision?"

Bleren nodded.

"I'm going."

The general rolled his eyes. "If I had known for sure you were going to choose that, I would have burned that message."

"Are you not curious about it?" His eyes turned back to the paper and lingered over the words.

"Of course I'm curious. I'm always curious about what their play might be, but that doesn't mean my questions should be satisfied. Don't go."

Karueq finished reading the message a second time. "You read this before you brought it to me." He quoted her message, "*I stayed my hand, and I will not dishonor his memory by betraying the Law now*'. She had the chance to kill me, Bleren. She almost did, but the Elequiri stopped her at the cost of his life."

"What makes you think there's anything stopping her now?" Bleren pressed. "He isn't there to stop her, and we can't know at all if the Mercy Law even stands now that he's gone. If you go, she will strike you down. Mark my words."

"You didn't see her face, Bleren. She was conflicted, and I was sure I would meet my end there in that tent. She may be brazen and unpredictable, but she will never be disloyal. If ever an Eleverian defected to us, she would be the absolute last to do so."

Bleren couldn't hide his disdain for what Karueq said. "You won a victory. You won an astounding victory. Do not throw it away because a little viper piqued your curiosity."

"You're confusing her with the trickery we attribute to Jezebel."

"She might as well be Jezebel at this point. We struck them hard, and they'll lash out accordingly."

"I'm still going. There's always a chance that this blow broke her enough that she may slip, revealing weaknesses we could only ever dream of. I will return to discuss our next move with you. Now leave me."

Bleren rolled his eyes and turned away, but his frustration rooted him to the floor. Karueq watched the small muscles in his neck war with each other to turn around or walk away. Finally, the younger man sighed. "Do what you have to, my lord." With his disappointment still hanging in the air, he walked out and left his commander to whatever end came.

Karueq left Xanadai with haste. It would take nearly all night to fly to the forest, and he remembered how long it took him to reach the ravine when he went to meet Aryngo. The Rale he was riding carried him over the lake straight to the tree line. The beast's squawking would alert the Captain to his arrival, but Karueq was confident that he was regarding the request correctly and wouldn't need to be careful.

He strode through the forest to the edge of the ravine. The orange light he conjured lit his way along the stream. The ravine was empty when he reached it.

"Thank you for coming, Karueq," a voice spoke beside him. His hand found his sword by reflex as he looked up, but he didn't draw it. It took him a moment to spot her sitting on a low branch in the tree to his left, arms crossed. She didn't look his way and just stared solemnly down into the ravine.

"I suppose congratulations are in order," she said, only then turning her head toward him slowly. He let go of his sword and let his hand fall to his side. Closing his other hand, he snuffed out his orange light and let his eyes try to adjust to the darkness.

A gentle blue light emerged from where Chelia sat. It shone quietly, reaching out until it illuminated the ravine edge, letting the two of them see each other. She seemed to consider him for a moment, then she drew her legs around the branch and let herself down to the ground. The light stayed in its place.

"I don't have long, Captain," he told her, letting his pride in himself radiate intentionally. He would command control of this meeting. "Speak."

His tone apparently had enough bite to erupt her stone expression. She looked away, her eyes swimming with emotions she couldn't conceal behind her solemn facade. Karueq relished it. He had waited a long time to break this unmovable woman.

When she finally spoke, her voice was small. "I'm asking you to return the mercy we've shown you since the institution of our Law."

"Denied. Until you surrender, you will continue to fall beneath our swords. Shatan will accept no less, and neither will I."

"I'm not asking for you to reciprocate the Law. I'm here asking you to give him back to us."

The request astounded Karueq. In exchange for not killing his men, they wanted a body.

"Also denied," he replied. "His body belongs to Shatan as the prize I won for him. Furthermore, I will not let you use it to make him a martyr for your people's morale."

"None of us become martyrs when we die, and the Elequiri is no different - but keeping him won't give you anything. It won't advance your campaign against us or against Seaga."

"You're not keeping your composure, Captain," he pointed out, smiling wryly. "That would be enough reason to keep him. Beyond that, he is the most valuable prize we have ever been after, and we won't give up any part of that victory."

"You've already won your victory. Give him back."

"My men haven't yet shared the triumph," he rebutted, coolly. "His presence will be good for morale, and they need that after what you did to us at Mount Caramel."

Her shoulders drooped, and her voice cracked. "What did you do with him?"

Karueq's face spread into a wicked grin. "Enough."

"Enough? I'm not here to fight with you or engage in a verbal battle. I am simply requesting honor and dignity for one of our own." Her gaze cut through him, and he felt exposed. His instincts told him to be wary of her and to brace himself under her intense gaze, matching her ferocity. However, this time he didn't see a challenge. Her piercing eyes invited him to search her in return, to probe her soul and believe in her sincerity.

He sighed, settling his inclination to fight back. "Calm yourself, Captain. I haven't let them near his body. I left it on the altar in Shatan's temple, and they wouldn't dare enter without consent."

Chelia took a moment to let out a tense breath, and when she did speak, she measured her words, careful not to stutter behind the emotion seeping back. "I appreciate that, Karueq. Thank you."

"I still do not yield to your request," he continued.

"Please, Karueq," she implored. "He was a son, and a brother, and a friend. I am here begging *your* mercy, not your master's. If you have ever loved anyone, you will know how much it would mean to lay him to rest."

Something overtook his desires against his will. It was slow and steady, and he couldn't place its source. He firmly thrust it away before it appeared on his face. "No, Captain. We have never given you quarter and you have never done so either."

She took a step forward, reached out, and pressed her hand firmly against the wound in his side. He grabbed her wrist, but she refused to budge. They were dangerously close, close enough that he distinctly heard her breathing. The last time those eyes locked on him so near, he had some control, and there was a sharp knife between them.

"This," she reproached him, pushing lightly against the injury for emphasis. "This wasn't giving you quarter?" She wasn't threatening him but that didn't ease the vulnerability he felt. She swallowed the beginnings of weeping creeping into her throat. "You owe him your life."

He looked up and glimpsed the loss in her eyes. Gone was the powerful, unpredictable woman he contended with in battle. Her statement weighed down on him. She really had meant to break the law that night to save her leader, and he shouldn't be standing here in the forest speaking with her. It was one command from the Elequiri that stood between him and his death.

Karueq had never been confronted with his mortality so harshly before. He knew the hazards that plagued his position, knew that he was a coveted target of these people. He'd only ever hoped his death would accomplish some goal he would have at the time. Reliving the encounter in the tent, he realized destiny had chosen that moment to end his story. In that moment, the Elequiri was more powerful than death itself.

His reflection of the scene reminded him of the aftermath. He reached around her back and pressed on the spot under her shoulder blade through which he'd skewered her. She made the smallest flinch at the pressure, partially healed but still tender. "If you're wondering, you only barely missed." Her admission would normally have frustrated him for being, yet again, just shy of some victory. This time, he found himself settling into a mutual understanding with her without an agenda, and he realized the vulnerability he was feeling ceased to bother him.

The ease in the tension made him consider the consequences of her earlier statement. "If I give him back to you," he began, "will it square my debt with him?"

She peered at him, a little surprised. "We hold no account of your sins, Karueq. We never have. If it is forgiveness you seek, you have it."

"I have no need of your forgiveness. I refuse to hold debts. Would giving him back to you settle this one?"

Her brow furrowed. "Are you looking for a reason to honor my request beyond showing mercy?"

"I never need to justify my actions."

Chelia constructed her answer carefully. "Then, if we ever held his death against you – if ever we held you accountable for the sins you've committed against us – we would indeed absolve you if you returned him."

Karueq nodded. "Then, I will sincerely consider your request."

Chelia's brow creased in disappointment at the delaying answer but softened again. "Thank you, Commander, this will mean so much to us. I'm sure I will see you again soon."

She turned to leave.

He stopped her. "What will you do now that he's gone?"

She turned around at his question. "We'll continue as we always have, fighting for the freedom of Seaga."

"How will you do that without your leader?"

She shook her head. "You haven't been paying attention, Commander. Your master has poisoned your mind so you can't see us as we are. You see us how you need to so you can despise us and fight against us without questioning why. Eleveria doesn't need the Elequiri because our purpose is not about fighting with you. We free souls."

"How do you win souls without fighting?"

"We're not winning them. They are not a prize to be won. You won't understand until you open your eyes to the truth."

"Truth is a matter of perspective."

"There is only one truth." She held out her hand to him. "Come with me, and we will show it to you."

"Never," he answered. "You may have swayed my men, but you will never have me."

"I'm deeply sorry for that, Karueq. I hope one day you will change your mind." She turned away. As she walked along the ravine edge deeper into the forest, the light dimmed and disappeared.

He remained planted where he stood. Part of him grew increasingly aware of the direction the meeting went. It unnerved him that he had ended up seriously considering her request. He swore when he ascended his position that he would never entertain concessions for the enemy, that he would fight mercilessly and scheme ruthlessly to serve Eleveria their damnation. His pledge was what he lived for, and his conviction to it made him powerful and feared.

The other part of him, the larger part, refused to let go of the conclusion he and the Captain had come to. The request was reasonable, simple even. They wanted to bury one of their own. Because of the mercy the Elequiri had shown him, he couldn't deny him to be laid to rest. He truly cared not for settling his debt to the man, but framing it in this manner might make it more reasonable to Shatan.

He shook his head. No, it wouldn't. There was no way to make it seem reasonable to the demon. Karueq would decide what to do about this predicament, but he needn't make a decision now. Because part of him wanted to honor her appeal, and the other part denied permission to accept it, he decided to quell his thoughts about it.

An excursion to one of his false nations would accomplish such a task. He had chosen the place before he emerged from the forest and kicked the Rale into the sky, heading east. The flight cleared his head somewhat, although the meeting still tugged at him gently. He arrived outside the city in the late afternoon, left the Rale in the hills, and took his time walking to the palace. A guard opened the doors to him after procuring his identity and led him to the great hall.

The crowd in the hall was rather sparse for an evening meal. There were neither dancers nor music creating the atmosphere he'd witnessed the last time he was here. Several of the lamps had not been lit. Grogun sat at the head of the table, staring at the wall, mindlessly elevating food and drink to his mouth. Those seated with him talked with low voices or didn't talk at all.

Grogun's eyes wandered to the new arrival with disinterest before he jumped up at once, recognizing his superior.

"My lord!" he cried emphatically. "So good to see you!" He clapped Karueq on the shoulder. "I apologize for the presentation. I did not expect such an honor this evening."

Karueq dismissed his apologies. "No need. I understand I've come unannounced."

"Please take my seat," the king groveled. "I will send for fresh amenities."

"What you have is fine. Sit."

Grogun furrowed his brow, but relented and returned to the table, Karueq following. Grogun ejected the man from the chair near the head of the table and sat down. Karueq took the head seat.

The king snapped his fingers at a servant near the wall and pointed to the plate in front of Karueq. The servant took his time meandering from his station to the table.

"How are things in the wide world, my lord," Grogun began, clearly trying to incite conversation. It seemed to take the servant even longer to clear the plate and set a fresh one. "I hear we've won Israel for good and that we're slowly winning the outlying lands."

"Your information is dated," Karueq answered. "We are struggling to keep the people in control."

"Isn't that high priestess in charge of the whole operation?"

"We do have a false queen there, yes."

"You'll hold it, laddy," the fat man snorted.

The servant began picking through the food and filling Karueq's plate, and he noticed the other men at the table were whispering amongst themselves and watching him. "How are matters here?"

The king's face turned red as he choked on a piece of dry bread. "Matters are good here," he sputtered. "Tell me about your last adventure."

Karueq turned his eye on the rest of the table, spooking the guests into private, averted conversations. His eyes turned to the food set before him. The dismal selection seemed to have been drying out for days.

He returned his attention back to the fat man beside him. He took a critical evaluation of this pawn, noting his dishevelment and the gray look in his eyes. "You're losing them," he appraised.

Grogun's eyes went wild. "Losing them, my lord?"

"The people. You're losing your hold over them."

"Not at all," insisted the worm.

Karueq slammed his fist on the table, making everyone jump. "Damn it, Grogun, you've lost your grip on these people!" His eyes flashed in anger. "What happened?"

Grogun glanced quickly at the others seated with them, doing little to keep his composure. "I'm sorry, my lord," he whimpered. "Truly, I'm sorry. There was nothing we could do, I swear."

"What happened?" he demanded.

Grogun's eyes fell to his hands cradled in his lap. "The Eleverians… they turned the people against our distractions. They rejected their riches and the decadence and put on sackcloth. They've been… turning their finery into charity. My advisors tell me the people are repenting their ways."

Karueq reached up to his temples and rubbed them. "How did they do it?"

"We're not exactly sure. They didn't leave anything behind, but they spoke with the people several times."

"You didn't alert me."

"We didn't know it was happening," he insisted. "We thought they left without doing anything."

"Clearly they did." Karueq kicked his chair backward and left the table. He stalked out of the palace and ran into the hills.

He remounted the Rale and redirected it toward Israel. The flight did nothing to clear his head and only seemed to further confuse his thinking. He left the beast outside the city and made his way toward the palace.

As he neared, he heard rumblings and angry shouts. A mob had closed in around the palace, preventing him from accessing the main door. Frustrated, he slipped through a side door and hastened up to Jezebel's chamber.

He burst through the door without knocking and braced for a tirade from the witch. Instead, his attention was stolen by the clarity of the air in the room. The haze and the smell of wine were gone. The room was tidy. The only sounds he heard were the muffled shouts of the mob below the window.

Something moved to his left. Jezebel was sitting down at the mirror, applying a red stain to her lips. She was dressed in all her finery with a large, ornate headdress balanced atop her head.

"Thank you for coming, Karueq," she said plainly, puckering her lips in her reflection to inspect her work.

"What's going on, Jezebel?"

"I am being executed by the man who killed my husband." Her speaking was eerily simple. "The people no longer believe in my rule."

She rose from her seat and walked over to him, holding a decorative neck plate. "They destroyed the temples and are building shrines to Eleh. Now, they are coming for me. Help me with this, will you?" She handed him the plate and turned around.

"What is all this charade for?"

She spoke without turning around, continuing to perfect her appearance from the front. "I can't hold this nation down any longer, so I will be sure I am remembered for ages to come. My reign over Israel is done, but my rule over Seaga has just begun."

Karueq reached over her shoulder and fastened the plate around her neck. His hand hovered over her for just a moment while he contemplated throttling her where she stood. Instead, he retreated his grasp and took a seat by the window. "I'll stay to watch your spectacle."

"Please do. You'll want to remember every detail when you realize the world will remember me and forget about you."

She left the room, her bangles jingling elegantly on her way out. Karueq peered out of the window and waited. It wasn't long before the priestess emerged on the balcony below and addressed her livid subjects. A pack of dogs barked viciously at the idol before them, and the horses screamed in excitement and pulled on their reigns.

A man riding a strong stallion pushed his way to the edge of the balcony.

Jezebel drew herself up and called down to him, quieting the thunderous shouts. "Is it peace, Zimri, murderer of your master?"

Karueq shook his head at the words she hurled at the man before her. This man was not Zimri. Zimri had only reigned for a week and was killed by one of Ahab's kin. Karueq doubted this newly anointed king would wither so quickly.

"Who is with me?" the man cried, ignoring the words of the queen. "Who?" The mob erupted again. Jezebel remained unperturbed.

"Throw her down!" he shouted. "Throw her down!"

Two men on the balcony rushed forward and seized her. She acted out a struggle before being tossed her over the rail. Immediately, the horde descended on her. The horses trampled her, and the vibrant colors of her attire disappeared in the cloud of dust they kicked up. The dogs lunged at their prey, baying viciously.

Karueq withdrew from the window. He didn't need to see the rest. Eleh had regained this people for now, and there was nothing he could do to stop it.

He made his way to the side door and left without notice. The whole city was gathered at the palace, so he returned to the hills without hindrance.

Upon reaching the Rale, he saw a slim figure seated on a rock nearby. It was Jezebel, clad in plain attire suited for travel. "Will you escort me to Xanadai?"

"Gladly, your highness," he replied with no lack of derision.

"Please continue to treat me with such distaste, Karueq. It will make watching your downfall that much sweeter." She mounted the snarling beast, leaving room in the front for him to slide in.

Karueq sealed his lips over his next retort. It wouldn't make the journey to Xanadai easier if the snake behind him concentrated her venom on him.

Their flight passed without hindrance and without any more words exchanged. Karueq was thankful for that. He needed the time to puzzle out what he had seen and heard while above ground. Part of him still conceded to Chelia's simple plea, but in light of what happened with both Grogun and Jezebel, he couldn't afford to show any good will to the Eleverians, not with teams of his men defecting and whole nations repenting their allegiance. Should events such as these dwindle, Karueq would consider handing Aryngo's body over to them as a consolation prize. Now was not the time.

They landed in the entrance to the city. Jezebel dismounted, regally accepting the offered hand of the guard at her side.

"Is there anything you wish for me to convey to the Prince, Commander?" Jezebel asked him.

Karueq looked at her questioningly. "You're going to speak with Shatan?"

"Yes, my dear. I must give him a report of my dealings in Israel before I return to my temple."

He concealed a cold grin, opting for a considerate nod instead. "Indeed, tell him I have a report of my own to give."

"Very well." The former queen and returning priestess turned on her heel and walked down the tunnel, her posture asserting her authority.

Karueq shook his head. He needed a good spar to cool his head and relieve the tension in his muscles. He wasn't about to discuss the happenings of Seaga in front of Jezebel, and he would hear Shatan's reaction to Jezebel's spectacle later. He held a sliver of hope that she would be reprimanded for her laziness and the loss of their most coveted kingdom.

The sweat clung to his skin when the messenger came to interrupt his sparring match. The four contenders settled down at the side of the pit, exhausted from the fight. With Karueq's skill he needed several men to keep his staff occupied, unless he was sparring with an elite.

He leaned on the wall of the pit and seated his elbows on the ground near the messenger's feet, looking up. "What is it?"

"The Prince has called for an assembly in the Great Temple," the man reported. "He has requested that you arrive early for instruction."

Karueq ran his fingers through his damp hair. So, the Prince had seen fit to reward the witch for her supposed achievements in Israel.

"Very well," he sighed.

With little time to waste, he bathed and dressed for an assembly in the Prince's presence, trading his travel and battle gear for less worn armor. When he arrived at the Temple, the Prince was already standing in front of the altar at the top of the stairs. Karueq noticed that the Elequiri's body still rested there. Seeing it now, the tugging at Karueq's mind rekindled.

"I understand you met with the Captain," the demon stated rather blankly. "Any news?"

"None worth our time, only that they want the body."

Shatan said nothing. He turned his eyes over his shoulder and looked at the body, his face unreadable. Karueq's own gaze wandered back to the body. It was uncorrupted in Shatan's presence, and his face still held that peaceful expression, not exactly happy but void of the end he'd suffered.

The demon turned back to him. "Why did you go to Israel afterward?"

"I have been receiving reports of our teams defecting. They are no longer taking individuals, they are converting groups of us now. I surveyed our holdings and ended up in Israel based on intelligence, and to possibly hear good news from the priestess."

Shatan considered his words before continuing. "I'm concerned about these reports. I am told by Bleren you consider this increased activity to be circumstantial, but we can't afford to let our advantage wane. We must be bolder."

"Agreed, my lord."

A low rumbling of voices raised in the dwellings on the shore of the lake. Karueq's attention stole to them. The people were beginning to pour out, making way to the Great Temple for the assembly.

Karueq turned back to his Prince. "I suppose those matters can wait until Jezebel's reward has been issued."

"Reward?" Shatan's fiery stare pierced him. "Why would I reward a queen for her eviction?"

Karueq's stomach dropped. Shatan's fury seared him, unnerving him.

The demon spoke again. "The reign of the priestess is over."

The people began to filter in. The whole of Xanadai was gathering quickly.

"What do you require of me?"

"Strip her of her riches," said the devil.

Karueq nodded and assumed a position at the bottom of the staircase. His gaze wandered through the gossiping crowd as they ordered themselves so each could see their powerful lord standing at the altar. Some of them pointed at Aryngo's body, a spectacle that had been denied them since it arrived a few days prior.

When it appeared all had arrived, a hush began to creep over them, starting at the rear of the hoard. The priestess had made her appearance, walking forward as if still a queen.

Every eye was on her, every gaze piercing the center of the assembly. Her garb was lavish, her skin oiled, her hair heavily perfumed. Just like in Israel, she was making sure this would be how the people remembered her - the seductive, powerful temptress who spent her spare time playing as Shatan's priestess.

She stopped and stood there on the center stone where the sacrifices were slaughtered. There was no fear in her eyes. No agitation of any sort.

"My lord and master," she spoke commandingly. "Call off this spectacle. There is no need for it."

"Silence!" the demon roared. "You think I will change my mind? While you were abroad you committed treason by your negligence and your stupidity."

"What treason?" she demanded.

"You cost us Israel!!"

The temple hushed. All of the blame for the loss fell on Jezebel, this one woman.

"I have cost you nothing," she stated boldly. "Israel and Judah are still divided, and they will not remain with the enemy long."

"Your task was to devote the nation to me, not to drunken yourself on their wine and their king." Jezebel shot a damning glare at Karueq, knowing he had reported on her leisure. "You were to purge them of their prophets. Elijah escaped along with a hundred others. Obadiah was right under your nose, and you failed to see him. Beyond these gross infractions, you defied the orders and counsel of your Commander."

"He is not my Commander," she hissed, icily.

"This is war!" Shatan snapped. "War on the nations of Eleh. You are a soldier sent to be a spy. You were to obey. Instead, you threw your station aside! Your Commander told you your hasty tactics would provoke the Eleverians. We had a chance for a victory! You threw it away because you were more concerned for your position."

Her eye twitched - fear.

Shatan's volume settled back down. "Your impatience after the challenge on Mount Caramel cost us even more. You chased after Elijah when he had gained the support of the people. In doing so, you turned the people against you and against me."

"They loved me!" she insisted.

"They dethroned you and threw you to the dogs!" Shatan shouted. "Your arrogance has cost you everything." He gestured to Karueq at the bottom of the staircase.

Karueq nodded and walked over to stand before the priestess. Her eyes were filled with terror despite her authoritative expression.

"You can't be serious," she beseeched him, quietly.

Karueq raised his voice so that all could hear him. "Jezebel, high priestess of Shatan, you are hereby stripped of your title and your possessions."

He grabbed her arm and gripped the bangles on her wrist. She pulled away. "Don't touch me!"

Karueq grappled her other arm to immobilize her and pulled the golden rings off, letting them fall to the floor unceremoniously. A desperate yelp escaped her. Karueq took hold of the lavish robes she wore and yanked them away from her body.

"You can't do this to me!" she shrieked.

Karueq continued with her humiliation, taking the knife from his boot. "You are no longer to serve as priestess to Shatan." He grasped her long, ebony hair. She squealed and struggled to pull away. The perfume filled his lungs, a pleasant odor, but a farce nonetheless. He lifted the knife to her and cut off all her locks.

"No! No!" she yelped.

The hair fell to his feet. She managed to break free for a moment, but he grabbed what hair she had left and pulled her back. He severed the last strands away from the base of her skull. She lifted her roughly shaved head.

"Stop this! Stop this right now!"

Karueq stepped back. She shuffled away from him and looked searchingly up at Shatan. Karueq looked at the crowd from his peripheral vision. The people were whispering to each other. Some pointing at her, some pointing at the riches that lay on the floor. She looked small without her luxuries, like a young girl just made an orphan. There was fear in her eyes. She looked to the people, silently pleading with them to help her.

It was Shatan's turn. "None of you are to give her aid under the penalty of the rack. Go."

The assembly drifted apart amid talk of the spectacle. Karueq gazed upon the wretch as she looked around at the dissipating crowd and left the circle to plead with them. The despair in her eyes intensified. She had nowhere to go. All of Xanadai was abandoning her. None of her many former lovers offered her a place to stay. She would wander the city like a beggar, hungry and poor, abused and exploited by those who would offer her help against the Prince's command. Perhaps she would become just another soldier once she had lost the will to beg.

Having been completely dismissed by the people, she returned to the center stone and attempted to scrape up the gold pieces scattered there. Karueq stepped to her head and kicked her away. She looked up at him in disgust, tears streaming down her face. Karueq nodded his head toward the temple entrance. She looked at him one more time with damnation, then she crawled away among the departing whispers.

The last of the murmuring died. The temple was deserted once more. Shatan descended the stairs and stood beside his servant. He spoke without turning. "We must be bold to stamp out Eleh's influence in Seaga."

"What would you have me do?"

"You came to me with a plan devised by the traitor Zokul."

The statement made Karueq's stomach sink, and dread made his throat dry. "You're asking me to deceive them into thinking I'm defecting."

"Yes."

A great apprehension took hold of Karueq's chest.

"You must not fail me," the demon warned. "You can't be allowed to turn. If she does not accept you, she must die. If she won't die, you must take your own life."

Karueq was puzzled to realize that he lamented this order, not the final part about him, but the order to kill the Captain. He didn't know if he could easily bring himself to kill her. She was bold, fought with fairness, and respected her leader's mercy. None of these concessions made her or her people weak.

He forced these thoughts away. Shatan said it perfectly while he castigated Jezebel - this is war. He bowed to his master. "You have my word, my lord."

CHAPTER TEN

A DESPERATE PLEA

Bleren slammed his fist into the wall of the training pit. "Tell me you're joking!" Karueq didn't return his glare, instead wiping his sweaty arms down with the cloth in his hand. The younger man barked again, "You can't be serious, Karueq!"

The news that Karueq was going to play a dangerous game with the Eleverians was not at all within Bleren's idea of a good plan. "This is the command of the Prince," Karueq explained very plainly as he wiped the sweat from his forehead. His voice didn't waver or hold even a shred of intensity. "I take orders from no one but him, and this is an order."

"The Captain spared your life because of some foolish loyalty she had toward the Elequiri. This time, you won't be so lucky."

"Whether or not they decide to kill me, this is the task I've been given."

"Shatan is scared!" Bleren hissed, and Karueq looked up at him, a little astonished. He had indeed taught this young man to speak brazenly in private. Harsh observations were often helpful when discussing harsh realities, but Bleren's treasonous words could be heard by anyone in the vicinity of the unoccupied pits.

Bleren continued, undeterred by his commander's reaction. "We have no reason to believe they won't turn you. We have every reason to believe that they'll kill you. Everything you have worked for will be lost."

Karueq interrupted him, firmly grasping the staff in his hand and giving it a testing twirl. "Which is why I called you here. We knew one day that my title and position would pass to you. That day may come sooner than we anticipated, but it cannot be undone. In the unlikely event that I fall to them, you are to succeed me and finish the work I started. You will win us the war if I can't break them from within."

He whipped his staff out at the man to incite a new duel, hearing the crack as the poles collided.

Bleren brushed the blow aside, his focus holding firm on the conversation. "And what of your reward? Should you fall, every merit you have earned will be given to someone else. Shatan will not forgive you in death. You have to win this impossible task or you will be detained on the rack in Hell for eternity."

Karueq understood Bleren's concerns. Shatan's word was final, and any command issued by him was obligatory, so Karueq had resigned himself to planning the task at hand instead of worrying over the consequences. Shatan was not forgiving. It was good for the people that Karueq led them directly. Any of the infractions they committed earned them imprisonment or torture, but Shatan would exact more. Since there was no buffer between him and his master, the punishment for failure would be severe indeed. That is why Karueq paid mind only to what he needed to do.

Bleren interrupted his brief thought. "Karueq, don't do this." In his eyes was the most desperate plea, reducing him to the likeness of the child he was before Karueq had selected him for greatness. He saw the deep respect this man had for him – and the loyalty.

"I can't defy an order from the Prince any more than you can defy mine."

"I'm not asking you to defy him directly. Change his focus. He'll listen to you."

"I've had more than enough of trying to change his mind over the way he wages his war. I will not do so again." In a way, Karueq was only saying this to convince Bleren that this was his choice and that he wasn't going to fight it. Unfortunately, he truly felt this way now about the demon.

Bleren sized him up. "What did the Captain do to you in the forest?"

Karueq scoffed. "You think she put her own spell on me?"

"That's the only thing that has happened since you brought the Elequiri's body down here."

"That isn't true. We've lost Israel, our men are defecting in droves, and our nations are failing. We're losing, Bleren; we are losing the war. If we're going to have a hope of halting their encroachment, I have to do this."

"No. You don't have to. You must convince Shatan that the way we have been fighting by means of deception and cunning is wrong. We must go back to the methods you used in the beginning. Be brutal. Be bold."

Karueq admired Bleren's fervor. He couldn't deny that he agreed with his assessment, but Shatan would rule the universe one day, and he demanded Karueq's compliance to the way things ought to be done.

He let his eyes fall on the staff in his hand, not being able to look this man in the eye. "Bleren, it is my command that you take my position while I carry out my mission. Your position will become permanent should I fail, and you will honor my appointment of you by defending Shatan's objective mercilessly."

With that, Karueq tossed the staff away and hopped up to the ground above, leaving Bleren alone with his protest in the pit. He was meeting with the demon soon, and he sneered at the irony that he preferred the company of that terrible beast to his closest friend right now.

The demon waited for him at the altar. The commander felt a slight disgust well up in his chest that the Prince should loom over the body so. Out of this sensation, or maybe because he was impatient, he cleared his throat to alert him to his presence.

"I know you're here," the demon uttered in warning as he turned around.

"You wanted to discuss the strategy behind my defection."

"Yes. I have already sent a summons to the Captain."

Karueq felt his self-control almost give way, but he gripped it tightly and pulled it back before it had the chance to escape him. "I would have liked to know what I'm supposed to have said to her to get her to come."

"Don't worry, commander, I made a copy." He threw a bit of paper down at Karueq's feet. Karueq only hesitated a moment at the contemptuous gesture before picking it up.

Captain,

Meet me on the island marked on this map before the sun

sets tomorrow.

K

Karueq's eyelids dropped, and he exhaled his frustration. "You're telling them to meet on an island, not the forest."

"That way we can remedy any losses we suffer before the festering spreads. I will fill the trees on the island with soldiers who will have orders to kill both you and the Captain should your negotiation go sour."

"You think so little of me."

"You've gone behind my back enough, commander. I will not let you be ensnared by them without having the ability to safeguard everything we've built."

"I have always remained loyal to you. How could I have earned such contempt?"

"Why did you go meet the Captain without informing me?"

"She put a time limit on the meeting, and I didn't have time to bicker with you over details."

"Your head has grown hot indeed to think you could make such a decision without me."

"Indeed. It has grown hot with your neglect of *your war.*"

Those eyes pierced him so that he could almost feel them searing his mind. "You repay me poorly, Karueq. All the honors and rewards offered to you, you have ungraciously rejected. Any latitude I grant you to contribute to the schemes I set, you have taken for granted. I will not have your inflated pride destroy what I've been building for longer than history remembers. You will obey your orders." His tone was overflowing with warning, bidding him to comply. Karueq stayed silent. His commanding influence did not extend to this creature, and he wasn't about to try to take control now nor become ensnared by the provocative challenge laced into the speech.

Satisfied that his pawn had been gagged, Shatan continued. "Chelia will come to the reef and bring the Eleka Guard with her as protection because the island is so near to my domain." Karueq had already calculated these predictions. "When you meet them, they will require you to renounce my name and swear your allegiance to Eleh. You will do so, but you will resist whatever He tries to do to sway your heart, and you will hold fast to the faith you have in my power. My Mark on your flesh will protect you. You will do this for the duration of your mission until you return to me with their secrets and the key to their downfall. Do you understand?"

"I do, my lord." His words felt dry and heavy. At the mention of the Mark, the image of Zokul standing before him with a disfigured arm flashed through his mind.

Shatan must have seen this play out on his face. "Why do you doubt me?"

"It isn't doubt in you. The Mark was removed from Zokul. What do you propose if they try to do so with me?"

"You'll comply. Your deception must be complete."

Karueq's mind couldn't help itself, and his glance wandered to the body that lay still as ever on the altar. Shatan's eyes followed him, moving over the body and then returning to the commander. "Speak."

Karueq cleared his throat before he spoke. "If total deception is our aim, then I have a proposition. The Captain's request was that we return the body. Both to make my defection believable and to account for this summons supposedly coming from me, I suggest we use her appeal as justification for this ruse."

Shatan looked him over carefully, the graveness in his expression deepening. Karueq fought the urge to fidget under such scrutiny and held his ground. He was making a fair point, one that even strengthened Shatan's original plan. Karueq wondered if Shatan would truly give up this prize for the opportunity of something far greater.

"Very well," the demon responded. "You may take the body with you and present it to her as a peace offering."

"Understood, my lord."

"Your task until tomorrow evening is to set all your affairs in order and to prepare your mind for your mission ahead. Go."

Karueq bowed deeply to his master, then turned and left. The weight of the mission ahead weighed on him. This was far more dangerous than any plan he had executed in the past. Neither of them spoke it during the meeting, but both he and the Prince knew they were going into this encounter blind. They had no way of knowing the outcome because they didn't know how the Eleverians turned their prey, if his death was again on the table, or if they would even accept him into their company.

He halted on the shore of the molten lake on his way to his chambers. The glow that reached far into the void beyond the temple had been a companion to him for many decades. The heat that seared his flesh, but didn't consume him, always surrounded him in this place. Standing here now, as if for the last time, he noticed he preferred to be here in the cavern as opposed to walking through the tunnels and halls of the underground network. It was the glow that he loved, a contrast from the shadowy lights flickering in their attempt to light his path. It was, perhaps, the darkness that plagued most of Xanadai that drove him to rise to the pinnacle of power so that he may walk where he wished, always coming back to the reliable light of the lake.

This reflection brought his mind to the moonlight on many cool nights he'd spent in Seaga. He closed his eyes and pictured the white light as it danced off the ripples of the lake near the forest. He pictured the smaller stars scattered in the sky that echoed the clear, cool brilliance of the moon. The vision brought stillness to his head and his heart.

His affairs were already in order since he'd left instructions with Bleren. So, he elected to sleep and charge his mind and body for the long and grueling mission he was about to undertake. However, sleep did not come easily to him, and after a few hours attempting to quiet his mind, he gave in and left the bed.

His feet carried him to the balcony where he swung his legs over the rail and sat there like a child, staring out into the cavern. Although he imagined he appeared deep in thought, his mind was disinterested in any coherent thinking. He simply peered around. Over the hours of the night, he would catch a wisp of a thought only for it to be shooed away by his indifference. The night was punctuated occasionally by a noise, perhaps a laugh or the shifting of the rocks about the city.

In the early morning, he finally caught a bit of self-awareness. All night long, he hadn't a thought, including thoughts of death. He realized death lurking in the schemes of today didn't concern him or make him ponder what his life amounted to. That didn't mean he was satisfied with his life. He hadn't yet completed his mission to bring the nation of Eleveria to its knees. Perhaps his indifference was simply years of being ground down by the constant battle with an enemy that matched him at every turn. He had grown accustomed to being defeated and then rising back up for the next punch. It didn't matter that he faced this threat again, however grave this one was.

By mid-morning, he had left the balcony and found himself wandering through the tunnels, not reminiscing but simply wandering. Sleep would not take him and there was nothing for him to do but wait. He doubted Shatan had given such a luxury to the soldiers he had stationed on the island. He guessed they were probably already there hidden among the trees, buried in the underbrush, or concealed in the water ready to spring up and attack the party that arrived. He chuckled darkly at the thought. Per Shatan's plan, they would be waiting to attack the Eleverians, yes, but he guessed they were also being given the order to cut him down if the trick did not play out. This was not simply a mission. This was a trial for his execution.

His musings stole away to the deep corners of his mind when he encountered Bleren in the tunnel he turned down. It was about noon, nearing the time for him to leave for the island with Aryngo's body in tow.

Bleren's stride halted upon seeing him. He didn't turn around or attempt to leave; he simply stopped where he was.

Karueq waited for him to say something. After a long pause unbroken by either of them, he realized Bleren was waiting for the same. His affection for the general beckoned him to oblige but nothing came, and he couldn't find anything to say.

Upon receiving nothing, not even acknowledgement, Bleren shook his head and continued walking. Karueq's chest tightened, telling him to say anything, but his feet remained still. When the last of Bleren's footsteps left the tunnel, Karueq's legs regained their purpose and carried him back to Sheol.

He arrived at the Great Temple, finding that the body had been removed from the altar, wrapped, and laid at the bottom of the staircase.

Shatan waited beside the body. "Are you ready?"

"Yes, my lord."

--^--

Everything was set. Karueq stood on the beach of the island
letting himself get lost in the scarlet horizon that the setting sun
painted. He was surrounded by an unseen legion of Shatanala soldiers,
who, this time, were not under his command. His stomach knotted against
this fact. Never had he felt so small when initiating a mission. He had
always been in control, always commanding his soldiers and never fearing
they would turn on him.

To counter his lack of authority, Karueq again focused on the
encounter due any moment now. He wouldn't simply bow to the
impossibility of this mission. He set his mind to winning a victory this
time. This time, he was solely responsible for conducting everything that
occurred, not relying on people with other ambitions and who easily
distracted themselves. This thought, the most coherent thought he'd had in
the last day, settled his mind on the mission.

Then, a dark streak appeared from around the north side of the
island followed by another. Two great beasts glided through the air down
the length of the beach, dipping low as they neared him. As they advanced
on him, he could make out long necks, heads like lizards, and brilliant
scales covering their bodies – dragons. Instead of crashing to the earth,
burdened by their monstrous size, they flared their wings back elegantly
and landed with ease several yards away.

Behind their folding wings, two figures slipped from their backs
and approached him. Karueq turned his whole body in their
direction. One of them was indeed Chelia, but he questioned why only one
man accompanied her and why he wasn't one of the Eleka Guard.

"Commander," Chelia acknowledged when she stopped in front of
him. Karueq glanced at the man with her and noticed that his eyes were
red and a little puffy. It was Alamar, a man seen frequently on aid
missions.

"This is Alamar," she continued indicating the downcast
man. "Aryngo's brother."

At the revelation of this kinship, Karueq stepped aside to reveal
the body lying behind him. "You understood why I called you here."

"We had our hope," she confirmed. Alamar's eyes glistened anew, threatening to burst the floodgates at the sight. Karueq had always seen him poised and relaxed, the lightheartedness playing on his face. This was a wholly different sight.

Karueq picked up the body with care and placed it in Alamar's arms. Then he unfolded the cloth away from Aryngo's face so they could see it was really him. The sight of his brother's closed eyes and the cleaned, dried-up gash across his cheek tugged at Alamar a little more. "Thank you, Karueq," he said, almost weeping. Alamar turned away and left him alone with Chelia while he secured Aryngo to the dragon.

"This means so much to him, Karueq, more than you may ever know. We will never be able to thank you enough." Her expression was sincere. It seemed that since the passing of her commander, Chelia had let herself be a little more readable.

Karueq cleared the silence clogging his throat and then began to play with her. "There is, I think, one way you can."

Her expression fell a little more serious. "What might that be?"

Karueq let his eyes wander over the dragons, faking an internal fight to what he was about to say. "Take me with you."

Her expression didn't change; she simply studied him. He began to fidget a little, ever so slightly, but she didn't respond. He spoke again, "Am I not welcome to come with you anymore?"

"Of course you are," she said. "You always are, but I don't believe that's what you want."

"I want to be rid of this life, Captain. For too many reasons to count, my life here is over. Not even the death of the Elequiri pleased him. He will never be satisfied until he consumes the world in fire and ash. He knows, too, that he is losing. We lost Israel, our soldiers are fleeing to you in great numbers, and he's afraid. There is little he can do to hide that now."

"You want me to believe that you're seeking asylum because you fear this is the end of the battle for Shatan?"

"I can help you," he insisted. "He's made you his next trophy. The offer he made to you for your loyalty has expired, and he wants your blood."

"Good. I was growing bored with his groveling."

"Please let me come with you."

She sighed and turned her eyes out to the sea, deep in thought. When she looked at him again, he couldn't read her, but that piercing gaze she gave him made him feel that same vulnerability he experienced in the forest. "I want to believe you, Karueq. I want nothing more than for you to know the truth and to find your freedom, but I can't accept your request when it is being played as part of a trick."

"I am not trying to trick you."

"Then renounce him now," she said abruptly.

"I do," he obliged. "I renounce Shatan, the Lord of Darkness."

"You really do want to play me for a fool."

"I renounce him," he insisted.

"Not with this trick, you don't."

He fell to his knees and raised his palms up in front of him, pleading. "I renounce him, Chelia. Please." He felt his gut jolt inside of him as he realized this whole charade was too easy for him to act out.

"If you are so keen on it, then reject his symbols. Anything that adorns your body in service of him, get rid of it."

"The Mark is permanently sealed into my flesh. I can't remove it."

"Your pendant, Commander," she tossed her chin at the winged beast around his neck.

He grasped it, lifted it off his head, and tossed it to her. When she caught it, a white light emitted brightly from it.

Chelia suddenly lifted her hand and thrust it out toward him. A burst of energy like a wave erupted from it and grazed over him. It made a wall like a shield around them. Then, it disappeared. Karueq took a second to recover from flinching. He wasn't injured.

Then her voice came, slightly muffled by whatever energy she had fixed to the air around them. "You're highly perceptive indeed to have trapped us like this," she said quickly.

"There is no trap, Captain," he argued, hearing his own voice muffled in his ears. She must have learned this trick from Aryngo.

"Your men surround this island ready to strike should this confrontation not go your way. Congratulations, Commander," she told him looking at the shining metal in her hand. "A great trick, indeed."

Karueq staggered to his feet and looked aghast at the pendant. Shatan had enchanted it before he killed the Elequiri. It was supposed to be a sign of something he refused to reveal. The sign revealed this woman, but there was no way to alert the demon from here.

"What are you?" he demanded.

She threw the pendant at his feet, the light fading promptly as it left her hand. "What do you think, Karueq?" she spat, disdainfully.

From the corner of his eye, he saw the underbrush moving and the water beginning to churn. He panicked. The Shatanala were on the move to follow orders.

He grabbed her arm and spoke quickly. "They're coming. We need to leave - take me with you."

"It's too late for that, Karueq."

"You are his greatest prize next to the Elequiri. Let me help you."

"You still think Aryngo was the Elequiri?"

The whole picture of the scene crashed on Karueq - the power cloud muffling their speech, her posture, the power she unleashed on Shatan in the prisons, her impossible loyalty to the Elequiri's plans. It was her!

The trees began to empty, and the heads began to appear in the water. The dragons fanned their wings, preparing to leave before the horde descended upon them.

Karueq's heart raced, and he shouted rashly through the muffle. "Captain, I need to come with you. They have orders to kill me."

Before he could react, she wound up with incredible momentum and swiftly punched him in the head. The blow brought him to the ground. He shook his head, but she had successfully disoriented him. He felt her spring onto him and place her hands on both sides of his head.

"Captain…" he managed to mumble.

She was mumbling something. but he couldn't make everything out. "…look on his repentance...safeguard him…"

He felt his awareness returning, heard the thundering of the Shatanala horde only yards away. Before any of his other senses returned, he felt the sharp kick of her boot and he blacked out.

--^--

Karueq opened his eyes, and the sound of his breath hushed any dreams he might have had while he slept. Silence and darkness surrounded him. His skin did not tingle in the heat. He felt at peace. Darkness, clarity, and cold seemed suitable companions for the moment.

He peeled back the hides that covered him and rose from the bed. His men had brought him to his chamber. He walked to the balcony, opening the heavy drape to view the cavern.

The lake was silent, nothing boiling beneath the surface. The glow was dimmed, and the shadowy darkness deepened. The fumes with their toxic strangle did not choke him. The vast cavern was captured in a sort of nervous tranquility. Trembling lights flickered from the dwellings carved into the rock. The faintest of chanting trickled from the windows. They were holding a sort of vigil, imploring their favorite demons and the powers of the earth to help their commander.

He rubbed the ache in his neck, remembering being knocked out. His memory was hazy; that woman knew how to deliver her judgment. He tried to filter out what happened before he was knocked out, but there was so much he wasn't remembering.

Something in the cavern lured his attention. He scanned what lay before him but didn't see anything. He wondered if it might be the demon beckoning him to the temple. Deciding that it might sort out his memory to talk to him, he returned to his chamber and dressed. Without having a clear reason why, he belted his sword at his waist and chose a few smaller weapons to bring with him. He decided that his reason would be the authoritative power he still needed to convey to his subordinates, should they look out the window while he walked to the temple.

No one met him along the shore of the lake or the bridge to the golden dome. His chest squeezed ever so slightly when he reached the threshold. His breathing hitched and the sensation in his chest gripped him tighter as he walked toward the altar. He stopped halfway, unable to go any farther. Shatan, who was standing at the bottom of the stairs, began to walk toward him. The grip increased as he drew near.

"No, my lord!" Karueq cried, throwing his hand out to halt him. He could hardly believe what he said, but at least it stopped the demon from coming any nearer. He pulled at the air, trying to eradicate the tightness and wondering what was happening to him.

"Forgive me," he apologized in a strained voice.

The demon remained silent. Karueq took one step backward, and his chest released him just enough to endure the pressure.

With the silence, Karueq figured he should start the conversation. "I'm here to give my report of what happened on the island."

"I wish you would," the devil snarled. "That wretched woman did something to you. We can't figure out what it is."

Karueq's brow furrowed. "What do you mean?"

"I've already received several reports of the fiasco on that island. Did she turn you? Don't lie to me."

Karueq was thoroughly confused by the question. No, no, he wasn't defecting. "I assure you my loyalty remains with you."

"General Bleren said she cast a spell, a white light that created a dome around the two of you. Then he heard no more of what you said though he saw the two of you speaking."

Karueq's memory jarred. He reached around his neck, feeling for the familiar chain, but couldn't find it. "The pendant," he stammered. "You enchanted it as a sign for something. It glowed for her."

Fear and disbelief assaulted the demon's features.

Karueq's mind grasped the other important fact racing along the boundary of his consciousness. "She's the Elequiri." His focus on the present returned. "Shatan, we were wrong about the Elequiri. We now know who he is...she."

"You're sure that it emitted a white light when she touched it?" the demon implored.

"Yes. I'm sure of it. She's the Elequiri."

"That enchantment wasn't directed at the Elequiri, you worm." Shatan's image flickered briefly, the beast beneath beginning to rebel. "It was a detection for the Crucible."

"The Crucible?" There was no shred of a memory that Karueq could count on for this. "Whatever that is, she's the Elequiri. I have no doubt."

"What did she do to you?" growled the devil, brushing aside his comment.

"She knocked me out," he answered, still itching to explore this revelation.

"I know that. What more?"

Karueq's mind combed the incident on the beach. All he could remember was the blow to his temple, and Chelia's mumbled words over him. "I think she prayed over me," he said finally.

"What did she say?"

"I couldn't make it out. Something about repentance."

"Did you repent?"

"I did. As planned."

"In your heart? Did you repent in your heart?"

The strange sensation wrapped around his chest again, but instead of pain and pressure, it felt more like an embrace.

A hand struck him hard in the face. The demon bellowed. "Did you repent in your heart?"

"I don't think so."

"There are no conditional answers to this, you dim-witted puppet. Did you or didn't you?"

The pressure in his chest gave way to frustration. He was trying to remember what happened on the beach, and knowing he was being harassed like a commoner made it insufferable to listen to the demon try to exact memories he didn't have. "What do you want me to say? I'm here."

He was struck again. "You are here and alive only because the General judged you to be uncorrupted and harmless. I will ask only one more time. Did you repent in your heart?"

"I didn't, but you're making me want to." He wasn't surprised by his daring attitude, only by the threat he made.

The demon's face twisted cruelly. "Then do it," he growled.

Karueq squared himself and felt the embrace in his heart rise. "Are you daring me to?" The demon only snarled, the image flickering horribly. Whatever restrain it still had was failing.

Karueq's resolve was failing, too. "I'll do it," he warned.

"Do it!" the thing snarled.

Karueq's blood boiled over. "I renounce you! I reject you! Go to Hell!"

With a roar, the beast sprung on him. It tackled him to the ground. It clawed at him as he tried to fight back.

The warmth in his chest spilled over him and exploded.

A deafening boom thundered and crushed the breath out of him. He gasped from the ground, his lungs sucking in any air it could. His breath finally returned to him, and he clambered to his feet, coughing.

Despite his state, he fought to stay in control of his senses and prepare for another attack. It didn't come. Instead, he found the Prince's royal facade overtaking the hideous beast within, staring sternly at him from those empty eyes. He coughed again and noticed a subtle sheen of anxiousness feathering the creature's powerful look.

"Go," the devil commanded, "before I try to kill you again." In a flourish, he furled his wings around himself and disappeared.

Karueq felt panic jump in his throat. What had he done?

Before he rightly knew what he was doing, he found himself running out of the temple and across the bridge. He raced across the lake shore and through a tunnel. Tears stubbornly sprung from his eyes and streaked his face. He knew the city well, but the tears blinding him and the emotional blow from moments before kept him stumbling into the walls and tripping around corners. He blinked away the tears and the confusion and realized he was going the wrong way. He spun around and continued running.

"Karueq!"

The voice was too muted by his confusion. He didn't hear it.

"Karueq!" the voice cried again.

Suddenly, a hand caught his shoulder and thrust him against the wall of the tunnel. Karueq blinked away his tears, but his sobs remained. It was Bleren.

"Karueq, what happened?" Bleren asked in a hushed voice. He knew something had gone terribly wrong, and no one should discover them.

Karueq's sobs continued, but it was now in pity for his second. Bleren should not see his commander like this, nor should he learn what he had done.

"Karueq!"

Karueq turned his eyes to the ground. He couldn't confess into those eyes that always trusted him.

"Bleren," he whimpered. "I renounced him."

Bleren let go of Karueq and staggered backward.

"I renounced him," Karueq sobbed. He buried his face in his hands.

Bleren glanced down the tunnel. He grabbed Karueq.

"Go," he hissed. "Run while you still can."

Karueq couldn't hear him, couldn't see what was around him while his sobs drowned his heart.

Bleren threw him down the tunnel. "Go! Before you can be hunted. Go!"

Karueq ran. He did not know how many teams ran after him. He didn't know if *any* teams ran after him. For all he knew, Shatan was too much in shock to do anything.

The floor in this tunnel was not as rough as the rest, but his continued weeping made fleeing difficult. He saw no one. They were still in prayer keeping their vigil. The narrow tunnel sloped up and away, taking him higher through the ground. Beneath him in the tunnels below were the halls that held his forces - the forces he'd betrayed. He must keep moving!

His strides brought him to the Rale cave. The beasts squawked at him angrily. He threw a hasty rope around the closest one, mounted it, and kicked it until it sprang from the cave.

The beast instinctively sprinted to the wide opening of the gullet and spread its wings. It flapped furiously at the air, both it and its rider ignoring the startled guards stationed there. Karueq held on with all his might to the scrawny neck as it rose higher.

Without giving the beast any more direction, he held on as it turned north and sprinted away.

THE MARK

PART TWO

CHAPTER ELEVEN

ESCAPE FROM HELL

----- ----- ----- ----- ----- ----- -----

In a blur of blind emotion, Karueq had ended up here. He wasn't exactly sure where he was, as he'd randomly turned the Rale in every direction until he became lost himself. He'd abandoned the beast some days ago, continuing to flee on foot in hopes that he would disappear while his pursuants looked for him on wings. He lost count of the days since his departure, too tired and confused to turn an eye backward.

With no sign of pursuit, he'd made it to this city. It was a port city with merchant ships leaving and landing every day. For the last few hours, he sat against the damp wall of an inconspicuous house, struggling to decide if he should board one and make himself that much more difficult to track, but the sea would make escape impossible if he was found there.

The strange warmth inside him that welled up when he left Shatan nudged him gently. He felt this feeling guiding him somehow, but in his sleep-deprived state he could easily be confusing vague bodily sensations for direction. He chose not to care about this technicality and instead followed the nudge wherever it took him. Now, it told him to board a ship.

The nudge didn't tell him which ship to board, and this made him a little uneasy. He didn't know if any of the crew would be Shatanala agents or if any of them would happen to find him stowed away.

He took a deep breath, banishing his apprehensions. He'd made it this far without his proper wits. If he regained his focus, he could last for years without the Shatanala finding him.

He swallowed and began soaking in everything around him as if planning an attack on the harbor just below the beach. The morning was far too young for anyone to be walking about. The full moon shone brilliantly from the west. He didn't have to run far to board any of the ships anchored there. He'd run much farther many times.

A shadow suddenly appeared in the street, blending in with the dark silhouettes around it. Karueq trained his eyes on its deceptive form for several seconds before he realized it was a scout.

He ducked farther behind the post next to the house and peered one eye around at it. For a few moments, it didn't move. Then, the shadow crept along the house two down from Karueq. It came closer, and then Karueq heard it – a quick, almost imperceptible set of clicks.

This scout was a blind hunter. They were an order of scouts that were most effective at tracking. Blinded at a young age, these creatures were relieved of the hindrances of sight. In this way, they honed their other senses - their hearing, their sense of smell, and the tremors in the ground.

The creature clicked again. Because they were blind, they had to find their way by other means. This one was creating a picture of its surroundings using its hearing.

Then, the scout's head snapped in his direction. Karueq stiffened and held his breath. It slinked carefully toward him.

Nine yards.

Another click.

Eight yards.

It waved its head left and right, gathering all the scents around it. Seven yards.

Its head stopped waving and snapped its focus again on the post in front of Karueq. Six yards.

Karueq's internal voice begged the creature to stop. Five yards.

Without a choice left, Karueq sprang up from his hiding and lunged at the stalking hunter. He pulled his knives. The scout leapt at him. He blocked the dagger. The scout kicked him. He wrestled the thing to the ground and trapped both of its arms. His knife found its throat.

The small nudge tugged hard at his gut. Instead of slitting its throat, Karueq threw his elbow at its head. With a sharp crack, he knocked the assailant out.

In his next breath, he realized that there may be a team in the city waiting for this creature to report back to them. He couldn't stay here with the unconscious predator. He needed to move. They might have heard the commotion and descend on the street any second.

He dashed down the street, pushing himself to run faster than he'd ever run in his life. His wild sprint brought him to the harbor. He darted down the dock to the ship anchored there. A rope dangled along the hull. He grabbed it and hoisted himself up quickly.

On deck, he dived low by the rail and waited. The waves lapping at the hull denied his ears a proper survey, so he raised his head until the beach just came into view. For an hour, he waited like this. Nothing came. No one followed him.

Close calls were bound to happen. He knew that, but he hadn't yet gotten used to the idea that his own men were chasing him.

His exhaustion nearly overcame him. He blinked the sleep away as long as he could. He couldn't rest, not until his body gave him no choice. As the moon drifted lower, he could barely keep his eyes open. The nudge pulled at him gently and led him below deck to a tangle of nets in the bilge, hidden in the corner. Feeling peace wash over him, he crawled under the ropes, concealing himself beneath them. Finally, he let himself fall asleep.

When he awoke, he was still tired but far less exhausted. The creaking of the ship frame gathered his sleepy attention. His body rocked up and down gradually. There were footsteps above him and a heavy thud every now and then. The ship was moving.

He didn't know how far from the port they'd traveled so far, but it settled his nerves to know that he couldn't be tracked now unless the Shatanala already knew he was onboard. If there were any common Shatanala soldiers on the ship with him, he could fight them off easily enough and subdue them.

He heard no one with him below deck, so he crawled out from under the nets. There was little light down here, and from the look of it, it was evening. He flexed his sore muscles and tried to soothe them. He breathed deeply, clearing his lungs and his mind. The belly of the ship was dank. The chill of the sea seeped through the boards, almost like the sea itself was leaking into the hold and displacing the air. The salty coolness was very different from the hot sulfur he left behind in Xanadai.

He tried to estimate the number of crew aboard. He heard a fair amount of noise and chatter. The company seemed a sizable group.

Then, a shadow crossing the open hatch caught his eye and footsteps followed, descending down the stairs. Karueq slipped behind a barrel out of view.

The footsteps halted for a moment before they reached the floor. Karueq kept his ears trained on their position and prepared to slip to a new hiding spot.

"I see you've come out from your hiding place. I wondered when you'd awake," came a voice. "You've been out for two days, and I was beginning to worry."

Karueq's heart quickened at being found out.

"I know you may be anxious right now, but you needn't worry about being tossed overboard. I sail with good company."

Karueq heard wood scraping and then a thud as a barrel was tipped to the floor.

"I once was a stow-away, and I know you have a right to your privacy. However, if you are so inclined, we are celebrating tonight, and you should join us for good food and good drink."

Without waiting for Karueq to acknowledge him, the crewman rolled the barrel to the stairs and shouted to his mates for a rope. Karueq waited until both the barrel and the intruder were extracted from the hold. Then, he breathed a sigh of relief.

He was safe aboard this ship. Any Shatanala onboard would have found him in two days, especially if a mere crewman had noticed his presence. Maybe he truly had escaped. The thought revived him.

His stomach growled. He had not eaten in many days while being on the run. Perhaps taking part in the festivities with the ship's crew wouldn't hurt. His eyes drifted to the ceiling, still clattering with the sound of busy feet. Yes, he would join them.

He rose and adjusted his cloak. He knew he would look out of place, but he couldn't mind that right now. He did, however, remove his weapons from view. He would keep them on his person, as he was still a fugitive from the world's most dangerous creatures, but he didn't need to give the crew a reason to mistrust him.

Karueq flipped up his hood and turned to the stairs. The hatch above showed a darkening sky, beckoning in the evening. The night would hopefully conceal his features, so if they were ever questioned, the crew would be safe not knowing they were sailing with him.

As his head cleared the deck through the hatch, a scream came from above. Karueq ducked instinctively, preparing to fight. Instead, everyone onboard looked up into the sail. One of the crew, a young man, had slipped and was trapped in a tangle of lines, hanging upside-down from his leg. He was in a panic, flailing against the dark sky, illuminated only by the merry lanterns aboard. Those on deck shouted and pointed.

A burly man near Karueq took off running to the helm and grabbed the wheel, freeing the man stationed there. This man raced toward the mast and leaped into the rigging with ease. He scaled the ropes and spreaders quickly until he reached the trapped young man. The frightened thing grabbed his arm tightly. The spider expertly loosed the trapped leg from the lines and hoisted him over his shoulder. The crew erupted into shouts of applause.

When the boy was safely back on deck, the older man put his arm around him and spoke with the voice Karueq had heard down in the hold. "Men! Break out the barrels and pour yourselves a toast! We have even more to celebrate tonight!" He clapped the sheepish child on the back and the crew gave three shouts for him.

There was a wild bustle as the men ran about securing the sails, putting their tools away, breaking out the celebration and tapping the barrels. Karueq took this opportunity to emerge from the hatch without much notice, take an ale, and slide himself along the rail. He huddled his face beneath his hood. The wind wasn't cold, but he welcomed the concealment of his cloak.

Music sprang into the air and food was passed around. It wasn't a rich feast with the kind of delicacies he'd seen from the royals and at some of the ceremonies Xanadai hosted. It was simple food, staples mostly, but there was plenty of it. Karueq's stomach settled as he ate.

A few of the men abandoned their meals and began dancing and singing songs to the entertainment of their comrades. Laughter and carefree heckling spilled over the deck. One of the performers challenged another to best him. The recipient accepted the challenge. He put his pipe down and sang a theatrical ballad of affection to a mop he picked up nearby.

"Stephen!" someone shouted. The rest of the crew joined him. "Stephen! Stephen!"

The cheers goaded the spider, who had returned to the helm, into a response. He secured the wheel and pranced his way to the center of the deck, playfully snatching the pint of another man on the way.

"You call this a party, you filthy scum?" he taunted them with a smile, the merry torchlight casting shadows all about. The men ridiculed him cheerfully. He drained the pint and tossed it back to its original owner, who promptly refilled it.

"It is such an honor," he bowed deeply to the crowd, "to be sailing with you on such a day. Unfortunately, I am not eloquent enough for a flowery speech, but I will tell you this. You are the finest crew I could ever hope to sail with."

"Is that what you tell all the girls?" shouted a heckler.

"You're the only woman aboard this ship, mate," Stephen teased.

The heckler faked a swoon and dropped onto the man standing next to him.

Stephen grabbed another man's ale. "Indeed, I am truly blessed to be among friends on this day." He raised the pint. "Eliuma."

The men raised their pints in response. "Eliuma." They drank the curious toast. Karueq, too, raised his drink to his lips, unsure exactly what he was drinking to. It occurred to him that Stephen looked familiar behind the clumsy shadows dancing on his face.

"Enough of my boring drawl! Musicians, give us a tune!" The playfulness returned to the men and the celebration continued on. New performers scurried to the middle of the deck. Stephen clambered his way through the gathering, participating in extra toasts and reveling with each man he passed. The crew took little notice of Karueq in their revelries.

Then, he felt a presence at his side. "Thank you for accepting my invitation, stow-away." Karueq lifted his eyes beneath the hood just enough to see Stephen's face. "Please enjoy yourself."

The man winked at him, and Karueq's breathing stilled. It was Quiron.

Quiron walked away without another word, leaving Karueq alone at the rail with his bewilderment. The most bloodthirsty assassin that

Xanadai ever produced was found engaging in a carefree party with a crew of Seagan merchants.

Karueq stared hard in his direction. There was no mistaking it. His mind raced back. The last time Karueq saw this soldier, a wicked malice burned in his eyes. In a private meeting, Quiron had renewed his blood oath to take the life of the Quiri and anyone who stood in his way. Then, he'd disappeared.

The former commander stood frozen against the rail for the rest of the celebration. It was hours before the crew grew weary of their merriment. Karueq barely noticed them start to retire for the night. He kept his eye on Quiron. He did notice when the last ones left the deck to dream away the night in peace, bidding the former assassin a good night as they yawned.

Quiron himself stayed above deck and moved about, inspecting the ship. Then, he turned to his mute guest.

"Too little fun to tire your mind, stow-away?" he asked him.

Karueq didn't respond. He didn't trust himself to speak.

"You can't be that shy, my friend. I know you're on the run from Hell."

Karueq's eye twitched. He'd forgotten that his clothing would give him away to a Shatanala, former or not. He tried to calm his nerves. There would be no way out, no escape for him if this man turned on him. He had to believe he would be received without retaliation.

"Your last words to me were a blood oath you have since forsaken." Karueq lowered his hood and let the lantern light shine fully on his face.

Quiron's eyes betrayed fleeting coldness at recognizing him, but in the next blink, it was gone. "Commander," he acknowledged.

"Not anymore," Karueq corrected him.

Quiron's mouth turned up in a surprised smile. "Of all the stubborn men to dwell in Xanadai, you shed the veil?"

"I'm not sure what you mean."

"You heard Eleh's call and answered."

"I received no call. I simply rejected Shatan."

"Eleh doesn't always speak directly. I heard it like a whisper in the thunder, almost completely imperceptible, but persistent enough."

"Is that why you left?"

Quiron chuckled and shook his head. "You wouldn't believe me if I told you."

"There have been a great many things I wouldn't have believed until recently."

"I suppose it came as a great surprise to you hearing of my desertion." The former Brehila slid onto the rail next to the commander and looked out at the sea across the deck. He crossed his arms thoughtfully. "I did indeed find the Quiri. It took me by surprise to know who he was."

A thread of shame crept into Karueq's thoughts. If Chelia was the Elequiri, that meant that the man he killed in the tent must be her constant protector. "It was Aryngo, wasn't it?"

Quiron looked at Karueq a little surprised. "Was?"

"He's dead," Karueq stated simply. He didn't trust himself to share further information.

"I'm sorry to hear that, but no, Karueq. The Quiri is his brother, Alamar."

The puzzle Karueq had been putting together in his head about the Eleverians shattered. He allowed Quiron to continue.

"I found him out a month after you sent me away. So fervent was my dedication that they couldn't hide him from me. He begged me to come with him to an Eleverian encampment. There, I might find freedom. I didn't listen to him at first. I tried to kill him, but Chelia stepped in. I hadn't known she was there. Instead of killing me, they simply begged me once more to see the light and come with them. That's when I heard Eleh whisper to me beyond the raging storm of hate in my heart. I listened to that faint, voiceless whisper and followed them. They removed the Mark, and I have been free ever since."

His gaze left the waves of the sea and the memory he was sharing. He looked thoughtfully at his former commander. "How long have you been out?"

"I'm not sure, perhaps a fortnight."

Quiron put his hand on Karueq's shoulder warmly. "Welcome to freedom, my friend." Then, his brow furrowed. He looked at Karueq's arm, sensing something was wrong. "You still bear the Mark."

Dread plowed into Karueq's mind. "I can't be rid of it. It goes too deep."

"Yes, it does go deep, but they should already have removed it from you," Quiron responded. He let go of Karueq and pushed his own sleeve up to the shoulder. A thick, ugly scar smeared the flesh like he had been severely burned, but the Mark was gone, just like Zokul.

Karueq's mouth dropped open. "Show me how."

"How did you get out? They would have removed it from you when you came to the light."

"I guess they didn't have time with an ambush upon them."

"It isn't like them to abandon someone."

"They didn't abandon me. I rejected Shatan a few days later. Can they really remove it?"

Quiron's grin widened. "Of course they can. I'll take you to them once we land."

Dread entered Karueq's thoughts again. "I'm not entirely sure I would be welcome, of all people."

"And what would make you so special in that regard?"

"The things I've done to them."

Quiron chuckled. "Your lowliness," he teased, "I had a personal agenda to kill the Quiri and succeeded in brutally killing many of their brothers and sisters. In their eyes, we are no different than the rest of Seaga. It is their mission to bring us to the arms of God."

Karueq's fear feathered away at Quiron's words.

Quiron looked at him thoughtfully again. "When you say they didn't have time in the ambush, what do you mean?"

"It was a trap set for them. Not the ambush, that was a failsafe. Shatan ordered me to feign allegiance to them, infiltrate them, and destroy them from within."

Quiron chuckled again. "They would have destroyed your plan from the inside, unless you were truly that stubborn."

"Then, the ambush began in order to kill me, ironically so I didn't defect, and I suppose they had orders to kill Chelia and Alamar. She knocked me out and prayed over me. A few days later, I woke up and rejected Shatan. Now I'm here." His eyes dropped to his hands.

"I imagine her prayer was a desperate plea for Eleh to open your eyes. The Eleverians can't force you to turn, and Eleh doesn't accept false surrender, but she must have pleaded with Him to give you a chance at freedom, especially if she knew your life was on the line. The rest is up to you."

Karueq thought about this carefully. "Does that mean that I didn't fully defect?"

"What do you mean?"

"I haven't formally given my allegiance to Eleh. I simply renounced the Shatanala."

"Yes, it is true that you have not given yourself to Eleh," Quiron clasped his shoulder and nudged him toward the helm. "But you are free to do that now; free of the binds Shatan placed on you. Most of those who come to the light surrender to Him right away. You may be an exception, but Eleh will welcome you anyway."

Quiron turned and walked up to the helm. Karueq followed and they leaned on the rail, looking out at the sea.

"How do I do that? What ritual do I have to do? What sacrifice do I have to make?"

"He requires no ritual, and the sacrifice you make is not what you think."

"What is that?"

Quiron paused, remembering what was told to him. "It's not simple, but the Eleverians told it to me this way. Eleh doesn't promise that walking with Him will be easy, but He promises it will be worth it."

"What does that mean?"

"Think about it. Eleh is so worth the pain and suffering that evil will inflict on you that there is no question in the mind of an entire nation that they would rather serve Him and suffer than have all the riches and glory the darkness promises. And even in the fickle states of Israel and Judah, you have never been able to starve, beat, or seduce His promises out of them, just sway them for a few years."

Karueq could barely absorb what he was hearing. Because he had renounced Shatan, he knew he had nowhere else to go, but Quiron's words were madness. From his experience with the Eleverians, the Shatanala, and the 'fickle state of Israel', he had grown to understand the world one way. Shatan had solidified his worldview with tangible rewards and consequences. From Quiron's speech, it seemed as if nothing Eleh promised could ever be grasped, playing contentedly in the intangible.

Quiron must have seen the puzzle in his eyes. "You're not expected to understand any of this to surrender. You'll understand eventually, soon enough with your intelligence. The Eleverians will help you if you ask."

"When do we land?" Karueq asked, a little too eagerly for his liking.

Quiron chuckled again. "It's a bit of a journey, but we'll be there soon enough. In the meantime, I'll answer any of your questions that I am able to."

The answer was enough to satisfy Karueq for the time being. He surveyed the deck and smiled in amusement at the night's festivities. "What was the occasion for the celebration? It seemed to center on you."

The corners of Quiron's mouth turned up, and he shook his head. He left the rail and strode to the keg next to them. "Indeed, it did." He filled two ales from the tap. "This is the day I defected from the Shatanala." He handed an ale to Karueq. "Cheers."

Karueq accepted the drink, but his brow wrinkled. "You told them your history?"

The grin spread wider. "No. They think this was a birthday celebration."

Quiron's eyes suddenly flitted to the rear of the ship, and his face darkened. "Karueq, what have you done?"

Karueq in turn looked to the direction in which Quiron stared. "What is it?"

"A team just boarded the rear. Did you bring them? Is this a trap?"

Something whistled through the still night and struck the mast. They both looked at it – an arrow, a warning shot.

Quiron grabbed Karueq and shoved him to the deck. "Karueq. Tell me once and for all that you didn't bring this team and I will believe you." His eyes teamed with earnest.

"I didn't bring them," he insisted.

Suddenly, the center of the ship exploded. Karueq was blinded by the green light erupting from the blast. Before his own quick instincts kicked in, Quiron grabbed Karueq again and shoved him against a pile of barrels. Desperate screaming from below deck erupted as the team began their assault on the crew in the bilge.

"Look at me!" Quiron hissed at him. Karueq complied, and the former Brehila searched him quickly. He must have found what he was looking for because he rushed to tell Karueq what he needed to know. "Pray to Eleh. Beg Him to help you. He will show you where to find them —"

A green blast exploded the helm. It cast Karueq against the railing. One thought raced through his mind. He couldn't be captured now. He couldn't give up on the salvation he'd hastily given up his life for.

He glanced over the edge of the broken ship at the debris in the water below. A piece of the deck, big enough to support two, floated just beneath him. The turbulent waves dowsed the small flames still clinging to the boards.

He turned back to Quiron, but his eyes fell on a body lying under a pile of debris.

A black shape sprang up from around the wheel. Karueq blocked the attack and jumped on it. He drove a punishing kick into its head, and the Shatanala fell to the boards. Karueq threw himself down next to Quiron.

"Quiron," Karueq managed.

The eyes didn't open. Then, Karueq saw the plank protruding from his chest. His heart fell through him. He couldn't leave him here among the choking flames. With all the strength he had, Karueq grabbed the limp body, shoved it overboard, and dove in after it.

In the water, he let himself be suspended below the surface. He tore off his waterlogged cloak. His eyes stung with the salt of the sea, but he forced himself to open them to watch for a following attacker. The surface splashed above him. The green and yellow fire consumed the wreckage. The light flared through the water, creating wavy shafts of light that illuminated the broken hull. The bow of the ship stooped below the surface, sinking faster than the stern whose silhouette stood black against the fires. The team was tearing the ship apart.

His lungs burned for breath. He spotted the raft of broken planks above him and clawed through the water toward it. Breaking the surface, he gasped for breath. His lungs filled and he pushed the air back out. He clung to the raft but kept himself as far below the water as possible.

His next priority was Quiron. He looked around but couldn't find him. He abandoned the raft and ducked below the water again. He forced his stinging eyes open and glanced around at the shadowy water. He saw planks, boards, ropes, and barrels strewn about in the water. Something floated in the water beyond his reach that could be a body. He prayed that it was.

He kicked through the water and grabbed the object, desperate to salvage it from the brine. It was indeed a body, and a board protruded horrifically from its chest. He clawed back through the water, dragging his burden. The raft had floated farther away. By the time he reached it, his lungs burned again and his arms were weary.

With everything he had left in him, he heaved the body up on the planks and dragged himself out of the freezing water.

He was still in danger. His eyes found the wreckage and scanned it. A black shadow stood on the small mast, which was all that still protruded from the water. It faced his direction. He flattened himself against the boards, praying he had passed beyond detection, but he knew the figure already had him made. It stayed there, focused on the lonely raft.

The man didn't move to alert the team to his escape. He simply stood on the mast watching his prey float away until it was out of sight. With enough staring and thinking, Karueq suddenly recognized the profile.

Bleren.

CHAPTER TWELVE

THE GATES OF ELEVERIA

----- ----- ----- ----- ----- ----- -----

Karueq's sobbing drowned his heart. His salty tears coursed down his face into the puddles surrounding him on the broken raft. He held tight to Quiron's body, forbidding the sea to wash him away to an undignified grave. He cried for this man. He cried for the many years he still might have lived, celebrating with the crew that had been so cruelly murdered during the night. He cried for the families they might have had who would never know what happened to their husbands and fathers and brothers on his account.

He cried for himself. He still couldn't fathom what had happened to him to set him forth on this path, unknown and without direction. He cried most of all for the poor soul that stood on the sinking mast watching him float away. Karueq recognized Bleren by the way he carried himself – sure, confident, and capable of accomplishing anything asked of him. He was capable of anything, that is, except killing his traitorous mentor.

There was no excuse for Bleren missing him and letting him get away. The team with him should have been split in two, half of them to clear the deck above while the rest slaughtered those below. Bleren made sure there were no survivors except for the single prize he had been tasked with.

Karueq wracked his mind trying to justify Bleren's loyalty. His allegiance by Xanadai law rested with Shatan, but Karueq had always known his true loyalty belonged with him. His weeping grew stronger as he imagined the heartbreak he must have caused the young general. Karueq's whole world had been upended, and so too had Bleren's.

The sobbing subsided just enough for Karueq to raise his head and peer blearily about. The deep fog of the early morning prevented him from seeing anything. His sighs spilled from his mouth in small clouds, mixing in with the thick shroud. He saw the dim light of the early morning beginning. The sun would rise and lazily burn away the moisture as it rose.

Karueq closed his eyes and released one more shuddering exhale. He was lost, utterly lost. He had no way of knowing where he would drift to. The thought of drifting helplessly to a beach controlled by the Shatanala frightened him. He didn't fear torture and death. He feared losing the chance to discover what Quiron had told him. He'd spoken of a life that was worth shedding Shatan's promises and enduring whatever the Shatanala could do to him. After everything that happened since Karueq fled, Eleh couldn't be what he'd lived his whole life believing He was.

He swallowed the overwhelming emotion in his throat and turned his attention to the Mark. He grabbed the knife from his boot and pulled his sleeve up. There it lay, the black ink gloating at him in continued triumph. The mighty beast smiled wickedly at him.

He thought first about cutting the cursed thing out of his flesh. He brandished the knife, ready to end its tether, but instead he lowered it. That would never work. The Mark ran too deep. He would gladly cut off the whole arm and be rid of it, but it ran still deeper. The brand was but a flower springing from a root that dove through him and wrapped itself around his soul. It bound him entirely, the chain Shatan used to shackle his spoils.

He couldn't remove it on his own. He put the knife back in his boot. He was ever so lost. Instead, he grasped the plank in Quiron's body and wrenched it free, tossing it away with a splash.

Then, he did something he hadn't done in a very, very long time. He shifted to his knees and bent his head over, pressing his face into his folded hands. The tears stung his weary eyes again. He swallowed.

"Eleh," he whispered. "I don't even know if you can hear me. I don't know if you would listen." He swallowed the sobs that threatened to burst forth again. "Please, don't abandon me. Please. Please, don't leave me on my own."

As he prayed, he felt the air change. Warmth seeped into his skin and feathered through his body. The salt in the air diminished, and the breeze tasted sweeter.

He opened his eyes. Light filled his vision. He raised his head slightly and saw that the water surrounding him was gone. Instead, the raft was surrounded by a sea of clouds. They burned gloriously with light. He gazed at them further. There was no sunlight and no sun. Something else was setting them ablaze.

"Karueq," a voice called gently to him. Karueq's heart skipped a beat. He felt he knew that voice. It seemed familiar to him, but he couldn't place it. His eyes wandered, searching for the source of the sound. He looked behind him, but nothing was there.

"Turn around," the voice called quietly, plainly coming from just outside his vision. Very cautiously, Karueq turned his head in that direction. He caught a glimpse of a man dressed in white before hiding his face in the boards of the raft. He trembled at the presence of the figure – Eleh.

"Do not be afraid," He said. "I am with you, and I will not abandon you." Despite the kind words, Karueq refused to look up. "I heard Chelia's prayer and opened your eyes. Now rise, and do not fear that you are lost."

Karueq remained bowed. He couldn't look up into the face of the One he'd sought to destroy for nearly his whole life.

"Karueq, open your eyes," Eleh whispered.

Karueq squeezed his eyes tighter, gathering his strength. He gave into the gentleness and the promise he had just received, filling up with hope that he wasn't lost. Then, he looked up.

Instead of the glorious, shining clouds, Karueq saw only the dense fog. It remained too thick to see where he was. He tried hard to squash the fear rising back up in his chest and to believe what had just been spoken to him. He held onto the hope that the vision wasn't merely a hallucination born from exhaustion.

Karueq's next thought was that he was soaked and cold. He looked down and saw that the cracked planks he and Quiron floated on were quickly becoming waterlogged and half of it was sinking. Drowning or freezing in the icy water, that is how he was about to die.

Then, there was a sudden jolt that threw him off balance. His rigid joints failed him, and he collapsed face first into the frigid water. He tasted the salty brine in his mouth as he clambered back to his knees. He looked around at the water. A reef had emerged from the depths next to the dismal raft.

Desperately, Karueq slid onto the reef away from the sinking planks and tugged Quiron after him. His options for death diminished to freezing.

This could be how Eleh was choosing to judge him. He would grow exhausted trying to remain warm as he shook in the icy water. His mind would be tortured mercilessly, having nothing to occupy it but the horrors he'd committed and his fear at what Eleh would do with him in death. The most likely outcome would be rejection from whatever Eleh promised his people, and he would be handed back to Shatan. His reward for defecting would be endless torment in Hell.

Just then, a dim glow trickled through the fog and grew brighter. It was the sun, fast burning away the thick clouds around him. The haze cleared, and Karueq stared in awe. All around him, the horizon glowed. The sun, just beginning its ascent into the sky, emitted a majestic light that scattered across the water and created a ring around everything Karueq could see. The sky above, too, captured a few distinct streaks of the radiance. Karueq's heart relaxed at the serene beauty, and his somber thoughts dissipated. It warmed him and brought him peace. He clung to hope once more.

Something caught his attention as he gazed around. Ahead of him was a curving white line sweeping up and away from the horizon, a bay flanked by two enormous pillars spiking the sky above the water. Land!

He took hold of Quiron's body and abandoned the reef, diving into the icy water and swimming as fast as he could. The farther he swam, the more he could distinguish on the shore. There was grass beyond the white sand beach. Farther still, a faint shadow stood beyond the beach against the sky that looked like it could be a mountain.

He made it to the edge of the pillars. They rose elegantly from the sea floor and gleamed in the morning light. Each one was banded with different colored stone – reds, oranges, browns, and whites. Karueq laughed warmly at the beauty and brilliance. They stood as if on guard over the bay, marking it like an entrance.

He swam at a sprint. Once past the stone guards, a thunderous clap startled him. He halted his sprint to the shore and looked up. The sound seemed to have shot up from the sea through the pillars. It sounded as if they were splitting, and he heard echoes of the clap shooting through the rock. The pillars remained whole. Confused but largely uninterested in the occurrence, he continued his swim to the shore.

Soon, he came upon another reef, this one almost submerged, and hauled his burden onto it. He, too, dragged himself to rest on it for a moment, thankful he would not have to face judgment yet. His body was worn out from the weeks of fleeing and the abuse he was putting it through now.

With his strength coming back, he sat up and again surveyed his surroundings. He wanted to miss none of the beauty surrounding him. The sky was fully awake. The low sun was warm, and Karueq noticed even the water was remarkably warm inside the bay. He looked down over the edge of the reef. The water was so calm he could see all the way to the floor. He estimated it to be at least a hundred feet deep.

He threw his head back and took a deep breath. The air was refreshing and only faintly salty. A smile was left on his face as he exhaled.

He looked to the shore again, his eagerness renewed, and dragged Quiron back into the water. He continued without stopping until his strokes clawed into the soft, white sand. He pulled the soaked body onto the beach. The lost assassin was safe now.

Karueq himself sank to his knees in the warm sand. He let go of his desperation and his fear. Relieved tears welled in his eyes. He, too, was safe for now. He allowed himself to believe this was a safe haven. He didn't recognize the beach or the pillars guarding it. The Shatanala were unlikely to be here.

Suddenly, a gust of wind drove across the beach. His head snapped up, and he blinked his blurred vision away. A gigantic beast landed down the beach a hundred yards from him followed by another. Karueq froze. They were dragons.

The creatures surveyed the bay and looked to the pillars. Their long necks curved forward, carefully inspecting what lay before them. The intensity of their gaze was broken only when Karueq couldn't hold his awkward posture anymore and shifted.

One of them snapped its focus in his direction. Karueq's heart seized with dread. The other dragon followed suit. Those burning eyes were upon him. The wings unfurled. They leapt toward him with haste. Karueq's hand found his sword.

With a great roar, the first dragon planted itself over him followed by the other. Karueq leapt to attack and fight for his life.

He swiped at one dragon's leg. It pulled the leg away and easily avoided the blow from its exhausted assailant. He launched at the other one.

"Stop!" he heard a voice cry out.

His sword hissed off the scales. The beast roared, its neck arched upward.

"Stop!" the voice came again.

A woman jumped from the dragon's back. Karueq swiped at her out of instinct. She blocked the blow with her arm guard.

A man jumped from the other dragon. He hurtled toward Karueq. Karueq thrust his blade at him. The man ducked and speared into him headlong, knocking him to the ground.

"Honai! Hold!" the woman ordered.

The men stopped struggling long enough to look at each other.

"Karueq?" the man said, a bit bewildered.

"Honai," Karueq reciprocated. He looked at the woman. "Henara." He recognized both of them from the Eleka guard. His heart rate quickened anew.

"What are you doing here?" Henara asked, a steely edge in her tone.

Honai released him and stood, but Karueq stayed on his knees. "How did you get here?" he asked, equally guarded.

Karueq looked at them searchingly. "What do you mean 'here'? Where are we?"

The pair looked at each other. "You don't know?" questioned Henara.

"You are within the borders of Eleveria," Honai answered him.

Karueq's jaw dropped open. Eleh brought him straight to Eleveria.

Honai's eyes squinted, searching him, his expression softening. "You had no idea where you are?"

Karueq shook his head. Henara's face remained unchanged by his admission. "How did you get here?" she demanded.

"I… drifted to a reef just beyond those pillars," Karueq stammered.

"The gateway," Honai corrected.

Karueq glanced at the pillars standing tall above the water. "Yes," he said, breaking the uncomfortable silence.

"Why should we believe you?" she demanded sharply. "You are armed."

"I fled Shatan. I renounced him!" he pleaded.

She turned to Honai. "We have every reason to mistrust him."

"But we might believe him," Honai replied to her. Then, they exchanged an entire conversation in a look that lasted but a few seconds.

Henara turned her stony face back on him. "You swear on your life that you are telling the truth?"

Karueq's heart pounded in his chest. "I do."

"Then we will take you to the Elequiri, and she will decide what to do with you." The woman's tone was still short and decided.

"No!" Karueq blurted. He couldn't stop himself. "I can't see her!"

Henara sighed, annoyed. "We haven't the wisdom to deal with you. My judgment is clouded, as you were my next mission, and we had no idea what sort of mind you had after that trick you pulled on the island. Honai has no desire to deal with you either because he just recently returned from searching for you. The Elequiri will decide what is to become of you."

Karueq felt defeated for the third time since dawn. He couldn't see how the promises in his vision could comfort him now. "Fair enough," he yielded, noticing he had no tears to shed. "I'll go quietly."

Honai glanced at the body lying on the beach a few yards away. "Who is that?" he asked.

Karueq's eyes fell on the slumped form. "Quiron, a former member of the Brehila."

Honai left the little group and walked over to it. He gently pulled the limp shoulder back and turned him over to look at his face. He reverently brushed the sand away from his face.

"Henara," he beckoned the woman. She left Karueq where he knelt in the sand and joined Honai over Quiron's body. They spoke quietly for a minute. Henara glanced at Karueq once. Henara nodded in agreement to something. At this, Honai gingerly lifted Quiron from the beach. The pair walked back to the dragons. Henara climbed onto the back of one and took Quiron from Honai, draping him carefully over the dragon's shoulders in front of her. Honai strode to the other dragon and held his hand out to Karueq.

"Come," he said.

Karueq rose from the sand, his legs heavy. He climbed onto the dragon with defeat still hanging over his head. Karueq noticed the enormous power of the beast as it breathed beneath him – slow, rumbling breaths that expanded its rib cage beneath him. Honai climbed in front of him.

With grace incongruent with its size, the dragon lifted its wings and pressed down on the air. With ease, it rose above the ground, climbing with each stroke of its powerful wings. Karueq's knees tried to grip the massive creature's body as if he were astride a Rale, but the smooth ride allowed him to balance and release the habitual grip, a welcome surprise to his tired body.

The shadow ahead and to the left was indeed a mountain as he had guessed. Its base was enormous and its peak was caught high in the clouds. Karueq looked also to the right and saw the silhouette of an expansive forest sweeping away from the bay. Between the two were rolling hills.

The dragons set down again shortly after, on a hill about a mile away from the beach. He saw a blanket spread out there, two waterskins, and a pack with food spilling from it. A small heap of various flowers lay in the grass by the blanket next to another pack.

Honai swung his leg over the dragon's neck and left its back. Henara helped him take Quiron's body from the other dragon. They set it down on the center of the blanket and wrapped it carefully. Karueq lamented at how skilled they were at accomplishing this funeral task. He shook his head at the hundreds and thousands of Eleverians he'd put in the ground where wrapping a body seemed as much a part of their lives as riding a dragon.

When they finished, they put their hands on the bundle and bowed their heads. Honai spoke a few words. Karueq wondered what they were. He guessed they were praying for Quiron. Hope squeezed his chest again at the sight. They prayed for a man that persecuted them with a cruel bloodthirst. Their mercy perhaps might also extend to him.

The two lifted their heads. Karueq prepared to continue the journey, but it seemed that was not the intent of his captors. Instead, they moved a few feet away from the body, where Henara turned around and sat in front of Honai. Karueq watched curiously as Honai began to untangle her braids. They talked in low voices to each other, and Henara's serious expression melted into a half-smile. Karueq grew self-conscious that he was intruding on a moment between them, and he looked away.

The dragons, too, were choosing to ignore their masters. They wrapped their long necks round their bodies and appeared to be dozing. The one Karueq was straddling idly lifted its wing, reached for it with its jaw, and scratched a spot on the membrane.

After a few more minutes, Honai and Henara got up and returned to their mounts. Henara's hair was free from the braids. The seriousness was gone from her face. She mounted the dragon again and Honai placed the now wrapped body in front of her. Honai returned to his seat in front of Karueq as Henara took flight, and they lifted into the air after her.

Karueq looked down. He couldn't help being marveled at the sights he saw below during the flight, despite his impending judgment. They flew past the mountain and the forest over a valley dotted with waterfalls and wildflowers. Imposing cliffs framed the sides of the valley. Beyond the valley was a wide open plain expanding beyond Karueq's vision in every direction.

Then a mountain range grew from the horizon before them. Karueq could make out a city carved in the foothills of the range, a mighty fortress rising from its center.

Before the city streamed a river. The dragons dove low so that Karueq could hear the swollen rapids teaming downstream. A mighty willow tree sprouted from the bank upstream. Its roots dived into the earth and into the river itself. Most trees would have given way to the river and fallen to join it. This one remained strong and erect.

Past the river, the dragons ascended a bluff upon which dozens of horses grazed and ran with each other. A young, white one raced after the dragons with all its might and whinnied playfully at them when it utterly lost.

Finally, they landed in the city outside the fortress. There were several Eleverians moving in and out of the gigantic building. The three travelers dismounted. Honai had a quick word with Henara and kissed her goodbye before ushering Karueq through the open doors of the great fortress. He led him past the courts and the wandering eyes of a few Eleverians going about their business. Karueq's discomfort mounted with each stare.

They reached a set of wide doors decorated with gold leaves and silver vines. White enamel lilies encrusted the center of each door. Honai opened the door and gestured Karueq inside.

Inside was a vast room that looked like the great hall of a palace.   The space rivaled the Great Temple of Sheol in size. Windows with clear panes of glass allowed the light to stream in from every direction.

Karueq's dread returned to him and forced the beauty of the place firmly from his mind upon seeing the three thrones against the far wall. Two thrones made of carved wood stood on each side of a grander throne overlaid in gold and standing tall above them.

His heartbeat grew quicker with each step and his mind buzzed with the atrocities he'd committed on her people. Yes, the Eleverians knew the cost of engaging with the Shatanala, and they willingly placed themselves in harm's way, but Karueq had ordered brutal punishment for such courage.

Honai stopped him before they reached the thrones.

"Wait here," he said. He left the uneasy man alone in the hall and walked out through a door in the wall on the right.

Karueq waited, shaking on the inside, frozen on the outside. He had never felt so alone and so frightened. He was a child again in the midst of war and pestilence. He tried to calm himself. This wouldn't end in death, and he had never known them to torture their prisoners. All the same, he trembled at the confrontation that was about to ensue.

Before his rational thinking could ease him, a loud clank broke the silence in the hall. He looked to his right.

Chelia walked hastily toward him from the door. Several others followed her, including Alamar and Honai. Her face was set, filled with not one, but a thousand emotions.

She halted in front of him. Her eyes flashed and pierced him. Those with her remained a short distance behind. Karueq could not break from her gaze.

Suddenly, she took a step forward and yanked his sword from his side. He startled. She flipped it around. The handle was within his reach.

"Take it," she commanded.

He stood frozen, powerless.

"Take it." Her firm tone jolted him, and his hand reached out automatically and took it. It never felt so heavy.

"Strike me down," she demanded. Her expression remained unflinching.

Karueq couldn't believe what he had just heard. His mouth fell open to protest, but his bewilderment swallowed it.

"Strike me," she repeated.

His voice came out small. "No..."

"This is what you lived to do for years. This is the prize you seek. How wonderful it will be for you to deliver the Elequiri and Eleveria all in one day! What riches await you! What power you will hold!"

"No! No, Captain!" he pleaded.

"Enough of your charade! Take your prize!" She spread her hands to the side showing no intent to guard her body.

Karueq sank to his knees, and the sword dropped with a clatter at his side. "No..." he pleaded. He found his tears again. The sobs wracked his body. His despair swallowed him. He had nowhere to go, and the woman he'd hoped would help him refused to acknowledge the change in him.

Then, he felt a hand gently on his head. "Karueq," she beckoned. Her tone confused him all the more. The sweat and tears drenched his face.

She spoke to him again, crouching down in front of him. "Karueq, dry your eyes and look at me." Her sleeve drew under his head and wiped his face. He sniffed back what he could. She turned his face up. "Karueq, look up."

He opened his eyes. A smile looked upon his miserable face. She wiped away the remaining salty trails. Embarrassed, he rubbed his face before she could finish.

"Your eyes are open," she grinned. "Please forgive my theatrics, but I had to test you. Some hearts are not easily rescued."

"You… you're not sending me away?" he stammered.

"You really haven't been paying attention over the years, have you? Of course we won't reject you!"

"But the things I've done…" His voice was small again.

"I told you in the forest, we won't hold your past against you. Stand up." She pulled him to his feet. "We've been searching for you for weeks." She placed her hand on his arm and looked at the Mark inking his skin, exposed under his torn sleeve. His gut flinched away as she looked at it.

She gave a decided sigh. "You stole back your heart, and you may give it away to whomever you wish. You have a second chance at the choice you made long ago. That being said, we can't allow Shatan's Mark to reside in our borders."

"Can you remove it?" he asked quickly.

"Is that what you want?"

"Yes."

"Then yes, we can remove it," she said with a smile. "You are exhausted from your flight. Tomorrow, you will be free of it."

"And we will take time to bury Quiron properly," Honai added.

Chelia glanced at Honai, puzzled. She asked Karueq to clarify. "What happened to him?"

Karueq's discomfort welled up within him again. His flight from Shatan brought nothing but tragedy. "A team managed to track me to his ship, and they killed him during the night. I couldn't leave him…" his voice trailed, and he didn't trust himself to continue speaking.

Chelia's gaze wandered away, and it looked like memories were teaming across her mind. Then, she turned to the Eleverians with her. "Send a team to the gate and scouts to the sea beyond it. Report to me any vulnerabilities and any Shatanala that may have followed him here."

"I'm sorry," Karueq managed.

"For what?" she asked him.

"I've put you in jeopardy."

She shrugged. "They were bound to figure us out eventually."

Karueq held onto that word in an absurd desperation – *they*. She didn't say *you*.

"Khana," Chelia addressed a woman who looked strikingly like her. "Take Karueq to recovery before you leave."

Khana nodded. "Come with me," she told him, picking up his sword.

Karueq's voice was lost, and he couldn't voice his gratitude for the kindness she showed him. He simply followed Khana to the back of the hall while the Elequiri and her people continued their discussion walking the other way.

Khana led him through the ornate doors and down a few hallways to a room containing stalls with deep baths. She took the rest of his weapons and pointed out a change of clothes on a set of shelves nearby. Then, she closed the door behind her and left him to clear the grime and salty water from his body. He rushed to do so, not wanting to keep her waiting.

Then, she led him down another hallway and up a flight of stairs. He wasn't really paying attention to where they were going, but they ended up outside another door, a simple one with a marking in the center. The marking consisted of two lines leaning against one another, evoking the shape of a lone mountain.

Khana opened the door and gestured him inside. The scent of fresh flowers hit him immediately upon entering the room. The perimeter of the ceiling was alive with flowers and greenery. The wide room was lined with beds and a long table stood to the side. The wall on the far end was opened to the air, the yawning doors paned with clear glass like he'd seen in the great hall. A wide terrace swept out from the doorway with a broad view of the plains beyond the river.

A man sat on the edge of the terrace, his feet dangling over the edge. He was marking on a piece of paper beside him.

"This is the recovery hall," Khana explained to him. "Those without or who heal from serious injury come here until they are well." She walked past him to a large set of cabinets and shelves against the wall. "You may choose any bed. Food and water are kept here." She gestured to the man on the balcony. "Hanai will be here for some time." Karueq's stomach twisted at the Eleka guard member's name. "So we stocked some of his favorites. Anything else you could need is in here too."

She reached for one of the many identical pendants hanging from several hooks on the side of the cabinet and held it out to him

"What is it?" he asked.

"It signifies that you are in recovery. For us, it means that for the duration you wear it you will not be sent on mission. It is also a symbol of honor for the task the wearer has just completed and how happy we are that they've arrived home safely."

Karueq's heart squeezed sickeningly. "I can't."

Khana squinted at him but returned the pendant to its place. "Let Hanai know if you need anything more. I'm sorry I can't stay long."

She squeezed his shoulder comfortingly, then called outside to Hanai. "Hanai, we're holding two ceremonies tomorrow if you want to join." The man raised his pen to acknowledge, and then Khana left the room.

Karueq remained where he stood. He didn't know what to do, and he felt that he was intruding.

"Pass me an apple, will you?" Hanai called from outside.

Karueq snapped out of his own head.

"And grab something for yourself."

He turned to the cabinet and the array of colorful foods spilling from the shelves. He took two apples and walked gingerly over to Hanai. The man was still busy marking the paper on the stoned pavement next to him. In his lap was a wooden flute. Karueq stood back from him a little so as to not disturb his final thoughts.

Hanai made a quick last note and then looked up at him. "Oh," he said, surprised. "Karueq." Without missing a beat, he eyed the apples in his guest's hand. "Mmm, apples." He took one from him with a gleeful look in his eye. He bit into it and then caught the stream of juice on his wrist that tried to escape from his chin. "Best apples in the north, though the south has sweeter ones." He bit into it again. "There's more juice in them the closer they grow to the mountains."

Karueq didn't have an appetite yet, though his icy journey since the feast on the ship should have made him famished. His current predicament froze his stomach. He took a small bite of the apple anyway to avoid being rude. It was indeed juicy, and the flavor was sweet with just a hint of tartness.

Hanai bit into his apple again. "Sit, man. I'm not going to bite, not with this gorgeous fruit in my hand." Karueq's hesitation was a little too long, because Hanai rolled his eyes. "Sit," he urged him.

Karueq lowered himself to the ground and let his legs hang over the edge.

"Welcome to Eleveria. How long have you been here?"

"I washed up on shore this morning."

"Washed up, huh?" He sized him up. "You must be the reason for the festivities. I gather you still have the Mark. That makes one. I wonder what the other could be."

"A funeral," Karueq informed him.

"A funeral?" Hanai's face was stricken with worry. "Henara? She wasn't supposed to leave until today."

"No, she never left. It's for a man named Quiron."

"Oh, Quiron." Hanai nodded after a moment. "We held festivities for several days after he turned to the light."

"He's returning here for a very different reason."

"Oh, he never set foot here in life," Hanai corrected him. "We just had a lot to celebrate. Alamar was safe from Quiron's bloodlust, and that meant Chelia was safer, and then there was obviously the miracle of Eleh turning a really, really evil heart. Oh! And a baby was born the next day. Mind you, those festivities by themselves lasted for more than a week -- Why are you so gloomy?"

Karueq came out of his head again. Hanai looked at him with a hint of concern. Karueq shifted uncomfortably. "It's been a long few weeks. I'm confused by the hospitality being shown to me." Karueq glanced back at the hall. "And I'm learning more than I can process about your people."

Hanai smirked. "Not who you thought we were, huh?"

Karueq shook his head.

Hanai elbowed him playfully. "Smile. You're free."

Karueq studied him. The joyful smile remained on his face. This was the same joy he'd seen many times in the field, but he never understood where it came from, and to be honest, he still didn't.

Hanai goaded him. "Come on. Eleh loves you and so do we. Smile."

For the first time in a very long time, Karueq's mouth turned up slightly into a genuine smile. He immediately felt sheepish.

"Ah, much better," teased the Eleverian. "I can't stand gloomy faces." He picked up the flute from his lap and blew a few whimsical notes. "I think you'll be the subject of my next piece of music. Brash tones to start," – he improvised an ominous line on his flute to illustrate, – "then a shrill section to commemorate your journey," – he played a taste of this section – "then a triumphant blast to announce your freedom" – he blew three loud tones in finality.

Karueq chuckled at the display despite himself. "I look forward to hearing it."

"That's the spirit." Hanai clapped him on the back.

Karueq's lighter mood ignited his appetite, and his stomach growled audibly. Hanai chuckled. "I knew that would work. Come with me."

Hanai led him back into the hall to the shelves. He pulled down an array of food and dumped it on the table. "Come. Eat."

CHAPTER THIRTEEN

THE BRAND REMOVED

----- ----- ----- ----- ----- ----- -----

Hanai spent the rest of the afternoon entertaining Karueq and raising his spirits. After several laughing fits at the Eleverian's antics, Karueq's eyes grew heavy, and he slumped onto one of the beds.

He slept peacefully that night, the most peacefully he'd slept in years. The next morning, the early sun woke him. Hanai was already seated on the terrace watching the sunrise. Karueq left the bed and joined him. He breathed the free air, drinking it in and taking notice of how it felt coursing through his body.

He surveyed all that lay before the fortress. The sun radiated quietly on the horizon and kissed the wispy clouds pink. The river glittered with the sunlight. The willow tree on the river's bank stood tall and cast its shadow toward the city. The horses grazed in peace on the bluff. The plain stood still, echoing the hush of the scene.

Hanai broke the quiet. "It didn't come today."

"What didn't?" Karueq asked.

"The ring of sunlight around the horizon." He looked to the right and to the left as if making sure he didn't miss it. Karueq remembered the

178

previous morning when he had seen such a ring while he was stranded in the bay. The rays of the sun had skated around the entire horizon as the sun sat low, and a few golden streaks had danced across the sky.

Hanai shrugged. "Still a beautiful sunrise." He smiled serenely. "Are you hungry?" He rose to his feet and walked back inside.

Karueq followed him, his stomach eager to join. They spread the food over the table again and began picking through it.

They were interrupted by the door opening. A man walked in slowly, limping on his right leg with a crutch under his arm. Hanai bounded up from the table and greeted him. "Nimera! You're here already?" He embraced the man, taking care to avoid his bad leg.

"I wasn't going to let them keep me down there for long," the man replied with a weary smile. He winced sharply. "Not when you're up here enjoying yourself."

Hanai reached behind him, grabbed a pendant from the hook, and helped Nimera place it around his neck. "Thank you," the man sighed. He turned on his good leg and limped to the table.

"Anything missing from the spread?" Hanai asked, reviewing the shelves.

The sick man looked over the table. "This is good, Hanai. Thank you." His eyes turned up to Karueq warmly. "Hello."

"Hello," Karueq returned the greeting.

Hanai returned to the table. "You're going to the festivities with us today, right?" he asked Nimera.

"Are you going to carry me down to the river?"

Hanai snorted. "I carried you out of Egypt. My task is done."

"Ha! Just because you knew your sister would beat you if you didn't get me out."

"She'll beat me anyway for letting you go it alone."

"She told me she was planning on it, regardless."

"Oh? When did you see her?"

"She took care of my leg."

Hanai looked under the table at Nimera's injured leg. "No wonder you were still down there until this morning."

Nimera elbowed Hanai in the ribs.

The door opened again. This time it was Chelia, carrying a bundle of white fabric in her hand.

"Good morning, gentlemen," she greeted them.

"Good morning, Chelia," said Nimera and Hanai in unison.

"How are the three of you doing?" she asked, sitting down at the table with them. She didn't touch the food.

"Khana made Nimera a cripple," Hanai blurted, a mischievous glint in his eye.

"You pick on her too much," Chelia scolded him, then looked under the table toward Nimera's leg. "Although she might have done better with her eyes open so she could see what she was doing."

"We could chop it off," Hanai suggested.

Nimera cleared his throat. "I'm sitting right here, you two."

"We can't chop it," Chelia went on, ignoring him. "Not when we can brace it straight. Then he can use it as a club."

"Oh, yeah, but what about when he rides? It'll flop around and cause drag."

"Again, I'm right here," blurted Nimera a little louder. He addressed Karueq. "Never trust Hondimai's children to ever make straight conversation."

"I'm telling Khana you said that," chuckled Hanai.

Nimera defended his aside. "She's the only one of you with a brain. She'll understand."

"Put that in your proposal," Hanai goaded.

Chelia shook her head. "Karueq, how are you feeling?"

"Better today, Captain. Thank you."

Hanai piped up again. "Captain, oh, captain!" he teased her.

Chelia giggled, shaking her head at Hanai, then turned to Karueq. "Please don't feel the need to address me as such, Karueq. You on the other hand," she rounded on Hanai, "will address me as either 'my lady' or 'my dear, dear, sweet sister'."

Hanai made a gagging noise. She returned to their guest. "May I have a word with you, Karueq?"

He nodded and rose from the table with her. They walked out of the hall into the hallway, and she closed the door behind them.

"I wanted to ask you again before we take you to the river," she began. "Is this what you want, to give your heart to Eleh?"

Karueq considered her words for a moment.

She spoke again before he responded. "This isn't just about removing the Mark. The Mark chains your heart and your soul, and nothing we can do can remove it. Eleh is the only one who can do that."

He gathered his thoughts before he spoke. "My lady, I fled from what I thought for years was the right company. I no longer believe in Shatan or his cause. I also know there is no middle ground. Everyone belongs either to Heaven or to Hell. I do not intend to go back, and when I consider what Eleh promises and the examples that your people have shown me, how can I refuse?"

"You know more than anyone who turned before you what is at stake. Eleh doesn't promise following Him will be easy, but He promises it is worth it. It is so worth it, Karueq. But know that for you, it will be especially hard. You will be hunted by everyone you know and persecuted with all the zeal you used to inspire in your soldiers. That is what awaits you in this choice, but I promise you it really is worth everything they will try to put you through."

"I have already made my decision, my lady," he responded, sincerely. "I know what awaits me at the hands of my former master. I would like to know what awaits me at the hands of my new master."

"King," she corrected with a smile. "He will be your King."

Karueq grinned, remembering the majesty from his vision in the sea. "I like the sound of that better."

Chelia handed him the white cloth in her hands. "These are for you - white for redemption. I'll collect you in an hour, and if my brother gives you any trouble in the meantime, feel free to tattle on him." She winked.

The trio in the recovery hall enjoyed the rest of their meal, and Karueq put on the white clothes. Hanai asked Nimera again if he would like to attend the festivities of the day, to which he replied that he would indeed, commenting on a need to return to normal life.

Chelia returned with Khana, who, with Hanai, assisted Nimera out of the room. Karueq followed them, nervous and thrilled at what the ceremony ahead would bring.

They walked out from the fortress and set Nimera on a horse. Khana guided the horse behind the little group to the south end of the city.

There, they entered an expansive and magnificent garden. Mighty trees produced a canopy that filtered the morning sunlight. Flowers burst from vines, bushes, carpeting plants, and tall stalks. Ferns shaded the soil. Gentle fountains watered the garden from underground springs buried beneath their feet. Tranquility nestled itself everywhere Karueq turned.

A large assembly gathered around a pool surrounded by blue and purple flowers. Quiron lay on an ornate blanket on the ground across the pool, dressed all in white. On one side of him, the earth had been dug up. On the other side stood Alamar watching the crowd gather. When everyone was settled, he began speaking.

"Today, we lay Quiron to rest. Quiron was everything we hope for when we minister to Seaga; a rescued heart utterly and totally devoted to God. I've heard the stories of those he himself rescued in the years since - men, women, and children all saved from the darkness. He is truly a wonderful example to us.

"In death, he claims his joy in Heaven. The lavish love Eleh poured out to him in life is ever more real to him now. Our prayer is that Eleh will transform every tear he shed into astounding joy and everlasting peace. He will forever be bound in endless love as he rests with Eleh for eternity."

Alamar turned to the body. "Go with God, Quiron. May you forever know the love He has for you."

Alamar bowed his head, and the crowd followed. Karueq too, bowed his head and offered a silent, clumsy prayer.

After several moments, soft music trickled through the air. All heads rose from their prayer and began singing. Alamar and several others scattered petals into the hollowed earth. Then, they wrapped the blanket around the body, picked it up, and gently lowered it into the grave.

The crowd began to move in a line past the grave, scattering a handful of petals over Quiron as they sang. Karueq followed them. Tears welled in his eyes as he passed by and let the petals fall from his hand. Quiron looked so peaceful, and Karueq tried to imagine that that face was mirrored on his face in Heaven.

Everyone returned to their place around the pool. The song changed. Alamar and the others with him moved the soil back in its place over the body. When they finished burying him, they erected a stone over it, a stone that bore a carving of Quiron's name and a symbol below it. Karueq noticed it was quite similar to the one carved on the door and pendants of the recovery hall, but not identical. This one had a third line in the middle, reaching up to the peak made by the other lines.

The song ended. Everyone gathered stretched out their hands toward the grave. "Eliuma," they all spoke in unison.

Then, they all turned to leave. Alamar made no motion to follow. Instead, he knelt down beside the grave, placed his hand on the stone, and bowed his head. Chelia walked through the departing crowd and knelt down beside him. Karueq looked on, thinking they must be offering their forgiveness for the sins he committed.

"They're standing in place of the family," a hushed voice interrupted him. Karueq looked up to find Hanai next to him. "The family stays behind to mourn for a while. Quiron has no family here, so Chelia and Alamar are staying behind to mourn him."

The sorrow in Karueq's heart tightened. "...May I?"

Hanai squeezed his shoulder and nodded. Karueq walked as softly as he could around the pool to the grave. He hesitated once he got near. He heard them talking with each other.

They looked up at him. "It's alright," Alamar beckoned him. "You're welcome to join us."

He knelt down by the stone. Chelia squeezed his hand.

"He sure had a fire burning in him," Alamar stated, staring warmly at the stone.

"He did indeed," Chelia agreed. "Almost took you out." She exchanged a nostalgic look with him. "His heart changed, but that fire didn't."

"No," Alamar responded. "He saved a great many people after he was saved. He was a very happy man in the last few years."

"Yes. I remember when he invited us to his first-year celebration. We hadn't planned on quite that much fun. The dancing alone..."

Alamar chuckled. "He danced you around more than I had in a while."

Chelia laughed. "I imagine he won't stop dancing for eternity now." She turned to Karueq. "What do you remember about him?"

Karueq was taken aback at the invitation. He wondered what he could say that wouldn't spoil the happiness of the memories these two had of him. "They... were celebrating him on that night. Such merriment as I had never seen." They nodded, encouraging him. "He was a happy man. His crew loved him..." Tears formed in his eyes. He couldn't help himself. "... I took it away from him. I'm sorry." He wiped his eyes, embarrassed.

He felt a hand on his shoulder. "This is what grieving is for," Alamar consoled him. "The dead are alive and happy. It is us that need the comfort their memories bring in their absence. What more do you remember?"

The shuttering ebbed away from Karueq's breathing. "Shatan was upset indeed to lose him. He was a valuable soldier with a stony conviction. I was surprised to be informed of his defection."

"I have to say it even surprised us," Alamar added. "I was sure that was the end of me." He looked over at Chelia.

The tears returned to Karueq's eyes. He cursed himself for ordering such evils, not just on the Eleverians but on every man, woman, and child who wouldn't bend to Shatan's will. He sat there, teary-eyed, deeply embarrassed at his state.

He could hold onto the pitifully dignified crying no more. He buried his face in his hands, ashamed.

Then he felt their arms around him. They held him for what seemed like ages as his eyes continued to drain. They didn't back away. They held him, warm and safe, until finally he could cry no more.

He stiffly wiped his face and rubbed his eyes. Chelia sat back from him to let him breathe, but Alamar kept his hand on Karueq's shoulder.

"My friend," Alamar began, "you are forgiven for everything." Karueq looked up at him hesitantly. The man gave him a soft, reassuring smile. "Everything," Alamar repeated, and Karueq was painfully reminded that this forgiveness included the death of his brother, Aryngo.

Karueq sniffed and nodded. "Thank you."

Alamar turned his attention back to the stone and placed his hand thoughtfully on it. "We'll give you a moment alone with him."

He and Chelia placed their hands on the stone for a moment. Then they rose and walked away around the pool.

Karueq sat in uncomfortable silence for a few minutes. He was unsure what he should do. The steely man he knew had been replaced years before. The Quiron he met on the ship was a stranger – a stranger who was intensely happy and full of vibrant life.

Karueq placed his hand on the stone. He apologized for all the things he'd made him do. He ended his little prayer by remarking on the peace that happy sailor found at the end of his life. With this prayer, he felt a weight lift from his shoulders. He sighed contentedly. If Quiron could find peace, perhaps he could, too.

He left the grave and walked back the way they came, the lightness in his steps renewed. Chelia and Alamar were seated on a pair of boulders not far from the pool. They both smiled and rose as he came around the bend.

"Are you ready?" Chelia asked, barely hiding her excitement.

Karueq nodded eagerly.

The trio left the garden and turned away from the fortress city. Karueq saw a crowd on the bluff before the river. His nerves trembled. Chelia and Alamar led him through the crowd. Those they passed smiled at him, and some clasped his shoulder.

At the edge of the bluff, he looked down. The ground between the bluff and the river was covered with more people. More found places to stand on the single, narrow pathway that led down the face of the cliff. Chelia, Alamar, and Karueq passed by these people, too, on their way to the river. More smiles turned on him. Many of the faces were familiar, but he failed to place their names. Perhaps he'd never bothered to learn them in the first place.

They reached the bank near the willow tree, and Karueq followed Chelia and Alamar in removing his boots. Here, the river did not run so wild, rather it was tame enough that Alamar and Chelia strode out into it until they were waist deep. They turned around and motioned for him to follow them.

He stepped in and sloshed through the water after them, trodding eagerly through the soft, sandy riverbed. Alamar turned him around to face the crowd. They all extended their hands toward him. Chelia and Alamar placed their hands on his shoulders.

Alamar spoke. "Karueq, may Eleh bless you richly. May you walk with him now and always. May you know His love and kindness and grow to know His heart."

Chelia took over. "Karueq, do you accept Eleh as the Lord of your life and your heart?"

Karueq responded. "Yes."

"Do you reject Shatan and all the promises of Hell?"

"Yes."

"Do you reject evil works and pledge to resist temptation?"

"Yes."

"By your promises and the decision of your heart, we wash you clean."

Alamar and Chelia took hold of his arms. "Deep breath," she whispered to him.

Karueq took a deep breath and closed his eyes. Then, they submerged him. The water rushed over his head.

A soft glow suddenly appeared around the edge of his vision, even though his eyes were still closed. It grew brighter and fanned across his eyelids. It continued to burn brighter with such great intensity, he heard himself screaming at the blinding light.

It only brightened, shattering his mind then reaching down deep into his chest. He felt as if he were about to explode. Something dark jerked in his chest like a stubborn root being forced to rip out.

The ripping continued, the light nor the dark giving way. The light tightened its grip and continued to pull. Suddenly, the darkness ripped from him. The light flashed brighter and speared his mind. Then he lost consciousness.

CHAPTER FOURTEEN

THE GATHERING STORM

Soft daylight glowed through the windows. Karueq's eyes blinked open sleepily. There was a dull ache at the base of his skull and his left arm was sore. He stretched away the fog from his mind and propped himself up. The ache in his skull spiked, forcing him to lay back down and rub his temple.

"You're a live one right away, aren't you?" a voice chuckled to his right. He turned one open eye in that direction to find Alamar seated on a stool near the opposite wall. "Do you always bolt out of bed when you're recovering?"

Karueq cast his eyes about the room, a fairly large chamber that housed many beds like the one from which he stared. There were windows in the walls on two adjoining sides. A large cabinet similar to the one in the recovery hall stood on the opposite wall. Shelves filled with blankets and bandages lined every wall. A shelf near each bed held a pitcher and a basin.

Alamar rose from the stool, walked over to Karueq, and examined him. "You've been out for more than a day, but you seem to have recovered well - except for the scarring. There's very little we can do about that."

Karueq's eyes widened, and he tugged at his loose sleeve. He ignored the throbbing in his head and peered at the flesh on his arm. A mass of scar tissue had taken the place of the flesh where the Mark had been – and the Mark was gone.

Karueq pinched and prodded the smear. It was real, at least it felt real. He could swear it was - no tricks, no illusions.

His memory crashed open, the bright light and the excruciating pain tearing through him. He turned back to Alamar, who had an unmistakable smile on his face. "What happened?"

Alamar pulled Karueq's arm toward him and inspected the scar. "The Mark was rooted in you very deep, so it was harder on you than most to have it removed. It was undoubtedly strangling you, but you never knew it. Most people don't have that extreme a reaction."

"Am I...?" Karueq's stammering question was lost in his disbelief.

Alamar's smile doubled. "You are free indeed, and you've chosen who you will serve."

Karueq's joy spread across his face, and he peered again at his scar in delight.

"Rest for now," Alamar said, reaching to the shelf next to the bed. He handed the free man a cup of water, which he took gratefully. "When you're ready, I'll take you to the recovery hall."

Karueq laid back down, his body still requesting a respite. He faded in and out of sleep for several more hours. By the time Karueq's aching head quit protesting him, the room was lit with the oranges and reds of sunset.

He propped himself up and found that Alamar was still seated on the stool, working with a tangle of leather that looked like a horse's bridle. Karueq's stirring borrowed his attention from his work. "Good evening. How are you feeling?"

"Much better, thank you," Karueq replied.

"Do you think you can manage yourself?"

"Yes."

"Take a minute to think about it," Alamar encouraged. "I can't know your body better than you."

Karueq was reminded of how Alamar had treated that Seagan man years ago at the broken canal system. Karueq took an inquisitive breath to explore his muscles and search out anything that might be alarming. "I'm much better now, thank you," he insisted, sure that whatever trauma the Mark had caused him was unimportant.

"Alright," Alamar nodded. "Come with me."

Karueq rose and followed Alamar from the chamber through a few halls and up the stairs to the recovery hall. The Eleverians they passed along the way smiled warmly at him and bid him a good evening.

Alamar opened the door, and the setting sun bathed the hall in amber light through the wide-open doors.

The room, however, wasn't peaceful as Karueq remembered it from days earlier. The sound of bitter weeping came from the man folded over on the edge of one of the beds. Karueq recognized him immediately from his bandaged leg. Several Eleverians surrounded him, not saying a word. Khana held him tightly. Hanai, Chelia, and several others Karueq didn't know sat around him with solemn expressions.

Chelia looked up at the sound of their entrance. She gave Karueq a half smile but put her finger to her lips. Alamar took down one of the pendants and motioned for Karueq to follow him quietly out to the terrace.

Once they were out of earshot, Karueq's curiosity couldn't be contained. "Alamar, what happened?"

Alamar looked back into the hall. "I'm not the right person to ask. I know he had a tough mission, but beyond that, I can't say."

Alamar looped the pendant over Karueq's head. Karueq started to protest, but he stopped himself. Instead, he studied it for a moment. He let himself accept their hospitable invitation.

"You still have full range of the hall," said Alamar, looking back at the group surrounding Nimera. "Just please be respectful of Nimera's recovery."

Karueq nodded. Indeed, he would. Alamar dipped his head to Karueq and then left the hall. Chelia followed Alamar out, but then promptly returned. Instead of rejoining her comrades around the utterly broken man, Chelia crossed the hall and joined Karueq on the terrace.

"Karueq," she smiled warmly. "It's so wonderful having you back." She embraced him for a moment. "Even better now that you're whole. Sit with me."

She crossed the terrace to the ledge and swung her legs over the lip of the wide apron. Karueq joined her.

"You're going to hear this soon enough," she began. "I would rather you heard it from me first. Nothing that has happened recently is your fault at all. Don't dwell on your part in it."

Karueq's stomach suddenly felt hollow.

"Tell me what you see," she inquired, turning her eyes on the expanse of the plains beyond the river. The sky was bidding its last farewell. The brilliant orange had given way to soft pinks with calm, gray hues gathering before them from the sun setting behind the mountains.

"I see the coming night… it's beautiful" he answered. He looked around, trying to find whatever she was trying to draw her attention to.

"Yes," she said, as if he had already answered her riddle. "The sunrises and sunsets are quite beautiful, but they're incomplete." She turned away from the wonderful spectacle and searched him. "Eleveria has always been hidden from the world. Eleh put a shield around us to protect this land, to provide us with a safe haven where the Shatanala can't reach us. The shield –" she looked around at the entirety of what they could see "– used to glow at sunset and sunrise, making a ring around the whole horizon. That ring is gone, as is our protection. It shattered when a Mark of Shatan crossed into our borders."

Karueq immediately felt sick. Before he could say anything, Chelia continued. "I left you on that island. The sin is mine. Never, ever think that you are to blame for this."

"…but it was my Mark," Karueq tried to argue.

"We are sworn never to abandon anyone," she refuted. "I was so angry at the trap that had been set for us and so afraid that we would be captured again that I left you there. I'm so sorry, Karueq. Will you forgive me for that?"

Karueq stared at her aghast. He couldn't fathom how she could possibly turn something like that into an apology.

She seemed to have read his thoughts. "I'm asking your forgiveness for betraying you, even if you didn't ask to be saved at the time."

"How could this possibly be your conclusion about the matter? It's natural to be angry, to be afraid, to make mistakes."

"Yes, it is. I don't deny that. We make mistakes all the time, but we are called to do better. Eleh has given us the privilege to take part in His salvation story. Our actions shape the stories of others. He gives us the opportunity to be His action to His people. *That* is what we do. The combat missions we launch against the Shatanala are merely a distraction against them so that we can bring aid to Seaga and share Eleh's love with them.

"To those who have been given much, much is asked in return. My people have been given vast gifts and talent and knowledge. We are asked to do more than nearly anyone in Seaga, because we can – and we love doing so. The work we do is so rewarding, it makes our suffering worth it. So, when we refuse to do the work, we expose ourselves to dangers such as the one I brought on us now. I refused to help you because of my arrogance and fear. I abandoned you, and I never should have done that. I'm better than that. Can you forgive me?"

Karueq was still in disbelief, but he was able to utter, "Yes." What she said seemed to make sense, though he didn't know what sense it was. He supposed he'd have to give up and think about it at some other point.

"Thank you," she said, sincerely. "It means a great deal."

"What happens now?" he asked. "With your protection gone, what will happen?"

She sighed, but there was still a sense of determination about her. "It will take some time for the Shatanala to find us, but they'll find us. I have no doubt they'll keep searching for you, and that alone will lead them here. To that end, we will defend our land whatever happens. This is our home and the place from which we aid Seaga."

"I'll help in any way I can," Karueq offered, earnestly.

Chelia smiled. "We won't enlist your help needlessly, and you owe us nothing, but if there is anything you could tell us, we would be glad of your insight."

Karueq nodded.

Hanai appeared on the terrace and sat down next to Chelia. He stared forward at the gathering twilight, the splendid colors having disappeared.

She turned to address him. "How is he?"

Hanai, with an uncharacteristically serious expression, glanced back into the hall. "He's asleep now. Khana is going to sit with him through the night."

"How are you doing?" she asked him.

He didn't speak for a moment, but eventually found the words he was looking for. "I'll return quicker than he will, but my days up here have just grown longer." He came out of his own head and made polite eye contact with Chelia. "I don't need anything from you tonight, but I want to be present for the Guard briefings as long as I'm up here."

Chelia nodded and hugged him. He hugged her back, and it seemed to be the thing he needed most in that moment. A faint part of his whimsical expression returned to his face.

Chelia planted a kiss on Hanai's forehead and then rose to leave. "Sleep well, you two." She returned to the hall and bid Khana good night before leaving. The rest of the group had cleared out as well.

Karueq was curious about the ordeal, but he hesitated.

Hanai spoke first. "You're awake," he observed, a half-smile spreading his mouth beneath his still barren eyes.

"Yes. Alamar told me I was out most of the day."

"I didn't expect to see you up here tonight. Welcome back." He clasped Karueq's shoulder.

Karueq returned the friendly gesture with an uneasy chuckle. "It seems that's about the only joy around recently," he noted, his eyes wandering back to the bed containing Nimera.

Hanai sighed. "It's not the only joy around. There are a great many things we still smile about. You've just seen a lot of our pain in a short time."

"May I ask what happened?" Karueq almost felt sick that he asked.

Hanai, however, seemed unphased by the question. "We were on an aid mission in Egypt. It wasn't supposed to end in combat. I only went because I hadn't done an aid mission in far too long. You were keeping the Guard so busy recently. Three of us - me, Nimera, and a man named Vyrion - were there to help a poor community learn trades and farming so they might make a livelihood for themselves and sustain their families."

Karueq's stomach twisted.

Hanai continued. "In less than a day of arriving, we discovered a slave trade the Shatanala were running out of the community - mostly children. We were greatly outnumbered, vastly outnumbered. Nimera was severely injured, and I barely got him out alive. I only ran from the battle long enough to get Nimera away - less than a minute - and by the time I returned, they had moved the children, and I couldn't find any of them. All they left behind was Vyrion's body."

Hanai paused, sighing the intense emotion of the memory away. "Aid missions always carry dangers with them. We know this. The Shatanala, and even some Seagans, attack us no matter our mission. Any mission to just go and help people can turn sour. But this mission looked much more like something I face with the Eleka Guard. The Guard, alone, is asked to do such awful missions because we know how to return home after such things. It will take a very long time for Nimera to completely return to us. He's resilient, so he will return, but there are some horrors in war - like not being able to help even a single child slave - that are better left to those who dive into them knowing there will be no perfect outcome."

Karueq's glance wandered to the sleeping man, Khana watching over him like a guardian.

Hanai continued, and it seemed like he was simply thinking out loud to himself rather than talking to Karueq. "He'll have good days and bad days. The bad days will outweigh the good for a while. He'll put on a brave face for Khana sometimes because he wants to be strong for her, but she knows what these missions entail. She may be the captain of the aid mission teams and never once thought of being in the Guard, but she's our sister. She's kept vigil for us far too many times in this hall. Especially when we first created the Guard..." He trailed off and sighed. "This is why Eleh is so important to us, Karueq. He gives us purpose and life and joy that no one can steal. People commit evil deeds, and they try to take away our joy, but in Him we stand firm and withstand everything they throw at us."

Karueq nodded.

Hanai glanced into the hall and then rose to his feet. "Good night, Karueq."

Karueq bid him a good night in return. He wasn't ready for sleep yet. Instead, he looked out on what lay before him, not committing to any of the thoughts swirling in his head.

A single star blinked at him from the sky, its brothers hidden in the darkening gray of twilight. A subtle breeze trickled through the evening and feathered his loose hair. At the lip of the bluff, the horses barely moved in their grazing. Even the rapids of the river were quieting for the night. Such a peaceful sight in the forefront of the sad scene behind him.

Then, a shadow caught Karueq's eye. It moved across the sky from the mountain. Another followed it. The dragons glided effortlessly across the river and out to the plain, almost lost to sight without the sun.

After several more minutes, his mind wandered to the beds in the hall. He glanced around at the land one more time then crept into the hushed hall.

Khana was still awake holding Nimera's hand, and he stopped at the foot of the bed. "I'm sorry," he whispered to her. Her expression betrayed her confusion. He glanced at Nimera's face. He wasn't sleeping peacefully, rather he looked consumed by his exhaustion. "I set up the trade in that region…" His confession needed no more detail than that.

"I think you'll find it exhausting to seek forgiveness for everything ever done under your command. We do forgive you, Karueq."

"I'm sure I'll learn to accept that someday."

Khana nodded. "He'll be alright you know," she said, tilting her head toward Nimera. "We're never down for long. I expect he'll be burning to go search for those children when his leg is healed."

"Is there anything I can do?"

She shook her head. "Not tonight. Get some rest."

He dipped his head politely and retreated to bed.

In the morning, he awoke to the sound of rain. The gray light illuminated the room through the closed door panes. A restrained laugh came from the table, and Karueq turned his head. Hanai and Nimera snickered at each other, trying to keep from getting too loud. Nimera noticed Karueq's rising first.

"Sorry, Karueq. Did we wake you?" he asked, coughing out another laugh.

"Not at all," Karueq denied. He threw off the blankets and stretched. The pendant around his neck drooped, catching his attention briefly. He managed a smile at this, deciding again that he could accept the Eleverians' goodwill and all the good that happened to him the last few days.

The men laughed again, and Karueq inspected what they were doing. There was a small pile of food separate from the abundant breakfast they were enjoying. Between them was a toppled stack of the foods from that pile.

"Go again, go again," Nimera egged. Hanai grabbed an orange and put his hand over his eyes. He waved his hand carefully through the air over the table.

Nimera snickered again. "Stop it," Hanai scolded him. "I'm concentrating." His fingers touched the stack, and he carefully lowered the orange toward the top of it. Nimera poked the fruit. Hanai cleared his throat in defiance and repositioned the orange over the stack. The bottom connected with the wide piece of jerky at the top. Hanai began to let go of the precarious tower slowly, monitoring every little movement of the orange with his finger pads.

Finally, the tip of his finger left the surface. Nimera scoffed at him, and Hanai took his hand away from his eyes. He pumped his fists in the air. "Ha! Beat that!" he exclaimed.

Nimera shook his head and chose a wide lettuce leaf.

"Really?" Hanai whined. "You're going the easy route?"

"My pride isn't as precious as yours. I'm not as foolish as you," he replied, covering his eyes.

"There's more fun in foolishness."

Karueq sat down next to them and began eating as Nimera began feeling for the stack. Hanai sneaked another orange from the pile and held it in the air just to the side of the stack. Nimera found Hanai's orange and proceeded to place the leaf carefully on top. As soon as he let go of it, Hanai dropped the orange and sent the leaf crashing into the stack. The tower tumbled onto the table.

Nimera quickly opened his eyes to view the unfortunate pile. Hanai bust up laughing. Nimera glared at the decoy fruit and tossed it at the imp. "Cheat," he chuckled.

Hanai retrieved the orange from the floor. "I used my resources. I never cheat."

Nimera shook his head. "You think being sly is the same thing as resourcefulness."

"I get it from my mother." Hanai peeled said resource and ate it.

"I'm sure she's never been prouder of her son."

It astounded Karueq to see the difference in Nimera this morning.

The door opened. Chelia poked her head into the hall. "Good morning gentlemen. I'm sorry to interrupt. Hanai, Guard briefing. Now."

Hanai rose from the table, taking a strip of jerky with him.

Chelia turned her eyes on Karueq. "Karueq, you're welcome, too, if you feel up to it."

Karueq nodded and rose, too. Without saying anything else to elaborate, she led Hanai and Karueq quickly away and to the great hall.

There, the Eleka Guard had gathered in the center of the hall, along with Alamar and a few others Karueq didn't recognize.

"Thank you for coming so quickly," Chelia greeted them. She wasted no time in moving on to the business at hand. "Shatanala scouts have found the gateway."

Those gathered exchanged rapid, concerned looks.

"They're not aware of exactly what they found, but they do recognize that this is territory controlled by us."

Karueq's mind automatically began calculating everything this could mean.

"We're detaining them elsewhere, as they're showing no signs of turning. We did find out who their team leader is – a woman named Ingana – but she wasn't among the party."

"How long until she notices they're gone?" Henara asked.

"As far as our intelligence goes," Chelia explained, "within a week." She turned to Karueq. "What do you think, Karueq?"

Karueq cleared his throat. "That would usually be a wise assessment, however, I know the girl in question. She's a new leader tasked with bringing in defectors, and her commitment to her orders should not be underestimated. She will investigate within a few days."

Chelia rubbed her head. "That leaves us with a day – two at most – to come up with something."

"Drive them mad," Karueq suggested.

Chelia turned a very serious look on him. "And how would you do that?"

Karueq shifted uncomfortably, keenly aware that he'd dipped into his old pattern of thinking while talking strategy.

"Out of the question," she said, shortly. "Any other ideas?" she asked the room.

"She's out for defectors," Honai reminded her. "Divert her focus to track the scouts instead."

"How long can we keep that up?" another Guard member asked. "She's looking for Karueq. Eventually she'll send another team."

"Or send another team right away while she's tracking these scouts down."

"We can detain that team, too."

"Right, and then eventually we'll have to detain all of Xanadai. Not to mention, we'll have to capture them at different locations in order to keep them from getting suspicious that there's something important here."

Chelia interrupted them. "We only need to buy time. We've done more with less before."

"Do you know how to repair the gateway and restore the dome?" Hanai asked.

"Not at the moment," she said, a hint of frustration. "We'll have to do our best to figure that out. If it becomes necessary, I'll stand in as long as I can." Several of them threw an odd look at her, but she continued unabated. "All else aside, we may need to prepare for war even earlier than we thought."

She turned to Karueq. "How soon would the Shatanala attempt to attack us once they found out where we are?"

Karueq pondered the question for a moment. "Shatan is like a wounded animal right now. He may attack the day he finds out."

"He can't muster a large number in such haste, can he?" asked one of the Guard.

"Unfortunately, he can. There are legions below ground waiting to taste blood. Many of them are out of practice, but just like you kept your strategies hidden, so have we."

Chelia locked eyes with him, and he watched her disassembling his statement while the rest of the group continued to argue strategy. In that formidable mind of hers, she was doing the very thing he never stopped doing as commander.

Then, she abruptly shook her head. The calculation was gone from her eyes, and she returned to the conversation.

"Is it really war he wants?" someone not from the Guard asked. "He wages open combat in skirmishes. He can't really want a larger confrontation."

"He's tried to wage larger battles before," said another. "Mount Caramel was just one of those instances. Knowing Eleveria is exposed would be the greatest motivation he has to gather his full power against us."

"Then we bring the fight to him," one suggested.

"How? We know nothing of their lair except where it is. Yes, we have an insider," the man pointed to Karueq, "but that will only take us so far."

"We fight him on Seagan soil. Rather poetic if you think about it," said Hanai.

Chelia chastised the idea gently. "We're not going to wage war in Seaga and risk lives."

Hanai nodded. "We lure him to a neutral site, away from any settlements."

"How do we do that if they want to attack us here? They would never meet us where we want to fight. They would instead take the opportunity to invade here while our forces are elsewhere."

"We'll have to make sure they don't find out we're vulnerable before we meet them."

"They won't come, regardless," Henara denied. "We have nothing to dangle in front of them."

Karueq refuted her. "That's not entirely true." He glanced at Chelia. The group followed his glance. Chelia looked at him, but her face was unreadable.

Honai asked, "What exactly is that?"

Karueq explained, "Shatan would consider listening to a bargain for the Elequiri, especially if you made it convincing, and especially if you offered her up as the Crucible."

Mouths stood agape. The looks they exchanged this time were stunned, searching, and unmistakably frightened.

Henara pierced him with her stare. "How do you know about the Crucible?"

"I only heard a rumor that such a thing exists," he replied.

Chelia held up her hand to silence further discussion. "I'll question him later about this rumor and brief the Guard. We won't discuss it now." Agreement murmured through the group, but the group remained a little tense.

"It doesn't make sense to dangle the Elequiri in front of Shatan," someone reasoned. "He has to know by now how resolute you are."

"We'll have to come up with something else."

"We're still going to wage war on him?"

They turned to Chelia for a decision. "You've brought forth excellent ideas. I'm not opposed to an open fight if we can fight on our terms. Convince me of a plan that you think will work and we'll implement it. In the meantime, we will use the detainees as decoys and prepare to have our borders threatened. Thank you all for coming. You're dismissed."

The group dispersed, most of the group leaving the hall through the front entrance. Two left by way of the rear entrance to the right of the thrones. Only Alamar and Chelia remained with Karueq.

Karueq looked between the two, waiting for them to speak. They were doing what Honai and Henara had done on the beach upon discovering him, exchanging a whole conversation without saying a word.

Finally, Alamar spoke to him. "You said you heard a rumor. Explain."

He said simply, "Shatan mentioned it before I defected."

Alamar waited for him to elaborate. Upon getting no answer, "What more did he say? We need to know everything."

Karueq rummaged through his memory, making sure he remembered everything. The problem was there was only one thing. "Shatan enchanted my pendant to detect the Crucible. I assumed it was to detect the Elequiri. He never told me anything about the Crucible until a minute before I defected."

"Who else is aware of it?" asked Alamar.

"Of this thing called the Crucible?"

"Yes. Anyone beyond you and Shatan."

"Not that I know. What is it?"

Chelia sighed impatiently. "It's me, Karueq. I thought that was obvious."

"Yes, but what does it mean?"

Alamar deferred to Chelia, but she only said, "Nothing I feel like divulging now. Maybe we'll explain another day."

"Is no one else supposed to know?"

"No one outside Eleveria and Shatan," said Alamar. "Now, of course, you."

"You're sure there is no one else among the Shatanala who knows and nothing else he said?"

"I'm sure no one else knew before I left. Being absent, I can't guarantee more."

"Thank you," she said shortly. "You may return to recovery."

Karueq stood planted where he was. His curiosity about the Crucible itched viciously. He almost voiced his question several times but swallowed it.

Chelia sighed softly. "You'll have to wait, Karueq," she requested. "Give me time to process this myself."

The itch eased, as he couldn't deny her request. He thought his admission was harmless, but of course she would need to deal with it, whatever it had revealed.

Karueq dipped his head politely and headed back to the recovery hall.

He spent the rest of the morning with Nimera and Hanai. When the rain stopped about noon, they opened the doors to let in the breeze and the sun that was pulling itself through the heavy clouds.

For the rest of the day, Hanai pointed out all the landmarks they could see from the terrace – the Glasphen River before them, the Lenara plains beyond, the Veranaz mountains surrounding them. He even told him about the dragons' colony that lay deep in the mountain range at a hidden place known as Zetha. He described the landforms Karueq saw on his way into Eleveria – Zarenvai Bay, Mount Cavraz disappearing into the sky, Montima Valley, the Ranovan Forest stretching beyond what he could see from the dragon's back.

At last, the day came to a close. Although the question about the Crucible still tapped on the door of his mind, he again slept peacefully that night.

CHAPTER FIFTEEN

WITH OPEN EYES

----- ----- ----- ----- ----- ----- -----

Karueq's legs dangled over the ledge as he drank deeply of the view from the terrace. He knew the sights by name now, and it brought a little deeper meaning to his appreciation.

In his mind, Karueq superimposed Sheol on what he saw. Everything was contrasted between this beauty and the murk of the underground – from the colors to the heat and the feeling of peace he felt. How very different it felt to be here, and how beautiful a sight he beheld. He locked these images and sensations away in his memory, along with all the nights during his internment as commander when the moon was clear overhead and the breeze was cool.

Today, Hanai wasn't on the terrace with him. He'd left the hall before either of the other men rose, and Karueq suspected he was meeting with some of the Guard. There were two others in the beds behind him, Eleverians coming back from their missions during the night. He didn't know their names, but he told himself to make a point of rectifying this as soon as he saw them awake.

Karueq left the terrace quietly, and, careful not to disturb the two new inhabitants, set out an array of food as he'd seen Hanai do every morning. He took special care in setting out those things Nimera seemed to enjoy most before the man joined him. They talked in hushed tones over their breakfast.

Karueq had made up his mind about something soon after the Guard meeting where they discussed the scouts. So, while he and Nimera ate, he asked him where he might find Chelia. The man's advice was to locate Hunga somewhere in the fortress. He would know where she was. It would be nearly impossible to tell otherwise if she was even within the borders of Eleveria. Karueq noticed happily that Nimera was having a good day and silently prayed that it would last until evening.

Karueq left and wandered through the halls, greeting passersby as he went. His leisurely pace let him admire the architecture of the fortress. The great hallways were constructed of white and tan marble and filled with light streaming in from the windows. The doors leading to halls and rooms were constructed with carefully carved wood. Gold and silver engravings decorated the doors, the walls, and the ceilings. The ceilings themselves swept up from the walls and came together to form a groove inlaid with silver.

He peeked quietly into some of the rooms in search of Hunga. The rooms, too, were ornate and inviting with the sun's light illuminating the space. Xanadai, in all its grotesque grandeur, could not compete with the beauty of this place.

He finally stumbled on Hunga a few hours later, conversing with a pair of Eleverians dressed for a mission just inside the main door to the fortress. They acknowledged his approach, and he stood off quietly while they finished their conversation. After a few minutes, Hunga clasped them on the shoulder, smiled, and gave them a few encouraging words before the pair left to wander back outside.

Hunga turned to Karueq and greeted him. "Karueq, it's good to see you awake."

"Thank you, Hunga," he replied.

"What can I do for you?"

"I'm looking for Chelia. I was told you would know where to find her."

"She's meeting with the Eleka Guard," Hunga informed him. "Alamar is with her, if you were going to ask for him next in her absence. Is there something I can do for you until she returns?"

Thought for a moment. "Perhaps," he said, removing the recovery pendant from around his neck and holding it out to Hunga. "I can do far more than sit in a room idling my time away. I would like to join one of your teams."

"That is highly generous of you."

"I was at the highest rank among the Shatanala for many years. I can be a great asset to you. Your hospitality is generous, and it has allowed me to find peace so quickly, but I must do something. I've put you in great danger, but I can help you protect yourselves from the armies I led against you. Please accept my help."

"We want you to know that it's not your fault at all what happened to the shield. Don't try to win favor and forgiveness. You already have it. We hold no account of your sins. However, if you wish to occupy yourself and work alongside us, we will accept it. What do you have in mind?"

"Let me go out and help you route the teams that come against you."

Hunga chuckled. "You may do that someday, but not now. Besides, missions strictly for combat are usually reserved for the Eleka Guard. I can only authorize such things of my own power in emergencies or when the Elequiri is long disposed."

"Then, I would like to do something useful in the meantime."

"Do you intend to remain among us?"

"What do you mean?"

"Do you intend not to return to Seaga and start a new life?"

The question startled Karueq. He'd been in this life so long, waging the wars of angels and demons, that he hadn't thought of claiming any other life. Still, he found he truly did not intend to forsake this life for the ordinary life of Seaga. "No, Hunga. I can't stand aside during this war - tilling fields and living in peace - when I can and want to do more, especially knowing what I know."

Hunga nodded. "We figured as much." He held out his hand and took Karueq's recovery pendant. "Relinquishing your recovery is not binding. Should you need to return to it, you are welcome to do so, however, you can't return during a mission."

"Understood."

"We will indeed send you out if you wish – a simple aid mission. I'll send a member of the Eleka Guard to accompany the mission, since you are an attractive and recognizable target for the Shatanala."

"When do we leave?" Karueq asked.

Hunga chuckled. "I admire your courage and eagerness. If you truly do choose to do this, meet me here at mid-afternoon for the assignment and briefing."

"Thank you, Hunga... and I apologize for all the injustice we did to you during your captivity."

Hunga clasped him on the shoulder. "All is forgiven." With that, he turned to leave.

"What shall I do to prepare until then?"

Hunga turned with a smile and a raised brow. "Pray."

Karueq stood there awkwardly, staring after the Keeper as he left. He didn't know what to do with such a suggestion, but he thought of a way to help him figure it out, so he turned to the open door and wandered outside.

His path led him to the gardens on the south side of the fortress. Instead of following the path toward Quiron's grave, he wandered around gazing at the beautiful colors and the wondrous displays. The individual gardens had themes all their own. The foliage and the rocks came together to suggest images of wheat fields and oceans and dragons and all manner of beauty.

His path led him to a particular garden bursting with brilliant oranges and yellows. In the middle was an open space with a petite waterfall on the far end. Surrounding this waterfall were more orange and yellow flowers in the shape of a sunrise. A border of yellow flowers surrounded the clearing. A little tree with thin leaves and slender, white flowers stood proud in the center.

A stone and new grass near the border on the left coaxed Karueq's eye away from the display. He recognized the symbol on it, the same symbol of three lines that was carved into the stone at Quiron's funeral.

He approached the stone, curious to know who would be buried here. Upon seeing the name, his shoulders sagged – Aryngo.

He sat down by the grave and whispered his regrets to the stone. His regret reigned in a little, reminded of the forgiveness the Eleverians lavishly bestowed on him.

Someone sat down next to him, and he startled at the sudden intruder he hadn't heard approach him.

"What brought you out here?" Chelia asked him.

His eyes fixed on the stone before him. "Just wandering...and now apologizing."

"If you took responsibility for every grave we've dug, you'd be here 'til even your bones turned to dust."

"I guess so." He turned an inquisitive eye on her. "Hunga said you were occupied meeting with the Guard."

"Yes. I had them meet out here in the gardens. We were just coming back when I saw you walk by." Chelia's eyes fell on the gravestone. "This grave, especially, is not your fault."

"I killed him."

"Yes, you drew his blood, but it was I who put him in the ground," she confessed. "There has been much happening here you don't know about."

Karueq's confusion reeled. He couldn't imagine what fault this woman could claim for what happened in that tent. "He saved you. If you're to blame for him pretending to be you when we thought he indeed was, you need a deeper share of this freedom and forgiveness you preach."

"No, that's not it," she dismissed him. "Alamar and I picked a fight after my actions at Mount Caramel. He was so fearful when I went into that tower with you and Jezebel. I was annoyed and blinded by my pride at his reproach - which was a reasonable reproach – so I refused to let him come with me on missions." She let a sardonic snort fly from her lips. "The Elequiri refusing the Quiri. So, Aryngo insisted that I take him along instead as a stand in for his brother. His pretense and death were his final act to protect me."

"We were tracking the Guard in hopes of catching him," Karueq countered. "He was dead as soon as he set foot in that area."

"Neither of us had any business being there. I knew it was a trap, though I didn't know the extent of the trap, and I insisted on going anyway. This is also why you're not to blame for the breaking of the shield. After Aryngo's death, I was in fear and doubt of my own judgment. That's why I left you on the beach. I came for only one thing and didn't listen when I clearly had another task to do in rescuing you. For that I'm deeply sorry."

Not for the first time did Karueq feel he was learning more than he could swallow. "I forgive you," he managed. This, his first offer of forgiveness, tasted strange on his tongue. He winced at the power he had to absolve this woman who had saved him. His uncomfortable thoughts automatically turned to something easier to grasp.

"What about the scouts?" he asked.

"Them? We decided we can detain them and confuse the search parties that come after them," she said.

"What about the battle?"

"I won't subject my people to such things needlessly. Right now, I don't have to."

"Because Shatan doesn't know where you are or that your shield is compromised?"

"Yes. As long as we can blind the Shatanala by other means, and as long as I can protect my people, I won't authorize open war."

This statement renewed the itch in Karueq's mind. He moved to ask his question, a question about the Crucible, but she rose to leave. "Don't sit with your guilt too long." With that, she left.

Karueq stayed there a while longer, contemplating what was revealed to him, but he still acknowledged his part in the death of this man buried in the soil before him. Finally, he offered a small prayer for the deceased and rose to leave.

It was several hours until he would meet Hunga, so he continued to explore the gardens. After a few hours of wandering, he found a narrow gap between the leaves in a hedge of berry bushes. His curiosity took him, and he peeked through the opening. It revealed a little glade with an enormous, hollowed out tree.

He slipped through the gap and inspected the fascinating tree. An opening that Karueq estimated to be large enough for ten men yawned at the base. Despite the lack of stability and substance this hole created, the strong tree boasted a canopy of leaves and appeared rooted firmly in the earth. Inside the space, Karueq found notches and footholds ascending and disappearing into the top of the tree.

He grasped the holds and pulled himself up through it. He climbed and climbed, looking down every so often to marvel at the height. Finally, he made it to the opening in the head of the trunk and pulled himself out.

Strong, wide boughs curled up and out from where he stood. They extended their many branches in every direction and formed a dome over the bare trunk pedestal. The sunlight streamed through the green, translucent leaves, creating a sparkling pattern on everything he could see.

He noticed in several places that the bark on the boughs was worn. The Eleverians must come up here often to sit among the leaves. Karueq chose a spot along a bough with a long horizontal segment. He sat down on it and stared through the lacey canopy, his hands supporting him on either side.

Then he closed his eyes, folded his hands reverently, and remembered the task he had been given by Hunga. He centered his thoughts, bringing them in from all the directions in which they pulled him. A few deep breaths pulled the strays in.

He again pictured the vision he had at sea. The rolling clouds burning with sunlight, but it wasn't sunlight. Instead, the light emitted from the figure in white. There was no face there in his memory, as he'd dared not look at the source of the stunning brightness.

Even so, he knelt his inner self down before him, Eleh, his King and Creator. Instead of being afraid, he boldly brought his heart to Him. He imagined it broken, burn marks scarring it from the wickedness he'd lived. He held it out to the faceless image.

Then, something reached into the relived memory. He felt a pair of hands surround his own and close them over the broken heart. He looked up and now saw a face. It was a handsome face, but also a plain one. The gentle smile beckoned Karueq to pour his heart out – to offer his gratitude and request his needs.

He bowed his head again. "Eleh, thank you. Thank you for hearing Chelia and giving me the opportunity to choose you. This is more than I deserve, far more than I deserve. I deserve abandonment and to be handed back to Hell. Thank you."

With his gratitude expressed, he ventured to bring his needs to this God who loved him. "I ask you to give me strength for the trials ahead that I face. I fight for you, now. Let that always be."

A sound pulled him from his deep reflection. A bird had landed on the branch above him and began singing into the leaves. He pondered his prayer while listening to its song, wondering if there was anything else he should be doing with his prayer. Not able to come up with anything, he

stretched his arms out wide. It was a silly gesture – but a symbolic one –
of his total surrender.

He climbed down from the tree and wandered out of the
garden. He spent the rest of the time exploring more of the gardens and the
fortress, learning its layout and what spaces it offered to its occupants.

At the appointed time, Hunga found Karueq at the entrance of the
fortress, leaning against the tall door frame and looking out at the
land. The Keeper looked noticeably pleased to see him. He was followed
by Honai, who was already dressed in mission garb, and three other
Eleverians, who were dressed plainly.

"You still decide to mission, then," Hunga presumed.

"Indeed."

At his reply, Hunga gestured for the group to huddle. "You are
being sent to help rebuild a community following storm devastation. Their
fields and homes were destroyed, and their water supply may have been
compromised. Finnah -" he gestured to the young woman in the group "-
has been told where to find it. Will you be able to leave in the morning?"

Each of the four Eleverians nodded. Karueq followed their lead.

"Then go with God and our goodwill." After his short blessing,
Hunga left the group.

Finnah cleared her throat. "We'll meet at Zarenvai Bay before
daybreak. I don't see the need for any extra provisions or tools. Especially
with two extra pairs of hands. It will be good to have you with us, Honai."

"It's been a while since you've been on an aid mission, hasn't it?"
rejoined the eager man next to her.

Honai smiled. "Yes, it has. It'll be good to see smiles on Seagan
faces for a change."

"Karueq," Finnah said, turning to their newcomer. "Welcome to
the aid mission. We were curious when Hunga informed us you wanted to
join. What prompted you to offer such a thing?"

"I just want to help, and I'll grow very bored indeed sitting up in
the recovery hall any longer."

"In that case, thank you for your help. I'll see you all tomorrow
morning." The group said their temporary goodbyes and dispersed,
however Honai stayed behind.

"You're very brave to request to help us," said Honai.

Karueq shook his head. "I've been fighting this war for my whole
life. This is nothing new to me."

"All the same, you're still being hunted, with a fervor we haven't seen since Quiron's attempt on Alamar."

"I was always under the impression your people were after my head. This means nothing."

"Fair enough," conceded Honai. He scratched his temple. "I've been assigned to you as protection but also as a guide. You're unfamiliar with our customs and the way we conduct missions."

"I've seen your missions," Karueq rebuked.

Honai chuckled. "It's been a common joke among the Eleka Guard that you never paid attention."

Karueq raised his eyebrow.

"There is quite a bit of preparation for a mission," Honai continued, "though, your preparation will be a little different because you're new and not a citizen. Come with me."

Honai led Karueq out of the fortress to a wide building set apart from the main fortress. They walked inside to a wide foray and then through a door on the left. Inside was an array of clothing and armor. The articles were stacked on dozens of long shelves and some were hung on the walls. Karueq recognized most of it from his time watching them.

Honai stopped next to a tall shelf holding piles of sand-colored clothing. Honai took a moment to size Karueq up and then removed two bundles of the fabric from a shelf above his head. He explained that this was the attire usually worn on aid missions in the region they were assigned. It was light and comfortable, and it would afford mobility and protection from the elements.

Karueq tried them on while Honai stepped out of the room. He inspected the fit, and it dawned on him what he must look like – the commander of the Shatanala being fitted in the attire of Eleverians. He tugged on the shirt to adjust it. Honai had chosen properly.

Then, Honai led him to another room filled with more supplies. He gave Karueq a supply bag and showed him the variety of goods held within. In one pocket were bandages, a pouch filled with strips of willow bark, a long cloth, a few strips of leather, and a few vials of liquid. Another large pocket held strings of beads and small figurines that Honai explained were gifts for children they met on missions. The pack was strapped with various tools Karueq wasn't familiar with, a square of flint, and two small knives.

Their next stop was a room stocked with neatly wrapped packages. Honai put several different shaped packages and a waterskin into the supply bag, filling the rest of the available space – the food ration for the mission. Then he showed Karueq a room to store his belongings. Karueq kept only his boot knife on his person.

With these preparations done, they left the building.

They stopped just outside the fortress entrance. "Is there anyone with whom you have a standing grievance?" asked Honai. At Karueq's mildly confused expression, he elaborated. "Because every mission is considered dangerous no matter what it is or how simple it seems, the team is given time beforehand to rectify any grievances they may have with anyone or things left unsaid. That way, they leave with a clear mind, and no regret should they fall."

Karueq considered for a moment. He'd already been forgiven for everything in his past when he entered the river. He didn't think he'd committed any grievances against anyone since then and no one had been anything but kind to him.

There was, however, one thing that had been left unsaid.

"Would I be able to speak with Chelia?" he asked tentatively. He wondered if she would be too busy to oblige his request.

"Of course," Honai said. He glanced at the sun making its way behind the mountains. "And I know just where to find her."

Instead of going into the fortress, Honai led Karueq around its north wall. There, they found a path up the mountain, which they scaled quickly enough. They came to an outcrop high above the foothills, with two people perched on the edge – Chelia and Alamar.

Chelia threw a glance over her shoulder at their approach. "Hello, gentlemen," she greeted them. Alamar, too, greeted them with a nod.

"Hello," Honai greeted them and tossed a vial from his pocket to Chelia. "Sorry to interrupt. Karueq is going on a mission with us in the morning and would like to speak with you, Chelia."

"So I heard."

Alamar pressed a kiss to Chelia's temple. Then, he and Honai retreated back to the path and wandered away.

Chelia patted the spot next to her that Alamar had occupied, and Karueq obliged. She sized him up. "It must feel very strange to be clothed for one of our missions."

Karueq looked down at the tunic, pants, and boots. "It's not all that strange."

She smiled. "What did you want to speak with me about?"

Karueq sighed, a strange feeling welling up in him over the new things he was finding himself doing in this land. "Honai informed me that everyone lays old business to rest before leaving for a mission. I know I've been forgiven for everything I've ever done…"

"You have."

A short laugh escaped him at her rabid insistence on the matter. "But I have yet to properly thank you for giving me a chance at this freedom."

Chelia smiled. "You are most welcome. I'm truly very happy you got your chance."

Karueq's smile grew wider. "I do wonder though. What did you pray over me on the beach?"

Chelia's face wrinkled as she tried to recall her exact words. "It was a hasty prayer. I asked Eleh to look on your repentance – your thrice renouncement of Shatan whether you meant it or not – with as much favor as He looks on true repentance. I asked also for Him to keep you safe until you made it out of Xanadai. He answered every part of my prayer."

She turned her eyes back on the open plain. The studying expression he'd grown accustomed to seeing on her was gone. She appeared every bit as though she wasn't contemplating war, but behind those eyes, she had to be. Karueq was reminded that this woman had been his unreadable adversary, both as Captain and Elequiri, never predictable but always remaining loyal to her cause.

This observation prompted him to speak further. "How many times did you even consider Shatan's offers to join him?"

She smirked. "I always considered them. It's unwise to not consider every proposal given to you, but I didn't consider them for my own benefit. I considered them in the light of pulling a ruse on Shatan, much like you did before you converted."

"Did anyone ever consider the offers we made?"

"I can't speak for them, but none of us have ever left Eleh for Shatan, so that must say something. I'm confident in my people's strength."

"They are wonderful people."

She smiled wider. "Yes. I love them dearly. There is nothing I wouldn't sacrifice for them."

Karueq glanced behind at the pathway. He should allow her and Alamar to enjoy their time outside of war. "Thank you for everything, Chelia. I hope to see you when I return."

"Before you go," she began, opening the vial in her hand, "I would like to honor you with our send off."

Karueq settled his seat again.

She turned the vial over on her thumb, wetting it with the oil. "Bow your head." He did so.

"Karueq, all of Eleveria loves you, as does Eleh, your King. You go with Him to do the work He has called you to do. Upon your return, you will be received with great joy. Should you fall, you will be dearly missed."

Then, she smeared the oil on his forehead, and he noticed its light perfume. "May the lavish love Eleh pours out to you in life be multiplied. May He transform your tears into astounding joy and everlasting peace. Go with God, Karueq, and may you forever know the love He has for you."

With her prayer done, Karueq opened his eyes. Chelia recapped the vial and smiled at him. "You're ready now. Get some rest."

He nodded and thanked her one more time. Then, he returned to the path. Honai and Alamar came over from the other side of the path. Alamar returned to the outcrop, and Karueq followed Honai back down the mountain and to the fortress.

Once back inside, they retired to a room that looked much like the healing hall. It was filled with beds and had shelves near each one. Finnah and several others were there sleeping.

In the early hours of the morning, while the room was still dark, he, Finnah, and Honai rose and flew on dragonback to the bay. One of their team, Tinorah, was waiting for them. The last one, Omri, arrived shortly after them.

Finnah reiterated the briefing they received the day before. She also assigned primary watch to Honai in addition to his charge of Karueq. Tinorah was in charge of procuring building materials upon arrival. Omri was assigned to the sick and injured. Karueq was to follow all directions given, contribute where he could best serve, and stick close to

Honai. Then, they bowed their heads, and Finnah uttered a prayer for a successful mission.

With that, they mounted the dragons and took off while the sky began to gray. Karueq was amazed at the efficiency with which the dragons pulled through the air. Their sprint could outrace a Rale with ease, and their flight was less turbulent even though they were flying fast. This was one of the many reasons he'd seen why the Eleverians were so good at their calling. The speed with which they reached their destinations made their small population seem a hundred-fold larger.

They arrived at the outskirts of the village before noon. They left the dragons there out of sight so as not to frighten the people. Upon reaching the village, Tinorah left to scout the town and the countryside for building materials. Omri asked where the infirm were being kept and went there. Finnah, Honai, and Karueq surveyed the damage about the community.

A small child stood barefoot by a collapsed home. She reminded Karueq of the time many years ago when, during a sabotage campaign, he almost kidnapped a boy about her age only to be stopped by the Eleverians.

He knelt down by the child and took one of the beaded strings from his pack. He held it out to her. She looked at it tentatively. Karueq encouraged her with a smile, and she took it, sheepishly returning his smile.

At the end of that day, the four companions gathered just outside the town to camp. Honai had counseled Finnah to make such a decision, stating that any Shatanala sympathizers among the town would have recognized Karueq immediately, and they would be vulnerable indeed in the center square - the Eleverians' usual place of encampment. Tinorah reported there were ample supplies from the wreckage that they could rebuild most of the community with what they had. The rest they could get nearby from the surroundings a few miles away. He also reported that the crops had been mostly spared. He showed Karueq a small bag of seed that, while not an ideal grain, would grow quickly and make up for some of the loss.

They arose early the next morning. Omri went back to the sick and injured for a few hours. The rest of them went about the community helping rebuild the homes and walls. The Eleverians encouraged the people with their words and their actions. Karueq awkwardly followed suit. At mid-morning, Omri rejoined them.

They spent the rest of that day and the next two days in a similar fashion. Karueq's pack was emptied of its treasures for the children. At the end of the third day, with the community restored by the work of many hands, the people held a feast with music and dancing. The team stayed until the torchlight burned low, then left. The people gave them a grateful send off.

Their journey back to Eleveria seemed quicker than the journey out. The team skipped over the Zarenvai shore and landed outside the fortress in the middle of the night. On their faces were joyous smiles. They all returned their provisions to the supply building, gathered their belongings, and then made their way to the recovery hall where they retrieved five recovery pendants, careful not to wake the sleeping dwellers.

Finnah ushered them all out to the hallway, away from the door. "Thank you all for making my first lead successful," she told them. "You made it easy to lead the charge."

"You were an effective leader, Finnah," Omri congratulated her. "We're proud of you."

All of them bowed their heads and Finnah offered a grateful prayer thanking Eleh for blessing their journey and the people they helped.

Then, they all said their goodbyes. Finnah went back into the recovery hall. Omri and Tinorah turned and went down the stairs, to Karueq's confusion.

Honai saw his reaction. "They're married and are going home to recover with their families. They do not need to be here. I'll be returning to Henara myself." He placed his hand on Karueq's shoulder. "You did very well, Karueq. Get some rest." With that, he turned down the stairs, and Karueq went into the hall.

Inside the dark room, Karueq found that Nimera still occupied the same bed. Another Eleverian was sleeping in a bed farther down. Hanai was nowhere to be found.

Out on the terrace, Karueq saw the outline of Finnah with her head bowed. Karueq did his best to not disturb her while he collapsed into one of the beds and fell asleep.

CHAPTER SIXTEEN

THE HORRORS OF WAR

By now, Karueq was almost unrecognizable from his former self. The Eleverians' characteristic smile played on his lips. When he wasn't out rebuilding homes and replanting fields, he'd become part of daily life around the fortress, spending his spare time exploring the land and resting in the evenings in the recovery hall.

Nimera had long left the recovery hall with his leg fully healed and his mind at peace. Karueq had gone on mission with him once, and the man's bleeding heart was evident. It was no wonder such a tragedy as Egypt had affected him so much. These days, Nimera's stays in recovery were minimal.

Karueq often encountered Hanai in the recovery hall. They made enjoyable company, though Hanai made a point to pull pranks on Karueq during his stay. Karueq himself brought back the choicest apples from around the country to present to him. The Eleverian became his close friend. He vented his curiosity on him by asking dozens of questions about Eleveria and life there. Hanai enjoyed the inquiries and made a point to say he'd never had to explain Eleveria to anyone because it was hidden from everyone who didn't live there from birth. His answers often procured more questions that frequently ended in fits of laughter.

Karueq felt such joy from all the good they'd accomplished on missions. He was still being assigned to the least dangerous missions, the ones that would have little likelihood of encounters with Shatanala. He made no protest. It gave him the opportunity to learn to take orders for a change. He was also learning how to approach Seaga without malicious intent, and it was incredibly freeing.

The Eleka Guard and some of the more brazen Eleverians not on the Guard occupied their time with luring the Shatanala away from the gates. They consulted Karueq's experience and his familiarity with their new leader, General Bleren, to make their missions most effective. So far, the Shatanala were kept unaware of Eleveria's vulnerability. However, it was becoming apparent that they would have to do something soon to satiate the rogue, Ingana.

As soon as he retrieved a recovery pendant and prayed after his latest mission, Karueq left the fortress and ascended the path to the outcrop on the mountain. A young boy had informed him upon arrival that Chelia requested his advice when he was settled.

On the edge of the outcrop, sat Chelia gazing mildly at the horizon.

"Karueq," she greeted him. "Thank you for coming." He took a seat next to her. "How was your mission?"

"It went very well, my lady," he replied.

"Good." She smiled. "You've helped a great many people while you've been here."

"I'm happy to do the work."

Her smile fell slightly, and she turned to the business at hand. "The Shatanala are threatening open war on Seaga. We can't let that happen."

Karueq understood the hidden ferocity behind her words. All the faces he'd seen on his missions and all the good and happiness that had been brought to their communities couldn't be sacrificed. "What did they say?"

"It was a messenger sent to one of the areas we protect, one the Shatanala haven't set foot in for years. They want our attention, and they're serious. Shatan knows you are with us and wants you surrendered. He also demands that we withdraw half of our protections in Seaga, or he will assault it with the might of Xanadai."

"I don't think he's bluffing," Karueq suggested. "He has the ability to do so. He will destroy everything and break as many spirits as he can."

"What do you suggest?"

Karueq sighed. It was truly an idea they had been discussing for weeks. "The scouts you captured when I came here - it's been a long time. Have they shown signs of conversion?"

"None. They're steadfast in their decisions."

"Have you tried what you did with me?"

"I did next to nothing by praying over you. It was all up to you. If you had not wanted to see the light even a little, Eleh would not have forced you." She silently pondered for a few moments. "It may be time to just let them go."

"Give it a little more time," Karueq protested.

"We don't have any more time. I refuse to let Seaga suffer."

"He won't attack right away."

"Can you assure me of that?"

He opened his mouth to say 'yes', but his voice was caught in his throat by her serious expression. He shook his head sadly. "No. I can't guarantee anything from where I am now."

"I appreciate what you have given us by being here, but I would need absolute assurance in this case."

"Agreed."

"As it stands, I think we can plan our own offensive with the time we will get by releasing the scouts. They'll have to relay what they know, their information will have to be investigated and confirmed, then they have to survey and come up with a strategy of their own."

"You know they've already been doing that. They wouldn't come to you like this if they hadn't been scheming already."

"Then we'll have to be quicker."

Karueq had come to learn this about her – there was always a way. She didn't shrink when the situation wasn't ideal. Even in impossible challenges, she found a way, and she instilled that confidence and attitude in her people. She was calculated, and that made her effective instead of being foolhardy.

"Thank you, Karueq," she said, "for your counsel while you've been here. I do very much appreciate it."

"You are most welcome, my lady. I wish I could do more."

"Good night."

He rose from the ledge and descended down the mountain slope.

The morning after his customary recovery day, Karueq accepted another mission and prepared to leave. As he had no family, spouse, or next of kin in Eleveria, his anointing always fell to Chelia when she was around. He relished his send off. She prayed over him in the name of Eleh and filled him with hope. By sweeping the oil across his head, she sent him off with the goodwill of all Eleveria, his adopted people. He thanked her each time, knowing she probably didn't know how much the little ceremony meant to him.

He and his team left the beach at Zarenvai Bay. They'd recently dismissed the Eleka Guard from accompanying his journeys as they were needed elsewhere. This mission was to save a village's crops and livestock from failing. Accompanying him were Dagar and Brynia with Koda leading.

They left their dragons hidden in the outskirts and walked toward the village. The morning was still, and the sky above was clear. When they reached the village, there wasn't a sound, and no one was seen milling about here or in the surrounding countryside.

"Where are they?" asked Dagar suspiciously. Karueq's heartbeat quickened. Dagar knew better than he that this scene wasn't normal.

Koda halted them, and they huddled together, facing outwards in every direction. Karueq noticed Brynia's hand find her dagger hilt.

After a moment, Koda crossed the path to a house and called quietly to whoever might be inside. He pushed the door away and took a peek inside.

Then, he motioned for the other three to disperse and check the other houses. Each of them approached a door and inquired in hushed tones.

Karueq stepped to the door of a small house and called out to the family that dwelt within. Upon hearing no answer, he cracked the door open and looked into the single room. No one was there, but there was ample evidence it wasn't just deserted. A pot had been kicked over into the coals of the cooking fire. Blankets trailed on the ground toward the door.

Karueq's eyes flicked around the village, zoning in on somewhere a whole village of people could be hidden. Karueq saw that Koda was doing the same. This was no mere aid mission.

Then, Karueq spotted the barns where the livestock were sheltered. He whistled low to get Koda's attention and motioned toward the barns. Koda signaled Brynia and Dagar to follow. The four of them approached the barns cautiously.

Koda made the decision to stick together in a group and all four lined up against the wall at the edge of the barn's opening. Koda at the lip of the opening briefly looked inside, then turned his head away towards them with his eyes closed. Whatever he had just seen was a terrible sight.

"Look for survivors," Koda whispered as he opened his eyes again. He drew his sword. "Be on your guard."

The three of them drew their weapons and followed Koda carefully into the barn.

Karueq's eyes stung from the stench. He picked his way among the slaughtered livestock and slain people piled up on the floors and against the walls. He prayed there would be one, just one, still alive and laying in agony among the corruption and the flies. None of the bodies breathed. He just met the frightened, still open eyes of the fallen.

At the back of the barn came a soft whimper. Brynia darted over to the source of the sound and crouched over it. The rest followed, their heavy hearts lightening.

"Shh, you're safe," Brynia cooed to the young man.

"Help...me," came his raspy whisper.

"We're here," she assured him. "We're here to help you."

Without warning, the man's hand emerged from under another body, wielding a knife, and stabbed Brynia in the belly.

She gasped sharply and fell backward. Koda lunged on the man and trapped the hand with his foot. Dagar dragged Brynia away from the fray. Karueq dropped his knee on the still struggling man while Koda relieved him of the weapon.

"What happened here?" Karueq hissed.

The man giggled with glee while choking on Karueq's weight. "We knew you'd come."

Karueq backhanded the lout. Rage boiled beneath his skin. "You want me? You have me."

The man spit full into Karueq's face. He wiped the filth from his eyes and wound up to strike him again.

Koda caught his fist. "Enough!" he barked.

Karueq swallowed his fury. He wouldn't forget his orders despite the devastation that lay around him.

"We have to move," Koda ordered him.

Karueq kept his weight on the scrawny man while Dagar helped Brynia to her feet.

"Brynia?" Koda asked in earnest.

"I can make it," she answered forcefully, her grit grinding her voice. "Just cover me."

With that, Brynia led the charge out of the barn, followed by Koda and Dagar, with Karueq coming last so the man was detained to the last possible second.

They had to cross through the village to make the quickest escape. Luckily, the Shatanala's strategy seemed to hide the army well away from the village in the hills so the party wouldn't see them if they grew suspicious. This gave them a little time to begin running. Now a Shatanala came at them from each side, beginning the assault. More poured from every street.

Brynia bravely dashed through them, leading the way. Koda, Dagar, and Karueq fought them away from all sides of her. They broke through the main assault and ran toward the edge of the village.

Another wave of Shatanala descended on them. Karueq saw Brynia begin to slow, and the others were occupied by the throngs of enemies. Karueq fought his way toward her, putting them all on the ground. Without thinking, he grabbed her by the waist and dragged her through the last of the Shatanala to the edge of the city.

"Go!" he cried. "Run!"

She complied and ran as fast as her weakening body would let her. Karueq turned back and helped free the others from the blockade. They sprinted after her.

Brynia was slowing down fast. Karueq and Dagar pulled her along so they didn't lose ground. Over their shoulders they found the Shatanala trailing them closely

Koda shouted a command into the air. The enormous dragons took flight over the hill and raced toward their riders.

The men hoisted Brynia onto a dragon just in time. The first pursuer sprung on Karueq and tackled him to the ground. Dagar pulled it off him and kicked it away.

Koda and Brynia's dragons launched into the air. Dagar's dragon leaped forward and fought back a wall of Shatanala coming at them. Karueq scrambled onto his dragon and pulled it around to face the oncoming Shatanala. It roared forward, giving Dagar time to mount.

Both dragons sprang into the air and sprinted away, Dagar and Karueq holding tightly to them to keep from slipping off. At this speed, they outran any Rales that could be following.

Koda set them down in a secluded region behind a low range of mountains. They dismounted, and Koda took Brynia from the dragon's back. Her face was ghostly pale and she was shivering.

He set her down gently and rolled her tunic away from the wound. Dagar and Karueq crouched beside her. Koda unloaded the bandages from his bag and set to work dressing the wound, Dagar assisted.

Karueq's mind got the better of him. "I'm sorry."

"Not here," Koda ordered. "Not now."

"It was a trap for me," Karueq explained.

Koda glanced at Dagar and tossed his chin away from the scene. Dagar stood up and motioned for Karueq to follow him.

They walked off a little way while Koda tended to Brynia.

"This is not the time or the place for such talk," Dagar told him.

"I never meant for any of this to happen…"

"We're not done here yet," Dagar interrupted him. "The mission isn't over until we cross the borders and get Brynia to the healing hall." He pointed back at her. "She's our mission now. You apologize for nothing, and you certainly don't do it in front of her. She has to focus on staying awake and not on consoling you for mistakes you think you've made or persecutions directed at you. Are we clear?"

Karueq swallowed his remaining qualms and nodded. He looked back to where Koda was inspecting the bindings. "Is she going to make it?" he asked.

"That's up to Eleh. We don't have the means to sustain her out here. The run exhausted her, and she has to make the ride back."

"What can I do?"

"Get her back home," Dagar answered.

The two of them returned to Koda and Brynia. She was still lucid but very weak. The decision was made to continue to fly her with Koda. Dagar and Karueq were to monitor the skies for unfriendly advances and to be prepared for any sudden stops should Brynia need more attention.

They took off from those mountains and sprinted toward Eleveria. Koda stopped only once, as Brynia had fallen asleep. It took a few minutes to wake her up, and Karueq had never been so worried. They made it past the gateway pillars and didn't stop until they reached the fortress.

There, several Eleverians helped them bring their injured friend to the healing hall where they began the long night's vigil for her.

Dagar took Karueq aside. "Who's your closest friend?"

Karueq was confused by the question.

Dagar questioned again. "Who is your closest friend? You need to talk to someone."

"You know what happened. What am I supposed to do?"

Dagar shook his head. "You need to speak to someone you trust and with whom you can speak freely about this."

Karueq shook his head. "Hanai is on mission."

"Who sent you off?"

"Chelia did."

Dagar nodded. "She'll want a report on this as well. Go. She'll be somewhere in the fortress." He left Karueq there with this task and hurried back to the healing hall.

Karueq didn't know where to begin looking, so he simply wandered the halls for a while. Undisturbed by anyone, his thoughts darkened bitterly with all he had seen.

It was then Chelia came down the stairway leading to the recovery hall accompanied by Alamar. Karueq couldn't speak. He stood at the bottom of the stairs, lost.

The pair reached him. "Karueq?" Chelia asked. "What's wrong?"

He couldn't answer her. Seeing this, Chelia sat down on the lower step and patted the stair next to her. Alamar left them without a word.

Karueq sat down tentatively next to her.

"I gather your mission didn't go perfectly," she ventured.

He said nothing.

"I can't know what happened if you don't say anything."

He let out a long breath. It didn't help to organize his thoughts. They remained scrambled in his skull.

"Start with your debriefing," she suggested.

"They're all dead," he blurted.

She didn't say anything for a second. "By 'they', you mean the people you were sent to help and not your team?"

"Yes." His eyes fell to his palms.

"No survivors?"

"No."

"Was anyone on your team hurt?"

Karueq's throat blocked up. He tried to clear it unsuccessfully. "Brynia… healing hall," he managed.

He saw her nod from the corner of his eye. "That isn't everything that's bothering you," she ventured.

He shook his head. She didn't speak. She simply waited for him to knit a sentence together.

Finally, he found a steady place to put his voice. "It was a trap. They set it for me."

Again, nothing from the Elequiri. This time, her silence was uncomfortable. It made him look up. She stared through her knees at the stair beneath her feet, deep in thought. He looked away.

After another minute, she finally spoke. "Are you sure they wanted you?"

He nodded. "The decoy told me so."

"Karueq, you won't be assigned to another mission for a while," she stated bluntly.

He stared at her, bewildered. "What?"

"We can't risk it."

Despair crashed in on him. "Chelia...I'm sorry. Please don't take this away from me."

"I'm not blaming you for anything. Please remember that. We can't risk your safety. If they killed a whole village and took down one of us to get to you, they're serious about taking you back. There's no way I'm letting them have you."

His heart waned at her words. "This is my choice, my lady. I know the price. I would rather die than go back, and death would be nothing for me now. Please don't take away my service."

"I'm not banning you for life, Karueq. I want you to stand down until their hunger for your blood tames."

He hung his head at her words. He felt her arm encircle his shoulders. "Your zeal for helping people is inspiring." His heart wouldn't quiet. "It won't be forever. Turn your service to us here in the meantime."

She planted a kiss on the back of his downturned head. "Go, get some rest."

Her arm left him, and he sat on the stairs alone blinking back tears. His feet almost pulled him away from his sulking to go check on Brynia. He felt he had to do something now that his joy had been stripped from him, but his shame took over and he dared not go back there.

Instead, he wandered forlorn to the recovery hall. He took a pendant down and went to the terrace to pray. He knelt down, but his grief brought him all the way on his face. He prayed earnestly like that for hours. The moon cast subtle shadows about him. His prayers were for Brynia, that she wouldn't die on his account. His prayers were for the people that lost their lives on his account. His prayers, also, were for himself, that he may continue to do the work of his King despite his new orders to stand down.

Then, he felt a hand on his shoulder. "Karueq, come get some rest."

The voice was that of Hanai. The Eleverian had come back early from his latest mission.

Karueq wiped his face of the salty tears and looked up. His weary legs wouldn't budge, or maybe it was his drowning heart. His sullen gaze fell on the nightscape before him. Hanai's face, too, turned out to the muted beauty of the view.

Another tear escaped down Karueq's cheek, and he caught it with his sleeve. "Please…tell me what I can do."

Hanai dropped to his knee and slid into a seated position. "You can rest in Eleh's promises."

"But what can I do here?"

"What happened?"

Karueq took a deep breath to steady his voice. "I'm not going out to mission again."

"I don't believe you're letting one difficult mission frighten you away from service."

Karueq shook his head. "Your sister is not sending me out again." When Hanai didn't say anything to this, he sputtered, "What am I going to do if I can't go out and serve?"

"There's work to be done everywhere, Karueq, including here. There are people here hurting and lives being challenged."

"There are more people hurting out there, out in Seaga," his dark thoughts surfaced, "because of things that I used to do to them."

"Yes, Karueq. Yes. They're hurting, but not just because of you. Eleh isn't asking you to save them all. He's letting you join His salvation story, but you're also meant to share in that story. The Shatanala want you desperately, and we won't sacrifice you for the work to be done in Seaga."

Karueq shook his head. "They're taking my new life away. They're spoiling what I've been given."

"Trust me, they can do nothing of the sort. Sometimes we are asked to simply be still."

"What do I do?" Karueq turned his tearful eyes on Hanai. "What do I do instead?"

The Eleverian turned the question around in his mind. "Sit with Eleh in stillness. Learn more about Him. You must still advise Chelia. Perhaps you should play a more active part in that." He put his hand on Karueq's shoulder. "Enough trouble for tonight. Come. Get some rest."

Karueq gave in to the invitation as he had nothing left and pushed himself up to standing. He and Hanai returned to the hall, and he dropped into the bed he'd essentially claimed for himself. He heard Hanai's blanket rustle in the next bed as he slumped into it.

Karueq's drowning heart floated on the waves of grief as he drifted. He kept his string of prayers going until he finally surrendered to sleep.

He awoke the next morning to the beginnings of a brilliant sunrise. He and Hanai joined three others out on the terrace to watch the sun peek over the horizon.

Karueq caught Hanai's eye wandering around the horizon. His heart twisted.

"Do you miss it?" he asked him.

"Hmm?"

"The ring."

"Oh," the man smiled sheepishly. "A little. It was quite a sight. Feeling the same today?"

Karueq nodded. "Maybe a little better. I'll have to make myself useful some other way."

The little group returned to the hall and spread the table with food. Karueq had taken a liking to the spicy jerky, but today, he couldn't consume much.

His heart lightened just a little with the banter over the meal. In his depressed state, he noticed better the inherent joy behind the eyes of the Eleverians. He remembered Hanai's encouragement the night before about nothing stealing his new life. This was a courageous mindset. Nothing, not imprisonment or torture or the threat of death could take away that joy the Eleverians found in their King. Hanai, he knew well, had experienced dire threats and the worst abuse the Shatanala could concoct. Yet, he remained hopeful and went out into battle with the Guard anyway.

The door opened to allow Dagar to enter. The Eleverian took a pendant from the hook and greeted everyone in the room.

He sat down opposite Karueq and addressed him immediately. "Brynia made it through the night."

At the news, Karueq's mouth turned up into a smile, and his eyes stung with hidden tears. "How is she?" he implored.

"She's a fighter," Dagar said, smiling. "I think she'll make it."

Karueq huffed in relief. "Thank you."

Later in the morning, Karueq made his way to the healing hall and found Brynia. She'd given him a sleepy, sideways grin and teased him that he never would have made it out without her. Her humor did more to lighten his heart than any amount of consoling could ever do. He didn't apologize, as he felt she'd find it just as inappropriate as Dagar and Koda had the night before. He'd done nothing to cause this unless he was supposed to be sorry for his mere existence. After their brief talk, he bid her well and left.

Karueq decided to clear his head by exploring more of Eleveria. He had yet to see the Ranovan Forest on the north side of the bay. As he made his way out of the fortress, he heard someone call his name.

"Karueq," Chelia called. "Might I have a moment?"

"Of course you can," he replied.

"Thank you." She sized him up. "Out to explore?"

"Yes. I've heard descriptions of the forest, but I haven't seen it for myself."

"It's quite a masterpiece. I'd plan to be occupied out there for the rest of the day. Make sure you get to see the old Eunara city in the center."

"What can I do for you, my lady?" he asked.

"It's not something you can do for me. I want to update you. We let the scouts go, but we sent them with a message. They're to report to Shatan himself that we have no intention of surrendering you."

It was a bold move, but Karueq lamented that it had to be done.

"We're ready for open war with them should they seek to destroy us. The fight is no longer just for Seaga. It's for you and for our home, and we will fight for it."

"I won't ask you to fight for me."

She smiled and then chuckled. "You really haven't been paying attention all these years, have you?" With that, she turned on her heel and left him to ponder her assessment.

CHAPTER SEVENTEEN

PURSUING BATTLE

The Eleka Guard was busier than ever. Even those not among the Eleka Guard were joining their daring missions. The scouts had indeed reported what they had seen, and it seemed Ingana herself had been tasked with investigating what it was they had found. Part of the Guard and their volunteers were stationed within fifty miles of the gateway, patrolling for her teams, luring and sending them away with their lives and without information. The rest were occupied with engaging the Shatanala forces out in Seaga to steal Bleren's attention away from Eleveria's vulnerable borders.

Karueq found his time to be heavily occupied despite not being sent on missions. Each morning, he awoke to view the sunrise and pray. He prayed for Eleveria, that his King would keep them safe. He prayed for the Eleverians out on missions, reminded from Hunga's imprisonment that prayer filled the void left in his absence. He had even begun praying for those under Shatan's rule. He asked Eleh to do for each of them what He had done for a despicable viper like himself. Then, he would meet with Chelia, Alamar, or Hunga regarding developments in their current strategy and to discuss details of the impending warfare. They agreed that they would have to wage battle with Shatan's army in order to secure the safety of Eleveria, and that battle would be fought on a site of their own choosing.

For the rest of the day, Karueq trained any available Eleverians in combat. They were all skilled fighters. They had to be, because they faced down enemy soldiers even when they were simply bringing food to poor families. They fought well, and Karueq's skills were tested with each spar, but there were obvious gaps in their tactics that needed to be remedied by him.

Late each night, he retired to the recovery hall, which had become his permanent home. He ministered to the temporary occupants when he could and tried his best to welcome them back home. Each night he slept peacefully.

Today, Karueq went to the great hall as he did every morning. He found Chelia leaning against a pillar, staring at the three thrones at the head of the hall. She heard him coming and looked over her shoulder.

"Good morning, Karueq," she greeted him.

"Good morning, my lady," he returned.

She held out her open hand to him. Laying neatly on her palm was a sparkling blue crystal attached to a leather cord. A strand of silver coiled around the crystal, attaching a rune to its face. The same rune was affixed above the central golden throne.

"This is for you," she explained. "A gift for everything you have done and continue to do for us."

Karueq took the jewel from her. "It bears your mark."

Her brow crinkled. "My mark?"

Karueq nodded his head toward the great throne. She looked up and saw what he meant. She smiled, amused. "You think that throne is reserved for me?"

"Is it not?"

She shook her head. "That is the throne of Eleh. Alamar and I occupy the lower seats." She pointed out the lesser, wooden thrones, both ornate in their own right. "Though they're largely symbolic."

Karueq nodded.

"You bear the mark of the King on your heart," she elaborated. "This is an outward sign of your redemption."

"Thank you," he said, admiring the crystal. She didn't speak for a few moments letting him inspect the gift she'd given him.

Then, she spoke. "Is there any way to storm Xanadai?"

Karueq was greatly surprised by this question. "That is a bold move."

"I want to cripple as much of Xanadai as we can before we engage them."

"How many of your people are you willing to sacrifice to do this?"

"I won't sacrifice them. But I want as little of Xanadai to join the battle, so we only fight those on the surface. You've said there are three assets Shatan has below ground that will cause us trouble should they engage us up here on the surface."

"Yes – the main army, the Brehila, and the host of demons they have."

"Part of our wager is to have the angels engage the demons as they did on Mount Caramel. I will not risk supernatural warfare with my people."

Karueq nodded at this. "There are weaknesses in the tunnels. Assuming we can get into Xanadai, we can collapse them and make it difficult to move the whole horde."

"What about the Brehila?"

Karueq shook his head. "They work alone. You would have to lure them all back to their lair and confine them there somehow. I don't see how."

"There aren't that many of them, though," she ventured.

"There are enough of them."

"But they're not very effective in mass combat."

"I suppose they wouldn't be as effective as they are with what they're trained to do, no."

"That's all we need."

"You're bold to think that." He considered her assurance for a moment. "What are you planning, exactly?"

"You'll find out soon enough," she said, patting his shoulder. "Something very bold indeed, and maybe very foolish." Then, she leaned off the pillar and strode to the door to the right of the thrones.

Karueq wasn't sure what to think of the short discussion. His calculating mind warped itself trying to imagine what she could possibly think could be done about the whole of the underground. After getting nowhere with his thoughts, he turned his attention back on the crystal still held in his grasp. The corner of his lip turned up. He would gladly bear this mark, an exchange for all the evil symbolage he bore during his enslavement.

He looped the leather cord around his neck and cinched it so the crystal hung at the base of his collarbone. With a cheerful smile on his face, he left the hall and made his way to the training grounds behind the gardens.

A few Eleverians in recovery were warming up with some light sparring when he arrived. Karueq noticed the pendants around their necks. He'd learned that recovery was not always a passive process for them. Every Eleverian completed some length of recovery after a mission, but it was up to them how they used it. Some needed to heal from their injuries or spend some time viewing the sunrises. For many Eleverians, their days of recovery were spent actively sharpening their skills, learning something new, or doing the work that had to be done in their own cities. When word spread that Karueq was holding these training sessions, many in active recovery flocked to the lawn behind the gardens.

It occurred to Karueq the Shatanala would never entertain an idea like recovery. Those deemed fit for reassignment were reassigned, and those deemed unfit were either given limited time to recover or sent out and used as bait. Karueq never gave thought to the health of his force's souls.

The training commenced, and he put them through tests of what he'd already taught them. He put a few to shame, but others shamed him in return. More Eleverians arrived during the session and joined seamlessly into the fray.

He let the last one up off the ground. Then, he showed them more tactics the Shatanala deployed. He mimicked different weapons with a variety of objects at his disposal. They listened closely while he took down each one of them with new tactics and armaments. They learned quickly from his demonstrations. Then, he challenged them to open duels.

His only lament of these sessions was that there weren't more of him. He could effectively instruct more people at a time and not tire by the time he dueled. He was grateful that some of the faster learners had no qualms with picking up his implements and dueling as a Shatanala in his place.

He saw on display at these sessions the adaptability for which he used to loathe them. Each of them had a favorite weapon and a distinct combat style, but they were completely willing to trade what they knew to try something more effective. He concluded the day well into the evening. He was exhausted and the sweat clung to his skin. Before retiring to the recovery hall for the night, he had a cool bath to prevent his muscles from stiffening while he slept.

Those in the recovery hall were sharing an evening meal by the merry glow of the table's lamp. Karueq gladly joined them at their invitation. They treated him to a few stories from the old country, before the tribes united under one oath. The storyteller of the group, Horan, accented his tales with shadowed figures courtesy of the lamplight's canvas on the wall.

Not surprising to Karueq, nor to any of his company, Chelia entered the hall and pulled him away. He thanked the group for their stories and the good company and then excused himself from the table.

In the hall outside the door, Chelia leaned into the wall, and he could tell he was in for a discussion.

"We're launching an assault on Xanadai," she announced. "I'm extending an invitation for you to join us, as we'll need help navigating both the route to Xanadai and the layout."

Karueq's mouth stood agape.

"I know," she said, shaking her head, "we only just discussed it this morning."

"And now you've just decided to attack them in their own lair? Since this morning?"

"Of course not. I've been considering it for a while."

Karueq was astounded at this move, though he felt he shouldn't have been. She was bold, he knew. Still, this was more bold than she'd ever been.

She cleared her throat at his silence. "You don't have to come with us. I know Xanadai used to be your home, and you had friends there. We don't intend to kill anyone. We're just stopping up the entrances."

For some reason, he was hurt by her words and what could be considered a question of his loyalty. "I know that. If you have concerns about me going, why ask me to come?"

She peered at him, catching the derision in his tone. "I'm not concerned about you joining us. What's wrong?"

He was taken aback at her question. He shook his head, figuring he must be tired from the long day. "I'm sorry – old habits."

"Have I caused you insult somehow?"

"No." He shook his head again. "How can I be of use?"

She peered at him again but seemed satisfied he wasn't hiding ill will. "We could use your knowledge of the place. I'll only ask for guidance from you. Guide us in so we know exactly where the weak points are and how to cripple them."

"I'll gladly do that, my lady."

"And Karueq, they're desperate for you. To take you to Xanadai I know is a risk, but they won't expect you there. I'm assigning a Guard member to your protection just in case."

"If I can help bring down Shatan's empire, I will gladly put up my safety and my life as a wager."

She smirked. "Most people would call you foolish. I consider you to be a brave man. Goodnight, Karueq. I'll see you in the morning." She left him with her words, and he, too, left the hall to rejoin the revelries in the hall.

He thought little of their conversation that night, but early the next morning, he rose to greet the sunrise and to pray to Eleh for the strength and wisdom for the Guard meeting.

When he arrived in the great hall, he found Hanai already there waiting. He was lying on the ground tossing an apple above his head idly. At Karueq's approach, he sprung to his feet.

"Karueq!" he greeted him. "How are you this morning?"

"Very well," Karueq replied. He grinned at his friend whom he hadn't seen in a few weeks.

"I've been assigned to your detail for this mission." Hanai took a healthy bite out of the apple. "I volunteered for it, actually." He smacked Karueq playfully in the elbow.

"I feel safer already." He rolled his eyes.

"Shouldn't be a terribly hard job. You're easy to throw around."

Karueq scoffed at this remark.

Then, the main doors behind them opened and a few Guard members came through it. Within a few minutes several more of the Guard filtered in, accompanied curiously by a few Eleverians who were not part of the Guard. Chelia and Alamar arrived to the meeting. She spread a chart over a table on the side, which Karueq had carefully helped them construct in recent months, and gathered them around. "Thank you for agreeing to join us, everyone. I didn't expect all of you to participate."

Karueq surveyed the group that volunteered for this crazy mission. There weren't but a dozen in attendance, including himself.

"In three days, we fly to Xanadai. We'll be partially concealed by a storm brewing in the area. Keep to the denser parts of this storm, but be careful." She pointed to a group of islands on the chart. "Karueq informed us that these islands mark a checkpoint for the approach to the city. They used to have guards stationed there, but we can't know for sure anymore. Our approach is to circumvent this group and avoid any scouts stationed here –" she pointed to two more islands "– and here.

"Once we get around them, the last point of attack will be the clusters around the gullet." She drew her finger around a dark spot in the middle of the chart, the entrance to Xanadai. "I want you to assume there are lookouts and assailants on each of them. Be ready for an attack at any one of these points as well as from anywhere within ten miles of the entrance."

She straightened up from the chart, propping herself up on both hands. "Rikhvera is your captain for this mission. You will escort the arrowhead along this path." She traced the path again. "Your charge before we breach the surface is to make sure the arrowhead makes it to the entrance. Those in the arrowhead are myself, Alamar, Hanai, and Karueq."

She flipped the chart over to another map, this one a convoluted depiction of the Xanadai underground. "Once the arrowhead has breached the gullet, your task is to keep it open for escape. The arrowhead will go under and compromise strategic points at the Brehila lair, the main tunnel out of Sheol, and the entrance to the city itself." She tapped each of the points.

"I expect we'll draw attention to our presence by executing this plan. Be ready for a gross assault to follow the arrowhead back to the surface. Once everyone is out, we will collapse the approach tunnels, block the entrance, and then race home."

She straightened up again and addressed them. "Rikhvera has split you into teams for the headcount. Do not leave your group behind."

They all nodded in agreement. This command needn't be stated.

"Rikhvera has been commanded that if after ten minutes we fail to surface from the city or the counterattack overwhelms you, the attack is to be suspended, and you will return here promptly. The continuity of command will initiate until we return."

She paused for a second and surveyed the group. "Now is the time for any questions you have."

A non-Guard member was the first to speak. "How long do we expect until they figure out we're there? There has to be an alert system of some sort."

Chelia turned to Karueq. "I'll let you answer that."

"Fortunately, there is no way of alerting the horde from the entrance, or at least there wasn't when I left." Karueq's mind ran through the strategy and the possible ways they could be caught. "Ten minutes is a good estimate owing to the size of this group. They'll be aware of us sooner, but we won't be pursued for a few minutes. Xanadai isn't exactly set up for defense against this kind of attack."

"I'll say that will be our best case," Chelia agreed. "However, Karueq is sure General Bleren has changed a few things in his absence. Assume they'll start organizing and time starts running out when we pass the last checkpoint. Just to be safe."

"Are you attacking Sheol first where the majority of the army is?" another asked.

"No. We'll attack the Brehila first. Unless any of you really wants to dance with them."

The group shook their heads in amusement.

"Will the arrowhead attack anything else if there's time and enough confusion among their ranks?"

"That would be ideal," Chelia nodded. "Those who have gone into combat with me before know my strategies are adaptable. However, this time we're traveling with their most wanted," she indicated Karueq, "and we don't personally know their city. I expect to keep to the plan this time."

It seemed after this question was answered, the group was satisfied. Confusion spurred into Karueq's mind. She hadn't said how the four of them were going to stop up the entrances, and none of the group was curious about it, though their other questions were thorough. That must mean they know.

Chelia surveyed them again. "Please come to me or Rikhvera with any other questions you have in the next few days. I need you all to take extra care to be highly prepared for this assault. Thank you very much for volunteering."

The chatter followed the group as most of them left. Only those mentioned as part of the warhead stayed behind. Chelia let out a long sigh and rubbed the back of her neck with both hands, preparing herself for perhaps the more serious part of the meeting. "Last chance to dismiss yourselves."

Hanai smirked and shook his head at her.

She turned her eyes on him. "Karueq, you're very quiet."

He replied. "What exactly are we going to do to stop up the tunnels?"

"We're using me."

Before Karueq could stop himself, he blurted, "The Crucible?"

"Yes,' she replied. "And before you ask, the Crucible is kept from common knowledge for good reason. The fact that Shatan let it slip shows his utter panic at your conversion. Don't mistake my decision to withhold it from you as an insult to your character."

He shook his head. "Shatan kept me well within his grasp by withholding information from me and by dismissing my concerns. You haven't dismissed me, whatever I've come to you with, but that doesn't mean I'm not curious."

"I understand that, Karueq," she said. "I don't ask you to check your brain at the door. In fact, I require you to bring it with you and ask questions. The only way I'm able to lead my people against the powers of evil is by Eleh's grace and the constant challenge of those smarter than me. So, ask your question."

"How will the four of us be able to cripple their infrastructure? We can't hope to be successful in collapsing the tunnels with weapons whatever tools you build. The tunnels might be haphazard, but they're still carved out of solid rock."

"I'm unleashing my power on the chosen points, thereby blocking up the passages."

"Your power. Why not vent such power on all of Xanadai? Destroy it once and for all?"

"For many reasons. One, I won't rescind the Mercy Law and kill people, even to our advantage. Two, not all the Shatanala are below ground. Utterly destroying Xanadai would lead to rash retaliations by those on the surface and result in more massacres. As long as they still have contact with their leaders below ground, they won't be so desperate and lash out. And three, my strength may fail me if I attempt such a massive attack, therefore, we're going to be precise and methodical. That's why we're bringing you, so you can show me where exactly to attack. Otherwise, I wouldn't ask you for such a risk."

Karueq nodded. "Thank you for explaining."

"I wasn't going to keep all that from you. Now," she said, turning back to the underground map. "We shouldn't have any trouble reaching the gullet, but once we're down there, we're on our own. There will be no one following us in. Like I told Rikhvera, we only have ten minutes to rendezvous with them before they leave. And Rikhvera has been ordered to leave without us."

She looked up to Hanai and Karueq. "You two will break with Alamar and I if we run up to the time. Whatever is the quickest way out, take it."

Karueq objected. "Why would we leave you down there?"

"Your task is to be our guide only, not to be bait for your captors. Although I don't expect a need for such a plan, Hanai will remove you by force if you don't comply. Are we clear?"

Karueq reluctantly nodded.

Chelia turned back to the map. "Once we enter the gullet, we run immediately to the Brehila lair. Do not engage anyone along the way. We don't have time to waste on them. This means we will be followed, so we outrun them to the lair at a full sprint," she pointed to it, "and you will subdue them there. Same goes for running to Sheol." She indicated the large hollow in the center. "No engagements until we get there. After that, we flee the hoard back to the gullet and close it. After that, we race home."

She looked up. "Any more questions at this time?"

Alamar and Hanai shook their heads and Karueq followed suit.

"Thank you for volunteering, both of you," said Chelia to Hanai and Karueq. "I do appreciate it."

"Well," said Hanai, tossing his elbow into Karueq's side, "I can't be letting anyone else have all the fun."

CHAPTER EIGHTEEN

THE CRUCIBLE

The three days leading up to the daring mission ran wild with activity for those that volunteered. The support team busied themselves with dueling practice, repairs, and memorizing the maps. Rikhvera met with them every day to drill the flight in. They discussed a variety of possible entanglements with the Shatanala, up to and including the plan being discovered ahead of time and a host of Shatanala waiting for them at the checkpoints. Chelia agreed that if this were the case, they would abandon the mission.

The arrowhead prepared by memorizing and drilling their own route through the city. Karueq did his best to describe what they would see and how the path would go. They, too, drilled a variety of scenarios every day.

Chelia gave her duties to Hunga for this time. She secluded herself when they weren't drilling. Karueq wondered what she was doing to prepare and concluded that she must be resting for such a large expense of her strength.

Finally, in the evening on the last day, they all bid each other farewell until the morrow at noon. They went about the preparations for their souls. They counseled with their friends and family, and they prayed earnestly for success on this mission.

Karueq, too, prayed heartily for Eleh to bless the mission. He had grown to love this God who wanted him despite the dirtiness of his life. The Eleverians taught him many wonderful things about this King and Creator, and Karueq sought His gentle heart in everything he endeavored to do.

Then, he approached Chelia to anoint him for the task ahead. She prayed the words over him and spoke encouragement to him, this being his first mission since the brutal massacre. When he lifted his head from the prayer, he noticed the inherent brightness of her eyes like all the Eleverians, so full of life and sheer determination, but also kindness and joy. He wondered if his eyes, too, now reflected this light.

At noon the next day, the mission group gathered on the beach of Zarenvai. Alamar prayed over them, for a successful mission and for a safe return for all those going on mission. As a final word, he prayed for the safeguarding of Chelia and protection from the wrath of the Crucible, something Karueq had never heard about before. When he looked up at the conclusion of the prayer, he noticed Chelia had a solemn face. He saw just a glimpse of why Rikhvera was leading instead of her.

They mounted the many dragons with them, Karueq seated behind Hanai and Chelia with Alamar. The rest took a dragon by themselves. On Rikhvera's signal, the beasts darted into the air and raced from the shore.

They sprinted for several hours through the afternoon daylight. The sun lit their way through cloudless skies until at last Karueq saw the beginnings of the storm ahead. The sky swirled with heaving clouds that darkened out the sunlight light night. The downpour and the sea were as one, a mass of water so thick he couldn't tell where the storm began and the ocean started. He braced himself for the turbulent ride in.

The rain hit them. The dragons heeded the storm not. They kept to their flight. Ahead, Rikhvera turned them this way and that through the torrent. Karueq and Hanai clung to the dragon to avoid slipping in the rain. The wind roared in his ears. His light clothing stuck wet against his skin.

They turned hard left. Karueq glanced below to see the faint smudge of the island checkpoint against the night sea. Then, they swung right, still following Rikhvera.

The dragon on their left point wobbled in a bout of sudden turbulence. They pressed on.

Rikhvera dove lower, the rest following. They looped wide of the second checkpoint. Rikhvera dove again, and the team joined her in the salty spray just above the seawater.

Karueq could no longer see. His eyes stung with the splashing mists that assaulted the falling rain. He held tightly onto Hanai and gripped the mighty beast with his legs.

He felt the dragon jerk backward and opened his eyes. Ahead, the support team darted back and forth above the gaping hole in the water. Purple and green flashed about. Of course Bleren had fortified the gullet in his absence.

Before he took in the fullness of the sight, Hanai spurred the dragon forward. They launched through the frenzy and slipped down the gullet behind another dragon.

They crashed to the landing below. Purple sparks flew at them. Karueq and Hanai leaped down and ran to the side tunnel, ignoring the attacking guards.

The arrowhead ran for their lives. Ahead, Chelia and Alamar sprinted away. The twists and turns down the dark passages did not slow the party down. They'd drilled for this. They knew when the turns were coming.

Chelia darted into an offshoot. The three followed her.

They emerged into another passage. They ran down this one, too. Karueq didn't hear anyone following them yet.

The passage opened to a small chamber. Alamar and Hanai jumped to their position at the tunnel on the right just past the lip. Karueq pointed to the jagged lair entrance ahead, then sprang into position with the others.

Chelia slid to a halt in the center, looking damningly at the lair and ignoring the other identical holes in the rock around her. She closed her eyes, crossed her forearms in front of her, and with a loud cry, she threw her arms out. A burst of energy exploded from her. It slammed like a wall into the lair. The rocks shattered and smashed to the ground.

Behind the settling dust, the entrance was blocked.

Immediately, Chelia turned on her heel and ran toward them. They turned ahead of her and sprinted down the tunnel.

They ran the route they'd practiced and turned into more passages. These ones held guards and loiterers. Those with enough awareness shook off their bewilderment and chased the intruding group down.

The arrowhead ignored them and raced to Sheol. Karueq felt the heat of the lava lake creeping through his wet clothes as they neared it.

Alamar turned them down the last tunnel. With their last bursts of energy, they emerged from the side passage into Sheol.

They ran through the crooked towers of dwellings, Karueq now leading them. The stiflingly narrow byways threatened to trip them, but with focused intensity, they sprang from the towers and down the shore of the great lava lake.

Karueq's attention stole to the alarming sight on the left. The bridge to the Great Temple held a small troop of soldiers standing in lines as if guarding the way to the temple. They filled the bridge from the shore to the threshold of the temple.

At first, those in front were confused by the small party. Then, with rage in their eyes, they peeled away one by one and ran at them.

Alamar and Hanai broke off and charged at the army. Chelia and Karueq veered right to the passage opening. He pointed it out and then ran ahead to the escape tunnel. Behind him he heard her cry out, then a deafening boom threw him to the ground.

He opened his eyes and reeled at the dizziness fogging his head. He hadn't gotten out of the way in time. Quickly, he rolled over and tried to push himself to his feet that way, but he lost his balance. He propped himself up on his side and rubbed his head. His faculties were returning.

His head cleared enough for him to get to his feet. He looked back at the frenzy in the cavern. The soldiers poured from the bridge. A few ran after Karueq. He whipped out his sword and attacked. He parried their blows, blows clearly meant to kill him.

Another thunderous blast exploded from near the bridge. It flattened him and his assailants in a cloud of dust and sprays of searing hot lava. A glob hit Karueq's temple, and he cried out as he clawed it away, burning his fingers in the process.

The hot burn kept him alert, wicking away the concussion fogging the periphery of his senses. He staggered to his feet. Shouting came from the threshold of the bridge. He whipped around and saw that the three

Eleverians were the only ones standing now. He quickly surveyed the wide shore and the soldiers that lay there.

Dead. All of them were dead.

Karueq's eyes then fell on the Great Temple now crumbling in ruins at the center of the lake. What had she done?

Then, from the towers, a clamor rose, resounding angrily through the cavern. The inhabitants, roused by the blast, streamed from the broken dwellings and descended on the shore.

Karueq shouted to the rest of the arrowhead. Their allotted time was surely coming to an end, but instead of fleeing immediately, they were huddled, not leaving where they stood.

Karueq shouted to them again. Chelia grabbed Alamar and kissed him desperately before the three of them broke the huddle and darted after him. Karueq barely noticed that Alamar lagged behind them considerably as his attention snapped into place again, and he fled ahead of them, entering the side tunnel before the wave of Shatanala crashed upon them.

With the horde on their heels, Karueq knew they couldn't take the time to weave through the predetermined route. They were probably already facing a flank from the Shatanala in the rest of the city. He turned sharply, leading them to a larger passage that would get them out quicker.

He turned up the direction of the gullet without looking the other way. The shouts coming at them told him they just cut in front of the flank.

The horde ran on fresh legs, and they were gaining. His tired muscles screamed their protest. Faster, he must go faster.

The tunnel swept upward, leading straight to the gullet. They were almost out. Chelia dashed ahead of him, and Hanai pulled up alongside him in the wide tunnel.

The two dragons roared terribly at the oncoming assault. The tunnel shook with their rage.

A sword sliced Karueq in the back. His cringe made him falter. Hands seized him. Hanai turned back around and launched his justice upon them. Karueq freed himself from the last pair of hands.

"Go!" shouted Hanai.

Karueq lurched forward. He didn't know how many he had to outrun yet, but he was almost there.

He glanced around briefly to look for Hanai following him, but he couldn't see him. Forgetting his orders, he drew his sword and turned back to the horde. He had to save his friend.

He fought viciously through the clog. Then, he heard his name, Hanai's voice. It came from behind him, near the roaring dragons. Hanai had made it out. Karueq swung around and ran to his escape. Just before he reached the landing, a hand wrenched him backward. Numerous Shatanala leaped on him and pinned him to the ground. He struggled with them, trying to break free. He clawed to his feet and threw them off, but there were too many of them. Then two large shadows skirted over them.

No, it couldn't be. Karueq yelled desperately for them to hear him. One dragon shot through the opening above. The other roared one last time and expelled a plume of fire toward the attackers below. Then, it darted upward and out of sight. A thundershock exploded on the surface. Rocks and a torrential wave from the sea poured down the gullet onto the landing ahead of Karueq, covering the Shatanala still attempting to aim their attack on the escaping team.

The Shatanala holding Karueq startled at the blast and looked up. Karueq's next decision was quick and full of determination. He was lost, he couldn't make it out on his own, but he was never going to back down as long as he had his strength. There were other ways out of Xanadai. He threw off the frightened soldiers and battered his way through them furiously. The men put up a hefty fight. His muscles screamed at him for respite.

Finally, a particularly vicious soldier leaped in his path and shoved his blade in Karueq's side. With a defiant grunt, Karueq tripped to his knees. The horde pounced on him, and in a frenzy, they beat him. The striking and kicking only fueled Karueq's determination, but his body gave out. He could no longer oppose them and instead endured the beating. A boot kicked his head, scraping the burn on his face, sending fiery shivers through his scalp and down his neck.

Then, they suddenly halted, and one of them put his foot firmly on Karueq's throat. He heard rapid shuffling in one direction as they parted. A gap opened up at his head, and a man emerged. Then, Karueq heard a familiar voice – one he thought he wouldn't hear for a long time – give a command he didn't expect.

"Detain him," Bleren ordered.

CHAPTER NINETEEN

PRISONERS OF WAR

----- ----- ----- ----- ----- ----- -----

Karueq leaned his head against the pillar with his eyes closed. He followed Hunga's example of imprisonment and filled the void he left behind with his earnest pleading. The assault team had probably reached Eleveria by this time, but he couldn't be sure, so he asked for their safe return. He asked for Eleh to give Chelia wisdom for the next move. He prayed also for Hanai, his dear friend, that he wouldn't let Karueq's loss dishearten him.

The wandering thoughts he couldn't control latched onto the circumstance of the escape. He didn't understand why Hanai had left so quickly without him. He'd been charged with Karueq's protection, and that was his task regardless of the outcome. This deeply puzzled and troubled him. Regardless of his orders, the friendship he shared with Karueq had to count for something. He wouldn't just leave him behind.

He redirected his unsettling thoughts, sending them in a different direction to dissect the strange occurrences of the mission. Firstly, there were four blasts. There were only meant to be three. The Great Temple had never been mentioned in the process of planning the attack but had ended up being a fourth strike. He couldn't fault her for that and made note that her strategies were admittedly flexible, but all the soldiers in Sheol had died as a result. In the private meeting with the arrowhead, Chelia assured him that the Mercy Law would not be suspended for this mission.

Another detail that nagged at him was Chelia's ability to outrun him to the gullet. Of great importance to her during planning had been conserving her strength, and she had even mentioned that it would fail her as a result of these attacks. Not only had she expelled a new attack, but she'd outrun both him and Hanai to be the first one to reach the dragons.

Then, he wondered how Alamar reached the gullet in time. He was slow leaving Sheol, far slower than he was when they arrived in the cavern. The horde had indeed caught up with them when they reached the last passage. He mulled it over but decided he must have gotten a second wind or latched onto his adrenaline just in time.

Karueq ran his parched tongue over his dry lips. They'd been keeping him here without food or water for maybe a day and a half. Their only care of him was stopping the bleeding from the wounds in his side and on his back. He stretched his chafing wrists in the iron chains that kept him secured to the post in the corner. His eyes opened, the skin around his right eye peeled the burn uncomfortably on his temple, and he surveyed the tiny cell. He'd never seen the prisons from this side. The sneers he offered the detainees were always from the other side of the door. However, it didn't worry him. This predicament wasn't enough to sway his heart to fear.

The sound of footsteps came down the hall. They halted just outside his view of the hallway. For several seconds, the person stayed out of his view.

Then, Bleren stepped in front of the door and turned the lock. His hardened face was aflame with a thousand emotions. He didn't even pause to relock the closed door. He struck his prisoner violently across the cheek.

"Why!" It wasn't a question but an accusation.

Karueq turned his head forward but didn't say anything.

"Shatan is demanding your blood! I'm using everything I have to stay his hand! Why!"

"I was given a second chance."

A fatal roar erupted from Bleren's throat, cutting him off. The man buried his eyes in his fists, his sides heaving. Karueq quelled his tongue.

With great effort, Bleren turned his red eyes onto Karueq, his mouth drawn tight. "You really are lost."

"No, Bleren. I was saved."

One shake of his head, that's all Bleren could afford. "I don't recognize you, but I don't accept that you can't be pulled back."

"Nothing will change my heart, Bleren."

"We'll start with your mind, then. I refuse to let you fall further. I'll do everything I can to convince Shatan not to drag you into the pit. That is my promise to you." He eyed him up one more time. "Don't get comfortable."

The general slammed the door open and left the cell without looking back at his prisoner. Karueq was again left alone.

Then he heard a faint, dry voice coming from the hallway. "Karueq?" At the sound of his name, Karueq's ears peeled open. "Karueq. Are you here?"

His breath caught in his throat, and his gut clenched horribly. "Alamar," he said. He heard the iron restraints shift.

"Did Chelia make it?" The weakness was evident in his speech, but he had no trouble hearing him. The cells were small and cramped enough that they couldn't be more than a few feet apart.

"Yes. She and Hanai both made it to the surface in time. Beyond that, I don't know."

"Hanai wouldn't leave without you. What happened?"

Karueq rocked as comfortably as he could onto his hip, giving his legs a rest but twisting his arms to do so. "They caught up with us and nearly had us routed. I was caught, Hanai freed me, but they caught me again."

"He wouldn't leave without you," Alamar repeated. In his voice, he seemed puzzled by this thought.

Karueq asked, "What happened to you?"

There was silence from the other cell for a minute. Then in a shaky breath, Alamar uttered. "Her strength failed her."

"She made it out, Alamar."

"Barely," the Quiri sighed. "I had to pass her much of my strength. I'm very weak, Karueq. I can't help you escape now, but I'm here for you. They'll take you to task for your treason."

"I know." Just like that, he had an answer to a question he didn't have. He was so dumbfounded by Alamar's capture, he didn't ask himself why he was up here in the forward cells and not in the stone encasings at the rear. The man probably couldn't break out of bindings a string much less an iron cell.

"Stay strong, Karueq. This is where you will show Eleh the depth of your love for Him."

Karueq's heart swelled at the thought. His King had reached into the pit of Xanadai and led him safely to Eleveria. Now, more than any aid mission he'd joined, he could demonstrate his conviction and devotion to Him.

Then came a curious question from the Quiri. "Why did you turn?"

Karueq was confused by the question. "It was Eleh's second chance for me."

"No, not that. We heard you were not born here. What drove you to evil all those years ago?"

Karueq glanced at his bare foot where his boot knife was normally kept. "My sister was sick. A witch came to the village and offered me the chance to save her, for a price. The witch did cure her, but she was killed a year later by vagabonds for what little we had. I don't think she ever knew what I'd done."

"I'm sorry, Karueq."

Karueq's brow knitted together at another thought. "What about the attack on the temple?"

The restraints scraped softly again in the next cell in hesitation. "I'm sorry, Karueq."

Karueq snapped his attention away from the subject. Any other time in the last few days, Karueq had the opportunity to ask them about the Crucible, whether or not he would get an answer. Sitting in this cell with the threat of torture and death ahead of him, it would be unwise to learn the truth now. The value of information in a cloaked war was indescribable.

Karueq knitted his resolve together. He wouldn't succumb to Shatan's threats. The demon was manipulative, for sure, but Karueq was confident he could withstand him. He'd been under his direction and conducted meetings in confidence with him for most of his life. There was nothing that would surprise him, and the beast had nothing to bribe him with.

So, when he was placed on the rack, his conviction held strong, and his heart would not be swayed. Their methods were cruel. He'd made some of the most sadistic of his men the butchers of the racks, and indeed, he'd chosen well.

The suffering his body endured was merely a prelude. He'd taught Bleren that a weakened – and especially damaged – body impaired the mind. This tactic he now employed on his teacher.

When the prisons were empty of their guards for brief periods, Alamar found his voice from the other row of cells between bouts of unconsciousness. Karueq could barely hear him, but the words he did catch were a balm of encouragement. He clung to that from the chaffing restraints of the rack.

After days of starvation and endless carving, Shatan came to his cell. The demon wore his royal facade, proudly brandishing his authority, an authority Karueq no longer respected.

His expression wasn't a smile, but there was no apparent malice there as he surveyed the gashes covering his body.

"This is a particularly poor way of repaying me, Commander," he began.

Karueq's voice cracked from anemia, thirst, and the endless screams that were released during his internment. "I'm not your Commander."

"You were, once. You held the highest place of honor in my ranks. You were owed everything I could ever offer."

Karueq didn't answer. He needn't waste his breath on this interview.

"I don't hold any of this against you," the demon continued. "You were tricked, seduced by a lie, and I'm sorry I drove you to such rash action. It is partly my fault."

Again, nothing from the rack.

"I won't even hold the attack against you. They convinced you that you were fighting for the right side, the side of truth and justice. They also have been lied to by Eleh."

"Eleh doesn't lie."

"Of course He hasn't lied to you. He doesn't even speak to you, but when He does, He always lies. He lied to me in the beginning, and now I pay the price for my decision to choose freedom."

"That isn't freedom."

"No," Shatan shook his head and cast a glance around the chamber. "This isn't freedom, far from freedom. That's why I continue to fight. I desire liberation from this prison."

The demon turned his attention to Karueq again. "I'm imprisoned here, Karueq. Why do you think I never go to the surface? Why must I wage war against the powers of Heaven with mortals and lesser demons? I'm trapped here. This is my only window from Hell where I'm being kept in perpetuity.

"Long ago, a small band of men saw through Eleh's lies, learned the truth of my captivity, and poured out their blood and souls in sacrifice to break open this small crack into Seaga. Their followers helped me build this city to shelter those that also accepted the truth, and from here, they wage war against Heaven and Eleveria on my behalf because I cannot reach the surface. That is the legacy that you ruled from, Commander."

"You have always been deceitful, Shatan, but I'll believe you about your confinement here. You won't give up your pride for much, certainly not to admit something like that. And I'm not your Commander."

"Eleh continues to lie to you, Karueq, and so does Eleveria. I doubt very much that they told you what the Crucible is, even though you were involved in a plot to use it against me."

"The plot succeeded."

"They didn't tell you, did they?" Shatan challenged him, ignoring the jab.

"No, and frankly I don't care."

"You should care. You think they're always honest with you; you think they've never lied to you, even lying by omission. They take you for a fool. Do you want to know why the Crucible is so valuable? Why they keep it a secret, and why I've never told you either?"

No answer.

"I've never lied to you without reason, Karueq, but I would be vulnerable if certain information is brought to light."

"Good. Tell me, so I can exploit it."

"If you can," replied the demon, a wicked smile fleeting across his eyes. "Your faith in the one they call Chelia is about to be broken.

"The Crucible is a volatile soul, capable of doing great work for either light or darkness. The power Chelia displayed in the attack is a poor example of her capabilities. She could fracture reality itself if she unleashed her full potential on the world. I need her allegiance because she has the power to free me, to fracture this prison I'm held in. Then, I can wage my war without using my followers. She is claimed by Eleh, but the allegiance of the Crucible is delicate.

"I said the Crucible is volatile. I meant it. The smallest temptation is enough to throw all conviction she has aside. When I say small, I mean perhaps even the most justified kill is enough to sway her to bloodlust. I reckon that is the main reason she instituted the Mercy Law. She is just as prone to choose her own side, or rather no sides, as she is to align herself with either Eleh or myself. What do you think now of your precious Elequiri?"

Karueq kept himself as neutral as possible. Inside, he now had a thousand questions, one of which was of the validity of what he was hearing.

The demon clasped his shoulder. "Karueq, I'm asking you to rejoin me. Eleh made an unpredictable weapon of flesh and bone, blood and power, and set it loose upon the world. What a cruel game." The demon's focus grew faint as he pondered his thoughts out loud. "She's a loose weapon capable of destroying the world, or she can save it and refuses to because Eleh commanded her. What a cruel game."

The demon shook his head for effect. Again, nothing came from his detainee.

Shatan looked him over thoughtfully and then left the cell. When Karueq thought it was over, he returned to the aisle carrying Alamar in his arms. Karueq's hatred for the demon inflamed as he shackled the Eleverian into the rack in the cell opposite him. The man rolled his eyes open and turned a dry smirk on the devil imprisoning him there.

"Good," he sighed. "I was feeling left out."

Without responding or bidding a final word to either of them, Shatan left, and they were alone.

Karueq looked the weakened man over. He was exhausted. A few bruises bloomed over his dirty skin. "I've looked worse," the Quiri said wearily.

"So have I," Karueq replied, "but a long night's sleep in recovery would do me good."

Alamar laid his head back on the rack. "Watching the sunrise."

"Yes," Karueq agreed.

"Breathing the free air on the plain."

"Listening to Hanai's stories."

A profound calm spread over Alamar's face. "Holding my bride."

Karueq smiled. "This is why Shatan can never break you lot."

"Nor you."

The statement lightened Karueq's heart a little.

They spent many hours nodding in and out of sleep not being bothered. Karueq was grateful to be free of the carving and the slicing for a time. His wounds scabbed over without the assault. When they were awake at the same time, Alamar encouraged him, and Karueq tried to do the same. With each kind word, the feeling of belonging in Karueq's heart grew, blossoming like a tender shoot. Even here in the ground, he was indeed a part of Eleveria now, part of the family that had taken him in.

Despite these wonderful things, Shatan's challenge crept into his thoughts. Thus far, he'd been able to keep that dirty trick away, but ironically with that feeling of brotherhood came the nagging need to know the truth.

"Alamar," he asked, unsure if the man was even awake.

A small murmur came from the rack across the aisle.

"Shatan told me about the Crucible."

The low murmur met his ears again, seemingly unconcerned by the admission.

"How much of what he said is true?"

Alamar cracked his voice open with a small grunt. "What did he tell you?"

"That Chelia is a weapon."

A low chuckle. "Of course he would see her that way. She's not a weapon, just a very powerful person and a strong leader."

"He said she is volatile and easily swayed."

"Not with her love of Eleh, nor her love for her people."

"But it's true?"

Alamar sighed. "Karueq, evil sees the world one way. He sees her as a weapon of unbelievable power, untapped and misused. Whatever

Shatan described to you is probably true. She is capable of a great deal, including, as he probably admitted, springing him from his cage. Temptation will happen to anyone, even a steadfast and unwavering woman like her, and falling to that temptation as the Crucible is destructive and could devastate nations. Imagine your ambitions and bloodlust while you were Commander combined with power beyond your wildest imaginings.”

Karueq relived the attack on Sheol in his head. “Inner strength. That’s what she meant - that’s what failed her.”

“Yes,” Alamar sighed. “She gave in to the temptation of wrath. She saw the splendor of the temple built for Shatan, a shrine of all that is evil, and her zeal overcame her. So she destroyed it, and it appears her wrath turned on all who bore Shatan’s Mark, too.”

“And you had to bring her back from the brink.”

“Yes. That is part of my duty as the Quiri.”

Karueq let himself settle on Alamar’s brief explanation. Of course, he wouldn’t get the full picture right now with Alamar in the state he was. If he was honest with himself, he knew they would both die down here, either giving out from the abuse or in an instant because of Shatan’s rage. He settled on this fact, too. He had the promise of Heaven from his King, and if Shatan sent him there soon, so be it.

“He offered you a chance to return, didn’t he?” was Alamar’s next question.

Karueq snorted. “He can keep his offer.”

CHAPTER TWENTY

THE BRAND REBORN

Footsteps echoed down the hall outside the chamber. It had been a day or two since Alamar had last spoken. His body lay limp on the rack, but he still breathed. The exhaustion had taken over, and he wouldn't wake up. Karueq was barely better. He slipped in and out of consciousness, his lips continued to crack and dry out, and his body sagged on his bound limbs. Dreams didn't come. Sleep merely provided blanks in the progression of time.

He barely heard the door open. Then, his wrists were loosed, his ankles freed, and he was dragged away from the rack. He caught glimpses of the passages as he was dragged through the underground. His bare feet and knees scraped along the rocky ground.

A wave of cold air hit him, sending a shiver through his spine. He opened one eye and surveyed his surroundings. They'd brought him to a chamber high in the earth. He could smell the salt of the ocean above and looked up. A dark opening wide enough for one or two people to go through reached into the ceiling and was swallowed in pitch black above. This was one of a few vents that led out of Xanadai to the cool ocean air on the surface. It emerged in a crack on the rock face of a small island.

Karueq was puzzled why he'd been brought here. A hand grasped his shoulder. He stared into the face of Bleren.

"Take the Prince's offer," he commanded him.

Karueq's thirsty voice cracked, barely audible. "He's not my Prince."

Bleren cracked him across the jaw. "Take his offer."

"No," was his answer.

With his free hand, Bleren reached to his side and pulled a limp body from the grip of two other soldiers. Alamar sank to the ground with a sickening thud. Bleren gave him one last venomous glare, then moved aside. Shatan stood before him. In his hand was a sword with a jewel-colored hilt and no cross-guards – Chema, the sword of the Elequiri. Karueq startled, even in his weariness, unsure of what this could mean.

"So that you may know that I'm playing no games with you," Shatan explained, holding the sword forward to show him. "Chelia is waiting on the surface to receive her Quiri back."

Karueq set his face. This was indeed a game, and he would not see it otherwise.

Shatan continued. "She is willing to sacrifice you to retrieve him. She will not get him back until you surrender. Fail to do so, and the cost is his life. Any breach of this deal on my end, and she will destroy all of Xanadai."

"He is prepared to die, as am I," Karueq said.

"How dare you put yourself above him!" Shatan hissed. "How dare you refuse to free him! Ask yourself what Eleh would think of you, a worm I used to hold complete claim to, sacrificing a righteous man who is the safeguard of His most powerful weapon. He will never forgive you for it. Alamar is more worthy of his life than you are of your soul. Bow to me."

Karueq flinched at such an accusation. "Never," was his small answer.

"You know I would be happy to leave his corpse rotting in the Rales' den. This is the one thing you can do yet for your precious Eleveria. Give them back the Quiri and give up your delusions. Your choice is clear."

Karueq's mind ran with him, and there was nothing he could do to stop it. He knew he was not of sound mind, but he couldn't truly hold on to anything. Then he grasped it, the reason for his conviction and his continued defiance. "I will never reject my King. I am His servant, and no threat of darkness holds sway over me."

"It is not the threat of darkness that should hold sway over you. You are nothing to Him, Karueq. He will never forgive you for the cruelty you exacted on His people, the thousands of Eleverians you put in the ground, the Hell you harbored in your heart all your life. Your soul has more rot in it than any other before you."

Karueq's inner voice grew smaller with the accusations.

"More than any before you, you fanned the flames of hatred. You cared nothing for anyone, including yourself. You took none of my rewards, not because of your piety or your goodness, but because your true prize was Eleh's undoing. You hated your God."

Karueq winced.

"You sought to destroy Him – with a bloodthirsty hunger. You let your hatred of Him prosper. You would spit in His face and drive your blade through His heart if given the chance. You would be sure you could watch the light and divinity leave Him and forego savoring nothing of that day. You hated Him. Even in what little salvation you may have gained by your false defection, you took it greedily. Nothing you did under His or the Eleverians' command was for love of Him. You did all of it greedily, thinking only of yourself. You are a poor, waste of a man. He will never have you – you selfish, hateful, deceitful sinner! I pity the Eleverians for what they wasted on you."

The accusations consumed him. He couldn't look up, couldn't look at the good man lying broken on the ground before him. Indeed, his past was heinous, hardly worthy of the love he'd been shown.

It was because of him, and the brutality with which he'd waged war on them, that Eleveria had to meet the Shatanala in so many battles, losing countless lives and suffering terrible sorrow. It was because of him that that village had been massacred – an attempt to find him – and Brynia had nearly died. It was because of him that Nimera had lost his friend and suffered terrible torment after a routine mission. It was because he entered Eleveria bearing the Mark that it was now exposed, and Chelia had made a rash attack on Xanadai in its defense – a rash attack that cost her her protector and love, Alamar.

His *never, never* weakened. It would be because of him and his selfish attempt to claim an inheritance with Eleh, that Alamar would die rather than have the chance to hold his bride again.

What little strength his resolve offered him gave out, and he sagged further against the grip of the men. They let him go, and he dropped to his knees, his face coming within a foot of Alamar's. After a brief look, he turned away. He couldn't face this man even if he was unconscious.

An object clattered obstinately near his hand. He turned a glance on it, and a tear sprang to his eye. The knife with the ivory handle, a gift from his sister, glinted daringly at him.

"Renew your blood oath to me," demanded the demon.

The knife felt so heavy. The cold handle sent its own accusations through his fingers. *Eleh, I am so sorry. Please...please forgive me.*

"Your oath, Karueq."

With every ounce of strength he had left, he lifted the blade to his palm and dug a deep, regretful gash into his flesh. The tears that blinded him from the pain in his heart, not the sting in his hand, were fitting. They preceded the blindness he was willingly taking into his soul.

On the rough floor at his knee, he wiped a crude image of the Mark from the cut in his hand. It was such a poor drawing that he briefly hoped maybe it didn't count. He knew, however, that it was the intent of the heart that counted, not necessarily the display of ritual. He did intend to make this trade for Alamar.

He placed his bloody palm on the center of the image and in a small voice with his eyes shut tight, he swore, "I renounce the light. Let darkness consume me. Deny to me the promises of Heaven and all its lies. I bind myself, heart and soul, to Hell for all eternity."

Upon his final word, a stinging sensation slithered through the cut in his hand. Then it violently seared up his arm through his veins and bloomed at his shoulder. He grunted at the sharp cutting in his flesh as the Mark branded itself deep into him. Just as the branding subsided, a sickening squirm erupted in his skin and the Mark sprouted a root that dove through his shoulder into his chest. There, near his heart, the root lay in wait.

A soft scrape tickled his ears. He turned his face toward it. The men dragged Alamar from the floor and hoisted him up through the ceiling. At the man's waist dangled Chema. Shatan was making good on his word.

With broken weeping, Karueq was dragged away, back down the tunnel through the underground. The soldiers brought him back to his place on the rack.

There, his uncertainty, his confusion, and the darkness of the prisons consumed him. The Mark took hold of him, and as his thoughts circled deeper into despair, loneliness, and deep regret, it slinked in and choked his heart.

His memories shifted. Beautiful experiences and moments that he held onto during torture blackened. His memory of the hospitality they'd shown him in Eleveria was marred by feelings of deceit. Of course they hadn't taken him in willingly. Of course they showed him kindness to keep him in check. He thought of his missions now marred with conflicts in logic. He'd gone to the same village more than once, and he shouldn't have had to. The blessings should have taken hold permanently and remained there.

Even his memories of Hanai turned toxic. He'd only pretended to befriend Karueq as part of the Eleka Guard. He was an assignment, a mission. At the brink of capture, Hanai had hastily thrown him aside and escaped Xanadai. Every conversation they'd had felt bitter now. Hanai's jokes and pranks were a farce, and he damned him for it.

His mind then turned over Chelia. The lying witch and her entire army were hiding such a powerful weapon. He mulled over Shatan's cautionary elaboration of this weapon. Indeed, she was either too scared, too proud, or too ensnared by Eleh's lies to wield it. That is until she feared invasion by the Shatanala and sought selfishly to circumvent it.

Karueq's old malice returned, and his spiny, scheming mind reemerged.

Karueq heard someone coming down the hallway and became aware of the exhaustion still deeply set in his body. He opened his eyes to find Bleren peering at him through the bars on the door, reminding Karueq of a curious boy peeking into a viper's den.

He grunted to clear his throat. "Water," he commanded in a rasp.

Bleren paused for but a moment, then unlocked the door and pushed it open. Karueq turned an eye on what was in the man's hand. A waterskin and a cake of ground meat were in his clutches. He held the waterskin up to Karueq's mouth.

He scoffed. "You think to sate me by your own hand? Take me down."

"Not until I know you've returned for sure."

"If I'm not, you can easily slay me in this state. I'm tired and broken. Take me down."

Bleren set the skin down and laid the cake on top. He gingerly undid the shackles holding Karueq to the rack and helped him slide down to sit upright against the rack. Karueq pulled the skin toward him and drew a pull from it, feeling it revive him even as it drained down his throat.

He looked Bleren over. "I'm glad it's you I see first."

"You're being detained until Shatan says otherwise," Bleren said abruptly, keeping to business.

Karueq's face hardened. "That's not going to happen."

"You committed the highest treason, Karueq. He's only keeping you alive on my account."

"I don't intend to take back my position immediately, but he would be remiss to leave me down here when I now have what we need to win this war." He lifted the meat to his teeth and tore into it.

"Yes, that was part of my bargain with him. You have valuable information, and it would be good to keep you alive as an incentive to divulge it. He would prefer to extract it from you in the pit."

"Not as a prisoner. Take me to his temple. He must have rebuilt it by now." He took another bite.

"The temple is still in ruins."

Karueq nearly choked on his mouthful. He'd been down here for a few weeks, and rebuilding the temple would have been Shatan's primary focus. "Why?"

"Whatever that woman did to the temple, the entrances, and the Brehila lair, Shatan can't reverse it. Nor can any of the priests or the demons, nor any creature at our disposal."

Karueq slammed his fist on the floor. It didn't make near the thud he'd intended, merely a thump. That was why it had to be Chelia, their ultimate weapon, to head the attack. He should have seen it. Simply collapsing key entrances wouldn't have stopped the Shatanala from repairing the damage. Such a plot would have only set them back a week. It had to be her not only blocking them up with rubble but fixing an impenetrable force over the rubble. They'd planned their attack well indeed.

"Then take me to his ruins."

Bleren stared at him for a moment, investigating the change he was seeing. Without a word, he left the cell. It wasn't long when Shatan materialized outside the cell. His expression was damning, daring Karueq to defy him. "You expect to appear before me without a summons, you worm?"

Karueq tossed the waterskin toward the door. "It's empty."

The beast beneath flickered into view briefly. "I will remind you that you committed treason."

"I will remind you that you are imprisoned down here, and I penetrated Eleveria's defenses."

The beast flickered again. "And you did not return willingly."

"And you let a precious bargaining tool slip through your hands to get this miserable, treasonous worm back. You need me. Why put up this charade when you know you will open that door and counsel with me outside of this barbaric lodging you've given me?"

Nothing came from the demon.

Karueq folded his bare arms, closed his eyes, and leaned back casually against the rack. "You're the one wasting our time at this point."

After several seconds, he heard the lock click and the door scrape open. He opened his eyes, pleased, and got up from the floor. He walked out coolly, dusting off his hands, despite not yet having all his strength. "Since your temple is still in ruins, where are we discussing?"

Shatan glared as they walked to the temple sector. Karueq didn't mind the silence. His faculties still failed him. They reached the ominous purple light of the sector court and turned to the temple of Madaka. Karueq felt that old, sickening feeling nauseate him. He truly did hate this demon.

The temple was deserted, and no one would interrupt them or listen in on this meeting. There were no fires lit on the side altars. The center altar was conspicuously bare. Karueq remembered the time the battalion slew the high priest on it and Zokul's rabid speech that followed. It was not lost on him that his honest defection had been the fulfillment of that rat's idea, and that this whole mess started here.

Then, a plume of smoke swirled in front of them and materialized the maleficent host demon. It gave him a glaring stare. "I would have had this pig in shackles to go with his rags," it spat.

Shatan ignored him. "Speak," he ordered Karueq.

"We must strike them now."

"How?"

"Eleveria was concealed by some form of a shield that kept them protected and hidden. It was broken when I entered while still bearing the Mark. They've been keeping you oblivious to its location ever since by keeping you distracted."

"You mean *you* have been keeping us oblivious," Madaka sneered.

Karueq ignored him. "With their shield down, we can penetrate their borders and fight them on their own ground."

"I won't fight in a territory I don't know."

"That's why you have me, why you're keeping me alive. Let me lead your men once more, and I will hand the Crucible over to you."

"Lies!" Madaka hissed.

This time Karueq did address him. "With all your power, with all your deceit, Madaka, you have no power to win your lord his prize. So, smite me or bite your tongue." He stood his ground daring the demon to make good on his challenge, but the demon couldn't dissuade the leverage Karueq now offered them. He simply snarled and glared furiously at the recovered traitor.

Shatan spoke. "I will not put you at the head of my forces. Your general, Bleren, has taken over such tasks."

"I will concede that if you make me his second."

"Careful, Karueq. You have already won your life by his hand. Do not provoke me to revoke such a gift by your appetite for power. You will counsel your old friend on this move. That is all. Now tell me, why must we strike them now when we are crippled?"

"The attack on Xanadai was just preparation for their plan. They intend to battle us on neutral ground without the full force of our armies behind us."

"They would never entice us to such a battle."

"Be careful in underestimating them, Shatan," Karueq warned. "Claiming foolishly that they would never come underground to destroy us is what led you to these desperate times."

A glare crawled over Shatan's brow, but he said nothing.

"If you have nothing further from me at this time, my lord, and if you must consider my counsel at length, I will retire," said Karueq. "Send the general to my chamber." He needed several hours of proper rest and food to renew his strength. Then, he would attack that miserable nation alongside Bleren.

He left the chamber, shivering off the ill feeling Madaka exuded as he escaped the temple. He found his chamber as he'd left it, but there was a new animal skin on the seat behind the low map table. He recognized it as Bleren's. Karueq pictured him sitting in that seat staring at the map for hours wondering where throughout Seaga his master could have gone. He imagined the young man falling asleep studying those lines so often that he'd brought that skin here to sleep under.

After eating what was left from the rations Bleren had left in the room, Karueq lay down on the bed and faded quickly to sleep. So deep was his slumber that he had vivid dreams – dreams that both tormented and delighted him. In his dreams he saw the burning sea of clouds from his vision, the figure dressed in white walking toward him. This time, Karueq viciously plunged his sword through the man's chest. A look of pity, a look he'd seen a thousand times from the Eleverians, stared back at him from the man's face, and to his horror, that face was Hanai's.

At first, that pity made him feel small, apologetic even, but by the tenth reenactment, Karueq felt nothing. Then he woke up, that sterile indifference following him. He puzzled over the sensation. Where was the rage and the anger? Where was the burning desire to destroy this God and His people? There was malice, sure, but the rabid desire he'd once had wasn't there.

The sound of someone shifting their weight brought him out of such analysis. He peered over into the room. Bleren was seated on the folded animal skin beside the table.

Karueq rubbed his temples to banish the sleep. "You're eager to start already."

"I didn't know Shatan released you."

"So, you moved into my quarters in my brief absence?"

"Watch your tone, Karueq," he spat.

Karueq's gaze froze on him. He didn't believe Bleren just challenged him. "Excuse me -"

"You will mind your tone when speaking with me. I know this is a charade trying to make everyone believe that you're back to the way you were because you feel out of place right now. You will not take it out on me. Am I clear?"

"You intend to keep my position?"

"If you remain a lost soul, then yes. If you speak with me on pretense and refuse to get your conviction back, then you will remain an advisor to me and no more. But, if you once again manage to inspire me in our crusade, you may again lead me."

Bleren's lecture reminded them of the bond they used to have. He saw a glimpse of hurt behind the hardened stare looking back at him. Bleren had gone through a proverbial Hell while Karueq was away. He'd seen his mentor flee the city on account of his treason. He'd had to assume command of all Xanadai before he could mourn the loss. He'd set assassins loose to hunt him down and then let him escape the ship as his last gift to a soon-to-be dead man.

Karueq looked away. Bleren was right, of course. He was compensating for his long tenure with the Eleverians. He was compensating for the lack of bloodlust, and he realized all he felt about Eleh and his people was betrayal. The betrayal was strong, nonetheless. Karueq was surprised to find that he wasn't just putting on a show for everyone else, he was putting on a show for himself.

"I apologize, Bleren." He threw off the blanket and swung his legs over the side of the bed. He was famished, but he would tend to that later. "Shatan must have sent you to discuss our next strike."

Bleren turned resolutely to the map. "You want to attack immediately, but all we have to draw on are the soldiers we have above ground. It's impractical to move the whole city through the vents. Once on the surface, our only way out of the sea is flight."

"-- and the Rales are trapped underground. What assets do we have?"

"Where is Eleveria?"

Karueq pointed to the general location on the map.

Bleren nodded. "We can draw out the armies stationed in these areas," he pointed out pockets of Shatanala plants, "and if there are any Brehila left there, we will send word to them. I wouldn't mind having a few in our arsenal."

"I agree."

Bleren pulled a piece of empty paper gingerly from under the map, careful not to disturb the stones. "What does it look like?"

Karueq drew out a rough sketch of Eleveria on the paper. He outlined the gateway of Zarenvai bay, the hills beyond that, the plains stretching to the river, and then the fortress nestled near the mountains.

"If we make it all the way to the interior there, they will be very unprepared indeed," Karueq mused.

They calculated it would take a few days to reach the gate by ship, as they had no way to go by air with the army they needed. They reasoned the attack would fail before they reached the bay if the Eleverians were aware of their presence at all. They would rain down on them on dragonback and force the army to float back to Seagan land on debris.

The two of them discussed countless scenarios in the bay. After a few hours, they were determined they could take the beach if they weren't discovered too early at sea. Once they took the beach, they would conduct a swift campaign to the fortress. It would be unwise to stay in the hills or even take control of them – same with the plains. Once at the fortress, they would lay siege to it. Karueq reassured Bleren the Shatanala could lay siege to the fortress for years, because he knew of the abundant food sources around the land to supply them.

Bleren pondered the drawing and asked what was on the other side of the mountains. Though Karueq hadn't been over the mountains, he pointed out that there was a vast desert that made up the western half of the country. Bleren asked about the possibility of the Eleverians fleeing there, but Karueq explained there was almost no chance of that happening. It was an unforgivable wasteland where no settlements had ever been made in Eleveria's history and no Eleverians ventured there now.

In the course of their planning, Karueq noticed their relationship revert back a little to what it had been before he left. Karueq's suggestions turned into him making the plans and Bleren happily advising and questioning his every move. It dawned on him while they schemed that he missed the young man and was happy to be back with him.

CHAPTER TWENTY-ONE

INVASION

The ocean waves were calm in the gathering light of morning. The fleet was close to the gateway now, and no attack had come to them. Karueq and Bleren kept their eyes on the sea and in the sky, watching carefully for any sign of the Eleverians. The Shatanala had hastily organized a moderate army and set them aboard ships commandeered from the coast, the same port Karueq had escaped from when he fled Xanadai. If not for Bleren's diligence during Karueq's absence and his zeal to ensure the Shatanala in the field were at the ready for anything, the force they gathered would have been much smaller. As such, the soldiers on the ships riding through the calm waters outside Eleveria were among the regular combatants they employed for such things as the contest at Mount Caramel. They were sharp and conditioned for the war they were about to wage.

Karueq and Bleren were together at the bow of a single ship. Karueq's defection, of course, was common knowledge, and he had been a wanted man, so Bleren kept him close. He was wary of his soldiers' appetite for him, and he was wary that Shatan was against Karueq joining the attack. Only by Bleren's insistence that his knowledge of the land was vital was he allowed to go. Karueq was pleased that Bleren had learned to be audacious in making demands to Shatan just like him.

The pair said nothing to each other the entire journey through the sea. It wasn't just the nature of the journey. Karueq could tell Bleren was uncomfortable and still held hidden injuries. His trust was bruised. Karueq left it alone because they had an immense task before them.

On the horizon, two spikes appeared. They protruded from the sea into the sky, and Karueq recognized them instantly from the many times he'd returned to them from a successful mission.

"Is that it?" asked the stoic man at his side.

"Yes," he answered.

Bleren left the bow and went about the ship whispering orders to the men above and below deck. Flag signals were waved to the other ships. The battle to the fortress was imminent.

The pillars drew near, and the beach came into view. All the men were at the ready. Bleren resumed his position at Karueq's side, his face set for war.

Just before they crossed the gateway, the ship slowed abruptly. It wasn't a sudden stop, but like a hook and line was dragging them to a halt. They looked around. Their lead ship was stilled directly between the pillars. Karueq looked up to see that the sails were slack. He looked behind, and the sails of the other ships hung limp from the masts.

Bleren kept his face forward, but an accusing look spread over his face. "What's happening?"

"I don't know," Karueq answered, his mind running wild with itself to come up with an explanation.

"Did you set this trap?" Bleren accused him.

"I swear I don't know what's happening."

Bleren turned to the men who'd begun whispering behind them and ordered them to silence themselves and stand guard. Karueq's only guess was that the barrier must have been reinstated with the reappearance of the Mark on his skin.

For several minutes, Bleren and Karueq conferred what could be happening, the younger man hesitant to let his guard down. Bleren came to the decision that they must turn around and go back. Karueq thought that unwise but kept himself from discrediting Bleren's command in front of subordinates by arguing so.

Just as preparations were being made to turn the ships around, a terrifying roar sounded through the air. All the Shatanala looked up to the sky. Five dragons darted over the beach into view straight toward the ships. The men cried out in a mix of fear and aggression and took up their arms.

The beasts flared their wings out and halted, hovering over the bay just behind the gate. Looking down from their backs, Karueq saw five familiar faces – in the center, Chelia, flanked by the Eleka Guard.

Her face was set, appearing every bit like the fierce and determined Captain they all used to know. After several seconds of pause, she locked eyes with Karueq, and shock spread over her face. She exchanged a look with her team and glanced back at him. Then she addressed Bleren, "Stand down and return your captive to us."

Karueq's brow knitted together, and he looked to Bleren, wondering if they'd managed to capture one of them.

Bleren answered her. "We have no prisoners of yours among us."

She pointed at Karueq. "Your former commander. He is bound to Eleh - return him to us."

"He's ours. He won't be leaving us again."

"He can't be yours unless he returns to Shatan."

"He has rejected your God, Elequiri!" Bleren barked.

Her expression didn't change, but she didn't answer him either. Instead, she turned her eyes on Karueq. Her dragon swooped forward, and she dropped deftly to the deck in front of Karueq. Bleren whipped out his sword to strike her. She caught it by the blade with her bare hand and turned a warning look on him. "Save it, General."

A hush fell over the men. She let go of Bleren's sword, a gash slashed into her palm. She turned her eyes back on Karueq. It was that piercing gaze again, the searching probe that he remembered from the forest when she begged for Aryngo's body back. Again, he felt vulnerable under her stare.

"Tell me you didn't," was all she said.

In defiance, he pushed the cuff of his sleeve up his arm as high as he could. Her eyes fell to his shoulder and instantly closed.

"Don't be surprised," he sneered. "You traded my soul for Alamar's return."

"Is that what they told you?"

"That was the price you agreed to."

"The price I agreed to was to not attack Xanadai for a hundred years."

Karueq's accusation halted. He searched her.

Bleren raised his sword again. "Be gone, Elequiri. We won't attack you today."

Chelia turned on him. "You wretch!" she barked. "You can't attack my land unless I let you!" Then, she addressed Karueq, "Come back with us."

Karueq's resolve held firm. "Never."

"You've been lied to, as have we," she shot another damning look at Bleren, "and your peace has been stolen once more. Come with us."

"No. Surrender yourself to Shatan, and your people will be spared."

"Shatan's army will not pass through these gates so long as I live. Come with us."

"No."

She continued to stare at him. Her inner war alighted in her eyes, and her questions burned through him. Finally, she said, "You are always welcome to return to us –" then, she said to Bleren, "– as are all of you."

Before they could openly deny her invitation, she jumped over the forward rail and ran across the bowsprit jutting from the front of the ship. The dragon caught her again when she leaped from the beam and returned to hover in its place. Chelia swept her hands through the air like she was drawing a curtain. As she did, a steady breeze filled the sails, and the ship was drawn backward.

The other ships, too, retreated in reverse. When they coasted to a standstill, Karueq realized that the shield had not been raised again, but Chelia was generating a barrier to oppose them. She'd blocked their way in case the Shatanala decided to attack.

Bleren turned to Karueq with a slightly softer expression and said to him quietly, "You have regained my trust."

Karueq nodded once to him in acceptance. This was a good test for him to establish himself once again among the Shatanala officers. However, his heart was troubled. What that woman said revealed a double-blinded plot both on him and the Elequiri. They'd leveraged Alamar to broker a hundred-year truce for Xanadai and bring Karueq back to the fold. He was impressed and would extol Bleren later for the significant part he undoubtedly played in it.

At the Seagan coast, Bleren sent the soldiers away, back to the stations from which he'd summoned them. He and Bleren flew back to Xanadai on Rales. Once they reached the island with the vent for their entrance, they returned the creatures to the scouts on the surface. How lucky it was that several of these beasts were stationed on the sentinel islands before the assault by the Eleverians.

Back underground, they gave their report to Shatan in Madaka's temple. Madaka himself was not present, but Karueq imagined the shade was none too pleased that the Prince usurped his abode while the Great Temple lay in permanent ruins. Karueq mused about Madaka's reaction should the Eleverians have attacked this temple, too.

After the report had been given, Bleren insisted to the Prince that Karueq be reinstated as an officer to avoid any unfortunate incidents with the armies. Shatan regarded him coolly for such a suggestion. Bleren argued that the three of them knew the plan to infiltrate Eleveria was dangerous and that they all agreed to it anyway. Karucq kept silent about just how unwilling Bleren was of the plan. Before departing, Shatan did indeed give Karueq a menial title with the promise of greater honor if their soldiers ever regarded him with adequate fear again.

Bleren spent the next several days informing Karueq of all that the Shatanala had accomplished in his absence. They'd made very few gains, as their staunch pride in the mission was shaken by their leader's downfall, but they were gains nonetheless. They lost ground here and there, and Karueq filled him in on what the Eleverians had done to win that ground.

Bleren asked about the things Karueq had seen and done while in the captivity of the Eleverians. He listened with great interest to the stories of the missions. It occurred to Karueq that Bleren was fascinated by the Eleverians, something he'd never noticed in the young man before.

He was most interested about the customs regarding Eleverian recovery. As Bleren's questions probed deeper, Karueq found that he was agitated by the memories there. He wasn't as disgusted as he'd like to be. He was dismayed to find that it was a feeling of loss and rejection. Halfway into his account on Nimera's struggle, Karueq abruptly ended the conversation, excusing himself to retire for sleep.

That night, he dreamed the same rerun of his vision, repeatedly stabbing the figure in white when it drew near. Only this time, the face wasn't Hanai, and it wasn't a look of pity. It was a face that, in the dream, Karueq recognized as Eleh, and He looked on Karueq with such profound sorrow. Those eyes pleaded with him to stop this desperate action he kept reliving to hold on to the bitterness in his heart.

He woke up drenched from sweat, his hand clutching tight to the blanket at his side. He stared angrily around the room, willing his head to clear and forget what he'd seen in his sleep. He forced it from his mind, willing himself instead to concoct new plots like he used to.

After a few brief minutes of his dark musings, he got up and strode to Madaka's temple. Those he passed in the tunnels didn't look at him. They avoided his stern glare, pleasing Karueq that his place among them might soon be restored.

He threw open the great doors to the temple. Only when he reached the center altar did he look around. The sinister quiet of the space was roughened only by the servants timidly tending the fires in the corner.

Irritated, he gathered the darkness that once again dwelt in his gut and let it surge through his arm. With all his might he raised it and slammed the surface of the altar. Bright purple light thundered from his fist and split the altar in two with a sickening crack.

Before he blinked, a whirl of smoke barreled forward and knocked him to the ground. "Fool!" hissed the shade.

The temple servants screamed and ran. Karueq stared up into that ugly face of fury.

"Smite me, and you'll have Shatan to answer to."

The demon crouched over him, snarling, but didn't move to kill him. When its upper lip stopped quivering, it slinked backward, letting him up. Karueq made a show of stretching his neck of the whiplash. Then, he addressed the seething creature. "Aid me, and I promise you a mightier haunt than this once we're finished."

It snarled again, indignant at such a request, but with one look at the desecrated altar and the deserted space, it conceded. "What do you need?"

"I need your support before Shatan for a plot to end this insipid war."

"If your plot is worth anything, you'll take it to him without me."

"I would, believe me. I've hated your presence from the first time I met you."

The creatures lip curled again.

"However, Shatan will not hear such a plan come from me or the General. I need your assistance."

"What is it?"

"The battle to end all battles. A wager of the highest stakes."

"Enough with the riddles."

"This is no riddle. We will wage one battle, a contest for the key to victory on each side."

"No," Madaka spat.

"No?"

"You do not have my support."

"Very well. Cower here in the belly of the earth where you belong. I'll offer your reward to the host of other spirits who will elevate themselves above you when we have won."

He turned to leave, but the demon flew forward in a cloud of smoke to block him, sticking his sinister nose inches from the fallen commander. Karueq smirked.

"What reward?"

"You're not interested," Karueq taunted.

"What reward?!" it hissed.

He sidestepped the demon and began circling him while he elaborated.

"Once we win the battle, the Prince will claim control over Seaga with temples and shrines of magnificence abounding throughout the nations. But you, Madaka, where will your place of worship be? Where will the peoples of all nations make pilgrimage to honor you, to pay tribute to you? Will you remain down here where you will be forgotten, or will you claim for yourself a worthy place to reside?"

"Where do you propose?"

Karueq squared himself in front of him. "Eleveria."

The demon's wicked eyes widened ever so slightly. Then, his lip curled up in the corner. This was indeed enticing. Karueq calculated well.

"Very well," it murmured with pleasure. "You have my support, but if this plan should fail and Shatan rightly condemns you, I will be your undoing. Do we have a deal?" Out of his hand rolled the end of a large scroll. This contract was a source of great pride for the demon. He kept a running account of his deals, adding the new to the old as a trophy.

Karueq lifted his calf and withdrew the ivory knife that Bleren had returned to him. He slit the tip of his little finger and, for the first time in his life, smudged a drop of blood next to the terms that appeared at the bottom edge of the shade's paper. It was a fairly empty deal. It promised support only. It said nothing about the fervor with which either of them would approach the Prince regarding the matter, but on their mutual understanding, it was enough.

Madaka summoned Shatan to their presence, to the temporary space they both occupied to receive worship, the Prince accepting honor from the Shatanala whenever he pleased and the shade lapping up what was left.

Shatan listened to the plot carefully. He probed it with a critical ear and challenged Karueq on every aspect. Madaka was silent until he was addressed to provide his endorsement. After several hours, the traitor and the shade convinced the Prince of Darkness to authorize the risky conquest against the people of Eleveria.

In response to this plot, or to continue to keep Karueq in line, Shatan presented him with the jewel Chelia had given him in his exile. The blue jewel still held the Mark of Eleh, but it was corrupted by a black metal that was forged over it, turning the mark into a poorly wrought version of Shatan's Mark. Karueq's heart flipped curiously at it for a moment, but he ignored it. Instead, he fastened the jewel around his neck where it had lain for so long before.

CHAPTER TWENTY-TWO

THE DEAL WITH THE DEVIL

Karueq approached the ravine, not caring to conceal his presence. Not since Aryngo's death had he walked this forest with confidence that he would leave with his life. He knew their mind now, knew they wouldn't kill him, not even to gain an advantage. The only guarding he needed was to be wary of any offers the Elequiri would make to him. Those offers, he smirked, would fall on deaf ears.

The silvery light glowed from the bottom of the ravine. He reached the edge, looked down into it, and scowled. She wasn't alone. Alamar stood at her side. He shook his head and scaled quickly to the ground below, allowing his footsteps to crash noisily and announce his presence.

"I told you to come alone," he barked forcefully at her as he rounded the pool where the ball of light was suspended.

"I agreed to nothing," she replied.

Karueq eyed the man at her side. The evidence of his internment in Xanadai was thick in his stilted posture and the weariness in his eyes. He couldn't fathom why she would bring him in this state, but he wouldn't be able to get rid of him now that he was here, so he said, "This is your decision, not his. The answer will come from your tongue, and yours alone."

"Karueq, come with us," she pleaded.

"You won't sway me back."

"You know I can't turn you by force. Just open your eyes and remember all you left behind."

"And follow you back to your den of betrayers? No."

"We loved you. We worked alongside you. You carried such a profound love of Eleh in your heart. He was your King, and you swore to me many times that you would never leave Him, that you would rather die."

At her reminder, his heart twisted, but the root inside him clenched him tight. "I didn't die, did I?"

"What happened?" she asked.

"I don't need to answer you for anything," he spat.

"You owe us an explanation of what you think I agreed to. I thought you were dead!"

He scoffed. "And you didn't think to beg for my body the way you begged me for Aryngo?"

"I did beg!" she blurted. "When Bleren came to this ravine with his lies, I begged him to give you to us even in death. He told me he was your very close friend and wouldn't give you up, but he promised me he would return your body if Shatan refused a proper burial for you. I did *not* abandon you."

He shook his head, the root stilled the ache in his chest. "And Hanai leaving me behind?"

"He was tricked by an imposter. Believe me I had the same questions you do about what happened during the attack. I was furious with my brother. He couldn't give me an explanation that satisfied him or myself. Then, Bleren admitted a Brehila enchanted himself to look like you, and Hanai left the gullet with that man instead, almost at the cost of his life." Her tone was icy now. "He mourned you bitterly, if that means anything to you."

Her explanation fell on deafening ears. He wouldn't be taken captive by these people again, not this time. "Nothing you say will ever make up for all the times you've lied to me. The Prince has never lied to me like you have."

"You call that viper 'the Prince' again," she lamented, shaking her head. "Karueq, come back to us. Come back to the love Eleh has for you."

"Enough!" he barked at her. "I've come here with a proposal, not to hear you lament your losses."

She bit her tongue and didn't challenge him again, though her eyes screamed at him that she still wanted to.

Satisfied he could continue with her interrupting, he went on. "We're all weary of this war, but we can end it. In seven days, you'll gather your army, and we'll gather ours. We fight one battle from noon until sunset on the plain outside this forest. That way you can't accuse us of being unfair. Congratulations, Elequiri, you have your open battle on some of your terms."

She glared at him, fully incensed by his mockery.

"We'll have no interference from you. You'll stay out of this one - the battle will be fought by your people only. That is the fairness you'll extend to us. You're much too powerful to allow in this fight.

"Now, this won't be a fight for surrender, but the objective will be simple. If Alamar survives the battle, –" he said, glancing at the Quiri, "– until the sun disappears from the horizon, you win. If he dies, the victory is ours.

"Your prize will be a complete cessation of our campaign on Seaga and total surrender of the living forces of Xanadai, including me, my lady," he sneered. "Our prize –" he stared at her pointedly, "– is you."

Her expression didn't change. He returned her stare, determined to hold his own against her, this time unflinching. He was disturbed to find that the probing vulnerability he usually saw in her eyes at these discussions was absent. Instead, he beheld her ferocity. Her fire blazed in her eyes, such a determination he would never see among the Shatanala.

"Why would I ever agree to such terms?" she hissed.

"If you don't, we'll retaliate. We'll attack any team you send into Seaga out in the open and burn your holdings to the ground. We'll find a way into your now precious, unprotected Eleveria and destroy it. You have my solemn word that nothing you attempt to claim or cling to will escape our hand."

"You only think you can wage such a war with us."

"Is this not what you want, Elequiri?" he jabbed. "To have nothing standing in your way of enslaving the world to your God? Of emptying Xanadai and crippling Shatan where he lays rotting in the earth?"

"None of what you're saying is true or even to the point. What did they do to you?"

"This is an opportunity for you to rid the world of all you deem to be vile and to be free of any competition with us."

"Karueq! What happened to you?" she screamed. "There's no way you can think like this. There's no way you *would* think like this. You can't have completely forgotten how we live and what we work for."

"And what do you work for?" he sneered.

She gave no reply, only stared at him with that blazing fire burning from her eyes. Such a stubborn fool, but what an awesome weapon Shatan would gain once he won and broke her. Karueq only hoped he would get to see that day.

He didn't get an answer to his question, so he ordered, "Your answer, Elequiri."

"You know I'll never accept such terms. And you know Shatan will drag you to the pit when you've gone back empty handed. Come with us now."

"Never."

The disappointment in her face was evident, but she simply turned around, and she and Alamar began to walk away.

Karueq tried to stop them from leaving. "You will accept, Elequiri!"

The two of them continued on their way. Karueq wasn't done yet. He yanked one of the daggers from the small of his back and flung it angrily at her. In one fluid motion, Chelia caught it and hurled it at his feet. It stuck resolutely into the soft dirt. She stood square to him.

"Accept the challenge and be rid of this war," he badgered her.

"Come with us," she implored.

"There's no way I ever will."

"Why?"

In answer, he pulled the corrupted, blue gem over his head and tossed it to her. She caught it and looked at it. A horrible look of bewilderment spread over her face. She was frozen, and she didn't even blink at the jewel.

Karueq said, "Your lies will never betray me again."

Chelia just continued to stare at the gem, and Karueq wasn't sure she heard him. Her amazement stilled her face. Not since Aryngo's death had he seen her in such shock. Alamar, too, noticed the change in her and peered at the stone. Then, he glanced up at her face, a fearful look springing on him, too.

For what seemed like hours, none of them moved. Karueq was struck by their expressions, as they hadn't quite processed whatever it was they were seeing on that stone. Alamar was the first to move. He glanced at the stone one more time and put his hand on her shoulder. Her posture sagged as his touch brought her back to reality, and she looked to him. The bewilderment was gone, and it was replaced instead by an intense anguish on both their faces. Chelia looked to be searching for some answer from him, or asking for him to tell her not to do something. He only gazed at her and nodded sadly.

Chelia looked one more time at the jewel and then clenched it in her hand. She turned a resolved but stormy look on Karueq. "Yes," she said.

Karueq's face mounted to confusion. "Yes to what?"

"Yes, I accept your challenge."

Alamar now looked at him, too. Karueq's focus shifted rapidly between the two.

"What?"

"You got what you wanted," she spat. "Seven days, one battle."

"Why are you agreeing now?" Karueq accused.

"Go. Tell your master he may have his battle."

"What--?"

"Go!" she cried. The storm in her had turned into a hurricane. Karueq found he dared not continue to berate her. He let himself be satisfied that he had succeeded in procuring their agreement to his scheme.

Chelia shot one more damning look at the gem and then chucked it into the dirt. She turned around and left, Alamar letting his gaze on Karueq linger but a moment before following her. Karueq was left rooted where he was.

Again, for the thousandth time in his life, he didn't have the whole picture. The turn he saw in her was unreasonable. He couldn't figure out how she'd come to the conclusion to accept his challenge because of that pendant. His mind repeated to him the same question she'd implored of him – *what happened?*

He didn't know how long he stayed in that spot, but when he emerged from the forest, the sky was graying, threatening the dawn. He shook his head of his confusion, of his ponderings, of the need to know that which he didn't know. He'd gotten what he wanted, and after the battle when they were victorious, he would have no need to know what they hid from him.

Upon his return to Xanadai, he called on Shatan in Madaka's temple. Bleren and both demons listened intently to the result of his errand, and Shatan congratulated him coolly on his little victory.

Over the next several hours, they discussed details of their strategy for battle. Per the agreement in the forest that, oddly, neither the Elequiri nor the Quiri had amended, their only objective was to kill one man. It was far easier to kill a man than it was to defend him, but the four conspirators needed to be absolutely sure. This was a risky, unyielding wager.

From Karueq's point of view, the Shatanala already had nothing to lose. The Crucible had been unleashed on them once, and they had been continually losing ground since the perceived stalemate years ago. He was sick of operating from the shadows of history. With one stroke of the sword or the flash of an arrow, they could win everything Shatan craved and the death sentence to Eleh that Karueq had worked his whole life for.

That evening, Bleren sent all the spies they had left to the farthest reaches of the world. Their instructions were simple and could not be ignored. All Shatanala in Seaga were to report to the battlefield with all haste. Those that would arrive late were still ordered to rush to battle. The orders contained the objective to kill the Quiri on sight. Thus, they would amass an army that would fiercely challenge the Eleverians, even with most of their forces trapped below ground.

On the second evening, Bleren held counsel at the battlefield with the officers and laid out the attack plan. He made it clear that any Shatanala found alive upon defeat would be executed before they could be surrendered to the Eleverians, so their troops must give limb and, most certainly, life in order to accomplish what their lord commanded.

Karueq surveyed the sky during this meeting. On the far horizon, shadows flitted around – the dragons of Eleveria bringing in the army. Karueq almost couldn't believe that they were here at the final battle to decide the fate of Seaga and decide which master would reign over all.

CHAPTER TWENTY-THREE

THE FINAL BATTLE

Bleren had the army marshaled and in formation by mid-morning. Unlike previous battles they'd waged, the forces would charge head-on and fight in the open, not needing to conceal the bloodshed from wandering Seagan eyes. Troops were still arriving and taking their places hastily behind the lines.

Karueq sat astride a Rale at the head of one column. He felt only slightly odd not being at the head of them all, although he admitted to himself that he hadn't headed a battle in a long time. Their last major clash was at Mount Carmel, and he'd been left in the tower with Jezebel.

This, he decided, was a fine position to take. He need not worry so much about monitoring everything on the field. He only needed to satiate the bloodlust now boiling in his reclaimed heart. His sword would once again taste Eleveria blood.

At late morning, the Eleverians gathered on the far side of the field, leaving their camp several miles away to muster for battle. Many of them were mounted on dragons, but still more would fight from the ground. It was a sizable defensive indeed. Karueq lamented the horde still trapped below ground. It would have been no contest if they had all their forces behind them.

When it looked like the Eleverians had closed up their ranks, Bleren alighted on his own Rale, and Karueq followed, as discussed. A dark blue dragon and a red dragon lifted into the air from the Eleverian army and glided toward them. The four beasts set down in the center of the battlefield, and their riders dismounted. Bleren, Karueq, Alamar, and Hunga came face to face.

"Where is the prize?" Bleren asked, at the conspicuous absence of the Elequiri from the meeting.

"She's not a prize, General," replied the Quiri. Karueq noticed he clearly hadn't recovered yet from his imprisonment, but his zeal for his wife remained. "She stayed behind in Eleveria." He held up his hand to stop the indignant men before they protested. "Our land, as you know, is close. She is waiting on the shore of the bay to hear the outcome. As you requested, she is not to interfere, so it is to your advantage that she stays behind."

Bleren relented, unable to do anything now. "Very well, Quiri. She will hear of your death on our terms and have no chance to mourn you before she is dragged into the pit. My terms are these. You may engage in battle yourself with your men, but they must stand down and surrender to us when you fall. The boundaries of the battlefield are the forest to the east, our camp to the south, the river before your camp to the north, and the hills to the west. The battle may extend outside these boundaries, but you, Quiri, are not to cross those borders. If you do, you forfeit. You may use any advantage at your disposal as will we. Are we clear?"

"Yes," replied the man. "Is that all?"

"Yes," Bleren acknowledged.

"Our terms are these," the Quiri began. "As your proposal set forth, the battle ends at sundown, when the sun touches the hills on the west."

"When the sun is no longer seen," Bleren corrected.

"You have already set your terms," Alamar countered. "This is one of mine. Sundown is decided thus. When the sun touches the hills, it is over. You will agree."

"Fair enough," Bleren relented, though his voice dripped with disappointment.

"You will also execute no scheme to drag me outside the boundaries, thereby forcing me to forfeit, as you discussed. This is to be a fair fight. Additionally, our law to extend mercy to you and your troops is suspended for the duration of this battle. At sundown, you and your army will lay down arms immediately and surrender as you proposed, and we will take up our law once again."

"Agreed," said the General.

The Quiri said no more, and the three men stood in uncomfortable silence for a few moments. Karueq noticed a bit of a faraway look in the man's eyes. Perhaps this battle, whatever the outcome, was destroying Eleveria from the inside.

Having no more to say, Bleren drew his sword, and Alamar drew his. They crossed their blades, a customary commencement for battle. Without saying a word, the three men mounted their beasts, and raced toward their respective armies. The battle had begun.

Bleren circled his Rale low over the columns, shouting commands to move forward. The troops complied. They raced ahead viciously, thirsty for the first taste of blood at the front line. The Eleverian line moved, as well. The dragons raced forward. The ground troops sprinted ahead.

Karueq led his column charging toward the fight. He kicked the Rale to surge forward faster. Ahead, the Eleverian battle cry resounded, drawing closer. He kicked the beast again – faster.

The armies clashed just in front of him. Karueq took aim at a dragon darting in his direction. The Rale took him under its wing and then veered over it. He whipped his sword at the two riders. He slashed the rear one in the shoulder. The dragon dove before he could double back around for another blow.

He chased after the next dragon and took to the fight in the air. The dragons were formidable. The Shatanala had never battled them head on before. They darted over the battlefield with a speed and agility that didn't match their size. The Rales were tiny by comparison. Karueq spurred his beast on, zipping back and forth over the battle. He punished it in his fervor to do unfathomable damage.

He narrowly escaped the flap of a wing. His sword just glanced off the edge of it when he twisted around. For an hour, he fought through the air. The Eleverians fought hard, too. He hardly glanced at the carnage below. The ground churned in his peripheral vision. The ferocity was matched on both sides.

He came into contact with Alamar's dragon many times, but the beast was too quick for him. When he did get to engage with him, another Eleverian would assault him and drive him out of the way.

His Rale noticeably slowed. It may be used to lengthy sprints, but it wasn't designed or conditioned to dart around in a battle. Karueq felt it slacken while its wings fatigued.

Then, a dragon crashed into him with its claws outstretched. It shook the tired beast once. Karueq's grip slipped, and he plummeted to the ground. His back screamed at him for the jarring assault when he hit the ground. Only, it wasn't the ground. It was an armored body. As quickly as he could, he scrambled to his feet and attacked. His sword was missing from his hand, so he picked up a weapon from the dirt. He fought as viciously as he did in the sky. He ignored the fatigue in his muscles. This fight was theirs to win.

Without the possibility of getting near Alamar from the ground, he cut through as many Eleverians as he could. He'd taught these people well when he lived among them. Their defenses were solid, but so was his.

Far to his right, a dark blue dragon lilted in its flight. It was Alamar's dragon. A silhouette fell from it. Several other dragons dove toward it. At last!

Karueq fought his way in that direction. A blazing fire erupted from the spot. It sprouted from the lizards' mouths. He could feel the heat from where he was. He parried and punched an Eleverian away, barely recognizing him and not caring to.

A familiar shape glinted from the ground - his sword! He snatched it up as he passed and fought with it toward the place where the fire blazed.

Another fiery torrent erupted from the dragons. More dragons descended on the spot. Above the clashing heads, Karueq could see they were creating a wall around what was no doubt the Quiri – a wall with flaming breath.

Those beasts couldn't keep up their fire forever. Karueq looked up at the sun, or rather toward the west. There weren't but a few hours left in the day. The long hard battle would come to a close, and the Shatanala would never breach the wall around the target.

A formation of Rales with mounted fighters attacked from the sky, trying to get into the center of the circle. They were blasted from the air, and one was snagged between the jaws of two dragons.

An Eleverian leaped upon Karueq. He battered it away. It knocked him to the ground. He deflected its blows and rolled away, springing to his feet. Instead of resuming the fight with her, he ran in the opposite direction.

He sprang on a wounded Rale lying on the ground and beat it until it got to its weary feet. Once mounted, he spurred it toward the north. The creature dipped every few strokes, but he urged it on.

Finally, he saw Bleren in the crowd below. He kicked the Rale hard in that direction and deliberately crashed it into a swarm of Eleverians near the general. He sprang from it just in time.

"Bleren!" he called. He battered his way over to the general. "Bleren! New tactic!"

"What is it?" he replied, driving a kick into a nearby head.

"Send me to Chelia!"

The general whipped around to him bewildered. "How?" he questioned, knowing exactly what Karueq meant to do.

"Send me!" he cried again.

"Go! End this now!" Bleren whipped back around and jumped back into the fight.

Karueq raced to the nearest Rale, kicked the rider from its back, and mounted. The creature squawked at him, but he drove it into the air without delay.

Leaving the battle behind, he sprinted the animal beyond the boundaries and the forest. He flew swiftly over land and then the sea. Before it was too late, he came upon the gateway.

The pillars stood steadfast above the water, their colored bands glimmering quietly with the retreating sun standing at their backs. The shore of the bay swept up away from the water, and there, a woman alone on the sand rose to her feet.

Karueq aimed at the gateway, hoping she had lifted the barrier she placed on it. To his relief, he made it through without stopping and guided the squawking, angry creature to the beach. The brute landed hard, squabbling at him for the hard flight. He dismounted the creature and turned toward the woman a few lengths down the shoreline.

"Your Quiri is dead, Chelia," he called to her. He stalked toward her. "You belong to the darkness now."

She simply stood there, watching him advance on her, not saying a word.

He halted before her. "Come quietly," he said, softly. "Don't make this harder on yourself." Still, she did not respond. He held out his hand to her. "Come."

She turned her eyes on the gateway and searched it. After a moment, she turned her gaze back on him. "You lie."

"You belong to Shatan now. Come with me."

"You didn't bring his body to gloat to me. You lie."

"I don't lie to you, Chelia. I know what he meant to you, but he's gone."

"No. He's still alive. The fight isn't over yet, and you've come here to steal me away before my people can win it."

"That's something I wish I could come up with. As it stands, I can't deceive you, because he's dead. His body lies on that plain waiting to be taken to Xanadai as Shatan's trophy. You'll join him there where I'll grant you the time to mourn him. It's the least I can do for the fair fight you've given me all these years."

"Silence!" she hissed. "I will not surrender under such pretense. Show me his body, then you may have my soul."

"Very well, I'll take you to him."

"No. You'll bring it here if what you say is true. You won't trap me when my people are sacrificing their lives to save your souls."

"There will be no more saving of souls."

"Karueq! Open your eyes! Shatan is using you. He's always used you. We gave you nothing but love and kindness. Eleh gives you that same love and kindness. He loves you, Karueq! Come back to Him!"

Karueq's blood boiled at the notion. "Never! You betrayed me many times, not the least of which was your trick on the island to blind me to Eleh's deception. He enslaves you, Elequiri! He created you to be a powerful weapon and then makes you frightened of yourself because of it. You are deceived!"

"I'm not afraid of myself. I refuse to give in to sin and the empty promises Shatan offers."

"And what is Eleh's offer? The promise of eternity you may never know. No, Chelia. It is you who are blind to it all. Come to Shatan, as

you promised in the forest and as Alamar agreed on the battlefield. Honor
your husband's word, and do not disgrace him in death."

"He's not dead! You're here because we're winning." She
pointed behind her. "Look at the sun! It's almost over. You have to see
that you will always lose in Shatan's company. He will never win, and he
will punish you for eternity for any slights he imagines. You may take our
lives, but you will never stop Eleh's salvation of His people or take away
the joy of my people. Come back to us."

His anger boiled over. He couldn't stop himself. He whipped out
his sword and swiped at her. He swung again when she sidestepped his
blow.

"Karueq!" she cried.

The root of the Mark clenched tighter, strangling him into
rage. She dodged the blade and tumbled behind him. She didn't pull a
weapon. She might not have had one.

From there, she jumped on his back and seized a full body grip on
him. He jabbed his blade at her, but her hold on his shoulder prevented the
angle he needed.

He dropped to the ground, slamming her into the sand. The jolt
knocked her hands just free enough for him to yank them away. He
elbowed her in the gut and sprang to his feet.

She rolled out of the way of his jab. The sword stabbed into the
ground. She sprang up. He swung. She darted out of the way.

His arm wound up to stab at her again, but he held it there. His
mind cleared a little from the adrenaline. "Enough. Shatan wants you
whole. Stand down and come quietly."

"You attacked me, Karueq."

"Even so, come quietly."

"No. You won't take me until you show me that Alamar is truly
dead, and when you can't, you will be forced to surrender."

Wild fury again blinded him at her words. He lashed out. The
Mark screeched its own rage at him. He would not surrender. His blow
landed on her arm guard.

"Karueq, stop!" she cried.

He whipped his sword away and thrust again. His stab shot
through her body.

Immediately, blinding pain stabbed through his chest. He cried
out. His hand clutched his heart, and he dropped to his knees. A piercing

ring filled his ears. The fiery stinging exploded through his body. He felt the fire scorch the root from where it strangled him through his shoulder and to the brand in his flesh. It burned every part of him, and those screams were his own.

Then it stopped.

Karueq opened his eyes. He was staring at the ground, doubled over on his knees. The sand fluttered away beneath his rapid breath. His head was in a fog, the root of the Mark was paralyzed, and he didn't know where he was. He smelled the dragon smoke on his clothing and remembered the battle on the plain.

This wasn't the plain. He brushed the sand from his lip with the back of his hand and lifted his head. The fog around his mind cleared. He was in Eleveria, coming to steal the Elequiri away to Xanadai.

Then, he saw the form sprawled before him. An agonizing breath escaped her, and his heart collapsed. Protruding from her body was a sword – his sword.

"No…" he whispered. Her breathing was shallow, and her eyes were closed tight. He almost reached out to her but couldn't. He was frozen, on his knees, begging heaven that what he saw before him was a trick, an illusion. Every muscle in his body fought him to run or to fling himself at her side.

For several minutes, she wept softly to herself, swallowed by whatever grief flooded her soul. Then, she turned her head toward him and opened her eyes, the agony radiating from her. He shrank under her gaze. She shuddered another breath and moved her hand toward him, beckoning him near.

He hesitated, every fiber fighting him to run away, but he pulled himself over to her. He took her reaching hand and cradled her head in his other hand.

A tear escaped down his cheek. "Chelia…I'm sorry."

"Come back to your King," she implored him.

His gut twisted. How could he return? How could he come back when he was beyond saving this time?

He sobbed. The tears blurred his vision, and he furiously blinked them away. "I do…I do want to come back."

She gritted her teeth and seized his arm over the Mark. The monstrous fire erupted over his skin again, swallowing his sobs. Again, he howled under the searing pain. Like a fast-burning wick, the root of the Mark was consumed by the fire.

Then, the scorching stopped, and her hand dropped from his arm. His chest still burned horribly, but he could tell he was free once again. The lingering pain reignited his weeping.

He felt her hand on his wet cheek and raised his pained eyes to hers. Her searching gaze was there behind her anguish. "Don't leave Him again," she whispered.

"I'm so sorry," he wept. "So sorry."

"I forgive you."

He closed his eyes, shook his head, and bit down on his teeth. "I don't deserve it. My lady, I could never deserve it."

"You really haven't paid attention, have you?"

He raised his eyes to her once more. Beyond the pain and the grief, he saw her sincerity. Mercy and love were extended to him, and he gathered her up in his arms to comfort her.

A sudden gust of wind and a thundering crash startled him. He clutched her tight and looked up, ready to defend her to his last. His attention darted up the beach to where a dark blue dragon had landed hard. A man stumbled toward them from the dragon, his gait broken by injury.

It was Alamar, and he threw himself down next to them. He gently pulled her away from Karueq, who backed away to give him space.

"Chelia," he begged her. "Chelia."

She looked up at him, and her face twisted horribly as she began to weep in his arms. He gathered her closer to him and then turned his face up to Karueq, already running with tears. "Get out of here!" he yelled, his voice tight. "Run! Someone will have followed me."

Karueq's heart plummeted at the mercy being shown to him again.

"Go!" he yelled again. "Take the dragon; hide in the mountains."

"No," he blurted. "I deserve to die."

"Not on our watch, Karueq. Never on our watch. Go!"

Chelia turned a tearful eye on him. He braced himself against the urge to stay and surrender to his captors. This was a last request from his captains, and he would honor it. "I'm so sorry."

He pulled himself away and darted past them toward the dragon before he could stop himself. He leaped onto its back, and it surged into the sky without direction from him.

It sped away with him over the hills and the plain. He didn't see where it was taking him, his vision was so blurred. He never saw the fortress, but he knew they'd reached the mountains because they climbed higher into the air.

He didn't know where they landed, but the dragon reached the earth gently and waited patiently for him to dismount. His sobs eventually quieted to unsteady breaths. At last, he wiped his eyes, threw a glance around, and slid from the creature's back. It took off and left him alone, flying back in the direction of the bay.

The mountains rose higher all around him. He stood on a stone pavement a hundred yards across. A few paths snaked away from the clearing through gaps in the rock. A deep pool of water lay, nearly still, against a cave that opened wide on one side. A faintly trickling stream issued from the pool, flowing down the side of one path out of the mountains.

He felt utterly lost. What transpired on the beach didn't feel real. With nothing left in him, he sank to his knees where he stood and did the only thing he could do in the dying light.

"Eleh," he begged. "Please hear me. I am so sorry. I never should have abandoned You. I have no right to ask anything of you after that, but please, please hear me. Don't let this prayer be in vain. Save her. Please, save her."

He prayed like this for a long time. When he opened his eyes, it was dark. Night had set in, and the air was cold. He noticed he'd been shivering. He looked around but saw no one. Defeated, so very defeated, he pulled his cloak around himself and crossed the pavement to the cave. There, he tucked himself away and wept until his battle-weary body made him fall fitfully asleep.

CHAPTER TWENTY-FOUR

THE DUST SETTLES

Early the next morning, Karueq woke up. He felt no different, still lost and utterly worthless. He glanced out of the cave. The pavement was still abandoned. Now, Karueq could see that the pavement was set in beautiful designs spiraling out from the pool. Karueq wondered what this place could be.

Having no opportunity for answers, his eyes left the pavement and looked up at the sky. It was pale, just beginning to welcome the day, a day which Karueq dreaded deeply. He heard no sounds, not even the dragon that brought him here. He was alone.

His eyes welled again when his heart flooded with the reality of what could be transpiring beyond these rocky peaks. They blocked his view so he couldn't even see the plain, much less anything happening beyond it. He fell to his knees beside the pool on a mosaic of yellow-gold stones and prayed. His prayers mirrored those he'd prayed the night before, not that his prayers were coherent or complete. His mind ran away from him, and he begged Eleh for every desperate thing it ran into in its mad flight.

Late in the morning, his prayers were interrupted by a gust of wind beyond the peaks. A rhythmic, gentle whoosh approached. Around the peak on the eastern shoulder, a dragon glided through the air, a dark blue dragon. Karueq held his breath as it landed a few yards from him. For a moment, he and the great creature stared at each other. Then, he saw a leg dangling behind its wing. He waited for Alamar to slide off its back.

But it wasn't Alamar. Instead, Hanai dropped from behind the wing. He glanced briefly at Karueq before pointing a far-off look at the pool. His eyes were red and swollen. The light from his expression was crushingly absent. Karueq's dread bloomed to despair. He croaked, "Hanai, I'm so sorry…"

Hanai closed his eyes and shook his head once, forbidding Karueq to speak further. They stood there in uncomfortable silence for several minutes. Karueq's throat was tight, and he swallowed back the audible sobs trying to break through his solemn face. In the silence, Karueq noticed several unattended gashes on Hanai's arms, evidence of the cruel battle he'd concocted against them.

Finally, Hanai spoke, still without looking at Karueq. "Alamar and Bleren rescinded the challenge. There will be no surrender on either side, but the shield is broken, and Alamar fears there is no way to protect us." He paused to rein in the quaver that crept into his voice. "We're going into exile today so we can't be targeted as a whole, and we can still help and protect Seaga."

Karueq hung his head. "You're fleeing, and so soon," he managed.

"Bleren gave us one day. Just enough time to bury her and leave."

Karueq's guilt and disgrace crashed through him. Tears dripped down his face, but no more leaving him empty than adding to his embarrassment.

"I'm here to bring you in," said the Eleverian. Karueq nodded his surrender to whatever fate the Shatanala would decide for him, but Hanai added, "They've put a heavy price on your head, and we can't leave you here vulnerable."

"What?" he asked, bewildered.

Through the puffiness around his eyes there appeared a very serious look from Hanai. "We would never abandon you, Karueq, especially not when part of her final act was to free you once more."

"How could you ever forgive me and show me such mercy?"

"Trust me, Karueq, it's hard. No matter the friendship we shared, you killed my sister in the name of Shatan. It's hard to forgive you for that, but I do forgive you." His eyes dropped to the ground. "It will, of course, be a long time before any of us trust you again or seek your friendship. Eleh teaches us by great example how to forgive, so you can be assured you have it, and one day you'll hopefully forgive yourself. Now, come."

Karueq couldn't move, couldn't fathom the unbelievable mercy extended to him. His eyes darted around the pavement and the pool.

Hanai sighed. "We don't have much time, Karueq. Come."

With heavy steps, Karueq walked to the dragon with Hanai. They mounted and took off. The dragon rose high into the air and lifted them over the tall peaks. From this high, Karueq could see the stream from the pool snaking down through the mountains along the path. They descended the mountain slopes, rising here and there for a hill and glided down the tall spires.

Eventually, they came to the foothills in which the great fortress was nestled. It cast its shadows onto the rock face at its back in the late morning sunlight. The river glittered gold. Such a peaceful scene as this couldn't tell the horrible story that played out yesterday.

Karueq expected them to continue on toward the bay, but Hanai angled the dragon and set it down below the bluff next to the giant tree that dug its roots into the riverbank with its tendrils falling into the water. This was where he had entered the water and given his life to Eleh, a promise he made that he broke too soon after.

Hanai slipped to the ground, and Karueq followed him. The Eleverian didn't move, just stared at the bank, and Karueq followed his gaze only for a lump to ram itself firmly in his throat again. Under the shade of the tree, near the bank of the river, was a stone, a stone with the burial mark etched on its surface. Fresh earth lay before the stone.

"We buried her early this morning," said Hanai, "but I'll give you a moment to say goodbye. Come to the mission hall when you're ready." Without waiting for a reply, he turned away and flew up over the bluff on the dragon.

Karueq's vision blurred then, but no tears fell as he approached the stone. He closed his eyes and did his best to remember the words of the burial rite. His utterance was mixed up with the mission rite he'd received from her so many times, but they were similar enough that he knew it was close to a proper recitation.

With his prayer said, he opened his eyes and stared at the stone. His betrayal still choked him like a noose. He let his mind wander through his memory of her. He lingered over the utter joy always contained in her words, her eyes, and that laugh when she was held prisoner in Xanadai. He held on to her determination, her conviction, and the strength of her heart. She was a strong example of grace and hope, a leader who fearlessly led her people against the powers of evil.

Then, he could no longer hold back his final memory of her. Her body lay on the beach. She clung to what breath she had left. The tears streaking her face displayed her agony, but so much more her despair. The joy was gone; the strength within her almost disappeared. Through the horror of that scene, she gave him – her murderer – a parting gift. She broke the shackles around his heart, removed the Mark, and freed the part of him that still clung to his promise to Eleh and the hope he'd found in this land.

He was grateful, ever so grateful, that his was not the last face she saw. Just in time, Alamar had arrived to hold his bride one last time and be a source of peace for her in her final moments. He, too, had given Karueq a parting gift. *Run*, he'd said, to escape the fate he deserved.

Karueq left the grave with a tear-stained face. He could feel the hot puffiness in his eyes. He picked his way up the bluff, his mind not having left the grave. If he was honest, he knew part of him would rest here with her forever. The tumbling pebbles his heavy steps dislodged did nothing to bring him back to where he was, or more importantly, where he was going. He found himself halted in front of the fortress. His attention was caught by a dark blue mass off to his right. The dragon lay there in front of the mission hall blinking at him. He sifted through his instructions from Hanai. The mission hall - that was where he was to go.

He wiped the embarrassing blur from his eyes and turned toward the hall. As quietly as he could, he slipped through the door. Hanai was there waiting for him, sitting on the floor by the wall, but he didn't look up. There was a pack at his feet, packed so tightly the seams protested their contents.

"Go change," he said, still not looking up.

Karueq glanced down at his Shatanala garb and flinched. He left the entrance quickly to avoid the awkward tension rising in the space. The room on the left was almost bare. He noted, grinding his teeth, that there hadn't been enough of any one type of mission clothing for all the Eleverians, and only some sections had a full set left. Remembering Hanai's words, he looked around, understanding that they'd broken up into teams and fled to many different regions. Some went to the desert, some to the coasts, others to the mountains, and all of them scattering throughout the world to avoid being attacked as one.

His eyes fell on a shelf that held a set of sand-colored clothing. It was the same make of the clothing he'd worn on his first mission to Seaga. *How fitting*, he thought. Yes, he would go to that region again. He could start somewhere where they knew God so that he would relearn what he'd lost. It was close enough to the desert that he could go there to seek Eleh when his mind inevitably became clouded.

He pulled the set on, noticing it fit him well, then slipped back into the entrance. Hanai lifted the pack into Karueq's hands, then led him outside to the dragon.

There, he stopped and turned up his face to look at Karueq for the first time since they left the mountains.

"Where am I taking you?"

Karueq looked down at his attire, and Hanai nodded.

"A good choice, but Karueq, we won't be able to protect you like before. If you need our help, we will indeed come to find you. Any immediate assistance, however, will be delayed, as we will not be with you. Not for a while."

"Indeed," said Karueq, sniffing, "I'm afraid it will be quite a long time before I seek your company myself."

Hanai said nothing to this. He studied Karueq, almost nostalgically, and Karueq understood that this was the last time he would see him, at least for a very long time.

The Eleverian's face twisted slightly in a fresh wave of anguish. He turned away and looked out to the plain. Karueq had seen this profile of him countless times as he loved looking out on his beautiful home, surveying the horizon and inspecting the colors the sun pulled through the sky at dawn and dusk. Even the clouds held his attention when they streaked the sky like sea foam. It occurred to Karueq that this was Hanai saying goodbye to his home.

Then Hanai turned square to the dragon, his eyes watery. "Let's go," he said simply and mounted.

Karueq pulled himself up behind him. From the dragon's back, he glimpsed a man standing in the open doorway of the fortress. His build gave him away as Alamar, and his dragging posture gave away his grief. Karueq almost fell behind when the dragon lifted powerfully into the air. Another piece of his heart stayed behind with that broken man.

The plains fell away. They crossed the valley. The country dropped behind them. Soon, they sped across the bay and beyond the gleaming pillars with their bands of red, brown, and white. Then, there was naught but the sea below them. Karueq held on awkwardly to Hanai. This was clearly a difficult task for Hanai, to rescue his sister's killer. To have Karueq clinging to his back while he fled from his own home and everything he knew must be the worst thing he'd ever had to do. Karueq tried for a while to keep his grip light, but the force of the dragon's wings made it difficult.

Along the way, a mass of clouds, heavy and gray with a building storm, created a wall in their path. They dived into it. Their skin wicked the moisture from the clouds and made them damp. It was the only incident on their journey, which finally ended on the outskirts of a quiet settlement.

Hanai set the dragon down, and they dismounted. "Wait here," he said. "I'll make sure it's safe."

Karueq protested. "Whatever awaits me, I deserve it."

Hanai turned on him. "My sister died saving you. Don't dishonor her memory with such words. I expect you to refrain from recklessness, too, for as long as you live." His eyes flashed with the beginnings of anger, but it quickly dissipated, replaced by a now empty look.

"I'm sorry," Karueq whispered. His own throat was tight, and he didn't trust it to be steady.

Hanai glanced at the dragon. "Stay here until I return." He left Karueq and walked toward the settlement.

Karueq sat down against a shallow rock wall and shut his eyes. It would take an hour or more for Hanai to survey the town and be satisfied that there was no immediate threat to his fugitive. Karueq filled the time just as he had since his crime. He prayed. He guessed, quite rightly, that he would find himself doing this always in the spare time he would have.

When Hanai returned, Karueq's head was still bowed into his hands, eyes closed. Hanai beckoned him to rise and retrieved a vial from the pack strapped to the dragon's leg.

"Karueq, all Eleveria loves you, as does your King, Eleh," Hanai began the mission rite. "You go with Him to do the work He has called you to do. Upon your return…" Hanai's words failed him for a moment, and Karueq's throat tightened again. This verse seemed to mock them both. Hanai quickly cleared his throat and continued. "Upon your return, you will be received with great joy. Should you fall and not return, you will be dearly missed."

He inverted the vial on his thumb and smeared the oil on Karueq's forehead. "May the lavish love Eleh pours out to you in life be multiplied. May He transform your tears into astounding joy and everlasting peace. Go with God, Karueq." He placed his hand on Karueq's shoulder and looked him in the eye. "May you forever know the love He has for you."

Karueq swallowed. "Thank you, Hanai. It means a great deal to me."

"Promise me something."

"Anything."

"Your soul is not a bargaining tool. It is never an option to hand yourself over to evil. You may forfeit only your body and your life. Promise me, as my friend and not my enemy, that you will not hand yourself back to Shatan, no matter what promises they make you."

"I promise," was Karueq's unmoving answer.

Hanai didn't smile, but Karueq understood he was satisfied with that answer. "I do hope to see you again one day, my friend," he said. Before Karueq could reciprocate – or before Hanai's tears flowed anew, Karueq would never be sure – the Eleverian leaped onto the blue dragon and sped high into the air. Karueq watched them disappear beyond his vision to the north. Then, he turned his face toward the settlement, shouldered his pack, and made his way toward his new mission

It was already past noon, and in the heat of the day, many of the inhabitants were taking shelter in the shade of their houses or the trees surrounding their fields. Karueq's survey of the place showed little sign of damage or disease. Indeed, as Karueq looked closer, it looked much the same as the day he'd left after rebuilding it with Honai, Tinorah, Omri, and Finnah. The holy house, too, was still intact, suggesting the people had not rejected Eleh since they left. This was not the sort of place Eleveria would send a team, as there were many other places in dire need of help. However, here he was, and he intended to do what little he could while he regained his faith.

He crossed a house on a street that was naggingly familiar. He took a long look at it, trying to place it, when someone walked up to him.

"Sir, can I help you?" came the young voice. He turned to her, a girl of adolescent age. Her mouth broke into a wide smile. "I thought it was you," she said knowingly.

"Do I know you?" he asked. She looked familiar, too.

"I don't expect you to remember me. You helped a lot of people the last time you came here, but I could never forget the face of a man who gave us such hope." She brushed the side of her veil over her shoulder and pulled a braid out into the hot sun. Woven into the hair were brilliantly colored Eleverian beads, the likes of which were given to children during missions.

Karueq glanced at the house again, and his mind filled in the picture – a little girl, barefoot and shy, standing on a pile of rubble that used to be her home. She'd grown up a little since last he saw her.

"I remember you," he said. He looked at her and realized he'd never asked her one important question. "What's your name?"

"Rayah," she answered with an even brighter smile. "Have you come to help us again?"

"I have, Rayah. I would be grateful if you would help me find those in need of my assistance."

"I will, indeed. You must need a place to stay." Her face lit up, though her expression was already so bright. "My family would be honored to host you –"

"Thank you," he said, stopping her, "but I'll make my camp just outside, like before."

She studied him for a moment. His hasty answer made her quick little mind tumble. "Is everything alright?" He guessed she probably saw the shadows of trauma hanging on his face.

"Yes," he said, making an excuse. "It's been a very long journey."

Karueq did indeed make camp outside the town. He spent most of the afternoon on his knees praying, hands resting open palmed on his lap. Rayah came out to find him, dragging the hands of a few younger children along with her. Some of them were shy, some were fascinated by this stranger who came with small gifts for them. It was second nature for him to reach into the front pocket of his pack and remove the beads and little figurines when there were children around. Rayah, so young as she was herself, wisely removed the youngsters from his camp when his forced smile and focused energy waned.

When dusk drew near, his eye fell on his pack. He swallowed. Though he hadn't eaten in two days, he didn't have an appetite. He reached for it anyway, as he would need his strength for this unending mission. Luckily, mission food was bland and dense. It would feel more like a task than actual eating. But when he opened the rations pouch, his eyes filled with tears anew, and he wept over the forgiveness and love that was extended to him for the third time. Nestled at the top of his rations was an apple.

--^--

News reached Karueq quickly in the following months that the days after the darkest tragedy in Eleverian history were the happiest the world had ever seen to date. Such an outpouring of love from them swept through all the lands, including those controlled by the Shatanala. A nation that showed no malice and sought no revenge turned their sorrow into joy for others.

No, the world would not know what had happened. There was no reason for them to question their quiet angels. Because of the daily threat to their lives, the Eleverians never stayed long in one place. Karueq crossed paths with a group every now and then. They were gracious to him, but he didn't keep their company. He couldn't bring himself to lay down his guilt just yet. What he did accept from them was news of their lives and advice to avoid certain areas where the search for him intensified. He never met any of the Eleka Guard. They elected to defend settlements where the Shatanala made brazen attempts at takeover, places Karueq absolutely avoided out of respect for his promise to Hanai.

The struggle once again hung in stalemate. Bleren must have taken his truce with Alamar very seriously. Retaliating by outright attacking Seaga must be very tempting, and Shatan would have demanded he do so. Nonetheless, the Shatanala kept to the old ways of scheming and secretive mischief. Karueq was relieved every day that went by without a massive assault somewhere in the world.

A long time after what Karueq decided was the worst day of his life, he found himself in a new area, a new city. He'd never been here either as Shatanala or missionary. Here, he was doing what good he could manage on his own without people he knew helping him navigate their homes. There was so much in this city he could do, and he wished for a team of dozens of Eleverians to help him do it all quickly.

Sweaty and exhausted from a full day of repairing houses for the city's poorest neighborhood, he dropped down next to the large shade tree that marked his camp outside the city limits. Even this long after his exile, he refused to camp among the people. Instead, he chased seclusion so that he could be alone with Eleh.

He also couldn't trust his dreams. Sometimes they were peaceful, mirroring the vision he had when he fled from Xanadai. Often, he woke screaming while he relived his torture in the prisons, murdering Chelia, or surrendering his soul once more to Hell. For this reason, too, he stayed away at night - better to sleep at the edge of the wilderness than to frighten his hosts.

He said a quick prayer in thanksgiving for the day, then he opened his pack and retrieved his meal. He'd run out of his rations ages ago. Now, he accepted food from out of the people's goodness, never as payment. He did hunt when generosity was scarce, but recently he'd received a great deal of charity. He saved what could be saved and ate what he needed. His pack today was as full as it was the day Hanai carried him out of Eleveria. He ate well, boosting his energy for the next day. He'd had his eye on a shack standing on the edge of a street in dire need of work. So far, he hadn't found enough material to rebuild it, but tomorrow, he decided, he would search all day until he had enough to do the job.

It was dark when he ended his prayers and slipped under a blanket that Rayah and the other children had made for him. The four corners had tassels with a few of their beads tied in. It had been a very long time since he left their town, and he thought maybe he would soon go to check on them.

His senses pricked up. He opened his eyes and flickered a glance around him. The sky was cloudy, making it too dark to see. He should be alone, but he felt he wasn't. He propped up onto his elbow and peered harder into the blackness, but he couldn't make out anything that might have stirred his instincts. Then, he understood.

"Come out of the shadows," he said.

After a few tense moments, six shadows stirred and moved toward him. Karueq pulled the blanket aside and stood. The shadows stopped suddenly. Now, he could make out faint distinctions in their form. Red sashes and dark hoods covered five of them - the Brehila. The other bore no such distinctions, but she was the only one who spoke.

"Come quietly," was her command.

Karueq peered at her a little closer in the darkness. A braid swept across her forehead. He knew her well by now.

"Ingana," he called her by name. "You finally found me."

"If the Eleverians hadn't kept us off your trail, I would have had you sooner."

"I believe you."

"Come quietly, or I'll return you dead."

Karueq wasn't surprised at all that his heart didn't quake. He figured this would happen one day, his borrowed time was temporary. There would be no way for him to get out of this standoff. He was unarmed, spent from the day's labor, and no longer conditioned for combat. He wouldn't be able to outrun them.

"Very well. Take me," he said.

Two of the shadows stalked toward him, laid their hands on him, and bound his hands behind his back. He made a silent prayer to Eleh, begging Him to use his death to save even one soul in Xanadai.

Ingana stepped in front of him and looked into his face. The naivete was gone from her own face, hardened by years of high order Shatanala commissions. "I respected you once. How far you have fallen, commander."

Karueq refused to reply.

--^--

The men laid into him, and their blows were brutal. He grunted with every strike, refusing to let any more than that escape him.

"Enough," Shatan ordered. The last man cracked him hard in the jaw. He tasted his blood and spit it on the ground. All of Xanadai was gathered in Madaka's temple. The violet light was brightened by torchlight this time that danced across Karueq's skin. His nose wrinkled at the putrid incense in the air. The great shade himself snarled at Shatan's side, glaring viciously at him with a mixture of glee and hatred.

Karueq caught Bleren's eye standing behind Shatan. In those eyes, he saw pleading. In his hands, Karueq saw the cruel sword he'd left behind so long ago on the Zarenvai beach.

"I do not like repeating myself, Karueq," the demon glowered.

"Neither do I. My answer stays."

"You have nothing in being an ally to Eleveria now. They've all gone into exile, and you have no one to save you."

"I don't want anything from you Shatan. I will not be turned back again."

"I can give you everything."

Karueq scoffed. "You can't. You're unable to leave this prison in the ground." He relished the disbelief that gasped through the horde gathered around them. "Even if you could, you wouldn't. For what I've cost you, you will drag me into the pit for treason as soon as I give you my soul again, and I will become the carrion of Hell in your hands."

"I'll make your days a *living* Hell if you don't submit."

"You may torture my body again, you may threaten and promise until my last breath, but I belong to Eleh. My heart is His, and I will not abandon Him again."

"You belong to me!" Shatan roared. "Eleh let you be dragged back here from hiding to be at the mercy of the forces you once led. He has no claim to you!"

"I will never surrender to you," Karueq declared, and he spat his bloody spittle at the demon.

The image of the beast flickered. The caged animal threatened to break loose in his rage. Instead, the angered demon set his face. "On the altar," he ordered.

The Shatanala holding him kicked his legs out from under him and dragged him onto the altar. Karueq smirked at the crack still splitting it in two as they yanked him to kneel on the wretched thing. One of the men behind him crawled onto the altar and yanked his head back so that he stared fully into the face of the demon.

Shatan held his hand out to Bleren without taking his gaze from the traitor. Bleren clenched the sword in his hand and silently pleaded with Karueq. Karueq, however, did not waiver. He'd made his choice. Kneeling here on a demon's altar in the belly of the earth surrounded by the host of evil, Karueq surrendered his soul and his eternity to a hope. His faithful friend would not be able to save him this time. Seeing this, Bleren bowed his head inconspicuously to him, and Karueq swelled with the hope that his loyal friend would consider giving Eleh a chance by his example.

Bleren slid the blade from the sheath and surrendered the weapon to Shatan. Shatan took it, wrapping his fingers firmly around the hilt. He held the blade low at his side, his eyes remaining fixed on the man who had once been his best commander. Karueq returned the gaze now with no fragment of fear or hatred in his heart.

"Give me your last words," ordered the demon. His eyes flashed with warning.

Karueq needed no time to think. "I am not innocent," he declared for all to hear, "by your laws, the laws of Eleveria, or the laws of Eleh, my King, but I pray in His grace He will not hand me back to you in death."

The burning steel shot through Karueq's chest. The clench of the blade forced the air from his lungs.

He looked into the fiery eyes of the devil one last time. "Long live my King..."

A NOTE FROM THE AUTHOR

Samantha Hurrle

Thank you for taking the time to read this book. I hope the story and the characters have entertained you and given you hope that you can share with those around you. I believe any wrong choice, bad mistake, or miserable situation can be turned into astounding joy and everlasting peace. I hope you can find the courage to live your life like an Eleverian – courageous, free, full of joy, abundant in hope, and with a purpose beyond anything you can imagine. Darkness rules the night, but the light comes in the morning – if only you keep your eyes open and watch the sun rising to greet you. You are precious and needed, more than you can possibly imagine. Go with God, and may you forever know the love He has for you.

(Eleverian for "Praise God")

www.ingramcontent.com/pod-product-compliance
Lightning Source LLC
Chambersburg PA
CBHW071243300726
48975CB00002B/534